Miryo s̶̶̶̶̶̶̶̶̶̶̶̶̶̶̶̶̶̶̶̶̶̶able to feel the dagger in her fingers.

She had thought she was prepared for the shock of seeing her doppelganger. She was wrong.

The doppelganger's flame-colored hair was cut much shorter, but the hue was like hers. Her body was hard muscle, but the proportions were the same. And the face Miryo saw was her own. Not similar: *identical*. Miryo's skin crawled.

The other's eyes—gray, like her own—widened in shock. "Who *are* you?" the doppelganger whispered, body tensed and wary. "My—my sister?"

"No," Miryo said, responding automatically. She couldn't make herself move. "Not sisters. You and I—we're the same person. But I have to kill you now."

PRAISE FOR
Warrior

"Good characters, action, originality, and a plot that keeps you turning pages. A remarkable first novel."
—**DAVE DUNCAN, author of *The Jaguar Knights***

"A startlingly original take on magic and its price—fast, entertaining, and full of new twists. I can't wait for her next book!"
—**RACHEL CAINE, author of *Thin Air***

BY MARIE BRENNAN

Warrior

Witch

Midnight Never Come

Doppelganger

Warrior

MARIE BRENNAN

www.orbitbooks.net

New York   London

Copyright © 2006 by Bryn Neuenschwander
Excerpt from *Witch* copyright © 2006 by Bryn Neuenschwander
All rights reserved. Except as permitted under the U.S. Copyright Act of 1976, no part of this publication may be reproduced, distributed, or transmitted in any form or by any means, or stored in a database or retrieval system, without the prior written permission of the publisher.

Orbit
Hachette Book Group
237 Park Avenue
New York, NY 10017
Visit our website at www.orbitbooks.net

Orbit is an imprint of Hachette Book Group, Inc.
The Orbit name and logo is a trademark of Little, Brown Book Group Ltd.

Printed in the United States of America

Originally published as *Doppelganger* by Hachette Book Group
First Orbit mass market edition, August 2008

12 11 10 9 8 7 6 5 4

To the usual suspects:
my family and Kyle.

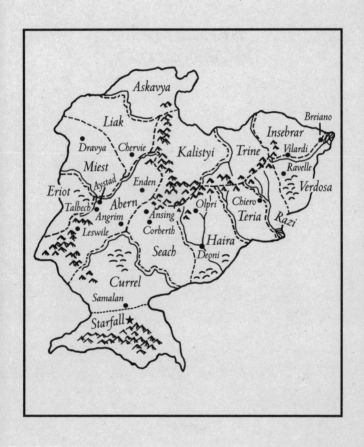

CHAPTER ONE

Commission [Mirage]

RAIN PATTERED STEADILY through the leaves of the wood and dripped to the ground below. Two figures slipped between the trees, all but invisible in the darkness, silent under the cover of the rain. The one in the lead moved well, but the one trailing him moved better, ghostlike and undetectable, and he never knew she was there.

Three men waited for him, crouching in a tight clump under an old elm and shivering in the rain. He came up to them and spoke in a low voice. "She's alone. And looks like she'll be bedding down soon enough. If we wait, she should be easy to take."

Hidden in the trees just a short distance away, the woman who had been following him smiled thinly.

"I still don't like this," one of the other men hissed. "What if she's got spells set up or something?"

The woman's jaw hardened, and the amusement faded from her face.

"She ain't a witch," someone else said, with the tone of a man who's said it several times already. "You saw her in the alehouse. She damn near cut that fellow's throat when he called her one. And Tre would have said if she'd been singing when he looked in on her."

"She wasn't," the spy confirmed. "Just talking to her horse, like anybody does. And besides, witches don't carry swords, or play cards in alehouses. She's just a Cousin."

"We're wasting time," the last of the men said. "Heth, you go first. You make friends with the horse so it don't warn her. Then Nessel can knock her out. Tre and I'll be ready in case something goes wrong."

"Some help that'll be if she *is* a witch," the fearful one said. "How else did she manage to get five Primes in one hand?"

The leader spat into the bushes. "She probably cheated. Don't have to be a witch to cheat at cards. Look, there's four of us and one of her. We'll be fine."

Ten of you wouldn't be enough, the woman thought, and her smile returned. *Not against a Hunter. Not against me.*

Mirage didn't object to being accused of cheating at cards, especially not when it was true. She *did* object to being called a witch—or a Cousin, for that matter. And she objected to being driven out to sleep in a rain-drenched wood, when she'd been hoping for a warm, dry inn. Now these idiotic thugs were planning on *jumping* her?

They deserved what they were going to get.

She slipped away from the men and returned to her campsite. Surveying it, she calculated the directions Heth and Nessel were likely to come from, then arranged her bedding so it would look as though she were in it. The illusion was weaker from the other direction, but with the fire in the way, any scouts on the other side shouldn't be able to see anything amiss.

Then she retired to the shadows and waited.

The men took their time in coming, but Mirage was

patient. Just as her fire was beginning to burn low, she heard noise; not all of the men were as good at moving through the forest as Tre. Scanning the woods, she saw the spy nearby, already in place. She hadn't heard him get there. Not bad.

Quiet whispers, too muted for her to pick out. Then one man eased up next to her horse.

Ordinarily that would have been a mistake. Mist was trained to take the hand off any stranger who touched her. But Mirage had given her a command before leaving, and so the mare stood stock-still, not reacting to the man trying to quiet the noises she wasn't making.

Mirage smiled, and continued to wait.

Now it was Nessel's turn. The leader, who had slid around to the far side of the fire, gestured for him to move. Nessel came forward on exaggerated tiptoe, club in his hands. Then, with a howl, he brought the weapon crashing down on her bedding.

Tre went down without a sound half a second later. Fixed on the scene in front of him, he never noticed Mirage coming up behind him.

"She's not here!" Nessel yelled in panic.

Mist, responding to Mirage's whistle, kicked Heth in the chest and laid him out flat. Mirage stepped into the firelight next to the horse. "Yes, I am," she said, and smiled again.

Nessel, a credit to his courage if not to his brain, charged her with another yell. Mirage didn't even bother to draw a blade; she sidestepped his wild swipe and kicked him twice, once in the chest and once in the head. He went down like a log. Mirage, pausing only to give Heth a judicious tap with her boot, leapt over the fire in pursuit of the last man.

He fled as soon as she appeared, but it wasn't enough of a head start. Mirage kept to an easy pace until her eyes adjusted once more; then she put on a burst of speed and overtook him. A flying tackle brought him down. She came up before he did and stamped on his knee, ending any further chance of flight.

Then she knelt, relieving him of the dagger he was trying to draw, and pinned him to the ground. "What did you think you were doing?" she growled, holding the dagger ready.

He was trying not to cry from the pain of his injured knee. "Gold," he gasped. "Only that. We weren't going to kill you. I swear!"

"I believe you," Mirage said. "And for that, you live. Provided you learn one little lesson."

He nodded fearfully.

"I," Mirage said, "am not a witch. Nor am I a Cousin. I have *nothing* to do with them. Can you remember that?" He nodded again. "Good. And be sure to tell your friends." She stood and tucked his dagger into her belt. "I don't like people making that kind of mistake."

Then, with a swift kick to his head, she knocked him out.

ECLIPSE SCOWLED as he shouldered his way through the crowds swarming through the streets of Chervie. The newer parts of the city, outside the walls built during the city's heyday as an Old Kingdom capital, were more open in their plan, but here in the central parts even carts couldn't make it down half the lanes. That had never been a problem for him before, but then he'd never been in Chervie this close to the Midsummer Festival. It seemed that every resident of the city had packed back inside the Old Kingdom walls, along with all twelve of their country cousins. The sheer press of people made him twitchy and irritable. It was a relief to step into the alehouse he was seeking; the interior was full, but it was nothing compared to the streets outside.

He scanned the patrons, dressed up for festival in bead-work and lace, and soon spotted a familiar and distinctive head. She found him at the same instant, and even across the room he could see her light up. He sidled his way between the tables and came up to her, grinning. "Sitting with your back to a door, Seniade? What *would* our teachers say?"

"They'd say I should have picked a different alehouse. Two doors on opposite walls, and hardly a seat to be found in the whole room. I decided to watch one and take my chances with the other."

He snagged a stool out from under a patron who had just stood to leave and settled himself onto it. "Well, I'll watch your back and you watch mine. Not all of us have your reflexes, Sen."

She quirked one eyebrow at him. "You know, you're the *only* one who still calls me that. Even the rest of our year-mates call me Mirage."

"And you still call me Kerestel. Old habits die hard, I guess. Or else we're slow learners."

Mirage grinned. "Can you believe this crowd? I'd forgotten how seriously they take Midsummer in Liak. I knew Chervie would be full, but this is ridiculous—and the festival hasn't even really started yet! It's a shock, after the quiet of the road."

"From what I hear, your trip wasn't what I'd call quiet," Eclipse said pointedly.

Mirage raised her eyebrow again.

"I came here by way of Enden. An alehouse maid there treated me to—well, several things, but two stories in particular. One about how a soldier playing cards was almost knifed in their common room, and another about how four village lads showed up the next morning, bruised, bloody, and stripped of everything but their skins."

"They were lucky to keep those. I figured they owed me their coin for trying to steal mine, and as for the other . . ." She shrugged. "I wouldn't have actually *stabbed* him."

"Your fuse has gotten shorter, I see. Or did he have an extra deck up his sleeve?"

"No," Mirage said, looking down. "In fact, I won the hand."

Eclipse leaned forward. "Void it. That again?"

"Yeah." She sighed. Eclipse noted frustrated fury in her eyes when she lifted her head, but it was soon muted. "Same with the four fools. Except *they* thought I was a Cousin."

"So they're idiots. Not all witches have red hair. And just because you *do* doesn't make you one of them, or one of their servants."

"Tell that to the idiots who panic when I lay down five Primes."

His eyes widened. "You did that? No wonder they were suspicious."

"It didn't take magic," Mirage said, and grinned wickedly. "Just agile fingers."

Eclipse swore a blistering oath that earned him a dark look from a prim-mouthed merchant woman at the next table. "Void it, Sen, you're going to get yourself killed! Cheating at cards is *not* going to improve your reputation!"

She shrugged. "I was bored."

"Bored?" He stared at her in disbelief. "Of all the people I know, you're the *last* one I would expect to court trouble just because you're bored."

Mirage gestured dismissively and looked away.

He caught hold of her arm, worried. "No, don't you brush me off. What's wrong?"

She pulled her wrist free of his grip and sighed. "Nothing. I'm just . . . bored."

"Haven't you had any jobs lately?"

"Plenty. So many, in fact, that I'm taking a rest; Mist and I have been on the road for months. Three hires, all back-to-back. Courier run clear across the land from Insebrar to Abern, for starters, and then they had word that a town farther out in the mountains was having trouble from bandits—ended up being some men they'd turned out of their town for thievery. Then *they* said a village even farther out needed a bloody *mountain cat* hunted down."

Eclipse smiled, hoping to lighten her mood. "Looks like they took the term 'Hunter' in the wrong sense."

Mirage snorted. "The saddest thing is, that bloody cat was the most interesting part of the whole series. It was a damn sight more intelligent than those so-called bandits."

"So that's why you're bored."

"Kerestel, I haven't felt *challenged* since . . . since I

got that commission two years ago. Remember, when I was sent to Hunt Kobach?"

"The one who tried to take the rule of Liak from Narevoi?"

"I went through seven domains after him. Finally caught him in Haira, not too long after I left you. That was *tough*, Kerestel. It made me work, made me actually use the skills I've learned. Since then, though . . . nothing. Routine. Boredom."

Eclipse eyed her and tried to gauge her exact mood. He had the answer to her problems tucked in his belt pouch, but right now, with her recent difficulties, might *not* be the time to bring it up. It might help, or it might be more trouble than it was worth.

And speaking of trouble . . .

Distracted as he was by his thoughts, he hadn't even seen the woman come in the door. Eclipse opened his mouth to warn Mirage, but it was too late.

"Well, if it isn't the witch-brat," the newcomer said, stalking up to them. She always stalked; he didn't think he'd ever seen her in a good mood.

Mirage's eyes sparked. She turned in her chair and leaned back with an air of pure, unadulterated arrogance. "Ah, Ice. So good to see your usual frigid self."

Ice's own blue eyes smoldered with a low fury which belied her name. Smoldering was her usual state; eye color was the only conceivable reason she'd ended up being called "Ice." Then she lifted her gaze to meet Eclipse's, and suddenly her expression held a different sort of fire. "Well met, Eclipse."

"Keep your claws off him, Ice," Mirage said, her voice

flat. "I just ate lunch, and I wouldn't want to lose it watching you try your tricks on him."

"Taken already, is he?" Ice asked with a malicious smile.

Eclipse stiffened. He considered Mirage a sister; most Hunters of the same school and year did. What Ice was implying was little short of incest. But Mirage, to judge by her own faint smile, had things well in hand. "No, dear. I'm not so desperate that I have to seduce my own year-mate—although from what I've heard about Lion, it seems *your* luck isn't so good."

Eclipse stifled a laugh. He hadn't heard *that* particular rumor. Mirage might be making it up, but Ice's expression suggested she wasn't. Now it was his turn to add fuel to the fire. "Come, ladies, this is no talk for the week before Midsummer. This is a festival! We should be celebrating! Ice, please, join us in a drink. I'm told this place has an excellent stock of silverwine."

He thought he heard a snarl. Silverwine—not a wine at all, but an appallingly strong vodka—was brewed in the Miest Valley, and was the drink of choice for Hunters from Silverfire, Mirage and Eclipse's school of training.

"Now, Eclipse," Mirage said reprovingly before Ice could get any words past her clenched teeth. "This may be a festival, but you know Hunters should try to keep clear heads. Silverwine is hard on those not used to it; we wouldn't want to lead Ice into trouble."

The inarticulate noises Ice was making were quite entertaining. She was such fun to goad; for some reason Hunters from Thornblood all seemed to have short fuses.

"I can drink anything you can," Ice snarled finally. Red mottled her face and neck.

Mirage smiled a touch too sweetly. "I'm sure you can, my dear." Ice could probably drink Mirage under the table; Thornbloods prided themselves on the amount of alcohol they could down. But Ice was too infuriated to think clearly. "I'm afraid, however, that I have important matters to attend to—ones that won't permit me to get drunk with an old friend."

"What 'important' matters?" Ice spat. "You spend your time catching wife-beaters and rescuing kittens from trees."

Eclipse hesitated. He and Mirage had played in these verbal duels before; it was his turn to attack. And he had a very good response to Ice's insult. The problem was, if he brought it out now, he might hurt Mirage more than Ice.

Recovering from his pause, Eclipse made his decision. He slipped one hand into his belt pouch and removed a tiny scroll. Keeping his fingers over the seal, he waved it to get Ice's attention.

Both of the other Hunters froze, looking at it. Eclipse nodded, smiling. "A two-person commission," he said, addressing the Thornblood. "Mirage and I will be handling it together."

The fury on Ice's face was profoundly satisfying. Official commissions were rare enough that receiving one was an honor; as far as he knew, she hadn't been offered one yet, in seven years out of Thornblood. This would be his first as well, but the second for Mirage.

Across the table, Mirage's expression was incredulous. Eclipse was pleased by the delight in her eyes; this was, he well knew, the answer to her complaints of boredom and inactivity. Commissions were always difficult, always a challenge.

He just hoped she wouldn't kill him when she found out who had ordered the job.

Ice was still apoplectic. "Who's it from?" she growled at last.

He pulled the scroll away when she tried to reach for it. "Uh-uh," he admonished her, waving one finger in her face. "Authorized Hunters only. I'm afraid you'll have to wait with everyone else to find out what we're up to." He tucked the scroll back into his pouch. Once he got Mirage alone, he'd tell her more.

Mirage had smoothed her expression by the time Ice looked at her. She smiled at the Thornblood. "Don't worry, Ice," she said. "I'm sure you'll get your turn— some day."

That, coming from a Hunter two years her junior, was too much for the Thornblood. Growling, Ice turned and stormed out of the alehouse.

As soon as she was gone, Mirage leaned forward. "When were you planning on telling me about *this*?"

Eclipse shrugged uncomfortably. "I was about to say something when she showed up. I'm sorry; I didn't mean to trap you into it."

"Trap me? As if I'd turn a commission *down*?"

He stood to hide his discomfort. "Come on. Let's go someplace more private to talk."

MIDSUMMER TRADITION IN CHERVIE meant that no one cooked and ate at home if they could afford not to, which meant that everybody with two coins to rub together was eating somewhere in the city's public quarters. Prices skyrocketed, and space at tables, along counters, and under awnings became harder to come by than fresh fruit in winter. Mirage had to pay through the nose for a small, private dining room in a place called the Garden of Bells. It was more like a private closet than a whole room, but the Garden's architecture was copied from an eastern style; the fretwork walls would be very cold in Chervie's northern winters, but on this summer day it was pleasantly cool. Besides, there was nowhere for an eavesdropper to hide.

Normally she wouldn't have dreamed of paying the cost, but she was starving, the Garden had good food, and the commission was sure to pay enough that she could indulge a bit. "So, what *will* we be doing?" she asked her year-mate once the maid bringing in the roast pheasant and fruit had departed.

Eclipse looked uneasy.

Mirage put her fork down and gave him a sharp look. "What is it?"

By way of response, he pulled the scroll out again and rolled it across the table to her. Mirage picked it up and froze.

The seal was pressed into black wax flecked with silver—a color only one group of people used. And the sigil itself, a triquetra knot intersecting a circle, would be instantly recognizable to even the most illiterate of peasants.

It was the symbol of the witches.

Mirage set the scroll down carefully and looked across at Eclipse. "This is from Starfall."

"Yes," he admitted.

Mirage stood and walked to the fretwork wall, putting her hands against it. Behind her she could hear him shift uncomfortably.

"You don't have to," he said at last. "No matter what we said to Ice. Everyone knows you stay away from witches; everyone would understand if you turned it down. Everyone who matters, anyway."

More silence. Mirage closed her eyes. "What do they want?"

"I don't know," he said. "I haven't opened it yet."

"How did you get it?"

"Jaguar. A Void Hand witch brought the scroll to him; he chose me to take it on."

Jaguar's not stupid, Mirage thought. *He knew Eclipse would pick me as his second.*

What's his motive?

"A Void witch," she said, turning away from the wall at last. "Then it's an internal issue."

Eclipse nodded. "Which might explain why they're hiring Hunters. They may not trust their own people to be impartial."

Mirage returned to the table and picked up the scroll. *A commission from the witches. I wanted a new challenge, but not from them.*

"If you're uncomfortable . . ." Eclipse began again.

Mirage broke the seal with her thumb and unrolled the scroll. Now she was committed; it was a hanging offense for such a message to be read by an unauthorized person. So absorbed was she in fighting down her irrational surge of uneasiness, she almost did not notice Eclipse rising to read over her shoulder.

The message was short, and brutally to the point.

"No wonder they wanted the insurance of two Hunters," Eclipse breathed into her ear. "Although what the

Key of the Fire Heart Path was doing out where she could be assassinated escapes me."

"Damn them to *Void*," Mirage growled, flinging the scroll across the room. *Surge of uneasiness, my ass.* It had been a spell settling into place. "They've enchanted us against speaking of it."

"Do you blame them?" Eclipse asked.

"No." She sighed and pressed her hands against her eyes.

Her fellow Hunter crossed the floor and picked up the scroll once more. "Blank."

No more than I expected.

"This could mean trouble," he said reluctantly.

"Trouble" didn't come close to describing the possible outcome, and they both knew it. The commission, before it had faded, had commanded them not only to Hunt the assassin, but also to seek out whoever had been behind the task. And only someone very powerful could afford to pay for the death of such a high-ranking witch.

"If we call Hunt on a Lord or Lady . . ."

Mirage would have preferred him to leave it unspoken. "They may not ask for that. The witches may prefer to take care of payback themselves."

"From your lips to the Warrior's heart," Eclipse murmured.

Grim silence followed his prayer, before Mirage rose to her feet. "Well. We're instructed to present ourselves in Corberth before the full moon. We've just enough time to make it. Unless you want to be late?"

"Not on your life," Eclipse said.

CHAPTER TWO

Oath [Mirage]

THEY MADE MISERABLE TIME on the road south. Rain pursued them through Abern and into the mountains of Seach, turning the road into a sea of mud the horses sank into; this was not one of the Great Roads, graveled and graded and maintained by the Lady who ruled the domain. Mirage, hunched in her cloak as Mist picked her way along, wondered if she would ever dry out again.

"Tell me again," Eclipse said, "why we picked Silverfire."

"It sounded glamorous," Mirage said wryly. "Life on the road. Not tied down to any one place. Adventures! Excitement!"

"Mud. Rain. I should have been a Cloudhawk."

"Ah, what a life," Mirage said in a mock-wistful tone. "Pampered and petted, some Lord's kept spy. You might never have set foot on the road, might have traveled in a carriage."

There was a brief pause. Then Eclipse snorted. "I would've ended up killing someone out of sheer frustration."

"As would we all," Mirage replied, referring to her brothers and sisters of Silverfire. "I hate this Void-damned rain, but I wouldn't trade it for a life bonded to one employer. I'd be even more bored then. At least as a freelance Hunter there's variety."

More silence from Eclipse. The reply hung in the air anyway: *But Cloudhawks never work for witches.*

They did not speak again until they reached the next town. Even so, and despite the rain, Mirage enjoyed the ride. Itinerant Hunters almost always worked solo; she was not used to having company on the road. Eclipse's presence, however, was welcome, even when they didn't speak. He had been the first one to befriend her when she came to Silverfire, and he knew her better than any of their other year-mates did. There was no Hunter she would rather work with.

They stopped for the night in Ansing, perched in the foothills a day's ride from Corberth. Mirage scowled; she had originally expected to reach Corberth today. The rain had changed everything.

Once Mist and Eclipse's gelding Sparker were stabled, the two Hunters took their belongings upstairs. The town was small, and not wealthy; the inn had no services for drying clothes, so Mirage left Eclipse laying damp clothes out around their room while she went to buy more grain for the horses.

When she returned a half hour later, she also brought up supper, which Eclipse took gratefully. Mirage nibbled her own sausage roll and stared at the floor, pondering what they would face tomorrow. Somehow, even though her intended rest in Chervie had been cut short, she wasn't tired anymore. She welcomed any challenge to break the monotony of the past year.

"Who do you think we'll be meeting tomorrow?" she asked Eclipse.

He shrugged. "Another Void Hand, I'd assume."

A reasonable assumption. A witch of that Ray and Path had brought the commission to Silverfire, after all.

"Do you expect someone else?" Eclipse asked when she didn't respond.

"Maybe," Mirage said.

"Like who? Someone from the Void Heart? I guess that's possible, but usually the Path of the Hand deals with the outside world."

"I was actually thinking of a Fire witch."

"Possible," Eclipse said after a pause. "The victim *was* one of theirs."

"No way to be sure," Mirage said with a sigh. "We'll just have to default to generic address, at least to start. I'd like to know who I'm dealing with, though."

"Understandably."

There was another silence then; Eclipse stacked their bowls in the hallway and Mirage circled the room, checking the state of their clothes. She lost herself in the routine task, and, accustomed as she was to being alone, she jumped when Eclipse spoke.

"Are you *sure* you're all right with this?"

Mirage turned and stared at him. "What? I don't have much choice now. I read the commission."

"They could release you from it."

She sat down slowly, not breaking her gaze from his. "Why do you keep bringing this up? Do you not want me with you?"

"Warrior, no," Eclipse said instantly. "It's just . . ." He hesitated before speaking his mind. "If anybody else told me that you were going to work for a witch of your own free will, I would laugh in his face."

And he would have cause. Mirage stood and paced a narrow circuit of the room, making herself consider his question seriously. If taking this job was a bad idea, this was her last chance to change her mind.

She'd avoided witches at every opportunity for years now; it had become reflex. It wasn't just the red hair, either, though that was part of it. Mirage had known since childhood that she was unusually strong for her size, and no one could match her reflexes. Red hair alone didn't mean anything, though almost all witches had it—but red hair with her physical talents looked strange. And a minor curiosity became a distinct problem when she entered a Hunter school, a place that, by ages of tradition, was not friendly to witches.

A lot of people at Silverfire didn't like her being there at all. And so it became habit to avoid association with witches whenever possible. Other Hunters might go to a witch for healing; Mirage had only been healed once, while in training, and then not by her choice.

She shook her head and laughed softly. There was really only one answer to Eclipse's question. "I just can't pass a commission up."

"Because it's a challenge."

She nodded. "It . . . draws me. I don't like dealing with witches, but I want to take this job. Gut feeling. I think this is going to test my skills to the limit. And commissions are what our reputations are *built* on; having a second one this soon would really help make my name."

Eclipse grinned and shook his head in resignation.

"What?"

"I *knew* you'd say that," he said, still grinning.

THEY REACHED CORBERTH early the next afternoon. That night would be the full moon. Mirage had intended to arrive a day early, with time to prepare, but thanks to the weather, they had only a few hours.

She felt edgy as they brought their belongings into the inn Eclipse had chosen, and she took a moment to chase the feeling down. Normally freelance Hunters like those of Silverfire set the place of meeting, made their employers come to them. She was used to having that measure of control over the situation. With a witch, though, everything changed. The two Hunters would have to go to their employer.

She didn't like it, but she couldn't change it.

They didn't speak much once they arrived. Even though Mirage and Eclipse had not worked together since their days as students, they fell into a comfortable rhythm. He went downstairs to fetch hot water while she got what they needed out of their bags. It didn't take much sorting; they both packed very lightly.

Without asking Eclipse, she got out the finer of the two uniforms for both of them. Every Silverfire Hunter took care to keep one set cleaner and less worn, for formal situations. If meeting a witch did not qualify as formal, Mirage didn't know what did.

Luckily the uniforms packed small, so they were not a burden to carry. Mirage shook out the individual pieces, each made of windsilk dyed so that its black shade did not reflect the light as ordinary silk might. Windsilk was so light it felt as though it might tear in the slightest breeze, but that delicacy was an illusion. Nobles bought it as a statement of wealth; Hunters used it for practicality.

Eclipse returned then with water. They stripped and bathed in their room, conducting their ablutions in silence; each used the washing as a chance to prepare for their task.

Mirage dressed herself with methodical precision. First the full breeches, cut so as not to restrict movement. She took a moment to arrange every pleat properly before donning the loose shirt. Then came the short jacket, cinched down with her weapons belt before she wrapped her waist in the wide sash. The boots she had been wearing were put aside for a pair unstained by mud. She practiced a few kicks and spins to make certain that nothing would chafe. Then a pair of supple gloves, and the mask and head covering that left only a strip across her eyes clear.

There was no mirror in the room, but Mirage still smiled at her appearance. Hunters in uniform were faceless and intimidating. The familiar costume helped to counteract the strangeness of not choosing the meeting location.

Eclipse finished dressing just moments after she did. And by then it was nightfall, and time for them to go.

The two Hunters slipped from shadow to shadow, picking their way across the town. Eclipse had gotten directions from a maid when he went down for the water; he'd managed to choose an inn clear on the other side of town from the designated location. Mirage didn't mind. This skulk through the shadows honed her focus, stepping up her excitement just a little bit more. Evading the excuse for a local watch was easy, but even so, it exercised skills she hadn't used much lately, barring the bandits and that one skirmish in the forest outside Enden.

When they arrived at the house indicated in the commission, they stopped to consider it. The place belonged to a person of some wealth; it was surrounded by its own wall, sculpted to mimic flowering bushes and trees. A pair of weary guards patrolled its top with less than full enthusiasm. Mirage and Eclipse exchanged quick glances. The sculptures made it all too easy.

The guards never noticed the two shadows flowing over the wall.

The small courtyard was edged with trees, but paved in the middle. There was no good way to approach the front door without stepping into the open—but then again, Mirage reminded herself, there was no need to. They *were* expected. And passing the guards in front, easy though it had been, was enough showing off for one night.

They stepped onto the cobblestones and headed for the front door.

It opened just as they reached it. A red-haired woman was inside; Mirage glanced at the short sword the woman wore and felt her lip curl. A Cousin. One of those lackeys she had been mistaken for in Enden, an obedient servant of the witches.

The Cousin bowed to them, showing no sign of fear or even surprise at finding two uniformed Hunters already inside the gate. Mirage swore inwardly, understanding. *Ward of some kind. No wonder the guards are so lax. With tricks like this, how did that witch ever get assassinated?*

They were conducted inside. The Cousin offered no greeting, and neither Hunter chose to break the silence. Intimidation was a useful tool, and although the woman was not outwardly cowed, Mirage could see the stiffness in her back. She smiled beneath the windsilk of her mask.

The Cousin led them to an elegantly carved door and opened it, gesturing them inside.

Given the sumptuous appearance of the rest of the house, the nearly bare room was jarring. A few high-backed chairs stood in a rough semicircle facing the door, and in the center of the arc sat a woman. The shadows of the chair's wings cloaked her, but Mirage knew without being told that this was the witch.

Both she and Eclipse saluted their summoner.

The Cousin shut the door, and the room remained silent for several long moments. Then the witch spoke. "Silverfire."

Mirage instantly tried to analyze that. Had she not known what school was hired? If so, the cut of their uniforms would have told her that. But the voice, almost devoid of inflection, was unclear; it could be that she *had* known, and was making some comment on the choice. Mirage could not tell.

"Have you been told anything?" the witch asked.

Her voice sent chills down Mirage's spine. Melodious and smooth, like any witch; they depended on singing to control their magic, and so they trained their daughters' voices from the time they could speak.

"No, Katsu," Eclipse responded, defaulting to the generic form of address for a witch of unknown affiliation. "The commission merely said that Tari-nakana, the Fire Heart Key, had been assassinated, and that two Hunters were to be assigned to investigate the situation. It instructed us to come here and find you, and bound us not to speak of it to anyone else until now. That was all."

The witch stood. She was taller than Mirage by a good bit, of a height with Eclipse. "Tari-nakana was returning to Starfall when she fell from her horse and broke her neck. A simple tragedy, or so it would seem. But the snake that startled her mount is rarely active during the day, and avoids open spaces such as roads. When the horse's saddle blanket was removed after it was put down for two broken legs, its back was inflamed—not seriously, but enough to make it more skittish than usual. And the girth strap was quite worn—again, not enough to look suspicious, but more than anyone recalls it being."

Mirage felt a flicker of professional appreciation. *So that was how it was done. Clever, and subtle. No one clue so glaring that anyone would point a finger at foul play, and no mischief strong enough to be caught before it could come to harm.*

"These three anomalies caused us to investigate," the witch continued. "There was no evidence of anyone planting the snake, or tampering with the saddle girth, but the blanket had been touched with a very mild powder that irritated the horse's skin. Given that, we suspect that the other two were also not chance."

"What's our assignment?" Mirage asked.

"Hunt," the witch said bluntly. "Hunt the assassin and capture or eliminate her; either is acceptable. But also Hunt the one behind the assassin, the one who ordered the killing done. That, more than the first, is of paramount importance. But exercise caution; we do not wish to alert the employer. Inform us of your discoveries before any action is taken against that one."

Eclipse nodded. "Who will be our contact?"

"Myself. Do you accept the commission?"

"We do," Mirage said, knowing she spoke for both of them. Her fingers tingled with anticipation of the Hunt. It was a feeling she had missed, these past months.

The witch ought to have taken their oaths then. But she didn't, not right away, and a chill prickled at Mirage's neck. Why was she hesitating?

"I must warn you," the witch said. "I will require a blood-oath. Do you still accept the commission?"

Mirage froze in shock. Many Hunters went their whole lives without ever taking on a blood-oathed commission. It was glory and death, all in one. Only the most delicate of situations merited blood-oaths, because they required the services of a witch to bind the Hunter to the task. If the Hunter completed the commission, he lived, gained great fame, and could ask three boons from his employer— whenever he wanted, no restrictions.

If he failed, he died.

If anything would require it, this would, Mirage thought. *But am I ready for it?*

Glory, fame, and three favors from some very powerful people.

Or death.

She had wanted a challenge.

Mirage looked over at Eclipse, and found him doing the same. She was not at all certain what his choice would be until their eyes met. An instant only; that was all it took for them to know their answer.

"We accept," Eclipse said.

The witch stood and beckoned them forward. She pulled a small table from her side to in front of her, and Mirage saw that it held a small dagger, a shallow silver bowl, and a faceted crystal. Witches' tools.

"Your weapon hands, please," the witch said.

Mirage's heart was beating rapidly with apprehension. This could make her name for all time, put her into legend with other great Hunters of the past. But she could not forget the danger, the threat of death. If they failed, neither of them would live to take another assignment.

But if we succeed, the reward is worth it. And I'm arrogant enough to believe we will.

The witch interlocked their right hands so they were gripping each other over the bowl. Their gloves had been tucked into their belts.

She slid the dagger carefully between their wrists, flat against the skin, and held the crystal in her left hand. Then, without warning, the witch flipped the dagger to its edges and drew it downward, opening up a shallow cut on the inside of each Hunter's wrist. Their blood dripped together into the silver bowl, forming a dark pool on the reflective surface.

The crystal the witch held began to hum as she held it above their hands. "You are charged with the task of serving justice to the assassin of Tari-nakana, Key of the Path of the Heart of the Ray of Fire, and of discovering the instigator of the murder. Should you fail, you will die. Should you succeed, we who have hired you bind ourselves to grant three boons to you, whenever you might require them. Do you accept?"

Mirage and Eclipse recited their responses in unison. "I swear, on my oath and my name as a Hunter, that I will devote my utmost efforts to the task, or accept the retribution of the Divine Warrior who holds my oath."

Right hand on the bowl, left hand holding the crystal, the witch sang a series of sharp notes in the language of magic. Mirage's stomach lurched as their commingled blood suddenly rushed upward, back through the gap between their wrists, to strike the crystal, where it was absorbed. The witch set the newly dyed ruby back onto the table and clasped their bleeding wrists in her own hands.

"Your oath is accepted. You are free to Hunt."

A sudden surge of pain made Mirage grip Eclipse's hand in resistance. And then it was gone, as quickly as it had come, and the witch was moving the table away.

Mirage released Eclipse's hand and examined her wrist. Even in the dim light, she could see the thin scar. It glittered peculiarly, with a greenish shade that seemed to be a reminder of the strangely colored magical fire that had sealed it shut. The scar would mark her for life, a sign that she had undertaken a blood-oathed commission—and, if all went well, survived.

They didn't leave the house immediately. Both Mirage and Eclipse had a number of questions they needed to ask; if they were to investigate the assassination, they would need as much information as possible. The witch answered readily enough, but Mirage still felt something off-kilter.

Is she keeping something from us? But why would she? Mirage considered the question even as she listened to Eclipse ask something else. *Is she afraid of being incriminated in something? In the murder? I doubt the guilty party's hiring us to investigate.* She frowned beneath her mask. *It's something to keep an eye out for. I don't like mysteries, not when my life is on the line.*

They departed before dawn, carrying the first part of their payment and an enchanted sheet of rice paper that could be used to ask the witch further questions, should the need arise. Mirage was certain it would. She didn't like the paper, though; it would send the words written on it to a matching sheet the witch had, certainly, but communicating through writing would make it a great deal harder to tell if the witch was equivocating or avoiding a subject.

Neither Hunter spoke until they were in their room again and had checked their surroundings for eavesdroppers. There were none; Mirage hadn't expected any, but it always paid to be careful. She just wished she had some way to prevent magical prying.

"What do you think?" Eclipse asked as he removed his mask and put it on the table.

Mirage had also taken hers off, and she turned it over in her hands as she replied. "It's the work of a Hunter."

He nodded. "My thoughts exactly. We're the only people who get that kind of training, to think it through carefully, and hide our tracks."

"So which school? Could be several—Silverfire, for one. Although we don't tend to do assassin work as often. Thornblood would be more likely. Or Stoneshadow, or Wolfstar."

"I'd favor those latter two. It strikes me as the kind of job you'd hire a specialist for; we're more jack-of-all-trades, and so's Thornblood. So it boils down to a question of freelance or bonded. Is this some Lord's permanent assassin, or a mercenary?"

"I've got the same gut feeling—that it's an assassination specialist—but we can't get locked into that," Mirage cautioned.

"Agreed." Eclipse sat down, then leaned the chair onto its back two legs as he thought. "The greyweed on the saddle blanket had to have come from out east, probably Insebrar—do you think that's where the employer is?"

"Maybe. Would Lord Ralni have any reason to assassinate her? Not that it necessarily was him, of course. But Lords are some of the only people with the money or influence to buy the death of someone that important; I mean, she headed an entire *Path* in her Ray. And besides, Fire witches are the political ones." Mirage paced the small room, mask still dangling from her fingers. There was a faint thought teasing at the back of her head. When she nailed it down, she stopped pacing. "He's patient, whoever he is. He couldn't be at all certain Tari-nakana would die in that accident—our contact said she was a good rider. She might have controlled her horse when it shied, or gotten clear as it fell. So he valued subtlety over immediate results."

"But he was almost certainly hired for the *job,* not the attempt."

"Which means he had a backup plan."

"Her home, you think?"

"It's where I'd go next, were I in his place. She was on her way back to Starfall. I just hope they haven't touched anything yet, or that our assassin friend hasn't gone and cleaned the place up. If we see another of his traps, we might have a better chance of identifying his school."

Eclipse nodded and dropped the chair back onto four legs. "Which brings up a question: How do you want to work this? Should we figure out who the assassin was, and track the chain back that way, or should we be trying to find out who would've wanted to kill her?"

Mirage leaned against a wall and considered. Eclipse waited patiently for her answer, not pushing; they were already falling into a smooth working partnership. "We could split up, with one of us chasing each. Two Hunters would be useful that way. But we don't have to decide now."

"Right. Either way, the next logical destination is Tari-nakana's house in Starfall, since that's where her office was."

Less than an hour, and already Mirage had a question for their witch contact. "Could you write and ask if the house has been touched?" She grinned. "I'd do it, but . . ."

"You sing like an asthmatic horse. I'd rather not hear you try."

Mirage mock-snarled at him and went to put her mask away as Eclipse wrote out their question in his elegant handwriting. Then he activated the sheet, singing under his breath the first line of the ballad "The Hawk of Fire." A sign that their contact was from the Fire Ray, or just a nod to Tari-nakana's affiliation?

The words faded off the sheet, but the response did not come immediately. Rather than wait idly, they both changed back into mundane clothing. By the time their uniforms were packed into their saddlebags, a line written in a spiky, backhanded script had appeared in place of Eclipse's question.

"As far as she knows, the house is untouched," he said, reading from the sheet.

Two copper disks dropped out of nowhere onto the table.

Mirage swore mildly in startlement as she picked them up. "She'd better not do that on a regular basis." The disks were identical; on one side they showed the triquetra circle of the witches, and on the other, a two-part glyph. "Name symbols, do you think?"

Another line had appeared on the paper. Eclipse read it aloud. " 'The tokens should get you past the wards on Tari-nakana's house.' " He took one and examined it closely, then compared it to Mirage's. "Maybe. Tari-nakana's name, with something else?"

"Don't lose it. I'd hate to have to pick you up in pieces."

"That would be messy. Don't worry, I'll be careful." He glanced out the window to check the sky. "Not quite dawn. I say we sleep for a few hours, then get on the road."

"Agreed," Mirage said. "It's a long way to Starfall."

CHAPTER THREE

Future [Miryo]

THE MOUNTAINS REACHED HIGH into the night sky, but the stars glimmered higher still. Miryo lay on her back against the slanted roof of the students' hall and studied them, trying to lose herself in peaceful stargazing. Her thoughts, however, would not leave her alone.

Her eyes scanned restlessly, picking out one constellation after another, identifying each, reviewing their cycles in the sky. It didn't help to look elsewhere. Turning her attention downward only showed her the nearby buildings of Starfall's major settlement: the students' hall beneath her; the architectural logjam of the ancient main building; the New House, where she would hopefully be living before much longer. All reminders of what was coming. There was no surcease to be found in looking downward.

All the same, though, it was better out here than in her room. Were she there, her bookshelves and desk would beckon her with reminders of all the things she still had to study, all the things she still didn't know. Out here, where the night breeze could refresh her, she could at least try to empty her mind, to find peace and forgetfulness.

She could try to ignore what was coming.

The wind blew more strongly, making her shiver.

Miryo tucked back strands of hair that had been teased loose from their braid and then wrapped her arms around her body. She should have brought a cloak, or at least worn warmer clothing. It might be the middle of summer, but here on the slopes of the mountains, the breeze could still be chill.

But if she didn't want to return to her room, there were still places she could go that would be more sheltered. Miryo rose carefully, mindful of the long plunge that awaited her should she fall off the roof of the students' hall. Despite the cool air, she removed her slippers and stuck them into a pocket; she preferred cold toes to the loss of traction on the slate roof.

She made her way up the slope to the ridge line where, balancing against the wind, she paused to look upward, at the structure she'd had her back to before. Star Hall itself, the ritual heart of this place, looming over everything else with its windows like watching eyes. Miryo shivered and moved hurriedly into the lee of a higher gable. A cautious slide down the opposite side took her to the base of another rise; the students' hall, though not as mismatched in its structure as the main building, boasted a crazy landscape of intersecting roofs that afforded all sorts of fun climbing and hidden nooks.

"Watch out!"

The hissed warning nearly made her lose her grip on the roof's crest. She caught herself in time and slid carefully into the cup formed by the intersection of several slopes. Some enterprising student long ago had put a wooden platform down there, making a comfortable hidden spot that was a favorite refuge of those students who found it.

"You almost made me break my neck," Miryo said to the other shadowy figure in the pit.

"If I hadn't said anything, you would have fallen on me," Eikyo pointed out. "I figured it was worth the risk."

Miryo shrugged. "You would have survived."

"With bruises. Pardon me if I didn't look forward to that." Eikyo sighed and leaned back, mirth rapidly forgotten. "Have you finished your essay for Yuri-mai?"

"I've hardly started," Miryo admitted. "I've been . . ."

"Brooding," Eikyo finished for her.

Involuntarily Miryo glanced upward again at the watchful bulk of Star Hall.

"Don't think about it," Eikyo said as soon as Miryo's eyes moved. "Worrying isn't going to help you any."

"Like you never think about it yourself."

"Of course I do. But not as often as you do; I've seen you obsessing."

"I think I'm justified," Miryo said sharply. "It is, after all, my *fate* we're talking about."

"And mine," her friend replied, unperturbed. "In another couple of months. We're all facing the same thing, Miryo. But plenty of women before us have done fine."

Miryo shivered and wrapped her arms around her legs. "And plenty have failed. You didn't see what was left of Hinusoka, after . . ." She closed her eyes, but it didn't block the memory of the appallingly small bundle the Cousins had carried out of Star Hall. And the way it had dripped. . . . "I just don't feel *prepared*. Study is fine and well, but in the end, they hand you power and you have to control it. Or else it controls you. And there's no way to practice for that, because only when the time comes will you *have* power to handle."

"You'll be fine," Eikyo repeated. "Gannu made it, after all; if *she* can survive the test, you'll have no problem." Despite her words, her body had tensed, and Miryo looked at her in curiosity. "All right," Eikyo admitted. "I worry, too. But not about dying. Is that strange?"

Miryo knew what she was referring to. Eikyo had a superstition about saying it directly, ever since the teachers told them what happened to students who failed the final test. Not everyone died. Eikyo thought the alternative was worse; Miryo didn't much want to think about either one.

"Worry about something more mundane," she suggested, to distract her friend. And herself. "Like failing the questioning from the Keys, and being publicly humiliated because they decide you're not even ready for the test. Stuck here as an old woman, with all the younger students laughing at you—"

"Oh, that's helpful," Eikyo said, but some of the tension went out of her shoulders.

Miryo grinned at her. "Come on. If one of us is going to worry about the questioning, it should be *me*. Your memory has mine beat. Think past the test; think about the future. Are you sure you want to be Earth Heart?"

"Yes," Eikyo said firmly, brightening. Her preference had always been for the company of plants and animals, rather than people; being in crowds made her uneasy. "What about you? Have you made any decisions yet?"

Now it was Miryo's turn to sigh. "No. At the rate I'm going, I'll be one of those witches they have to push into deciding. You may hate the idea of having to wait a year before you're allowed to officially choose, but I'm glad."

"Don't you have *any* idea?"

"Nothing I can go on." Miryo gestured in mute frustration. "None of them seem right. None of them really call to me, and isn't that how you're supposed to decide?"

"To the Void with what you're *supposed* to do. Approach it from a different angle. Whom do you wish *not* to serve?"

The inversion of the ritual question was an interesting one, and it woke Miryo's mind up a little. Choosing a Path within a Ray was relatively easy. If you wanted to carry out the fieldwork of your Ray, you chose the Hand. If you wanted to do research or recordkeeping, you chose the Head. And if you wanted to administer your Ray's affairs, you chose the Heart. Most people knew where their talents and inclinations lay early on. But who you'd be working with, what tasks you'd be handling—that was organized into the five Rays, and for Miryo, that was harder.

She applied herself to Eikyo's question. "Not the rulers, I think."

"I can't see you playing at politics with Lords and governors," Eikyo agreed. "Fire's out, then; four Rays left."

Miryo leaned back and brushed strands of hair back behind her ears. "I don't think I could do Water, either."

"I was going to say that if you didn't. You're not suited to living your life out in a village, finding lost livestock and curing the pox."

"Well, no one said I had to choose the Hand."

"True, but you're not really organized enough for the Heart, and you don't have the patience for the Head. You're going to be a Hand, no matter what Ray you choose; I'd bet on it."

Miryo couldn't argue that. "The rest . . . I don't *know!*" She got up and paced as best she could around the tiny

platform, feeling the weathered wood rough under her
bare feet. "I don't think I'd want Void. I don't want to get
stuck in internal troubles. That's politics again, only our
politics instead of everybody else's. Earth? Maybe, but I
don't have the knack for nature that you do."

"Which leaves Air."

Miryo paused, thinking about it. The Air Ray didn't
have as clear a purpose as the others; they served whoever
needed it. "They travel a lot."

Eikyo laughed. "I can't tell by your voice whether
that's a good thing or a bad one."

"I don't *know* which one it is."

"You've complained enough times about never getting
to leave Starfall. I'd say you have the traveling bug."

Miryo wrapped her arms around her body, trying to
imagine that life. "But I've never actually *done* it. Not
like they do, always on the move. I think I might like it;
sounds better than my other options, anyway. But what if
I don't?"

"You *do* have a year after the test before you can officially choose," Eikyo reminded her. "That gives you
a chance to find out, before you get locked into anything . . ." The end of her sentence trailed off into an enor-
mous yawn.

"Up early again?" Miryo asked.

"Was I *ever*," Eikyo said feelingly. "Ruka-chai had me
help with one of the mares. She dropped a *darling* little
colt this morning."

"So that's where you were," Miryo said, sitting once
more. "I was wondering. You didn't come to breakfast."

"No, Ruka-chai had one of the Cousins bring food out
to us. We were covered in muck; believe me, you didn't

want us at breakfast." Eikyo yawned again, and flapped one hand in apology. "Sorry. I should get back to my room, though."

"As should I," Miryo said heavily. "I have to finish that essay for Yuri-mai, after all. You'd think that we'd be *done* with essays at this stage, but no."

They both climbed to their feet, and Eikyo gave Miryo's arm a squeeze. "Don't worry. We'll astound them with our knowledge during the questioning, and then breeze through the final test. *Both* of us. And then you can figure out where you want to be."

"Thanks, Eikyo." Miryo gave her a quick hug; then they began the steep climb back out of the cup. The wind bit into Miryo as she crested the top; she shivered in her thin clothing. "I'll see you tomorrow," she said to her friend. They split up then; their rooms were not far apart inside, but a crumbling bit of roof in between them made it safer for Eikyo to take a different path.

Miryo made it back to her side of the building without trouble. She leaned over the edge to make sure Teruku was not looking out her window; her fellow student knew Miryo and nearly everyone else went climbing on the roof, but she disapproved, and let everyone know it. Teruku was at her desk, with her back to the window. Miryo wrapped her hands firmly around a sculpture of a falcon and swung her legs over the roof. Her feet touched onto a knot of vines and, balancing on these, she inched her way over to her own window and climbed through.

Her half-finished essay for Yuri-mai was on her desk. Miryo gave it a sour look and stretched out on her bed instead.

Lying there, she could look directly across at her

shelves. They held pages and pages of notes, all tied into tidy sheaves; a good portion of her education was there, neatly stacked. Not all of it, of course; her education had begun as soon as she could speak, with simple etiquette. The sixteen forms of address proper for witches of various affiliations. How to bow. Where she could and could not go in Tsurike Hall, her first home.

Most of the material covered in her first ten years was not there. Those years had been spent on simple things, letters and numbers, the specialized language of magic. And voice lessons, of course; those had begun as soon as she could speak, so that when the time came she could shape her spells without waver or hesitation. The rest of her early training, in basic history and geography and the like, was deeply enough ingrained that she didn't need to go back over it.

Miryo rose to her feet and went to the shelves, where she ran a finger down the stacks of notes from her Elemental studies. She had finished reviewing them a few days ago: the symbolic associations of each, the foci that could be used to channel them, the magical effects they were suited for, their reflections in human society, their philosophical meanings. All five Elements, even the Void; it might not have any magic associated with it, or any foci to channel that magic, but it had everything else. Endless floods of detail. Once she finished her essay, she would go over it again. And again, and again, until time ran out and they put her knowledge to the test.

Scowling, Miryo went to her desk and glared at the sheets there. For a moment her own tight, slanted handwriting seemed hateful to her. She wanted to climb down the side of the students' hall and run away, down the mountainside, out into the night.

But there would be no point to doing that. She was a student here, the daughter of a witch, and in a month's time, barring failure, she, too, would be a witch. There wasn't any other path to take, not that she would choose voluntarily.

She kicked her chair abruptly. For the last year she'd gone through this cycle; every few months she would turn maudlin, questioning her purpose and her odds of success. It would pass before much longer; it always had before. Most of the time she enjoyed the challenge of her studies. Her mood would clear; she'd go to the tests with her determination restored and do just fine.

And if I tell myself that often enough, I might even begin to believe it.

"Oh! You surprised me, Narika-kai."

The words were swallowed up almost immediately by the shelves that filled the library. Narika looked up from the book she was holding and smiled at Miryo. "Are you so jumpy today?"

Miryo straightened from the bow she had dropped into when she rounded the corner and saw the witch. "I'm just a little tired, Kai."

"I'm not surprised." Narika closed her book and eyed Miryo, who tried not to flinch. "I think every student begins shorting herself on sleep as her trial approaches. Tell me, what did you stay up to study last night?" Her eyes went to the book in Miryo's hands. "Plagues?"

"Oh, no, Kai. This was for an essay I was writing for Yuri-mai."

"But I bet you *were* studying," Narika said, smiling.

"Yes, Kai. Healing spells."

"Ah, a wonderful subject. Not one I have any particular knack for, which is one of the reasons I didn't choose Water, back when I was your age. They do more healing than any three of the rest of us. Does healing interest you?"

"I'm . . . not certain, Kai."

Narika nodded. "You have time before you must choose. Of course, I'm not supposed to be trying to encourage you in any direction yet, since you haven't been tested, but I don't think you're likely to fail. So I'll go ahead and say that I think you would be admirably suited to Air. You strike me as the sort of woman who would do well with variety and adventure. Of course, you wouldn't *have* to be a Hand—I myself enjoy keeping the Ray's records, which is a good deal more sedate—but I think you would enjoy it. There, now I'm done proselytizing. Have I convinced you?" Narika smiled again, quite disconcertingly.

"I will consider it, Kai. But to be quite honest, I have *no* idea what I want. Air might work, but I'd have to travel first to see if it's what I want to do."

"Very sensible of you." Narika put her book back on the shelf and held out a hand for Miryo's. She flipped through it rapidly before shaking her head. "Things like this are depressing to me. I would *not* have wanted to be Ashin two years ago, finding that outbreak of red cough in Razi." Snapping the book shut, she walked farther down the library aisle to shelve it. Miryo followed her uncertainly. "To be quite honest, I can't abide being around sick people. I would have made a very poor addition to the Water Ray."

They emerged out the end of the aisle into an open space filled with tables. A twelve-year-old student Miryo recognized only faintly was asleep at one of these, her head pillowed on an open book of maps.

"Are you nervous?" Narika asked suddenly, rounding on Miryo.

"I beg your pardon, Kai?"

"Nervous. About the testing. It's only a month away, as I'm sure you know all too well. Are you worried?"

Miryo looked at the witch, considered dissembling, and abandoned the idea. "Yes, Kai. Very much so."

"I can't say for certain, of course, but I don't think you need to be. Well, a little worry won't hurt you—it will keep you alert—but for the love of the Lady, Gannu made it through. You're a good student, from what I've heard and seen, and level-headed. Don't fret too much, and *do* be sure to sleep. You'll need your energy, if you want to pass."

"Yes, Kai. I'll be sure to rest."

"Do that." Narika turned again and sent a disapproving look at the sleeping twelve-year-old. "Not, of course, to the detriment of your remaining work." She sang a short phrase under her breath; Miryo immediately identified it as a simple spell of levitation, with the ending flourish that would fix it for a period of time. She felt no movement of power, of course, and would not until after her test. But she needed no special sense to see the spell's result; the chair the student was in, and the table her head was resting on, rose smoothly to hover in midair.

Narika turned back to face Miryo. "Have you further studying to do here?" Miryo nodded. "Then tell her, when she wakes, that I will see her an hour after First tomorrow.

I don't side with those who would drive students until they drop, but neither will I tolerate laziness." That said, the witch disappeared down an aisle and out the door.

Miryo eyed the floating student with some amusement. Narika was unpredictable, but reasonably pleasant, as long as you didn't cross her. She felt some pity for the girl. With the spell fixed as it was, it would last for at least half a day. The girl would have to find a way down, or be in trouble from her teachers for missing class.

She fetched a book on spells of communication from a back corner of the library and brought it to one of the tables to read. After about three pages, noises from above told her the student was waking up.

The girl stretched, yawning, and rubbed at her eyes. Miryo stifled a snicker. Scratching one shoulder absently, the student opened her eyes blearily and looked around.

And then she looked down.

Miryo's laughter escaped her as the girl yelped in fright. The poor thing clutched at the arms of her chair, looking panicked. "You're not up *that* high," Miryo said calmly. "You can probably just jump down. Of course, I suggest you remember to take the book with you, or you'll be in trouble with Tomichu-ai for not returning it to the shelf."

"I'm afraid of heights," the girl whispered in a strangled voice.

"I'd say you have a problem, then. You can't levitate yourself down. If you don't jump, you'll have to stay there until the spell fades—which it should do an hour or so after Low, if I'm any judge—and every one of your teachers will assign you extra duties for missing class." Miryo stood, closing her own book; if the silly chit was going to keep having muffled hysterics up there, she would have to take her reading elsewhere. "That on top of whatever Narika-kai assigns you for falling asleep in the library in the first place. You're to see her an hour after First tomorrow."

The girl gave a little wail. From her expression, she'd run afoul of Narika before.

"Look on the bright side," Miryo continued, smiling. "Even if you can't find the guts to jump, the spell will fade before you have to meet Narika. I wouldn't recommend missing that appointment."

Then she left, shutting the door quietly but firmly on the girl's rising wails.

MIRYO HESITATED in one of the hallways of the main building, next to a bust of some long-dead witch. What had seemed like a good idea following the encounter with Narika lost some of its shine now that she was trying to follow through on it.

Come on. She doesn't bite. I think.

Straightening her back and lifting her chin, Miryo strode forward and knocked crisply on the door of Ashin's office.

In the silence that followed, Miryo prayed that the witch had not left Starfall again. As the Key for the Air Hand, in charge of the most mobile third of the most mobile Ray, Ashin was gone from the domain more frequently than any other ranking witch, and often with little warning. If Miryo had missed her chance . . .

Then you'll talk to her later, Miryo told herself irritably. *You haven't even passed your test yet. If she isn't here, then you'll just put the cart back behind the horse, where it belongs.*

But as the silence stretched out, Miryo could not shake her feeling of disappointment.

"Can I help you with something?"

Miryo turned to find the very witch she was looking for coming down the hallway toward her with what looked like a saddlebag draped over one arm. The Key stopped abruptly, staring at her. "Miryo, isn't it?"

"Yes, Kasora," Miryo said. "That is—I'm sure you must be busy. I can wait until later—"

"No, no, come in," Ashin said with surprising eagerness. She shifted the saddlebag over to her left arm and dug out the key for her door. "You—that is, you haven't been tested yet, have you?"

"No, Kasora." Miryo followed her in hesitantly, and stood with her hands clasped to keep them still as Ashin moved about lighting lamps with quick spells.

"I thought not. I would have remembered the questioning session." Ashin dropped the saddlebag onto a nearby chair, atop the pile of things already there. Most of the offices Miryo had visited in Starfall were cluttered to one degree or another, but usually with papers; Ashin's was crowded with all manner of other stuff instead. A lantern, a compass—there was a saddle on the floor. "What do you need?"

"Oh, I don't—that is, Ashin-kasora, I'm here more for curiosity than anything else. You see, I'm considering joining the Air Hand after my test, and since you're at Starfall right now, I thought I might take the opportunity to talk to you about that."

Ashin stopped abruptly again, as she had in the hall.

Her voice, when she spoke, was oddly tight. "After your test."

Miryo hastened to explain. "I'm sorry, Kasora. I know it's early for me to be thinking about that. But you're so rarely here—I apologize if I'm overstepping my bounds."

The Key began moving again, rummaging through piles as if searching for something, only she seemed to have no clear idea what she was looking for. "Oh, no. Not a problem. A lot of students start thinking about it early. It's good to be optimistic, I suppose."

Optimistic? Miryo's nerves returned full force. No one would ever quote an exact statistic on how many witches failed the test. It wasn't many; she knew that much. But Ashin's words were hardly encouraging.

Ashin glanced up and must have seen something on Miryo's face, because she smiled. Was it Miryo's imagination, or was the smile forced? "You'll be fine, I'm sure. The questioning is nothing to worry about; we just want to make sure you know what you need to, before you go into the test."

But the questioning wasn't what she'd been referring to a moment before. Miryo laced her cold fingers together. "Kasora—"

"After your test, why don't you come visit me again? We can talk then about your Ray and Path. The Air Hand might be an ideal place for you. You'll know better afterward, though."

And again that edge of artificiality. As if Ashin were not half so sanguine as she was trying to appear.

What did she know that Miryo didn't?

Miryo could not come out and ask; the Key's tone was

too clearly a dismissal. She made herself bow politely. "Thank you, Kasora. I'll be sure to do that."

Ashin came around the desk and led her out to the hallway. "I look forward to it." And then the door closed behind Miryo with a thud.

CHAPTER FOUR

Investigation [Mirage]

"HAVE YOU WONDERED at all why Jaguar picked us?" Mirage asked as they rode.

They were well into the plains of southern Currel by the time she made up her mind to air the question, but it had been on her mind since they left Corberth. She asked it now because they were nearly to the domain border of Starfall, and once they got there they'd have other concerns to keep them busy. Riding, however, had been dull and uneventful, and had left her time to wonder.

Eclipse gave her an arch look. "'Us'? What's this 'us' I hear? As I recall, the commission was given to *me*."

"Right. And Jaguar no doubt expected you to pick Willow as your partner."

He shuddered. "Warrior's teeth. I haven't seen that girl since we left Silverfire, thank the Warrior. No, you're right; it never occurred to me to look for someone else, and he probably knew that."

"So why us?"

Silence for a moment. Their horses ambled on in the late afternoon sunlight, surrounded by the greenery of ripening corn. Then Eclipse shrugged. "Why *not* us?"

"We're *young*."

"But not inexperienced. You've had a commission before, after all. And did it ever occur to you that *you* were the one he really wanted, and I was just a way to you?"

"Okay, two answers to that. First, as you said, the commission was given to *you*."

"Jaguar knew where I was. You were harder to find. And they say a witch has to know where you are, to send things to you. Besides, how would you have reacted, if the commission just showed up in your lap that way, by magic?"

"Is that how it was delivered?"

He nodded. "Dropped out of thin air, with a note from Jaguar explaining the situation."

If Eclipse was right about witches needing to know their target, that meant the witch in Corberth had known where they were staying. Mirage ground her teeth. He had a point about her probable reaction, though, if the commission had been sent straight to her. "All right. Second point, then. What's so special about me?"

"You're a damn good Hunter."

Mirage shook her head. "I'm a good fighter. That's all. When it comes to skulking and spying and all the other things we do, I'm no better than anyone else."

"Well, you're better than *some*." He grinned at her. "Willow?" It had the desired effect; Mirage began laughing. "You're not bad at the skulking and spying. And Jaguar's got some kind of liking for you; always has, what with letting you into Silverfire late. Maybe he wants to see you get good opportunities."

"Or maybe he expects danger on this job."

That sobered both of them up. They rode silently for

a moment before Eclipse shrugged again. "Bring it on. I haven't had any excitement in a while, either."

THEY FOUND NO EXCITEMENT on the remainder of the ride. But both Hunters sat straighter in their saddles when they approached the border of Starfall; riding through the witches' domain in a daze would not be a good idea.

After a night in Samalan, a town just on the Currel side of the border, they rode east, then left the road and crossed the border when there was no one in sight. Mirage half expected to feel something marking the boundary, but there was nothing; she was only certain they were in Starfall when they reached the foothills. Soon they were riding through a sparse forest of cypress and pine, and she felt uneasy; large areas of the domain were supposedly uninhabited, and she had seen no one, but what if someone was spying on them magically? Camping that night was worse. Even though they lit no fire and were as silent as possible, she felt as though their presence must be glaringly obvious. Surely their trespassing would bring punishment.

Now why would I feel that way? We're here on Hunt, after all. It's not trespassing when you have permission.

With that thought, she was able to see her emotions as if from the outside, and it became much clearer. *More spells. Bloody witches. It makes sense, though; nice security measures, which make anybody skulking around suspect every shadow. I assume it doesn't affect witches or Cousins.*

She voiced her thoughts to Eclipse, and his face lightened. He, too, had been feeling the pressure. Understanding its source did not make it go away, but they were better able to ignore it after that, and managed some sleep at last.

The next day saw them winding through increasingly higher peaks, these covered in more obviously cultivated forests, with orchards of apple, pear, and pomegranate. They kept an eye out for Cousins tending the groves, and gave the highest peaks a wide berth; that was the heart of the domain, the one large settlement. The Primes who ruled the witches lived there, along with their daughters in training. Neither Hunter wanted to approach the seat of their power.

By midafternoon they were near the valley that held Tari-nakana's private house, from which she had conducted much of her business. Among the many benefits of magic was the ability to work from a place other than an administrative center—which, along with other perks, was why every Lord in the land, and half their governors, took on witches as advisers.

After a short debate, they agreed to rest for a few hours, and continue on once night fell; even though they were entering with permission, they preferred to do so in relative secrecy. Mirage took the first watch, and spent it in a tree. It wouldn't protect her much from magic, but it would do nicely against roving Cousins, if they had such things as patrols. She would, were she in their shoes.

But no one appeared, either during her watch or Eclipse's, and after night fell they approached the house.

It was small, and much less sumptuous than Mirage had expected from the witch whose prominence in the Fire Ray had only been exceeded by that of her Prime. She had not indulged in the kind of extravagance some of her sisters did. There was, however, a lovely garden in front, filled with hyacinth and other blooming flowers, which Mirage saw as they scouted the surrounding area. It had not yet had time to become overgrown. The witches had hired them quickly in the aftermath of Tari-nakana's death.

Eclipse was a short distance away, barely visible in the gloom. His uniform blended into the shadows; she wouldn't have seen him if she didn't know he was there. Glancing at him, Mirage signaled in Silverfire's hand-code. *See no tracks. Go forward?*

He signaled agreement, and they slipped through the garden into the house.

In retrospect, Mirage realized they were lucky there had been no traps in the garden. She wasn't sure what there could have been—snares or falling trees would have broken the presumed mode of subtlety—but if the assassin had gone for more direct methods, they might have found out the hard way. *Start thinking, little girl. You're not on a picnic ride in the sun anymore.*

The house had the dead feel of a building that is deserted. Mirage was relieved, even though the hairs on the back of her neck kept expecting someone to jump out. But there was no one there, and the copper disks apparently kept them safe from Tari-nakana's wards. She wondered briefly what the wards would have done. Then she wished she hadn't. She could think of far too many gruesome possibilities.

Front hall, sitting room, kitchen. The food, protected by spells, was still fresh; Mirage and Eclipse sniffed and tasted it cautiously, but could find no evidence of poison. *Makes sense. If he used a quick poison, it would have been blatant, but a slow one probably would have been stopped in time. And then she would have been* very *suspicious.* Laundry, maid's room; Tari-nakana would have been unlikely to go there, but the Hunters checked both rooms nevertheless. Nothing.

Her personal quarters had to be upstairs, then, as Mirage had expected. They headed for the narrow staircase that arced gracefully up from the sitting room.

When she was almost to the second floor, Mirage stopped.

She could feel Eclipse freeze behind her. "Don't worry," she said, speaking for the first time since they had entered the house. "I think I've found something, is all."

She lifted her right foot very cautiously from the step it had just come to rest on. Reaching down with one gloved finger, she touched the nails that held the board in place. They showed patches of brighter metal as if they'd been hammered recently. And the board, when she pressed gently on it, gave beneath her hand.

Four steps in sequence showed the same. Mirage looked to Eclipse for confirmation; he nodded, and she stamped on the lowest one. It splintered beneath her foot without much force.

Eclipse moved up beside her and examined one of the fragments. "Termite damage."

"But not accidental." Not with those nails recently hammered in. Mirage glanced at the line of the staircase, calculating. "We were going slowly. Someone at normal speed, especially if they weighed enough—" She put one hand on the banister, heard it creak.

Eclipse bent to examine the near end of that section. "Some nails missing. This gives way, and she falls to her death. Or so our assassin friend hoped. He's running a risk, though—Tari-nakana would have looked a little accident-prone, after the horse and then this."

"But lucky for us, he didn't have a chance to come back and replace the nails and the original boards." Mirage broke out the other three damaged steps. She and Eclipse had to edge their way past the gap along the wall, but it was safer than risking that they might forget where the trap was. And the rest of the staircase was safe.

They found the upstairs destroyed.

No trap had gone off there; the chaos they found had been caused by someone searching Tari-nakana's belongings. Whoever it was had been thorough, if not particularly methodical. Papers were strewn everywhere. Mirage and Eclipse picked their way through the mess, not disturbing anything yet. No part of the bedroom, bath, or study had remained untouched; even floorboards and pieces of wall had been torn out.

"Well," Mirage said at last, "someone certainly didn't care if we found *this*."

"Must have happened recently, too," Eclipse said. "Our contact would have mentioned it, otherwise."

Mirage crouched to scan the scattered papers, then picked up a single sheet. Under it lay a small pile of ash. "Whoever it was already burned at least one thing."

Eclipse glanced out the window at the rapidly lightening sky. "It's almost dawn. I say we pull back to the woods. We can watch the house in turn and get some rest, then come back when it's dark again and search this mess."

Assuming there's anything left to find. Mirage sighed, but her interest was piqued. Who was responsible for this destruction? The assassin? Or someone else?

"Agreed," she said at last. "We'll come back at dusk."

*   *   *

MIRAGE TOOK the first watch again, but this time she explored a bit. She never went far enough to miss anything that might happen at the house, but she did climb up to the valley's lip, to where it ended abruptly in a crumbling cliff. From there she could see down into a lower, wider valley, more sparsely forested, with fields between patches of trees. Just before noon she saw figures out there, too far to be distinguished. She guessed them to be Cousins, farming the land.

Watching them drive a wagon across the valley, Mirage found herself grinning. People thought her one of *those* creatures? A tame pet of the witches? Not for all the money in the world. There was a reason she had chosen not to train at Cloudhawk or Stoneshadow. Mirage would no more want to be bound to a single employer than she would want to live her whole life in the same place.

The Cousins' situation seemed even creepier. In her few encounters with them over the years, they'd hardly spoken. Maybe their reticence only applied in front of strangers, but still—where did they come from? There were a dozen popular answers to that, but no proof. Did the witches really build them out of twigs and hair? Or were they the revived bodies of dead witches? She'd never seen a male Cousin, any more than she'd seen a male witch; either they never had sons, or they kept them all hidden here, in their home domain. Maybe as one of her three boons, when she finished this commission, she could ask their employer. Despite trying to stay mostly away from witches, she *was* sometimes curious about them.

Not long after that she returned and woke Eclipse, then lay down to rest. Her sleep was even lighter than usual;

her nerves were tight enough that it was all she could manage. She didn't mind. This edge of excitement was what she had been lacking.

In the late afternoon Eclipse nudged her awake and offered her a meal of bread, raisins, and cold sausage. They ate in silence, then waited for the sun to set.

"I'm leaning toward Wolfstar," Eclipse said as they waited.

Mirage nodded. "I am, too. The pattern seems like them, with things 'accidentally' failing—the banister, the step, the girth strap. A Stoneshadow would have used poison, I think."

"You're probably right. Which means we can tentatively take the domain rulers off the suspect list. They all have bonded assassins; they would have used them."

"True enough. And a pity, too." Eclipse raised an eyebrow, and she elaborated. "We know who employs Stoneshadows. So find the assassin, and you find the employer, and vice versa. It might have made things easier."

"Yes. And there's an unpleasantly large number of people left to suspect—pretty much any person or group of people who could afford to hire a Wolfstar."

"On the other hand, it does make some things simpler."

"Like what?"

"Repercussions. We can worry less about having to call Hunt on a Lord or Lady."

Eclipse looked puzzled. "You did that before, didn't you, with Kobach?"

"That was different. He was a usurper, and by the time I was hired all his allies had abandoned him. So that was less tricky. But we have *no* idea what the politics are here—why Tari-nakana was assassinated in the first place. I'm just as glad the employer is someone less influential than a Lord."

"I don't know about influential—there are some merchant consortia that have more clout than their supposed 'rulers.'"

Mirage rose and dusted off her hands. "We'll worry about that if we come to it. If we don't start searching that mess, it'll be a moot point. We won't know who's behind it anyway. Let's go."

SEARCHING TARI-NAKANA'S private rooms was a frustrating task. Mirage was not certain what she was looking for, or even if there was anything to find; she knew all too well that whoever had ransacked the place had probably taken or destroyed everything important. Assuming they had found anything. Assuming there had been anything to find.

They split up the task; Mirage searched the bedroom and the bath, while Eclipse took the study. When they finished, they would switch and search again, each hoping to find something the other had missed the first time around.

It promised to be a long and tedious night.

Mirage checked the clothes first, examining them by the light of her shuttered thieves' lantern, piling each garment into the corner as she finished with it. They had not been treated with anything as far as she could tell; perhaps the staircase had been the assassin's last planned trick.

She headed for the bath next, looking again for assassin's traps. She found nothing beyond a palatial setup powered by spells that provided heated, running water.

Moral superiority and envy warred with one another in Mirage's heart; envy won out. It would be nice to always have a hot bath. She frequently had to make do with streams, snowmelt as often as not.

Well, this job should pay enough that you can winter somewhere comfortable. Assuming it's finished by then. And assuming you actually succeed, and don't get killed by the blood-oath.

There were few belongings left to search; some jewelry, and a couple of things that looked like sentimental keepsakes. No sign of traps. Now it was time to look for clues, things that might tell her why Tari-nakana had been killed.

The most obvious thing to search for first was a secret compartment, which might hold important papers. The previous visitor had already done that, though, if by rather less delicate methods than Mirage herself would have used. She picked through the detritus, trying to see if any of it *had* concealed such a compartment, but everything seemed to have been normal before it was ripped apart. And none of the holes in the walls and floor held any remains of hidden contents.

Eclipse was still working in the study, so she turned her attention to the intact parts of the room. None of the walls held compartments she could find, and the same with the floor. The furniture, which the previous searcher had not thought to destroy, was similarly clean. *Of course, if she hid anything with a spell, I don't stand a chance in the Void of finding it.*

Standing with her hands on her hips, Mirage surveyed the room and tried to decide if she was missing anything.

"I think you should come look at this," Eclipse called from the adjoining room.

Grabbing her lantern, Mirage picked her way through the papers to Eclipse's side. He was holding a scrap of paper, quite small, with something written on it in an illegible scrawl. Eclipse tapped the signature scribbled at the bottom, but try as she might, Mirage could make nothing of it.

"You never could read his writing," Eclipse said with a grin. "It's Avalanche."

Avalanche. Six years their senior at Silverfire; he and Eclipse had been friends despite the gap in their ages. Mirage had never known him well, though, since he graduated not too long after she arrived. She peered at the note and supposed she could see his name in the scribble. "What does it say?"

Eclipse snorted. "Not much. 'Nakana: Back tomorrow.'"

Mirage blinked, and looked at Eclipse in mystified surprise. "He was working for Tari-nakana?"

"Looks like it."

Witches hardly ever hire Hunters.

Not that you could tell by their behavior lately. Next Ice'll show up with a commission of her own. Mirage took the scrap of paper and turned it over in her hands, but there was nothing beyond those three words and Avalanche's signature. "What could she have wanted him for?"

"Your guess is as good as mine."

"Protection?"

"Could be." Eclipse cracked his knuckles; there was a gleam in his eye. "We could always ask him."

"Do you know where he is?"

"Not at the moment, but one of our agents might know."

Mirage looked around at the chaos of the study. "Should we keep going through this stuff?"

"I'm pretty much done in here. Want to switch?"

"Not particularly, but I guess we should." Mirage stretched and eyed the papers balefully. "Warrior's teeth—did this woman never throw any papers away?"

"Give her a break. She was a high-ranking witch. This place is no worse than Jaguar's office would look if you threw everything *he* owns on the floor."

Left alone in the room, Mirage scowled at the papers. If only she had some idea of what to look for; searching blind like this was annoying. And the scattered, tiny piles of ash were testament that some important things had already been destroyed. Then she swore. "Kerestel—we're going to have to check downstairs again, too. If she had anything hidden, she might not have kept it up here."

"True enough," he said from the bedroom. "Looks like the last visitor didn't think of that."

"Who do you think he was?" she asked as she picked up a stack of papers and flipped through them.

"Not sure. The assassin, maybe; he might have wanted to take away any evidence pointing at his employer. And whoever it was knew to avoid the doctored steps."

"It doesn't seem like his style, though. He's been subtle up until now, so why rip this place apart? Especially since he's a Hunter. Even assassin specialists are taught to be more delicate than this."

Eclipse appeared in the doorway. "Who else, then? The employer himself?"

"Maybe." Mirage moved on to the next stack of papers. They looked like economic reports on the earnings of various Fire witches. "I'm tempted to bag half this stuff and take it with us back to Silverfire. Jaguar would like to know more about the witches."

"Uh-uh," Eclipse said, pointing a stern finger at her. "We're on hire. You don't spy on your employer."

"Thornbloods do."

"And Thornbloods are soulless mercenaries. What's your point?"

"Fine, fine, I'll leave the papers here. Go search. If I have to work, you do, too."

He vanished back into the bedroom, leaving Mirage with the papers. She made it through more than half of them before taking a break. *Plenty of interesting things I never knew about the Fire Ray, but nothing that seems relevant. Tari-nakana wasn't doing anything special that I can see.*

She went to the doorway. Eclipse gave her a mock-glare. "If I have to work, you do, too."

Mirage lifted one lip in a delicate snarl and he grinned. "Okay. What is it?" he asked.

"Why would someone kill Tari-nakana?" she asked.

Eclipse sat back on his heels. "You mean generically?" He began to tick the reasons off on his fingers. "Revenge for some personal or professional action. Prevention of some personal or professional action she was about to take. Political maneuvering—maybe someone wanted to see a new Fire Heart Key."

"We need to find out who replaced her."

"Definitely. And if the new Key has made any significant changes in the Ray's policy. You done with the papers in there?"

"Not quite. I was going to check the room for compartments, then finish them off."

"Okay. Then we'll look downstairs."

Mirage returned to the study and surveyed the walls and floor. There wasn't a lot left intact; the searcher had been more thorough—or desperate—in here. She checked nevertheless, and examined the desk as well, but found nothing. With a heavy sigh, she faced the remaining papers and set to work.

A paper covered in scribbled calculations; a personal letter from a Water witch informing her that the cat was doing well in its new home; a list of towns and domains that she scanned quickly. Breiano, Insebrar; Ravelle, Verdosa; Chiero, Teria; Olpri, Haira; a row of question marks; Ansing, Seach; Leswile, Abern. More question marks.

The names were familiar; she'd traveled too much to not recognize them. But why did they ring such a loud bell?

Breiano. Leswile.

Mirage leapt to her feet and went into the bedroom.

Eclipse glanced up, then rose hastily when he saw her eyes. "What is it?"

Wordlessly she thrust the sheet at him.

He scanned it and shrugged. "An itinerary?"

"*My* itinerary," she snarled.

"What?"

"Breiano to Leswile. That was the courier run I did, and those are most of the major towns I stopped in along the way. The question marks between Haira and Seach are probably where I cut through the tail of the mountains;

they must have lost track of me." She held up two more sheets, both covered in names. "This is more of the same. She's been tracking me for *years*."

He crossed to her and took the papers. "Why?"

Mirage threw up her hands. "I'm supposed to know?"

Eclipse gave her a careful look. "You're really upset, aren't you?"

"Wouldn't *you* be? I spend half my time trying to convince people that I have nothing to do with the witches, and now I find out they've been tracking my every move!"

"Well, not your *every* move. It looks like you lost them a few times." Mirage snarled at him, and he put up his hands defensively. "Okay, okay. Poor choice of joke."

Mirage spun away and kicked a wall in fury. The board cracked under her foot.

Eclipse's hand clamped down on her shoulder. "Calm *down*, Sen."

She took a deep breath, held it, then let it out slowly. "Sorry. I'll finish in the study. Then we can go downstairs."

"Avalanche may know something about this," Eclipse said, holding up the papers.

"He had better," Mirage said, her voice still tight. She could practically feel the eyes on her, and it made her skin crawl. "Because if he doesn't, I'm going to hunt down someone who does."

CHAPTER FIVE

Test [Miryo]

MIRYO WAS ON THE ROOF again when Eikyo found her, this time on a slope that had her facing Star Hall directly.

"You're brooding," her friend said in accusation, when she rounded a gable and found Miryo there. "*And* you made yourself hard to find."

Miryo just shrugged.

"Don't think you can get rid of me that easily." Eikyo came up and sat on the tiles next to her. "What's wrong?"

"Just thinking."

"While staring at Star Hall."

"I'm worried about the test, okay?"

Eikyo peered at her. "No, not okay. There's more to it than that. Has something happened?"

The sun-warmed tiles were soothing against Miryo's hands. She picked at a leaf that had become caught between two of them. "Maybe. I don't know." She caught sight of Eikyo's face, and sighed. "All right. I talked to Ashin-kasora a while ago, because I was thinking about maybe joining the Air Hand."

Eikyo's expression became sympathetic. "Did she turn you down?"

Miryo laughed without much humor. "She may not have to."

"What?"

"She . . ." Miryo searched for words to describe the Key's behavior. There really was no gentle way to say it. "She thinks I'm going to fail the test."

Eikyo stared at her in complete shock. "You can't be serious."

"And the funny thing is," Miryo said, not finding it funny at all, "just a few days before that, Narika-kai was telling me she thought I would be fine."

"Well, there you go," Eikyo said. "Who says Ashin's right? And for the love of the Mother, why would she even *tell* you that?"

"She didn't say it outright. Just acted like it."

Eikyo brightened. "See? You were probably just imagining it."

"I wasn't." Miryo shook her head, eyes on Star Hall again. "I don't know. Maybe it wasn't quite that. But . . . she was on edge about *something* having to do with my test. And she did a miserable job of hiding it."

Her friend ran her fingers down the cracks between the roof tiles, one by one. "Maybe she did it on purpose," she said slowly.

Now it was Miryo's turn to stare. "What?"

"Well," Eikyo said, "most of the time I've seen you fail at something, it's because you didn't think it was going to be a problem. So you weren't prepared. But if you expect a challenge—well, that's the quickest way to make you succeed. You put your head down and run at it, and Goddess help anything that gets in your way."

Miryo rolled her eyes. "You think she did it just to make me work harder?"

"Maybe."

It was better than the alternative. *And Eikyo's right about me, I guess. I left Ashin's office and went straight back to my room to look over my notes again.*

She was only up here brooding because that morning she'd received her script for the ritual that framed the test. It told her some, but not much. From the terse lines of her responses, she guessed that the test somehow involved trials of character, before it opened her to power.

Do I really think I'm going to fail that? Do I think my character isn't strong enough? Given some of the witches I've known here at Starfall?

But that wasn't really the question.

Am I going to back down from this—from what I've worked for all my life—just because I might fail?

Even if she could, she wouldn't.

Miryo smiled at Eikyo, and meant it. "I'll find out, I guess. In the meantime, it's back to studying for me. I'm damned if I'll fail the questioning, and miss the chance to prove Ashin wrong."

"WHY IS AMETHYST UNSTABLE in certain Fire spells, and which are those it can be used in?"

Miryo's heart clawed its way into her throat. Amethyst— Fire—Misetsu and Menukyo help her, she didn't know! Given time, maybe, but they would tolerate no delay!

And, for the thousandth time that day, even as Miryo's mind froze in terrified paralysis, her mouth gave the answer. The Fire Hand Key who had asked the question showed no reaction whatsoever, but Miryo knew it was correct. Again. Luckily.

The room was cool, but she was drenched with sweat, as if she had run a dozen circuits around Star Hall. And all she had done was sit in a chair and answer questions! Miryo felt drained. And still the questions came, steady and remorseless, and still she gave the answers, without quite knowing how.

Arrayed against her were fifteen women, each with a gaze piercing enough to have nailed her to the wall twenty feet behind her. Three from each Ray of Star Hall; they were the Keys to the Paths, and stood subordinate only to the Primes who led the five Rays. They must be passing some manner of signal among themselves, for the questions never paused, and no two witches ever spoke at the same time; they merely continued at the same measured pace, wringing every last drop of knowledge out of Miryo, including some she never knew were in her. Ashin was among them, of course, but her unusually dark eyes betrayed no hint of anything.

"When will the next lunar eclipse come, and how extensive will it be?"

"It will come forty-three days hence, and cover three-quarters of the moon, Itsumen-akara."

"During what part of the year is the constellation of the Hunter visible in the sky?"

"From the spring equinox to the winter solstice, Kimeko-akara."

Two in a row from the Void Ray. There was no pattern to the questions, no rhyme or reason to how they came. Miryo could never be sure where the next one was coming from, or what it would concern.

"Eliseed can be used for treating shortness of breath, but never with pregnant women, or those suffering heart troubles, Atami-makiza."

Without so much as a glance, the cue passed from the Water Hand Key to the Earth Heart. Would Atami be upset that Miryo had given too much information? The witch had not asked for exceptions to the use of eliseed. Even as Miryo said how many hot springs were in the domain of Trine—"Seventeen, Ueda-chakoa"—she slipped a glance back at the witch who had asked the previous question. Atami did not look irritated. It was probably better to tell more than less.

Miryo spared a moment to think of Eikyo. She hoped her friend was studying hard. The questioning was far more brutal than either of them had expected. How had Gannu ever passed?

"Lightning may be directed only in conjunction with Earth, Onomita-nakana. If the witch is not properly grounded, it may recoil back on her."

It took a heartbeat for Miryo to realize that no one had followed the Fire Head Key's question with a new one. She reached for her water glass; her mouth was dry from speaking, and these pauses came all too infrequently.

The Keys stood.

Miryo stared at them for an instant before leaping to her feet. The questioning was over. Now the Keys would announce their evaluation of her performance. Except that they hadn't discussed it among themselves at all; didn't they need to talk it over?

Then Miryo remembered her part, and turned to look behind her.

The five women who served as Primes for the Rays

stood behind her in an impassive line. Miryo bowed to
the Keys, then to the Primes, and moved to one side, out
of the way.

"This one has brought her mind to you for testing,"
Satomi-aken, the Void Prime, said into the quiet of the
room. "How do you find it?"

Hyoka-akara answered her, the Key of the Head for
Satomi's Ray. "Her mind is sound and well-prepared. We
commend her to your trial."

First stage down. Now, the one that matters.

Miryo approached the Primes and bowed again, trying to keep her face calm. They did not speak to her, but
merely turned and led her out of the room.

The six women passed down a hallway and through a
door, emerging into the crisp evening air. To her surprise,
Miryo saw that full dark had just set in. Even though she
was aware of the prescribed timing, it felt as though it
should be noon the next day. The questions had gone on
forever.

The Primes split up. One by one, they walked to the
four doors of Star Hall, until each stood at the door for her
Ray. Miryo was left a few paces behind the Void Prime.
Satomi stepped forward at last, and Miryo saw with some
interest that the woman chose the arm of the Hall dedicated to Air. Rumor had it that the branch you approached
from was indicative of which had shown the most interest
in you, the one they believed you showed the most talent
for. But it was only rumor.

In silent procession, Satomi walked down the lofty
corridor of Air. Miryo restrained her urge to gape around;
she and the other students were in here only rarely. She
kept her eyes glued to the Void Prime's rod-straight back,

until they stood in the center, where the arms of the Hall crossed.

The witch guided Miryo up onto the dais at the center, then turned to face her.

"Remain here in vigil, and contemplate that which you face. At midnight, the ritual will begin."

And then I find out what Ashin was afraid of.

"I hear and obey, Satomi-aken," Miryo said softly. The witch turned away and left the dais, walking out through the north, and the door of Earth.

Leaving Miryo alone in Star Hall.

From now until midnight, when the Primes would return, she would not speak. The silence of the Hall was oppressive, suffocating, until she wanted to talk, shout, sing, anything to break it—and yet she was forbidden to do so.

Miryo realized her breathing was quickening. Concentrating, she forced herself to calm down, and looked around the Hall.

It was a work of breathtaking beauty. Crafted from silvery stone, the Hall soared upward on impossibly slender supports, until it seemed to be reaching for the very stars it was dedicated to. Graceful rib-vaulting made a delicate pattern across the ceiling, fanning out across the bays, until at the crossing it leapt even farther upward, into a blackness the witchlights could not even touch. The crossing was devoted to the Void.

The four arms of the Hall, by contrast, were a riot of color. Each was built of the same silvery stone, clean and unadorned by even the simplest sculpture, but the walls between the piers of the arches were almost nonexistent, replaced instead by rank upon rank of exquisite stained-glass windows. In the west, where Miryo had entered, the colors of Air were all of the most delicate hues, barely even detectable, but the light that came through them turned everything sharp-edged and preternaturally distinct. She wondered what spell managed that. It was full dark outside, yet somehow the windows still shed light, still touched the silvery marble with their colors.

In the south, the hall of Fire was colored in all the hues of its namesake, red and orange and gold, until the light falling on the floor seemed to be pure fire itself. North was Earth, resplendent in rich greens and warm ambers; East was Water, all shifting blues.

And in the crossing itself—

The heart of Star Hall, dedicated to the untouchable emptiness of the Void, defied all the laws of nature. Somehow the color of the four branches, their light, their *life,* did not reach here. The air was peculiarly gray and washed-out, and the arches soared upward from the clerestory level into blackness. In the four arms, the windows depicted symbols of their Elements; in the center, Miryo could not even make out the windows, despite her best efforts. They faded away in an odd and disquieting manner, although she was sure they were there.

She shivered and looked away.

They wanted her to meditate on her future. *What a wonderful idea* that *is. All I can think about is what might go wrong.*

As far as she knew, there were two ways to fail the test. She didn't know how either of them *happened*—just the results.

She might die. It wasn't common, but it did happen,

and supposedly in a variety of ways. Though that might just be student rumor. Certainly Hinusoka had died.

The other possibility would make her a Cousin.

Most of those who served the witches had never been witch-students. They were the children of other Cousins, as Miryo was the child of a witch. Mostly daughters; a rare scattering of sons, which was more than the witches had, but not many. But ultimately they were all descended from failed students, and sometimes—when something went wrong in the test—new ones joined them.

Eikyo feared that more than death. Miryo wasn't sure which way to feel. If you ended up a Cousin, you didn't remember anything, which presumably meant you didn't care about your failure. But there was something appalling about the thought, about losing your mind—

Miryo's breathing had sped up, and she forced herself to calm down. *Don't think about that. Maybe fear is how it happens.*

You'll find out soon enough.

She concentrated on her breathing, focusing her mind, slipping into a light meditative trance where she thought about nothing at all. And, without her being aware of it, time passed.

Between one heartbeat and the next, they were there.

Miryo's breath caught in her throat. The five Primes had appeared silently, simultaneously; they might have been statues were it not for their glittering eyes.

Satomi was on the dais with her. The others stood at four points around the dais, each on a circular patch of floor inlaid with the color of her Element. In wordless unison, without so much as a sound to direct their power, they began to rise, until they reached the level of the dais, each standing on a coruscating column of Elemental light.

"Who comes?"

The sung phrase, five voices blending as one, broke the crystalline silence.

"A sister." The solo response came from Arinei-nayo, the Fire Prime.

"Who comes?"

"A student." This time the Air Prime, Shimi-kane, answered.

"Who comes?"

"A daughter." That was the Water Prime, Rana-mari.

"Who comes?"

"A candidate." Koika-chashi, the Earth Prime.

"Who comes?"

"One of ours, who is not one of us; one who would join us under the stars, who has not been tried." Satomi's voice rendered the peculiar intervals of her response without hesitation; the words floated upward to be swallowed by the blackness above.

The four other Primes sang in return. "Let her be tried; let the testing begin."

There was a pause. Miryo took a deep breath and braced herself.

"Aken, I stand in protest."

The chanted line stopped Miryo's heart. Shimi looked across at her with eyes like chips of palest blue ice; the woman's expression was antagonistic as she addressed the Void Prime in a monotone.

Was this what Ashin feared?

"This student is not fit for testing. She must not be allowed to continue."

"Shimi-kane," Miryo responded before she could think, "the Keys passed me in the primary testing."

The Air Prime gave her a frosty look. "They are Keys, and not Primes." She continued to speak in a single tone; Miryo had unconsciously echoed it. The music was the framework of the ritual, and despite this interruption—her heart skipped another beat in horror—it must not be broken entirely.

"That may be so," she said as steadily as she could. "But the Law of this Hall states that a student who has succeeded in the initial testing is eligible for the final stage. You may not agree with their decision, but the Law grants me the right nevertheless."

"The Law is not supreme. I am the Prime of the Air Ray; I have the power to alter it."

Arinei broke in now. "Sister, do you challenge a Prime?"

Miryo's jaw worked up and down a few times. Contradicting a Prime was unthinkable—but she couldn't let Shimi destroy her chances! "Arinei-nayo, my apologies, but the Law gives me the right to undergo this testing, and I cannot allow that to be taken from me. I have not come this far to give up."

"As my sister says, it is within the power of a Prime to alter the Law."

"But is now the time to do it?" Miryo shot back. "The ritual has started. It should be finished."

"It is not the place of a student to dictate policy to us, candidate," Koika said in a frigid voice.

Miryo spun to the north to face the Earth Prime, then bowed her head at the rebuke. "I understand, Chashi. But I will not back down from what I believe is right."

"Even though it may bring more trouble than you expect? Even supposing you pass the ritual, I fear my sister may never accept you. You build difficulties for yourself, candidate."

"I hardly expect every witch of the sisterhood to view me as a friend, Koika-chashi." Miryo lifted her chin. "If I cause trouble with authority, so be it; better that than to relinquish my convictions."

"Why do you wish to continue?"

The question, almost whispered in the chant all the Primes and Miryo were continuing to use, echoed fleetingly around the crossing. Miryo shifted to look at Rana.

"If I may be blunt, Rana-mari, I have not spent all twenty-five years of my life studying for nothing."

"You may die."

That short declaration made Miryo's skin crawl. She remembered what little had been left of Hinusoka when the ritual was done, and the other students who had not survived. Her fate might be like that. Or worse.

"Perhaps, Mari," she said quietly. "I am willing to take that chance."

"The Goddess smiles; the ritual continues. The sister, the daughter, the student, the candidate; she has been tried, and not found wanting."

What—oh, Misetsu and Menukyo, the ritual—that was it, part of it—all a test—

"Let the testing continue," the other four Primes sang in response to Satomi, in melody once again. "Will you begin?"

Miryo just barely remembered her own part. "I stand ready for Earth. May the Goddess as Crone be at my side, and lend me determination."

The Hall disappeared.

A crushing, lethal pressure was on Miryo—not physically; there was no physical element to this, but it was nevertheless horribly real and present, moving inward, forcing the life out of her. Its strength was terrifying. Miryo shoved back reflexively, trying to fight against the deadly attack.

Determination. Strength. Attributes of Earth—

Miryo braced herself, no longer trying to push the pressure back, merely concentrating on holding her own. It made the heaviest burden she'd ever shouldered feel light.

Goddess, Crone, I'm not strong enough—

That defeated thought sparked a sudden reaction in her; perversely, it made her that much less willing to give in. Eikyo had been right. *I made it this far; I'm bloody well not going to give up now.* She hardened her focus even more—

The pressure vanished. The Hall reappeared.

"I have mastered Earth," Miryo sang unevenly, her voice barely able to render the response. "Its strength is mine."

"The Crone smiles," sang Koika. Did she look pleased? Impossible to tell; the Primes were all impassive.

"Let the testing continue."

Miryo was not ready. She wanted nothing more than a moment to catch her breath, to recover from the ordeal of Earth. But she feared that any hesitation might undo her, might allow the terror to take control.

"I stand ready for Water," she sang before the doubts could rise up further. "May the Goddess as Mother be at my side, and lend me flexibility."

The words were scarcely out of her mouth when the Hall went away.

A fierce wind sprang up, seeking to rend her apart, to snap her in half. Miryo felt like a tree in a hurricane-force gale. Trees—they broke in storms, they were too stiff. She tried to bend with the wind.

She couldn't make it work. Like a tree, with its grained wood, she could not give way. The wind increased in force, and Miryo felt pain, as though her spine would snap, her branches break off.

Mother, Goddess of Water. I know what I should do—these tests are, in a way, straightforward—but I can't do it!

Slowly, painfully, she relaxed the nonphysical part of herself, moving in the direction the wind drove her. *Be a willow, not an oak.* It was working. The Goddess was with her.

"I have mastered Water," Miryo sang when the Hall was once more in her vision. "Its flexibility is mine."

"The Mother smiles," Rana sang. Two Primes had passed her; leaving three. And then—

Don't think about that.

"Let the testing continue."

"I stand ready for Air. May the Goddess as Bride be at my side, and lend me clarity."

This time Miryo was assaulted, not by a wind, but by an unreal barrage of—she could not put a word to it. Ideas, images, sounds, all flocked around her, flashing back and forth too rapidly to be comprehended, blurring into a demented collage, a howling demon of chaos.

It began to erode her sanity.

*Like studying—information—all those bits and pieces—
all at once—too many to control!*

The torrent continued. Miryo fought to put the thoughts
into order, to force them into some kind of sanity; she
fought and failed. Her own mental balance was rapidly
disappearing beneath the onslaught.

I have to stay calm!

She felt a scream building in her gut, fought it back.
She could not make a sound. It was forbidden to do so,
except in the responses. Not just for discipline; any ex-
traneous noise could disrupt the power of the ritual. The
wrong sound could be death.

This and a thousand other thoughts flew past in a mad-
dening flood.

And then it was over. Miryo drew a deep breath. "I have
mastered Air. Its clarity is mine." *Or so I hope. Misetsu's
faith—that was closer than I would have liked.*

Shimi appeared to find her performance good enough.
"The Bride smiles."

"Let the testing continue."

She feared this one more than all the rest—all the rest
save Void. Singing the next lines took more courage than
she could have imagined. "I stand ready for Fire. May the
Goddess as Maiden be at my side, and lend me courage."

Frigid chill. And a wind, again, this time bringing the
ice of the far north, like a blast of air off a snow-covered
mountain peak. Miryo's first instinct was to curl in on herself, pull her insubstantial body into a ball, but it did no
good; there was no shelter.

This was not what I expected. Goddess, I'm so cold!

The more she tried to hide, the worse it became. Her
bones ached at the cold. It grew steadily more painful;

her body was freezing solid, turning her into ice. Miryo huddled in on herself, almost weeping at the cold.

I'm going at it wrong. Obviously. Maiden, Lady of Light, what must I do?

Fighting back at the ordeal of Earth had failed. But Earth was not about fighting; it was about enduring. Fire, on the other hand—*that* was where you fought.

The fury she had held back, slowly building since Shimi had pretended to deny her right to be here, came bursting forth. It was more than anger, more than determination; it was her burning drive to undergo this ritual, and the dedication that had carried her through twenty-five years of training. To this point. This test.

I'm not going to give up now.

The passion of her emotions flared against the cold, pushing it back. Miryo straightened, lifted her chin. She had barely held on in the trial of Air, but this one was *hers*.

The Hall appeared once more.

"I have mastered Fire," Miryo sang, and this time there was real conviction in her voice. "Its courage is mine."

"The Maiden smiles," Arinei responded. She *did* look pleased; Miryo could see just a hint of it around her eyes.

"Let the testing continue."

This time the response was not Miryo's. She faced Satomi, who met her gaze as she sang the words. "No one stands ready for the Void. The test begins. May the Goddess as Warrior have mercy on your soul."

Everything vanished.

There was nothing. Not only was the Hall gone, and the Primes who stood in it, but nothing came to replace it.

There was no wind, no images, nothing at all. Miryo had been struck deaf and blind—more, even; her skin felt no sensations, she smelled no odors, even her own sense of her body was gone. There was nothing.

And Miryo knew it was the Void, but even that thought would not come, would not form in the emptiness. There was nothing.

Not even herself.

Her heart would have beat faster, had she a heart. She would have been terrified, had fear been able to exist. Her mind, were it not gone, would have dissolved into shrieking insanity. But it was gone, they were all gone; there was nothing except the Void, and the Void was nothing.

Her scream rang in the vaulting of the Hall.

Miryo stared around at the five women, the stones of the Hall, her own body. Her eyes drank in the images. The sound of her own panicked breathing was music; the touch of the air pure bliss. The world had returned.

She had screamed. Perhaps she had failed. But at the moment, Miryo could not bring herself to care; nothing mattered except the return of the world.

"You have glimpsed the Void, for an instant only, and it has marked you," Satomi sang. An instant? Eternity, and no time at all. Miryo's mind flinched back from it. "The Warrior has tested you, and you have not been destroyed."

"Let our newest fly on the wings of power."

The five women sang that phrase as one, and as the last syllable was released, something flooded into Miryo.

Pain annihilated the world.

CHAPTER SIX

Ravelle [Mirage]

MIRAGE AWOKE with a start, and didn't recognize her surroundings.

She sat up swiftly, battle instincts leaping into readiness. No one else was in the small, plain room. It was sparsely furnished, with just the bed she had been lying on, a small wardrobe, and a chair. The wardrobe doors were closed.

Moving as silently as possible, Mirage rose and stepped over to the wardrobe. Then, after taking a single breath to steady her muscles, she threw the door open.

No one was inside.

Reassured that she was alone in the room, she turned to survey it once more. Her saddlebags were there, piled on the chair; their presence did not clear up her confusion in the slightest. Where was she? And how in the Goddess's many names had she gotten there? Her blades were with everything else, so whatever had happened, she wasn't a prisoner.

Did I get roaring drunk, and just don't remember it? I don't have a hangover, though. Headache, yes. There was a mildly painful lump on one side of her head. *Was there a fight? What happened?*

There was a tiny window on one wall, but it only looked out onto a narrow alley and another building beyond. Nothing moved in the alley save for a stray cat. No clues there to help her figure out where she was.

Which left the door.

She belted on her sword and dagger before trying the handle. This situation might turn out to be harmless, but she'd rather be overarmed and laugh at herself than walk into trouble unprepared. The handle turned easily, and she stepped into an unfamiliar hallway.

Other doors lined its length; she put an ear to each one briefly, but heard no sounds from inside. When she came to the end of the hallway she found a staircase leading downward, curtained off by strings of enameled beads. *Teria, then. I recognize the style. What am I doing in Teria? And where in the Warrior's name is Kerestel?*

The stairs threatened to creak, so Mirage took them slowly, shifting her weight onto each one with exaggerated care. The effort made her head pound. It took forever to get downstairs. When she reached the next-to-last step, she flattened herself against the wall and peered through the beads into the room beyond.

She was looking into the common room of an inn. It was filled with trestle tables, each flanked by a pair of benches. At the other end of the room, a few comfortable chairs made an arc around the hearth. The fireplace was cold and empty right now, but Mirage saw a familiar blond head over the back of one of the chairs.

Alerted by his own instincts, Eclipse rose and saw her through the beads. "Sen!"

Mirage relaxed her weary muscles. She pushed through the curtain and walked to the middle of the room, surveying it. "At the risk of sounding like a minstrel's bad tale, where are we, and what happened?"

He gave her a careful look. "I can answer that, sort of, but not really." Taking her arm, he pulled her gently toward a chair. "Come sit down, and I'll tell you what I know."

"This isn't reassuring me," she said as she followed his pull.

"I bet." They sat down, and he looked directly at her. "I can't really answer your question because I don't understand what happened. We were riding along, doing nothing special. It was pretty far into the night, but we were trying to get to Chiero, and neither of us was tired—or at least you said you weren't—so we kept going. Then you pitched headfirst out of your saddle onto the road."

Mirage's eyes widened.

"I think you were unconscious before you hit the ground, but if you weren't, the fall certainly put you out." Eclipse shrugged. "We were almost to Chiero by then, so I tied you onto your saddle and brought you here to Marell's. That was yesterday."

Marell. A Silverfire agent, though not one Mirage had ever dealt with personally, hence the unfamiliarity of her surroundings. He owned this inn; it gave him a good means for gathering information that he could then pass along to the Hunters.

"Do you remember *any* of this?" Eclipse asked, worry lining his face.

Mirage leaned forward, putting her elbows on her knees, and stared at the floor. "We left Starfall. There was nothing else important in Tari-nakana's house, not after the itinerary." In her peripheral vision she saw Eclipse nod, but he did not interrupt her. "We went to Nasha in Handom; she told us Avalanche had last been seen on the road to Insebrar. On the way east, we wrote to our witch contact, because we wanted to ask about the new Fire Heart Key. She said she'd meet us in person in Ravelle. We agreed because it was on the way to Insebrar. She hadn't known about Avalanche working for Tari-nakana."

"What about the fall? Do you remember that?"

It was hard to pick any one day or night of riding out from the rest; the last five years of her life were a smear of roads, inns, towns, saddling her horse, unsaddling her horse, building campfires, being rained on, with only occasional landmarks to distinguish one bit of traveling from another. She closed her eyes, but it didn't help her memory. Riding, riding, then a blank. "No. I don't."

A short, tidy man came into the room then and introduced himself to Mirage as Marell. After reassuring him of her health—she felt fine, aside from the lump on her head—she asked about Avalanche.

Marell nodded briskly. "Bodyguard job in Vilardi. The Silk Consortium is there, negotiating with some of the major shipping companies. There's a lot of bad blood, so the head of the Consortium hired Avalanche to keep poison out of his food and daggers out of his back."

"How long are they there for?"

He tapped his fingers against his chin, head tilted back, apparently doing mental calculations. "They broke up recently over some argument, I believe, but it was a temporary halt only. They're aiming for an agreement within the next week."

That gave them just enough time to meet the witch in Ravelle before heading on to Vilardi. Mirage was relieved;

she had been afraid her mysterious blackout would make them miss Avalanche. He was their best hope for figuring out the motive behind the assassination. "What time is it now?"

"The temple rang Light an hour or so ago."

More than half the day wasted. Mirage wanted to swear, but restrained herself; Marell looked too proper for that. "Well, we can still get a few hours of riding in."

Eclipse shook his head before she even had the words out. "No. You need to rest some more."

"I've just slept for a full day. That's plenty of rest."

"You don't know that you're well yet!"

Mirage brushed one hand against the opposite wrist, drawing his gaze. Her sleeve covered the scar, but he understood. They were blood-oathed to their Hunt. Catching Avalanche in Vilardi was more important than pretty much anything else.

Eclipse sighed. "We'll saddle our horses ourselves, Marell. Thanks for your help."

THEY CAMPED ALONG the road that night, having ridden as long as they could without endangering Mist and Sparker in the poor light; the road here was not well-maintained. Mirage toasted bread as Eclipse saw to the horses, then passed him food silently when he sat down at the fire.

"What do you think caused it?" he asked between bites of bread and cheese.

She didn't have to ask what he was referring to. Her blackout had been on her mind all afternoon, too. "I have no idea."

"You might have been poisoned," he said. "I can't figure out how, though."

"Not poison," Mirage said, shaking her head. "Can you think of anything that works like that, delaying for however long, and then taking the victim down between one breath and the next? I know I didn't feel myself fading. It was sudden."

Eclipse considered it for a moment before shaking his head as well. "No. I don't know anything that would do that."

"Not to mention that there's no good reason I can see to poison me like that. What did it accomplish? It delayed us for about half a day. That's it."

"Maybe delay *was* the point."

"But only half a day? I can think of six different ways to slow someone down, every one of them more effective than that."

They ate in silence for a while, listening to the crackling of the fire and the small noises of the horses shifting around. The weather was hot and still, with scarcely a hint of a breeze. Mirage suddenly missed Silverfire, far to the west; it generally had cool evenings, with a breeze off the nearby river.

"What if it was a spell?" Eclipse said.

Mirage stared at him. "What?"

"A spell. That would explain the speed, and also why neither of us noticed anything. A witch might have knocked you out."

"And why would she do that?"

He shrugged. "I didn't say I had it *all* figured out. Again, maybe someone wants to delay us."

"Kerestel, we're working *for* the witches. One of them has been killed. They want to know who did it. Why would they slow us down?"

Eclipse put his hands up. "Fine, fine. It was just a random idea. I never said it would clear everything up."

Mirage took a deep breath. Snapping Eclipse's head off wasn't fair, even if he should have known that was a sore spot. His suggestion of magic had touched a nerve already raw from her discovery in Tari-nakana's house.

"Sorry," he said, before she could say anything. "I should've thought before I said that about a spell." He paused, and looked down at his hands. "It *is* something we should keep in mind, though."

Mirage touched his shoulder. "It's all right. We have to consider this from every angle. If the plausible explanations don't make sense, it's time to look at the implausible ones. And I'm going to have to stop twitching at every mention of magic; I'm working *for* a witch, for crying out loud."

He grinned. "Old habits die hard."

"But that doesn't mean they shouldn't be killed." Mirage stretched and tossed the heel of her bread into the fire. "You want to take first watch?"

They settled themselves for the night, but Mirage did not fall asleep immediately. She couldn't. Lying with her back to the fire, she stared into the shadowy underbrush and brooded.

Fine talk you make. "We have to consider this from every angle." And yet you don't tell him the whole story.

It was easy to rationalize her silence. She herself didn't understand what she had felt in that instant before she fell from her saddle. It had flashed in her mind and then vanished without a trace, leaving her unsure she'd felt anything at all. But the memory had branded itself vividly enough in her mind that she couldn't quite dismiss it as imagination.

Lying in the darkness, she closed her eyes and retreated into her mind, summoning the memory back. What *had* she felt?

The closest analogy she could find was the feeling she'd had a few weeks before, riding to Corberth with Eclipse. For the briefest of instants, it had felt as if an old and well-known friend, absent for many years, had been at her side again, as Eclipse was. There and gone, all in a heartbeat. And then, before she could do more than register the flash, she had blacked out.

And I suppose it's too much to hope that the two are unrelated.

Could it possibly have something to do with Eclipse? He was the one person she would consider an old and well-known friend. There was no one else, either from Silverfire or the years before that, whom she had felt particularly close to. Certainly not her parents, whom she had seen only a few times since being sent to the temple at the age of five; and they were dead now anyway. *Maybe I was visited by their spirits. Wouldn't* that *be a neat trick.*

It had felt familiar. But Eclipse had been there, just a few steps behind her on the road. And it hadn't felt like him anyway.

Mirage shivered, then made herself lie still. She heard Eclipse shift, but he said nothing. *I don't want this to have anything to do with the witches. Bad enough that I have red hair. Worse still that Tari-nakana was tracking me. I'll work for them, but that's the extent of my involvement. I don't want them interfering with my life. Any more than they have already.*

She took a long, slow, deep breath, and exhaled it carefully. Then, putting such thoughts firmly aside, she cleared her mind and went to sleep.

THEY PRESSED THEIR PACE to Ravelle. Eclipse still showed worry for Mirage's health, but her only concern was getting to Vilardi before Avalanche left. They'd already been weeks on the road since taking the commission, and she didn't want to waste more time chasing their fellow Hunter across the land.

Before they continued on, however, they had to talk to their witch contact. So Mirage and Eclipse dressed once more in uniforms and masks, and slipped through the nighttime streets of Ravelle.

The house they went to this time was smaller and less wealthy than the one the witch had used in Corberth, though the town itself was larger. It had no retaining wall, and also no guards; Mirage and Eclipse went directly up to the back door, where they were met once more by a Cousin. It was a different woman from before, Mirage noticed, but she was no more surprised at their arrival than the first one had been.

The witch rose when they were conducted into the slightly shabby parlor. The lighting in here was brighter; the witch had been writing, but Mirage could not see the page clearly enough to read it. She took a closer look at their contact, though, as the room in Corberth had been too dim to afford a good examination. Her hair was darker than most, more of a red-brown than a true red. Wide-spaced, large eyes gave her a perpetual look of surprise, but it was betrayed by the harder set of her mouth. If she controlled her expression, though, she could trick people into thinking her less than shrewd. Mirage wondered if she knew that.

"Sit down," the witch invited, gesturing to the hard-backed chairs.

"We have several questions," Eclipse said as he seated himself. The witch nodded for him to proceed. "First, is it possible to knock someone unconscious from a distance? Is there a spell that would do that?"

Mirage would have cheerfully strangled him. She clasped her hands in her lap instead and vowed to have a little "chat" with him later.

The witch seemed confused by the question. "From a distance? It depends on what you mean by distance. You have to be able to see them with your own eyes. It can't be done from across the city, or from a different domain. Why?"

If you tell her, I'll break your elbows, Kerestel. This is my business, not yours.

"It might be useful for capturing the assassin," he said smoothly.

"Oh. Well, it could be done, if I were close enough. Have you found the assassin, then?" A hint of eagerness crept into her melodious voice.

Eclipse shook his head. "Not yet. We're getting closer, though. As I wrote to you, we're fairly sure he was trained at Wolfstar. That narrows the field considerably."

"And what about the employer?"

"That's what we wanted to ask you about," Mirage said. "Who succeeded Tari-nakana as Key of her Path?"

"Kekkai-nai. I mean, she's Kekkai-nakana now."

"What was she doing before she became Key?"

"She was the regional coordinator for the north—Askavya, Liak, and Miest."

Mirage remembered the name now; she had seen it on no small number of papers in Tari-nakana's study. Closing her eyes, she thought back to those reports; had there been anything of note in them? Nothing came to mind. "Has Kekkai-nakana made any noticeable changes in the policies of her Path since she became Key?"

"Not that I can think of. But she hasn't been in office for very long, of course."

"What about Tari-nakana?" Eclipse asked. "What projects was she engaged in before she died?" The witch hesitated, and he lifted his hand in reminder of the blood-oath. They had every right in the world to know.

The witch nodded. "I'm sorry. In truth, though, Tari-nakana wasn't doing anything at all—nothing significant, that is. She was doing her job, obviously."

"Not 'obviously,'" Mirage said. "Was there something she *wasn't* doing? A duty she was neglecting, or a request she was ignoring? Can you think of anyone who would have wanted to remove her from office for ineffectiveness or incompetence?"

"She was quite competent," the witch said, her voice sharp.

Mirage made a conciliatory gesture. "The assassin's employer may have been unhappy with her failure to do something. Or perhaps he expects her successor to take a particular action that Tari-nakana wouldn't."

"Do you know of any projects Kekkai-nakana has been working on?" Eclipse asked. "Tasks assigned to her by Tari-nakana, or by her Prime? Did *she* have a pet project that might gain in importance now that she's a Key?"

Their contact shrugged, looking slightly hunted. "I don't know. Really. That's the kind of thing you'd really have to ask Kekkai-nakana."

"Then we need to meet with her," Mirage said.

The witch's control of her expression was greater than Mirage had thought; she quelled the flicker that ran across her face to the point where its nature could not be identified. Surprise? Unease? "Perhaps," the witch said slowly. "I'll have to write to her and ask. Heart Keys don't travel often, and Kekkai-nakana is particularly busy right now, as you can imagine."

They should have tried to set this up while they were still in Starfall. "Perhaps some magically arranged audience," Eclipse suggested. "Is there any way to do that? Talk to her at a distance, and not through one of those sheets?"

"Maybe," the witch said. "I'll have to ask. When I get an answer . . . I'll send the answer to your paper. You do still have that?"

"Of course," Eclipse said, and to his credit did not sound irritated by the question.

"Good," the witch said briskly. "I'll write to you, then, when I know about Kekkai-nakana. Until then, do keep looking into other clues. The Hunter bodyguard, for example."

They stood and saluted her, then left without another word.

"THAT WASN'T the same woman," Mirage said as they rode out of Ravelle's eastern gate in the predawn light.

Eclipse glanced at her. "You think so?"

"She looked the same. And her voice was the same. But the way she spoke was entirely different."

"Much faster, and less formal. I agree." He fell silent for a moment as they prodded their horses into a trot to pass three empty wagons trundling along the road back to their farms. When they were alone once more, he picked up where he had left off. "Why, though?"

"Depends on which one that face really belongs to. If the first witch looks like that, and the second was using an illusion, it may just be that our real contact was occupied elsewhere. Since she couldn't meet us on our way to Insebrar, she delegated someone else to take care of it."

Eclipse pondered that for a moment. "That makes sense, I guess."

"Unless neither one of them really has that face. That could be blamed on simple, standard-issue witch paranoia. If we can't identify our contact, that's one less bit of information we have."

"Did you get the feeling this second witch wasn't a member of the Fire Ray?" Eclipse said suddenly.

Now it was Mirage's turn to ponder. She hadn't considered that at all, but now that she did . . . "I think you might be right. She knew precious little about what was going on with Tari-nakana and Kekkai-nakana. Not that I expect leaders of any stripe to tell their subordinates everything they do, but she seemed particularly clueless. Which could be her natural state of mind. Or not." A thought struck Mirage then, and she pulled one glove off, cuing Mist with her knees to stop in the road.

Eclipse circled Sparker back to her side. "What is it?"

She extended her right wrist to him. "What color would you call that scar?"

"Sort of a faded brown—but there's a hint of green in it, too. Which is how it'll be recognizable as a blood-oath scar. It doesn't look natural."

"Now, I might be wrong about this, but I seem to remember a conversation back when we were trainees, where Talon mentioned that you can tell the Ray of the witch who cast the blood-oath spell by the color of the scar it leaves."

Eclipse looked at the scar again, then at her. "Greenish brown. Earth?"

"That would be my guess. It's certainly not a fiery color."

"So if our second witch wasn't Fire Ray, neither was our first."

Mirage pulled her gauntlet back on and kneed Mist forward; they couldn't afford to waste all day sitting on their horses in the middle of the road. "We thought she might be Void Ray, remember. And maybe we weren't wrong. But if she *was* Earth, and this second witch was something other than Fire—why are so many witches of other Rays involved in this investigation?"

"Tari-nakana was an important woman. Her assassination might mean trouble for all of them."

"Maybe. But it seems too pat."

More silence as they rode. Mirage kept quiet, for she could feel Eclipse was working through something in his mind. Morning had come in full by the time he had his thoughts together. She looked up sharply when he spoke again.

"Do you remember anything odd about those papers and letters in Tari-nakana's study?"

"I assume you mean the ones besides the itinerary."

Mirage considered it, then shook her head. "Nothing jumps to mind. It looked like routine paperwork and correspondence."

"Who was she receiving letters from?"

"Witches, mostly. Also Lords and Ladies of domains, of course, and some of their more important ministers and governors. But the bulk of it was from witches."

"Which makes sense, given that she was a Key, and of the Heart Path to boot. She was responsible for coordinating the activities of her Ray, and sending out orders that came down from her Prime. But what I want to know is, why were so many of those letters from witches— unranked ones, no less—*outside* her Ray?"

Mirage closed her eyes and summoned to mind as many of the endless sheets of paper as she could recall. She supposed Eclipse was right, but still— "Most of those letters were unimportant. Personal in nature. Like the one about the cat."

"They *looked* unimportant."

"You think they were in code?"

"I don't know. Maybe. We may have to ask our contact—or whoever it is we're dealing with now—to send us the papers from Starfall. I think I'm going to want another look at them."

The thought of having to cart the contents of Tarinakana's study with them across the land made Mirage cringe. "Let's at least wait until we've spoken to Avalanche. If there's something hidden in those letters, he may know about it."

CHAPTER SEVEN

Double [Miryo]

MIRYO SCHOOLED HER FACE to calm, her eyes in soft focus on the far wall. Once she might have paced, might have bit at her fingernails or her hair. The ritual had changed her, though; the calm of Air was in her, and she knew it now. She needed all its help to stay tranquil.

I have been marked. But in what ways? Goddess, Lady, I don't understand—have I passed, or not?

What is to become of me?

Miryo had not seen many people since the ritual; for a while it had just been Nenikune. Then, when the healer was satisfied with Miryo's physical health, Satomi's secretary Ruriko had come to summon Miryo.

Summon me to judgment?

Just then Miryo would have given a great deal to talk to Ashin. She wasn't certain of her own status, but it didn't much matter; whether she was a witch or not, she would have cornered the Hand Key and forced information out of her. Ashin had suspected this was coming. And Miryo wanted to know why.

She wondered how long she had been unconscious. No way of knowing; Nenikune had refused to say, and Miryo had known better than to ask Ruriko. The summons had been too formal. For all she knew, it could have been a week since her trial. The room she'd woken in had no windows, but if Nenikune had been bringing meals at regular intervals, then Miryo had been awake for two days.

The double doors, each carved with the symbols of the five Elements, swung open. Miryo rose to face Ruriko and bent into a tiny bow. Even if Miryo was a witch—and she wasn't at all certain of that—it couldn't hurt to be polite. The secretary gestured wordlessly for Miryo to enter, and exited after she passed, closing the doors with a final-sounding thud.

Miryo had never liked the hall she stood in now. Though beautiful, it lacked Star Hall's aura of magic; it was merely a place for mundane ruling, and not a space for ritual. Its intimidation was grimmer.

She walked the hall's length, hearing her footsteps echo coldly off the stone. In the floor beneath her feet were five parallel ranks of marble slabs; beneath them lay the bones of early Primes. The inscriptions were nearly illegible on many of them, worn smooth by generations of footsteps. It was a stark reminder of age and endurance, and it made Miryo feel small.

At last she came to the front of the hall and sank without hesitation into a full bow. Even if she was a witch, she was facing the Primes now, and respect was still required.

"Rise," Satomi said.

Miryo forced her knees straight and lifted her chin. She had no idea what was going on, or what had happened to her, but she was damned if she'd cower.

The five Primes eyed her from their thrones on the dais before her. Behind each of them hung beautifully stitched banners in their Elemental colors. Satomi's pale, fiery hair stood out starkly against its black background. It did nothing to soften her unreadable expression.

"You do not know what has happened to you," the Void Prime said at last.

Miryo remained silent, not knowing what she should say, or if she should speak at all.

"You could not have known," Satomi continued. "The information necessary to understanding has not been made available to you. We will give it to you now, so you may know what it is you must do to fix that which has gone awry."

Her voice had the measured cadences of formal words. Miryo forced herself to breathe, and did not look away from the Prime's pale green eyes.

"Five days after a witch gives birth to a daughter, before the infant is exposed to starlight, before the eyes of the Goddess bestow a soul upon the child, the witch performs a ritual that will, in the full course of time, allow that child to work magic. A channel is created. It is then blocked, that the child may learn the patterns of magic before its power is thrust upon her. And that block is not removed until the child is twenty-five."

None of this was new to Miryo; it was a part of the general course of study. She kept her eyes on Satomi, waiting for the new information that must be coming, the information that would tell her why she had suffered so terribly in Star Hall.

"But this ritual has a second effect. It creates a doppelganger—a second shell, a copy of the first, identical in every way, save that it lacks the capacity to work magic."

A second shell—Cousins? But no, Cousins are different—what happens to the other child?

Satomi answered the question for her. "This copy is a danger to the witch-child. Thus it is always killed."

Miryo's hands curled into fists at her sides.

"Your doppelganger is alive," the Void Prime said, her words whispering in the vast spaces of the hall.

And Ashin knew it. I'd swear my life on it.

She *swore my life on it.*

Miryo forced herself to breathe again, and wondered what, if any, of her thoughts had shown on her face.

"You must kill your doppelganger," Satomi said, not a flicker of an eyelash betraying any emotion other than cool practicality. "This is your task and yours alone. You may enlist others to your aid, but it *must* be your hand that strikes the blow.

"If you do not kill your doppelganger, then before much longer your magic will kill you. You cannot control it so long as your double exists; its continued life puts yours in danger. Until it dies, you must not use magic save in utmost defense of your life, and even then, be warned that your spell may kill you just as surely. You may not use your magic to kill your doppelganger.

"Once you have accomplished this task, you may return directly to us and take up life as an ordinary sister, choosing a Ray and a Path."

Only then did Satomi blink. The motion, jarring after the absolute stillness of everything in the hall save her mouth, jolted Miryo. She stared at the Void Prime, looking for words.

But it still was not time for her to speak.

"A horse will be prepared for you, and an escort. You

shall have such supplies as you need. In addition, you may choose one witch to be your counsel, answering what remaining questions you have until you depart. Whom do you choose?"

"Ashin-kasora, Aken."

Miryo didn't even have to think about it. This was a golden opportunity to get answers from the Hand Key.

Satomi blinked again, once, before answering; that was her only reaction. "Ashin has departed from Starfall on other business. Whom do you choose?"

Gone. Conveniently. And after saying she wanted to talk to me. Miryo controlled her anger. "Narika-kai, Aken."

"Narika will be your counsel. You will depart in two days. You may wear this." Satomi extended one arm, and a small object drifted through the air to settle in Miryo's cupped hands.

It was a pendant, crafted of silver: a three-cornered knot, laced around a thin circular band. Miryo's breath caught in her throat. *Despite my doppelganger—despite everything—I am a witch.* Satomi would never give her the triquetra sigil unless she had passed. She might not be able to use her magic, but she was a witch.

"Thank you, Aken," Miryo whispered.

The Primes rose to their feet then, startling Miryo; they had not moved throughout the proceedings. "Go forth and hunt, and return to us as one of our own," they sang in a unified monotone. Miryo bowed deeply to them and, torn between elation and sick dread, left the hall.

MIRYO SAT ON THE EDGE of her bed and stared at the floor. Around her were small trunks, empty, that she needed to pack; after she left Starfall they would be taken to the New House, where women just past their tests lived until they had homes of their own. On the bed next to her were saddlebags, likewise empty. These she would take with her to hunt her doppelganger.

Her stomach clenched at that thought. She could not imagine killing someone, not with her hands. Magically, maybe; there were always brigands stupid enough to attack witches. But not with a knife. Not that *close.*

A soft knock made her jump nearly out of her skin. Smoothing her hair back, Miryo took a deep breath and went to answer the door.

Narika was outside. "I expected you would be here," the witch said. "May I come in?"

She would never have asked permission before. It was another sign that Miryo was, despite her difficulties, a witch. The victory, sought ever since Miryo could remember, tasted like ashes in her mouth. "Please," she said woodenly, and opened the door wider.

Narika eyed the empty trunks and saddlebags, but did not comment. Miryo gestured for her to take the chair, and sat on the bed herself. At least she *could* sit, now; once she would have stood for the whole conversation.

"Satomi-aken told me of your situation," Narika said. "Do you have any questions?"

Miryo stared at the floor for a long moment, trying to focus her thoughts. They ran about like confused mice, chasing themselves in little circles. With an effort she brought them together, and asked the first thing that came into her mind. "Does this happen often?"

"No," Narika said grimly. "You did well to pick me; a lot of witches don't know much about this. But it's something my Path is familiar with, though not even all of us. You might have done better to ask one of my sisters in the Void Ray, but I can tell you almost everything we know."

"How did it happen to *me*?" Miryo said. It came out almost as a wail.

"No one knows. Perhaps your mother simply made a mistake. I didn't know Kasane well, but she never struck me as one so overwhelmed by sentimentality that she wouldn't be able to kill an empty shell. She knew the consequences of letting it live all too well. Every witch who has a daughter knows that."

"Do you think she knew, though? That it was alive?"

"Who can say? Kasane never gave any sign that she did, at least not that anyone has admitted."

Miryo tried to ask her next question, but felt her throat close up, blocking the words. She swallowed hard, disgusted with her own pitiful wailing. *For the love of the Goddess—if I can't even discuss this without falling apart, how do I expect to go after my doppelganger? At this rate, I'll not be able to see it through the tears, even if it were in front of me.* Miryo swallowed again and squared her chin. "How am I to find it?"

Narika sighed. "It could, in theory, be anywhere. You have at least one advantage: It will look exactly like you. So you can circulate a description, or even a sketch, to help track it down."

"That could take forever."

"It's possible. But I believe—although this is mostly speculation—that it won't be quite so difficult as you think. You and your doppelganger are joined in some way we don't fully understand; it's this joining that puts you in danger. But it can also work for you. I think that, if you trust your instinct, you'll find yourself traveling in the right direction."

"But you don't know for sure."

"No. I don't."

Miryo considered this for a moment. No immediate path of travel leapt to mind; she felt as lost as before. "I don't know if you can answer this—you said not all of this is understood—but what is it about my doppelganger that is dangerous?"

"It prevents you from controlling your magic."

"I know that," Miryo said, curbing her impatience. "But *how*?"

Narika sighed again. "In short, because it's a part of you, though separate from you. Controlling power takes perfect concentration, and your doppelganger is a part of you that you cannot focus at will. Thus your control is not strong enough."

"Even though it can't work magic."

"Even so. And you must hurry because—as you will, unfortunately, discover—though Satomi-aken has forbidden you to cast spells, her order will be hard to follow. Can you feel it?" Narika's eyes bored into Miryo. "Can you feel the power around you?"

Miryo swallowed painfully. Yes, she could. She'd been trying to ignore it. The power witches channeled came from the world around them; she could sense it with every breath she took, every touch of her hand against an object.

"Don't reach for it," Narika told her grimly. "You've been warned about the consequences. But that'll be hard to remember when you find yourself in trouble.

"You *must* be vigilant against this. Small spells you

might work without terrible backlash—if you're lucky—
but fine control is something that takes time to acquire.
You would likely turn yourself into a human torch when
you meant to light a candle."

Miryo nodded, her neck muscles stiff with tension.
*I'll not fall into that trap. I mean to see this through to
the end.* Narika was eyeing her as though hammering her
warning home by sheer force of gaze.

"Is there anything else?" Narika asked.

"Not at the moment," Miryo replied softly.

The witch nodded and rose. Then she hesitated. "For
what it's worth," she said, looking down on Miryo, "you
have my sympathy. And my prayers."

Narika was at the door when the words leapt from
Miryo as if of their own accord. "Why *do* all of this?"

The Air witch looked puzzled. "I beg your pardon?"

Miryo rose with a swift, choppy gesture. "The whole
thing. Doppelgangers. What's the purpose? Why did the
Goddess set it up this way?"

"Do I look like a priestess to you?"

"No, but they don't know anything about us anyway.
We're the only ones who would know."

Narika shrugged. "Ask one of my Path sisters in the
Void Ray, perhaps. One or another of them—I recommend Baira—can no doubt engage you in a long, philosophical debate about the Goddess's purpose for us in
this world. You'll probably not find any answers, but then
again questions like that rarely have any."

Miryo recognized the bite in Narika's tone for what it
was, and took a deep breath. "I'm sorry. I shouldn't have
asked. When Satomi-aken said I might have someone to
give me counsel, I know that's not what she meant."

Narika crossed back to Miryo, looking rueful. "I snapped your nose off, didn't I? I apologize. You don't need that, not right now. I have little patience with that sort of question, but I understand why you ask it. I don't have any answers for you, and I don't know if there are any to be found, but I wish you luck if you search for them."

"Thank you," Miryo said.

The witch returned to the door. "If you need anything further," she said, "send . . . a Cousin. I'll do what I can for you."

Send a Cousin, Miryo thought bitterly as the door closed. *"Send word," she was about to say. If I were really a witch, I could spell the message to her.*

And thoughts like that *are getting me precisely nowhere.*

Tossing her hair from her face, Miryo turned to the empty trunks and began to pack.

THE DOOR TO MIRYO'S ROOM was flung open so quickly it rebounded against the wall and nearly hit Eikyo as she dashed through. Miryo, who had leapt up from the floor at the sudden entry, was almost knocked down again as her friend hurled herself forward and enveloped her in a crushing hug.

"I was worried you'd be gone already," Eikyo said into Miryo's hair.

"Not until tomorrow," Miryo said faintly, still dazed.

Eikyo stepped back and squeezed Miryo's shoulders. "Nobody will tell me what's going on. I've never hated being a student so much—nobody tells students anything." She reached out and touched Miryo's triquetra pendant with one finger. "You *are* a witch, right? Some people don't seem to think you are—but you have this."

Miryo laughed shortly; it sounded bitter even to her own ears. "They're half right. I have the pendant, but what does it mean? Nothing, except that if I die I'll be buried as a witch and not as a student."

Eikyo's eyes widened. "What?"

"Sit down. It'll take a while to explain." Miryo swept a stack of papers off her desk chair, threw them into a trunk, closed the lid, and sat on that herself. Her bed was covered with saddlebags and clothing; she'd have to finish dealing with that before she could sleep tonight. "I'm technically a witch, but I'm not allowed to work magic yet."

Eikyo listened to her explanation, her blue-gray eyes solemn. When Miryo finished, there was silence in the room; the chirping of a cricket outside the window was shockingly loud.

"Well," Eikyo said at last, her voice heavy with unexpressed emotion, "I guess that's pretty cut and dried. You find it, you kill it, you come back and everything will be normal."

"Assuming it's that easy."

"What complications could there be?"

"Finding it won't be simple," Miryo said, rising. She tried to pace, but her scattered belongings got in the way. She controlled her urge to kick them across the room. "And killing it . . . I know I have to. But the thought of actually *doing* it, with a knife or whatever . . . I'm not *used* to that. It's not like I was trained as a soldier or an assassin; I'm a witch, for the Maiden's sake! I'm not supposed to kill people!"

"But crying over it won't do you any good," Eikyo said,

sounding more like her usual solid self. "It's the only way through this. So you grit your teeth and do it anyway."

"I know. I'll deal with it when the time comes. But that still doesn't clear up *anything* about Ashin."

"Have you talked to her?"

"She's gone. Satomi-aken told me I could choose a witch to answer my remaining questions; I tried to pick Ashin, but she apparently left right after my testing."

"Who did you choose in her place?"

"Narika."

"Does *she* know where Ashin went?"

"I didn't think to ask," Miryo said thoughtfully. "That's a possibility. I'll find her tomorrow morning, before I leave. If Narika knows, I might try following Ashin."

"What will you do if she doesn't, and can't find out? Where will you go?"

Miryo shrugged. "Narika thinks that if I choose at random, instinct or some such will lead me toward it. But she admits that she doesn't know if that will really work."

"Have you tried it?"

"Not yet. I don't know how I go about 'trying' to do something instinctively."

"We could go up on the roof; then you'd at least have a clear line of sight."

They did not head for their usual sheltered pit; instead Miryo and Eikyo climbed to the highest point they could easily reach. Above them Star Hall vaulted up into the night sky, blotting out stars, but neither of them was about to attempt that climb.

"All right," Eikyo said when they reached the top. "Which way?"

Miryo glanced around. The peak the students' quarters and Star Hall were perched on was the highest in the immediate region; to the east and west the mountains marched on in a jagged line. South, the land rose up into the bulk of the mountain range, then fell away sharply into a narrow coastal plateau; that region was inhabited by witches and Cousins and no one else. To the north the heights shrank to foothills, and then to plains, until they spread out into the patchwork of domains ruled by various Lords and Ladies, which spread out for weeks of travel in all directions.

And my doppelganger could be anywhere out there.

It was unlikely to have chosen the south. So Miryo would have to head generally north, but she could tend to the west, the east, or any line in between. None of them stood out in her mind as being more likely than any of the others.

I guess I just pick at random, then. Miryo thought about reciting a children's counting-rhyme to choose, but discarded the idea. *I have to head somewhere. I guess it'll be west.*

Miryo raised her arm to indicate this, and found herself pointing east instead.

Eikyo looked at her. "What's wrong?"

Shrugging, Miryo lowered her arm. "Nothing. East it is."

Avalanche [Mirage]

VILARDI WAS A much smaller town than Breiano, and seemed an unlikely place to hold such an important series of meetings. But Breiano, perched on Insebrar's coast a few days' ride away, was the headquarters of the Silk Consortium, and as such was hardly neutral ground.

So they made do. Vilardi did not have enough inns to house everyone, but the shipping families didn't care; they were accustomed to living in their wagons and tents, leaving the much pricier hotels for the silk men. Mirage and Eclipse, approaching the town from the west, encountered the perimeter of the tent city long before they reached Vilardi itself.

"Looks like most of the major overland shippers in the east," Mirage said to Eclipse as they drew closer. The large wagons at the heart of the tent circles had sprouted poles from which an assortment of banners flapped. "What do you want to bet there are at least three Windblades in there?"

"Might be some other Silverfires, too," he replied, scanning the area.

"Marell would've mentioned it if there were. Most of them are probably hiring bodyguard specialists." That might very well be why the Silk Consortium had gone for Avalanche; Hunters were dedicated to their employers above their schools, but not everyone believed that. "Let's go ask a few questions. Vilardi's not large, but they could save us some searching."

The perimeter guard eyed them suspiciously as they approached; Mirage belatedly wished that she had covered or dyed her hair. Then again, maybe that wasn't what was putting him off. Neither of them was in uniform, but it didn't take a genius to recognize Hunters, or to at least guess that they were dangerous. She relaxed her posture and held both hands out wide; beside her Eclipse did the same. The guard did not seem reassured by this indication of goodwill.

"What're you after?" he muttered, flexing his hands on the grip of his pike. The man was thick around the middle, but he still looked like he meant business. "What business do you have here?"

"None in your camp," Eclipse said. "We're not trying to enter. We're just looking for where your leaders are meeting with the Consortium's men."

Mirage knew it was the wrong thing to say the moment the words came out of his mouth. The guard's eyes narrowed further, and he stretched the pike forward threateningly. "I'm not telling you that. Get gone, before I call more guards on you! And if you show your faces around here or near any of our people, it'll be more than a warning!"

Swearing inwardly, Mirage nevertheless composed her face and bowed in her saddle. "We apologize for bothering you."

"Get out of here!"

They wheeled their horses and left the camp's entrance at a fast trot. Once they were a safe distance away, they pulled up and eyed each other wryly.

"Stupid of us," Mirage said. "They're so nervous they're hiring bodyguards, and we ask them where they're meeting?"

"Not the brightest idea we've had," Eclipse agreed.

They veered south, giving the encampment a wide berth, and circled around to the eastern side of the town. Mirage fumed at the delay, and at their own foolishness, but there was no help for it now. They'd just have to hope the shipping guards didn't cause them any trouble in the town itself.

Inside Vilardi's walls, the streets were packed. Not only had the Consortium and the shipping companies brought their people, others had flocked to the town in hopes of parting the visitors from their coin. The result was a madhouse.

"We'll be lucky if we can find a room *anywhere!*" Eclipse called over his shoulder, his tone sour. Mirage silently agreed. She had forgotten how small Vilardi was. Had there been a Silverfire agent here, they might have had a hope, but the town wasn't usually important enough to merit one.

The day had grown old and Mirage's patience had frayed to the breaking point before they found a place to stay. Tiny, with only one bed to split, and with more than a fair share of vermin. Her lip curled, but she said nothing. *We're lucky we've got even* this *much. However little it is. And you've slept in more disgusting places—that flophouse in Liak, before you got the first commission and had enough coin for something better.*

Her wrist tingled at the reminder. This assignment was definitely important enough to be worth enduring a few lice. Or even an army of lice.

A handful of men in the common room made lewd comments to her every time she walked through; she smiled and returned them in kind, although she had no intention of following through. It was the safest way to handle this type of thug; if she looked intimidated, or too defensive, she'd identify herself as an easy mark or a target in need of taking down. As it stood, they grinned, and winked, and left her alone.

As soon as their things were settled, with the bill paid in advance, of course, Mirage and Eclipse took to the streets once more. Their innkeeper had no more idea of where the Consortium and the shippers were meeting than how to spell his own name, so they'd have to search for it themselves.

A second tour of the town brought no more results than the first had; despite the cramped quarters, the leaders involved were doing a remarkable job keeping things secret. Mirage would have been impressed, had it not irritated her so much. *I'm not here for their Void-damned meeting. I just want to find Avalanche, talk to him, and get on with this job.*

The Warrior, it seemed, heard her prayers. When they turned onto a street they'd walked six times already, they found a procession coming from the other direction. Guards formed a thick wall, shoving the crowd back, keeping a protective space around the core of their ring. At the heart of it all was a palanquin, richly hung with embroidered silks. That was, no doubt, the leader of the Consortium. Mirage couldn't have cared less about him, though; it was the riders that interested her. One of them, dressed to match the rest, was nevertheless recognizable.

"Follow him," Eclipse said in her ear.

They tailed the procession discreetly; it went straight to the richest inn Vilardi boasted. The grounds were swarming with more guards, which didn't surprise Mirage in the least. If they were to get Avalanche's attention, they'd have to do it out here.

The two Hunters quickened their pace accordingly, working their way ahead of the slow-moving procession until they were as near the inn wall as they could safely get. Then, as the riders around the palanquin approached, Eclipse gave a piercing whistle.

It caught Avalanche's attention, of course; he was watching everything, from the rooftops to the windows to the beggar children in the alleys. In a crowd like this, his nerves had to be hair-triggered. The whistle brought his head around with a snap. He spotted Mirage and Eclipse and gave them one curt nod. Then he was through the gates and into the courtyard.

Mirage and Eclipse settled down to wait.

Avalanche was quick; he was back outside before a quarter of an hour had passed. The three Hunters withdrew to a nook not quite as exposed to the watching eye.

"Make it fast," he said, still scanning the crowd. "It's supper soon, and I have to be there to taste everything."

"The joys of bodyguarding," Eclipse said wryly. "We need to talk with you, though. Can you come meet us? We're in—What's the place called?" he asked Mirage.

"The Barmaid's Bosom," she said, keeping her face bland.

Avalanche grimaced. "I wouldn't visit you there even

if I could. But I can't leave him alone for that long anyway. You'll have to come here; I'll tell the guards. What do you need to talk about?"

"We've been blood-oathed to investigate Tari-nakana's assassination," Eclipse said.

The words made Avalanche go pale. Mirage would have been more subtle about it, but after all, Eclipse knew the other Hunter better than she did. "Do me a favor and don't mention that too loudly around here," Avalanche said. "It doesn't look good if they know the last person I protected ended up dead."

"So you *were* bodyguarding her," Eclipse said.

"Yeah. And I don't mind saying I feel like shit about what happened. Here I am, the only one she trusts to keep her safe, and I fail miserably at my job." He sighed. "Come back at Low. I'll be up; his lordship sir grand master high-and-mighty Consortium won't. The guards will let you in, and we'll talk." His eyes slid to Mirage. "I can't promise I've got answers for you, but I do have some things you'd probably like to know."

Then he was gone, pausing only to speak with the captain of the guard. Mirage glanced at Eclipse, and they left silently, melting into the crowd.

"SOUNDS LIKE AVALANCHE isn't enjoying his job," Mirage remarked later, in their room.

"I'm not surprised. I've heard about this Consortium leader. He's a real bloodsucker; cares more for his money than pretty much anything else. And he's used to having things done when he wants them, the way he wants them. He's probably running Avalanche ragged."

"Warrior's teeth. He's one of those who figures it's the

bodyguard's job to protect him, and doesn't do anything to make the process easier."

Eclipse nodded ruefully. "I'll wager you the palanquin and its curtains were there to shelter him from the noise and stench of the streets, and not rooftop archers. People like that hate to change their behavior just because of some vague, nebulous, maybe-there-maybe-not danger. They never believe they're at risk."

"Lucky for him he's got a sensible adviser in there somewhere, or he'd probably not even have hired Avalanche."

"Yeah. I just hope he's paying well. I'd ask a hefty fee, to put up with that kind of shit."

Outside, a bell tolled the third hour of Last. One more hour until they had to meet Avalanche. Mirage was glad she'd learned patience in Hunter training; a lot of her time was spent in waiting or monotonous riding. "Let's go get some food."

The common room was packed, even though it lacked just an hour to Low, but they employed intimidating looks to good effect and got a tiny spot to themselves along one wall. The table was none too steady—it looked to have been one end of something longer, before it was broken off—but it was theirs alone, a luxury they appreciated in the close quarters. Eclipse ordered food for them both, and they leaned against the wall to survey the crowd.

Men from the Consortium's lower ranks were sitting cheek-by-jowl with locals, and there was a scattering of shippers throughout as well. The atmosphere, luckily, was amiable, if a bit too drunken to rely on. Mirage just hoped the good humor would hold until she and Eclipse got out of there. She'd been in more than one barroom brawl, and they were never much fun. Even with all of her training, brawls were so chaotic and unpredictable that she usually ended up taking a chair to the back of the head before it was all done. Not her idea of a pleasant way to spend the evening.

The serving girl arrived with some indefinable sludge on thick pottery plates and went away again to fetch them beers. The supposed dinner was disgusting; Mirage picked through it with the point of her knife, looking for edible bits. She left most of it on the plate. The last thing she wanted tonight was a sick stomach.

Actually, that goes for pretty much any night.

Then there was a commotion at the door, and Mirage realized heavily that there was indeed something she had wanted even less.

Trouble.

A knot of men-at-arms from the shipping companies stood in the doorway, scanning the room. Mirage held still and prayed that they were looking for someone else—a friend, maybe, or a prostitute, of which there were plenty in the room. But she had barely finished the thought when the lead guard's eyes found her and narrowed in anger.

"Oh, Crone's stick, no," Eclipse muttered.

"You!" The guard advanced across the room, stabbing a finger at the two of them. *Just my luck. It would be the one from this morning.* "I told you to leave. I told you not to show your faces!"

"We're just having a drink and a meal," Eclipse said. "We'll stay the night, and then we'll be on our way and trouble you no more."

The guardsman bent to put his unshaven face right in front of Eclipse. "You'll leave *tonight.*"

"Funny," Mirage drawled, pulling his eyes to her. "I

don't recall any edicts from Lord Ralni forbidding us to be in this town. Nor from the mayor, either. I'd say we have as much right to be here as you do. More, given that you're disrupting the peace and we're not."

His scowl warned her. She seized his hands as they reached for the front of her shirt and twisted them around, bending them backward until he was in a reasonable amount of pain. "Don't touch me," she said softly.

The action set the guardsman's friends off. They stepped forward threateningly, hands going to the hilts of their knives. Mirage thanked the Warrior that wearing swords inside town walls was forbidden while the meetings were going on. Even so, their motion brought the Consortium men to their feet, which in turn sparked the other company men, which had the locals looking for a quick exit.

Then, unfortunately, a Consortium man chose to take Mirage's part. "I suggest you leave the lady alone. Unless you really need to prove to the world that you're uneducated, drunken boors not worth the effort to spit on."

Mirage used her leverage on the man's hands to throw him backward into his friends, buying herself time to get out of her chair as the room exploded. Eclipse rapped the one company guard who charged for her behind the ear, and he went down like a felled log. *One less in the fray. But there's plenty more where he came from.*

The tension she'd felt earlier had snapped, creating a full-fledged brawl in the space of a heartbeat. Mirage jumped out of the way of a local bent on finding an escape, but in doing so put herself in the path of another Vilardi resident too drunk to care whose side he was on.

She spun out of his path and found herself face-to-face with the guardsman who had started it all.

"Bitch," he snarled.

Mirage smiled at him and kicked him in the knee.

He went down, but someone else's elbow caught her in the head, full force.

Void-damned brawls! Mirage growled away the stars and turned on the owner of the offending elbow, slamming the palm of her hand into his nose and then kneeing him in the stomach where his too-small leather breastplate didn't cover. A swift punch to his kidneys as she threw him behind her finished him off, for the moment at least, leaving her still in the middle of the very brawl she had not wanted to see.

The sound of a breaking chair brought her around swiftly, but it was only Eclipse taking down another guard. He grabbed her wrist; she went along with his pull and flew out of the path of another attacker's downswinging fist. Eclipse kicked him in the stomach, chest, and head, and then they were gone, pushing through until they reached a wall, and then sliding along it until they found their way to the back door and made it outside.

"I hate brawls," Mirage growled, feeling the side of her head carefully. A noticeable lump was forming.

"They're not my favorite, either. Come on—it's almost time to meet Avalanche anyway. He won't mind if we're a few minutes early."

The brawl was already attracting a crowd of spectators outside the inn. The two Hunters eased their way out of the growing ring and took to the shadows; neither wanted further trouble. They moved to the middle of the street before they reached the Consortium inn, though. Provoking the already jumpy guards would just start another fight, this one much more serious.

They endured an extended scrutiny, but were finally passed along inside. Guards were camped out all over the courtyard, and another pair flanked the door, while a score or so filled the common room with quiet talk. Mirage found the atmosphere a relief after the fun in the Barmaid's Bosom.

"We're here to talk with the leader's bodyguard," Eclipse said to the door guards.

One of them grunted; the other nodded. "Upstairs to the second floor. Third to last door on the right."

Not an interior room. Mirage guessed that the Consortium leader was in the room just beyond. She could imagine Avalanche trying and failing to convince him to take a room without windows and a balcony. At least they were on the second floor, rather than the top or the ground; it lessened the risk of someone coming in from outside. Still, it wasn't the kind of setup a bodyguard would pick.

Better Avalanche than me. I might have staged a fake assassination attempt just to prove to this idiot that he is vulnerable. But if he wanted to take the job, that was his business. They were here to ask him about Tarinakana. And Mirage most expecially wanted to know why Avalanche had glanced at her like that, earlier in the afternoon.

The upstairs hallway was quiet, and dimly lit with elegant lanterns. Everything was peaceful.

Mirage stopped Eclipse with a touch.

He glanced at her and raised his hands to sign. *Trouble?*

Maybe. Go quietly.

They crept along the hallway, carefully placing their boots to minimize the floor's creak. The inn was well-built and well-maintained; the floor beneath the runner rug was solid enough not to make much noise. They flanked Avalanche's door, and Mirage put her ear to it.

Silence inside. Then a faint noise.

Mirage kicked the door in.

For just an instant, she could see a figure silhouetted dimly against the night sky over Avalanche's balcony. Then he was gone.

She was after him in a heartbeat.

There was just enough time, as Mirage vaulted the balcony railing, to realize that the inn's retaining wall was within reach for a good jumper. She landed well enough on its top edge to keep her balance and her momentum; her boots thudded onto the cobblestones a moment later, and then she was off down the narrow alley beyond, pursuing the just-visible figure of the other Hunter.

This was a quieter part of town; there was no one on the street besides them. Mirage gritted her teeth and poured her energy into running. She was fast, but her quarry had long legs and a head start. She was gaining ground, but very slowly, and he was nearing the town wall.

He veered suddenly to the left. Mirage took the corner fast and made up ground. Just ahead she could see another low wall, with ivy growing along it. He began to claw his way up it. She made a tremendous leap as she neared the wall and seized hold of his torso.

The other Hunter tried to dislodge her without losing his grip on the ivy, which was already threatening to tear out. She tried to pull him loose; she also spared a moment to tug at his mask and head covering, but they wouldn't come off easily. The struggle persisted for a few moments, during which neither made any real progress, and then the ivy rendered the situation moot by ripping loose.

The fight to put each other on the bottom as they fell ended in a draw; they landed together on their right sides and rolled apart. Both drew knives, which went flying a moment later as each chose to concentrate on disarming the other instead of holding on to the weapon in hand.

Mirage's opponent snarled and came at her in a rush.

She ducked his double kick and then tried to sweep his legs out as he landed. The attempt failed. He threw a backhanded punch at her, which she blocked, slamming his elbow as she did so. He grunted and pulled back, then came forward kicking once more. One foot caught Mirage in the ribs; a right punch clipped her head again, worsening the headache and disorientation from the brawl not long ago. She snarled away the pain and sweep-kicked again, this time taking him to the ground. He rolled out of the way of her descending kick and vaulted to his feet again.

Mirage had anticipated that; he took a fist to the face that sent him reeling backward. He blocked her next two punches, though, and then pounded her bruised ribs again.

Adrenaline kept the pain away. Mirage, turning to cushion the hit to her ribs, threw a left-handed blow that connected solidly with the side of his neck. Continuing with her momentum, she turned and delivered a hook kick, then a side kick from the other foot. The other Hunter reeled backward, hand dropping to his belt, and she knew she had the upper hand.

Then he threw a handful of ash in her face.

She leapt back, coughing, and tried to clear her eyes. But in the moment that she was distracted, he struck—not to her head, but to her left knee. Pain shrieked up her leg. And by the time she could see, he was gone into Vilardi, and she didn't have a hope of catching him again.

THE TRIP BACK through the town was a slow one. Mirage had washed the ash out of her face at a well, but the adrenaline had long since faded, and she felt every hit she had taken. Her knee was throbbing with every step, her ribs twinged with every breath, and her head alternately ached and plagued her with fits of dizziness. She staggered like a drunk until her fury overcame the pain; then she clamped her jaw shut and walked as steadily as possible, through the unfamiliar streets, working her way back to the inn by vague memory and no small amount of guessing. She just hoped Eclipse was still at the Consortium's inn; he hadn't followed when she jumped out the window. And what had happened to Avalanche?

Movement in the shadows; her hand leapt for the dagger she had not retrieved and closed on air. But the figure melting out of the shadows was only Eclipse, and she relaxed as much as she could without falling over.

"Where's Avalanche?" she asked as he approached, even though she could already guess the answer.

"Dead." Eclipse's face was a stone mask. "The killer?"

"Wolfstar, by the cut of his uniform. Gone, though. I caught up to him, but he blinded me with ash and kicked my knee out to stop me from following again." The admission galled her, even though she knew Eclipse would never blame her for her failure.

"Can you ride?" he asked.

Mirage blinked. "Why?"

"The inn's in an uproar, and men from both sides are all over this area of town, looking to cause even more trouble. If we don't get out of here, we're going to find ourselves blamed for Avalanche's murder."

Mirage considered it. She hurt like fury, and was still fighting dizziness. *Oh well. I can always tie myself to the saddle.* "I can ride."

"Good. We get the horses, then, and get out of here."

CHAPTER NINE

Departure [Miryo]

THE DAWN LIGHT was only beginning to peek through the stable doors, but Miryo had been up for an hour already. She dropped her saddlebags on the dusty floor, gasping from carrying them this far, and went to look for a Cousin.

The two who were to be her escorts were in the tack room, fetching saddles and bridles for the horses they would ride. Miryo asked one of them to deal with her bags, then went back inside to find breakfast.

Narika was not in the breakfast hall, but Miryo knew she was up; the witch had left a note under her door saying she'd be there this morning to see her off. Miryo hoped she would; she still needed to ask about Ashin. *And what if Ashin went in a different direction? Will I change my path to find her, or go with what I chose last night?* Miryo honestly didn't know. She put the problem aside to be dealt with when and if it arose.

She seated herself on one of the benches in the empty hall and nibbled on a hard roll. Motes of dust drifted through the early morning sunlight, mesmerizing her. It would be easy to fall asleep right here, were her mind not racing.

She couldn't believe she was about to leave Starfall. She hadn't left it for more than a few days at a time since she had come here from Tsurike Hall fifteen years ago.

And yet, if she were to join the Air Ray, this would be her life. Assuming she was a Hand, of course, but as she had said to Eikyo, most of the Air Ray acted like Hands anyway. Which meant a lifetime of traveling, always on the move, lending her skills wherever they were needed, to whomever needed them. Within reason, that was; no witch was bound to aid a cause she deemed unjust.

Was that the kind of life she wanted? It was more uncertain than most of the other Rays. Fire witches received food, housing, and pay from the Lords and Ladies they served; Water got the same, on a much smaller scale, from the villages they watched over. The Void Ray was supported by the labor of the Cousins and the tithes paid by domains for the aid they received from other witches. Only those of the Earth Ray had a lifestyle at all like that of Air; they lived off the land. If Miryo were to follow this path, her life would be like that: traveling, living off the land as often as not, receiving occasional rewards for her work, but unable to depend on such generosity. The people the Air Ray served often had little or no money to spare.

With a start, she realized the beams of sunlight had moved. Time was passing, and she was wasting it. Rising to her feet, Miryo scanned the few women down at the other end of the hall; Narika was still not among them.

Nor was the witch outside, nor was she in the stables. Miryo bit one knuckle, wondering if she should go seek Narika out, or send a Cousin to find her.

"Good, I was hoping you hadn't left yet."

The sudden sound made Miryo jump. "You startled me, Narika." She managed to swallow the "kai" just in time. It wasn't wrong to address a fellow witch with the honorific, but neither was it necessary, and Miryo was determined not to do anything to reinforce the idea that she was not really a witch.

"I do apologize. You don't look like you slept much last night."

"Packing took longer than I had expected." That, and she had spent well over an hour poring over a map, trying to figure out where she was headed in the east, where her doppelganger might have holed up. Assuming her choice wasn't really random.

"That's why I'm not a Hand," Narika said with a smile. "They all quickly learn not to pack more than necessary, I'm told, but I take forever to get myself together."

Miryo smiled and tried to figure out how to broach the subject of Ashin.

"Do you have any further questions before you leave?" Narika asked.

Well, that made it easy. "I was wondering, actually— do you happen to know where Ashin-kasora has gone? Satomi-aken told me she left not that long ago."

Narika looked thoughtful. "I'm not certain. She travels so much, and she's not *my* Key. She might have gone up to Askavya; Geike was saying there had been some troubles up there."

Askavya was due north. Miryo sighed. "Thanks."

Narika gave her a curious look. "Were you hoping to talk to her? I can try to spell to her, if you'd like."

"No, thank you. That won't be necessary."

"Are you traveling toward Askavya?"

"No, I was thinking of heading east instead."

"Does something draw you there?" Narika's ears all but pricked.

Miryo shrugged helplessly. "I honestly don't know. It doesn't seem *wrong,* so I guess it's as good a direction as any."

Narika looked disappointed; Miryo supposed she had been hoping for some great revelation. "Very well. I would offer you a searching spell, but it would be confused between you and your doppelganger. You'll have to trust instinct."

Let's just hope it's doing something worthwhile for me. "I will. At least until I have something better."

"Very well. I suppose I should let you go; you're losing valuable traveling time, and if I keep talking like this, you won't even make Samalan before nightfall." Narika followed Miryo out of the stables into the early sunlight, where the Cousins waited with saddled horses. "Goddess go with you, Miryo. Travel swiftly, and return to us soon."

"Thank you, Narika." Miryo was surprised when the witch hugged her, but she returned the embrace. Then, before anything else could delay her, she mounted and turned her horse's nose toward the road. She did not look back toward the students' hall.

TREES ENVELOPED THEM a few minutes into the journey. Miryo and the two silent Cousins rode through green shade dappled with pale, sharp morning sunlight. She let her horse choose its own pace; the road was well-built, but the rocky mountain soil here made for poor footing, and she had no intention of laming her horse on the first day out.

The ride was quiet and soothing. Given the Cousins' habitual unobtrusiveness, she felt almost as if she were on the road alone, with no one around save rabbits, squirrels, and her horse.

"Miryo!"

Eikyo materialized out of the bushes so suddenly that Miryo's horse almost reared. Her friend had the bridle in a heartbeat, though, and she soothed the animal with a soft word. "Sorry. I didn't mean to startle you like that. I was just practicing moving quietly in the woods."

Miryo smoothed her hair back with one hand and shook her head. "I'd say you don't need much more practice."

Eikyo eyed the Cousins, who were sitting impassively on their horses, and edged closer to Miryo. "Did you ask Narika?" she said in a low voice.

Miryo nodded. "She thought maybe Askavya, but she wasn't sure."

"Are you going to go north?"

"Not without more confirmation than that. If it's just one hunch against another, I'll stay with my own."

"That's probably good." Eikyo gave the Cousins another sidelong glance and lowered her voice even more. "Do you—do you want me to come with you?"

She didn't even have to think about her answer, but she did, just to be fair to her friend. It didn't change. "No. This is . . . it doesn't get more personal than this, Eikyo. I'm only taking the Cousins because I *have* to. Besides, you have your own test coming up."

"Not for a while. You won't be gone *that* long, will you?"

"I don't know."

Miryo's words fell more heavily into the silence than she'd meant them to.

"And don't follow me, either," she added firmly, to quash any rebellious ideas lurking in Eikyo's head. "I mean it."

Eikyo looked unhappy. "I just wish I could help you somehow."

"You can," Miryo said. "Pray for me." She shook her head when her friend laughed. "I'm serious. I'm going to need it."

Eikyo sobered up and nodded. "All right."

"Thanks." Miryo leaned down from her horse and gripped Eikyo's arm. Her friend squeezed hard, still looking worried.

"Goddess be with you," Eikyo said. Then she released the bridle of Miryo's horse and stepped aside so she and the Cousins could pass.

THEY RODE THROUGH the day, stopping briefly to eat and rest the horses, and came into Samalan in the late afternoon. The town, which sat just on the Currel side of the border, was a natural stopping point for people traveling to and from Starfall. It had taken a rare collaboration on the part of the Fire, Water, and Void Rays to keep the prices in Samalan fair; too many merchants saw it as a golden opportunity to gouge all who passed through.

But thanks to the work of Miryo's sisters, she was able to find lodgings for the night at a reasonable price. The Primes had given her a purse of money as well as a packhorse laden with supplies, but she had no idea how far she had to go. She could, of course, ask for more should she come to need it, but Miryo was determined to put that off as long as possible.

One of the Cousins saw to the stabling of the horses while the other took their bags upstairs. They had dinner in the common room that night. Miryo hardly received a second glance from the other patrons there. Witches might be an unusual sight elsewhere in the land, but in Samalan they were commonplace.

The reverse was not true for Miryo. She was twenty-five years old, but the world outside the halls of the witches was nearly as alien to her as the moon. She'd studied the domains in excruciating detail—their histories, their peoples, the ways of life in each place—but that was not the same as going out into them. Not the same at all.

Miryo couldn't imagine trying to learn everything she had to know to be a witch without isolation and intense study. Still, looking at the prospect of now having to face a world she'd never seen, she was inclined to seriously question the teaching methods of Starfall. Farmers, herdsmen, weavers, carpenters, merchants—such people were strangers to her. It was enough to make her want to choose the Void Ray, just so that she could spend her days talking to witches and Cousins, who were familiar.

The thought made her glance at her two silent companions. *I'd almost feel better if one of them would ask me where we're going, or say something*, Miryo thought. *I hope I adjust to them quickly; somehow I never noticed before how silent they are. Mother's mercy, I don't even know their* names. *I assume they have some. I should find out. Except it would feel weird to ask; at home Cousins are about as noticeable as the furniture. They're the perfect servants—except this silence is getting on my nerves.*

"We're likely to be traveling for a while," Miryo said abruptly, causing the Cousins to look up from their food. "And I don't even know your names."

They exchanged swift glances. Miryo wondered suddenly if Cousins had any kind of society, if they relaxed together when they weren't serving the witches. She had absolutely no idea.

"I am Kan," the taller of the two said. It was the first time either of them had spoken since Miryo had met them this morning. "This is Sai." The shorter Cousin nodded, but said nothing.

Miryo nodded back. "I'm Miryo." The Cousins glanced at each other again, then went back to eating their food. "We'll be going east at first," Miryo continued, determined to get some kind of conversation started. "I think we'll take the coastal road. We might have to change our path along the way; I don't really know." She wondered if Satomi or anyone else had told them what she was doing on this journey. Whether they knew or not, she wasn't about to broach the subject in the common room of an inn. "Is there anything we need to buy here?"

"I don't believe so," Kan said. It looked like she was going to be the spokesman for the two of them. "But I may go through the market tomorrow morning to be sure."

"All right. The market opens at First; if we leave an hour after that, will it give you enough time?"

Kan nodded.

"I'll see you in the stables an hour after First, then. In the meantime, I have an errand to run." Miryo rose to her feet, then stopped as Kan also stood. "Is there a problem?"

"I'm going with you."

Miryo stared at her. "What?"

"The Primes have charged us with keeping you safe, and it's getting dark out."

"Samalan is the safest place in the world, except for Starfall itself. No one would dream of giving me trouble, not so close to our domain."

Kan merely shrugged.

Miryo continued to stare at her, but the Cousin ignored it. *Misetsu and Menukyo. I probably couldn't get her to stay here if I tied her to a ceiling rafter.* She eyed the Cousin's muscles. *As if I could.* "All right. I don't think it's necessary, but it doesn't look like I'm going to change your mind." Kan didn't answer that.

They went out into the evening light, Kan walking a few steps behind Miryo. Glancing back, Miryo saw that the Cousin was alert, keeping one hand near to the handle of her short sword. *Maiden wept. She's probably going to act like this the whole trip, too.*

Shaking her head, Miryo turned her head and paid attention to where she was going.

It was a fair walk; lying in the grasslands as it did, Samalan had all the open space it needed to sprawl through. The directions she had been given led her finally to a modest-looking house near the north edge of town. Both the Water Ray and the Void Ray had representatives in Samalan: Perachi, a Hand of the former, lived farther to the east and served the people of the town. Morisuke, however, was responsible for monitoring who came and went from the witches' domain.

Kan hovered behind Miryo as she knocked on the door.

A moment later she heard the lock turn. A tall blond woman opened the door and took in the two of them with a quick glance. "Miryo, I presume. Satomi-aken spelled to say you might be coming to see me. Do come in."

With a start Miryo glanced at the woman's neck. The triquetra pendant hung there openly enough; Morisuke was apparently one of that minority of witches with blond hair. "Thank you," she said, realizing she had yet to move or speak, and stepped over the threshold. Kan followed silently.

"May I get you anything to drink?" Morisuke asked, gesturing Miryo toward a chair in her small sitting room. Her house was modest but obsessively tidy; even the fireplace, unused right now, was swept spotless.

"No, thank you," Miryo said.

Morisuke nodded and seated herself. Kan took up a sentinel position against one wall; Miryo resolved to speak to her about that. There was no need for the Cousin to behave as though she expected an assassination attempt any minute.

"What can I help you with?" Morisuke asked.

"I was hoping you could give me some idea of the road conditions we'll be facing."

"Which direction are you headed?"

"East, through Haira and Teria, but I don't know how far."

Morisuke closed her eyes and looked thoughtful. "There have been some storms in the coastal hills, but any damage to the road will likely have been repaired by the time you get there. If you go as far as Razi, that's the only place you might find trouble. Cano is not as good about keeping up his duty of road maintenance as he should be. But the storms were mostly west of his domain, so even if he hasn't yet seen to the roads, they should be in passable shape."

"Is there any political unrest?"

"Not in that region. Ruitte spelled earlier today to say that Lady Chaha of Kalistyi is claiming some of Seach's men-at-arms caused havoc on her side of the border— Lord Mimre is, of course, denying the charge—but that's up near the mountains. Southern Seach should be quiet. The only other trouble is up in Askavya, well out of your way."

Askavya again. And if anyone would know where Ashin went, Morisuke would; wherever she went, she almost certainly passed through here. "Narika said something about that as well. Do you happen to know if Ashin-kasora went there? She left Starfall about a week ago."

"Yes, she went north, and very suddenly. Did Narika by chance tell you what's happening up there? I've received very little word."

Miryo shook her head. "I'm afraid not. She wasn't certain herself."

"Pity. Well, it may just be some internal Air issue."

Morisuke was good at keeping a smooth expression,

but Miryo caught the slightest flicker of vexation. She had to suppress a laugh. Witches of the Path of the Head always hated not knowing things, and the Air Ray's habit of not telling the Void about their affairs probably drove Morisuke crazy. The witch no doubt prided herself on knowing a great deal of what was going on in the land, even if decisions about how to react were not hers to make.

"Indeed," Miryo said when she was sure she would not laugh. "Has anyone in the Earth Ray sensed any further weather problems?"

Morisuke shook her head. "Rain along the coast, which is to be expected for this time of year. But it shouldn't be more than an annoyance."

Miryo nodded and rose to her feet. Kan stepped forward. "Thank you for the information. I'd considered taking the northern route east, but I'll take rain in the hills over raids in the mountains."

The Void witch also rose. "I'm glad to be of help."

And glad to know that the new little half-witch is going east. Now if anyone asks, you can tell them. Miryo had no reason to hide where she was going—she doubted her doppelganger would hear of it—but the prying habits of the Void Ray irritated her.

She walked slowly once they were back outside, lost in thought. Kan followed her as before, keeping an even sharper eye out now that it was fully dark.

Her steps took her, not to the inn, but to the fountain that stood in the center of Samalan. It was not elaborately carved, but a spell cast by an Earth witch many years ago had arranged for it to never run dry. Even in the depths of winter it flowed, the water always warm enough not to freeze over.

Miryo stood next to it in the moonlight, watching the water leap and dance. She was aware of no sound save for its splashing, until Kan spoke. "Katsu?"

The quiet word made her blink. It was, she realized, the first time anyone had addressed her by that honorific. That pleased her unexpectedly; every sign that someone considered her a proper witch was encouraging.

"Yes, Kan?" she said at last.

"We should return to the inn."

"Not yet, Kan. No one's going to attack me out here, I'm sure, and I'd like a moment to sit." Behind her she heard the Cousin's footsteps, backing away. *No doubt she'll stand like a guard dog in the shadows now. Well, she can if she wants to.*

Miryo continued to watch the water, listening to it play. She was torn by indecision, unsure of her path.

When it was one hunch against another, I trusted my own. But now I know Ashin went north—she's probably into Abern by now. I could try to follow her. It would be a lot more logical than wandering vaguely off to the east, following a choice made at random late one night. Ashin might even know where my doppelganger is. She might be heading toward it right now; maybe that's why she left so suddenly. But if that's the case, why wouldn't she tell someone?

She seated herself on the edge of the fountain, trailing her fingers in the cool water. Kan was a barely visible shadow at the edge of her vision. *If I follow logic, I should go north.*

And yet . . .

Miryo knew she had no reason beyond gut feeling to think there was anything for her in the east. The river lands were more populous, it was true, so simple probability was on her side if she went in that direction. But she could hardly examine every person living in the eight domains that lay that way.

So the question is, how much should I trust my gut feeling? Do I believe Narika, and believe myself? Or do I take the safer, more assured path, and follow Ashin?

Miryo stood abruptly, making Kan shift. "Let's go back to the inn. I've changed my mind; tomorrow we'll go north to Askavya."

KAN WENT the next morning to buy a few more supplies; the lands to the north were less heavily settled than those to the east. Miryo and Sai took their bags down to the stables and rearranged the packhorse's load to make more room for the additional food.

The Cousin was back not long after the town bells rang First, and before the scheduled hour was up, they were ready to go. They led their horses through the market crowd, then mounted up as they neared the edge of town. Miryo cast an eye to the west; Morisuke's house lay not far in that direction. If they were going to head north, they should ask about the conditions in that direction.

She and Kan left the Void witch's house not long later, leaving Morisuke manifestly curious as to why they had changed their path. Miryo knew she'd pass the information on to others. Morisuke probably suspected she was following Ashin, and that was excellent gossip. She put the woman's machinations out of her mind, though, as they went to rejoin Sai on the main road and begin their trip north.

Ten steps into that trip, Miryo sawed her horse's reins around so sharply that it almost reared.

The Cousins glanced at each other, then watched her as she sat in the middle of the road, biting her knuckle in indecision.

Ashin's in the north. Goddess only knows if there's anything useful to me in the east.

"Misetsu and Menukyo save me from my own stupid impulses," Miryo muttered. Then she raised her voice so the Cousins could hear. "Forget it. I've changed my mind again. We're going east."

CHAPTER TEN

Witches [Mirage]

THE MOONLIGHT WAS STRONG enough to show the road, so the two Hunters rode away from Vilardi without stopping through what remained of the night. An hour or so before dawn, as the sky began to lighten, Eclipse left the road and found a tangle of brush where a tree had recently fallen. He set about constructing their camp while Mirage eased herself out of the saddle and fought down pain and nausea.

She woke at midmorning and felt better. Her head would take a while to recover, but the pain in her knee and ribs, while still there, was at a level she could cope with.

Coping with her memories was harder.

Eclipse was not inclined to blame her; in fact, he was generous with praise for her quick thinking and quicker feet, catching up to the other Hunter at all. The blow to the head she'd taken in the brawl, in his opinion, excused her failure to win the fight.

Mirage didn't agree.

"Tell me about the Hunter," he said, when it became obvious she wasn't going to leave off accusing herself anytime soon. "You said he was a Wolfstar. What did he look like?"

Mirage closed her eyes to concentrate, searching for details her mind had subconsciously recorded during the fight. "Tall—a bit taller than you, and slightly broader in the shoulders. Hazel eyes, close-set, with long lashes. Most of his height is in his legs, which makes him a *fast* runner, even though his reflexes aren't anything special. He favored kick-fighting a lot; makes sense, given his build."

"But it's unusual for a Wolfstar. Anything else?"

There was something . . . ah. "You remember what I said about the way we fell? We both fell onto our right sides, and I know *my* arm wasn't happy about it. Yet he still punched more from the right than the left. Which suggests his ambidexterity leaves something to be desired."

"Useful to know, though I'm surprised he made it through training with a flaw like that." Eclipse chewed on his lower lip, then shook his head. "No one's coming to mind. We can send a message back to Silverfire, once we get to an agent. They may be able to identify this guy there."

"Let's not waste time, then," Mirage said, and stood to begin saddling Mist.

Eclipse opened his mouth, and then closed it again. Mirage was grateful for his silence. She wasn't in great shape, but right now they needed speed more than anything else. The sooner they got to an agent, the sooner they'd know who the Wolfstar was.

And, since I can't believe that it's pure coincidence Avalanche was killed, chances are we'll have found Tarinakana's assassin as well.

*   *   *

"SO HERE'S A THOUGHT," Mirage said when they were two days away from Ravelle. "I'm not so sure that brawl was an accident."

Eclipse gave her a startled look, which changed to thoughtfulness. "Delay?"

"The way that guard showed up—it looked *purposeful*. He was looking for us, I'm sure of it. And while he might have just been spoiling for a fight, it seems too convenient."

"Because if we had gotten to Avalanche's room just a minute or two later, we'd never have seen the Wolfstar."

"And we might well have gotten pinned with the murder. At the very least we would have been under suspicion, and detained, and there would have gone any chance of catching up to the killer. It almost worked anyway."

Eclipse pulled Sparker to a halt and crossed his arms over the saddlebow. "All right. So what are we doing?"

Mirage blinked. "Explain?"

"The guard is behind us, back in Vilardi. He may know something worthwhile. We left to avoid getting arrested, but is there anything worthwhile in this direction? We need to decide where we're going and what we're doing before we ride any farther."

He had a good point. Mirage leaned her head back and considered it. And, out of the corners of her mind, a thought emerged. "We keep going this way. We're going to Miest."

"To Silverfire. Why?"

"Because I'm going to talk to Jaguar. I can't accept it as coincidence anymore that he chose us for this job, or explain it away with a simple desire to see us get an important commission. Tari-nakana was *tracking* me. I don't know if he knew that, but I'm sure he had a reason for choosing me. And I want to know what it was."

"Not good enough," Eclipse said, and his voice hardened to match her own. "Miest is a damn long ride from here. We can't waste all that time on the road without a better reason than that."

"Here's two more for you, then. Tari-nakana's successor, Kekkai-nakana, is probably in Starfall. If we're going to arrange any kind of face-to-face meeting with her, it'll happen there, or at the very least somewhere west of here. And second, Jaguar is the one who got the commission to begin with, who talked with the Void witch. He might have picked up some extra details, from what she said or how she said it, that could be useful. Remember that there's already something strange about this. A Fire witch was assassinated, but a Void witch delivered the commission, and it looks like one from the Earth Ray sealed it. I don't think inter-Ray scheming like that is common."

He looked at her steadily, and Mirage held his gaze without blinking. This was part of why Hunters often worked alone; in a situation like this, with no one possessing clear-cut authority, conflicts of will could cause real trouble. *I'm not going to back down. Will he?*

"Let's go," Eclipse said, and touched his heels to Sparker's sides.

Mirage stared at his back, then belatedly cued Mist forward. They rode in silence for a moment before she cast a sidelong look at him. "That was easier than I expected."

Eclipse shrugged without looking at her. "The first

reason didn't outweigh the benefit of questioning the guard, but all three together did."

"Not good enough," she said, deliberately mimicking his tone from a moment before.

That made him grin, and his stiff back relaxed. "All right. I also trust your instinct. There was a look in your eye when you said Miest, one that said *some* part of your mind had made a connection I hadn't. Once you had a few decent reasons, I couldn't argue anymore."

"Connection?" Mirage said, and shook her head. "Not that I'm aware of."

"Probably not. But you made one, I'm sure of it. We'll figure out what it is eventually."

Mirage shrugged and let him get slightly ahead of her on the road, so that he could not see her face. A connection? No. But some instinct, yes. She wanted to go west, and she didn't know why.

Except that something that way drew her. And she had no idea what it was.

THAT NIGHT Eclipse brought out the enchanted sheet of rice paper that was their link to their contact. Before he could begin to write on it, though, Mirage put a hand on his wrist.

"I have a different idea," she said.

He leaned back and eyed her. "Yes?"

"The house where we met the first witch, in Corberth— that wasn't her house. I'm fairly sure of it. The way she stood—she was a stranger there, and it showed."

"But . . ."

"But the second witch was different. That place fit her, shabby as it was. She lives there. Which, come to think of it, suggests she might be Water Ray, serving the people of Ravelle. It's a big enough town to merit its own witch, though just barely. But anyway, my point is, I think that if we go back to that house, we'll find her there."

"Go back unannounced, you mean."

Mirage nodded. "If she *was* wearing an illusion, this is how we can find out. If we don't warn her we're coming, we should be able to see who she really is."

The look Eclipse gave her was equal parts amusement and wariness. "You do remember the wards, yes? How neither of the Cousins was surprised to see us at the door? I'm betting that warning systems are the least of their defenses. If we show up without an invitation, we may get fried."

"I doubt it. Especially with a Water witch; they have sick people coming to them at all hours of the night. I don't think she'd have a ward that hits people with lightning bolts just because they didn't announce their visit in advance."

"That still doesn't mean she won't do something herself, when she sees us. Unannounced sick people are one thing; unannounced Hunters are another."

Mirage shook her head. "Gut instinct says she's not that kind of person. She won't kill us." Then she grinned, a swift, wild expression. "Besides, where's your sense of fun?"

MIRAGE'S HEART BEAT at an accelerated pace as they approached the house. Beneath her mask, she was grinning again. Reckless as this plan was, it was also *fun*. And they would come out of it okay. Probably.

I'm just lucky Eclipse is as stupid as I am, to go along with this.

She half expected lightning to strike them down on the way there, but nothing of the sort happened. They crossed into the garden without any trouble. The back door was locked, but that didn't stop them for more than a moment. Then they were into the house, moving fast, looking for the witch before the alarm ward that surrounded the place could summon anyone to stop them.

They were in the hallway, on their way to the parlor, when a creak and a singing voice behind them brought the two Hunters spinning around.

Their muscles froze in mid-movement, but by then they had turned far enough to see the witch who had cast the spell.

As Mirage had expected, she looked nothing like the woman they had met in Corberth and, supposedly, here as well. Her hair was much lighter, and shorter; she looked younger as well, with a weak chin and a thick scattering of freckles. The way she moved, though, identified her as the second witch.

"What are you doing here?" she blurted out, looking shocked to find them in the hallway.

Shocked and—relieved? I think she really is. As if she's not happy to see us, but we're not as bad as whoever she was expecting.

"Among other things," Eclipse said, indistinctly, since the spell had his face nearly immobilized, "we wanted to ask why you disguised yourself the last time we were here."

The witch blinked and tried to pull herself together. "I

don't know what you mean. I've never seen you before in my life."

"Give us some credit," Mirage said, putting as much bite in her tone as she could given the constriction on her jaw. "You can recognize a person by more than her face. You're the witch we met here less than a week ago. Why were you spelled to look like the witch we met in Corberth? Was that even *her* real face?"

"Of course it was," the witch said, but Mirage strongly suspected she was lying. "I'm sorry we misled you, but your original contact couldn't travel out here to meet you in person, the way you wanted. We thought you'd be more comfortable if you thought you were meeting the same witch."

"Would you mind releasing us?" Eclipse asked mildly.

"Oh—sorry." She whisper-sang a soft phrase, and they could move again. Mirage's skin shuddered all over in relief as the spell vanished. "Um. Come into the parlor and we'll talk."

Watching her go past to lead them into the parlor, Mirage became more certain than ever that their appearance—or rather, its unexpectedness—had given the witch quite a scare. Whom had she expected to find in the hallway?

"So," the witch said with false brightness when they were seated, "do you have more information for us?"

Eclipse related everything they knew about the Wolfstar. The witch didn't recognize the description, but they hadn't expected her to. It was simple courtesy, and proof that they were making progress.

"If you don't mind, Katsu," he said suddenly, in the

middle of his description, "may we know your Ray? I would prefer to be able to address you properly." Not as good as knowing her name, but they had figured she probably wouldn't tell them that.

She opened her mouth, paused, reconsidered, and finally nodded. "I am a witch of the Water Ray."

"Thank you, Mai," Eclipse went on, and Mirage brooded. *A Fire witch assassinated, and women from the Void, Earth, and Water Rays are involved. Why?*

"Now," Eclipse said when that matter was done, "have you gotten in touch with Tari-nakana's successor, Kekkai-nakana? It would greatly help our investigation if we could talk to her. In person, preferably. I know she can't leave Starfall for long, but is there a spell she could use to bring herself out here? Or to take us to her?"

"No," the witch said curtly. "Living things cannot be moved like that."

"Then if we could just talk to her, even at a distance. We *do* need to question her."

"I'm afraid that won't be possible," the witch said, even more curtly.

Mirage's eyebrows rose. "It's necessary, Mai."

"You'll have to do without it. You will not question Kekkai-nakana."

"Why not?"

Beside her she felt Eclipse twitch at the utter lack of deference in her tone. Mirage had come to some conclusions about this Water witch, though. She lacked the self-assurance of the Earth witch they had met in Corberth; she could, Mirage was sure, be put off-balance enough to reveal more than she wanted to. She might resort to using magic on them if they pushed too far, but Mirage felt it was worth the risk. After all, they'd already broken into the house. *Hanged for a fleece . . .*

The witch's mouth was working up and down; her expression had turned hunted. "You just can't."

Young, and without the other's composure. She'll crack. "It's necessary to our investigation," Mirage said, hardening her voice. "If you get in our way, you're interfering with the oath we swore, and slowing our progress. Which, incidentally, could get us killed. Do you want us to solve this or not?"

"You can't talk to her! She doesn't know!" The witch looked horrified as soon as the words were out of her mouth.

Eclipse pounced. "She doesn't know? No one's told her that her predecessor was assassinated?"

The witch swallowed and lowered her hands from her mouth. A deep breath failed to restore her shredded composure. "No. They haven't. And she is not to be told. These orders come from beyond me."

Beyond her. A Key? A Prime? Of her Ray, or another? This just gets more tangled.

"Why hasn't she been told?" Eclipse asked. "We still don't know why Tari-nakana was killed; someone may go after Kekkai-nakana next. She should be informed, for her own safety."

"She has Cousins to guard her," the witch said hastily.

"Cousins weren't enough for Tari-nakana," Mirage reminded her. "Even a Hunter wasn't enough. You can't assume Kekkai-nakana's safe from attack. Besides, she may have information crucial to our understanding of why Tari-nakana was killed."

"She doesn't, I swear by the Mother. Please believe me. Kekkai-nakana is safe, and she knows nothing."

"How can you know that?" Mirage demanded.

The witch's expression grew even more desperate. She stood up abruptly, knocking over her chair, and then, before either Hunter could move to stop her, began to sing.

THE HUNTERS' VISION and hearing returned, and the room was empty.

"That was unexpected," Mirage said, standing up.

Eclipse shook his head to clear it. "To say the least. She's gone, isn't she?"

"Gone, and not likely to come back anytime soon." They did a circuit of the house, but found no one, witch or Cousin, and enough personal belongings had been removed to confirm the witch was gone for good.

"We ought to apologize to the people of Ravelle," Eclipse said as they returned to their inn. "We've just robbed them of their witch."

"Though I have no idea why. What in the Void was going on there?"

"Your guess is as good as mine. That witch is running scared, of us and of something else. But I'm glad it was her we faced down, and not the one from Corberth; she would have been a damn sight harder to crack."

"True. I just wish we knew what *caused* the crack."

They took to the road again as soon as dawn broke. Eclipse pulled the sheet of rice paper from a pocket in his cloak as they rode and raised one eyebrow at Mirage. "Think I should send a message to our dear contact? Or do you think she knows already?"

"That Water witch ran so fast, she's probably in Starfall by now and has told everything," Mirage said with a grin.

He laughed and tucked the paper away. "Pity. I was going to ask her to send the description to Jaguar with a spell. It would be a lot more reliable than homing pigeons."

"I'd rather you not ask," Mirage said. "I don't want one of them serving as a go-between for our messages. We keep to ourselves, and they do the same. Most of the time." Although that formerly clear-cut situation was becoming murkier all the time.

"All right, fair enough. Still, think how convenient it would be, if magic were more common. You could send messages from Insebrar to Abern in an instant—no need for pigeons or couriers."

"I'd be out a hire or three."

He laughed again. "Well, maybe there *would* be need. After all, you wouldn't want to trust a witch with really private messages. They've got their own priorities, for all they talk about serving people."

"It's a moot point anyway," Mirage said. "There aren't enough of them to make things like that common."

"True. And I wonder why?"

Mirage shrugged. "They don't have many children. Maybe magic somehow causes miscarriages, so they don't carry most of their babies to term."

"Or maybe they just have half as many because they don't ever seem to have sons."

"We don't *think* they do. Who knows what really goes on in Starfall? For all we know, they kill off all the boy children."

"You have such a cheerful imagination, Sen, you know that?"

"All right, all right. Maybe they miscarry when it's a boy. It could be a magic thing. Who knows? Ask them, if you really want to know."

He shuddered. "I've had enough of facing down witches for information, thank you."

The conversation died then, but Mirage kept thinking as they rode. What *would* things be like, if there were more witches? She didn't like the idea, but she was biased. When she thought about it logically, it might not be so bad. Witches *did* do healing, for example; they could do a lot of good if there were enough of them in the Water Ray to cover the towns properly. And the Earth witches worked to prevent droughts or blights, and they kept the starving wolves at bay during harsh northern winters. Fire witches she had less use for; they served the rulers in their political games, and Mirage tended to think the rulers didn't need any encouragement or help. She also didn't particularly care about the Void Ray, which did very little to touch the outside world.

Of all the Rays, she felt the most affinity for Air. They were like Silverfire Hunters, traveling constantly, addressing problems where they found them, no matter who it was that needed help.

She envisioned ordinary people having houses with the hot water spells Tari-nakana had set up, spells to keep food fresh, spells to make life a little easier or simpler.

And deep in her mind, something clicked.

Mirage realized that she had stopped Mist, and Eclipse was staring at her. She glanced forward and back up the road; there weren't any travelers in sight, but some might come along.

"You've thought of something," Eclipse said.

"Let's get off the road."

They dismounted and led their horses through the thick trees until they found a good place to pause. Mirage tethered Mist and hopped up onto a boulder, where she bit one knuckle and stared at the ground.

"What is it?" Eclipse asked when his patience ran out.

Mirage started, then looked at him. "If you were searching someone's belongings and found papers you wanted to destroy, what would you do with them?"

He blinked. "Burn them, probably."

"Where?"

"Where? As long as I didn't care about hiding it, on site. If there was a fireplace."

"*Exactly.* You'd burn them in the fireplace. So would I. There's no point in going to the trouble to light a splinter from a lamp or whatever and burn each paper individually, where you found it."

He saw the connection now. "Yet the ashes in Tarinakana's house were all over, in tiny piles, no more than a sheet's worth or so in any one place. Why?"

"Magic," Mirage said.

Eclipse's eyes widened, then narrowed, considering it.

"I can't imagine it would take more than a tiny bit of power to light each one. A witch wouldn't think twice about it. She'd find a paper, conjure a lick of flame, and up it goes."

"So you think a witch trashed her study."

Something else occurred to Mirage then. "And another thing—how did that Wolfstar get into her house in the first place? It's one thing for that Water witch to leave her house lightly warded; she expects mundane visitors, living where she does. But Tari-nakana lived in Starfall, and whatever her wards are, they're strong enough that our contact felt the need to protect us from them. What about the Wolfstar? How did he get inside to set up his second trick, if he didn't have help?"

Eclipse stared at her. "You think he was *hired* by a witch?"

She hadn't considered it until just now, but . . . "Maybe."

"Why? And why would they then hire us to investigate it?"

"I can't answer the first, but for the second . . . we tend to think of the witches as all getting along. Why should they? Do the Hunter schools?" They both knew how ludicrous that thought was. Even within Silverfire, there were rivalries. "It's flat-out *stupid* not to expect factionality within them. So maybe one faction had Tari-nakana killed, and the ones who hired us are on the other side. Assuming there's only two sides."

He exhaled slowly, thinking it through. "Warrior's blood. I thought this might turn out to be messy, but this is . . ."

"Ugly."

"Uglier than the Crone with leprosy. Before, we had to worry that we'd die if we didn't solve this. Now we have to worry that we'll die if we *do*."

"It could explain lots of things, though. Like why witches of so many different Rays are involved in our side; these factions don't necessarily stick to Ray boundaries."

"And why our Water contact bolted. Do you think Kekkai-nakana is on the side that hired the Wolfstar?"

"Maybe, maybe not. Our contact might fear that, though. It's too simplistic to assume right now, but Kekkai-nakana might have had Tari-nakana killed out of ambition alone. And if our contact knows, or at least suspects, that other witches were behind the assassination, no wonder she's afraid." Mirage whistled suddenly. "And it explains Avalanche, too. Remember what he said? He was the only one she trusted. Tari-nakana had to have known the ones after her were witches; that's why she couldn't rely on Cousins as her bodyguards."

It was making more and more sense. Mirage wished Avalanche were alive to confirm it, but even without that, the explanation was becoming more and more plausible. And more and more frightening.

"Do we say anything yet?" Eclipse asked.

Mirage chewed on her knuckle for a long time before answering. "No. Not until we talk to Jaguar. He can tell us about the Void witch who delivered it, if she behaved oddly or seemed to hold any information back."

"And now we have another reason for going to Silverfire," Eclipse said soberly.

"What?"

"Protection. If we're right, and witches are behind this, we're going to be very unpopular with that faction. We may have no choice but to ask for shelter from Silverfire—since I *don't* want to depend on 'our' side to keep us safe."

Mirage shivered. Eclipse was all too right. She could

feel the eyes upon her already, hunting her, after her blood, like a palpable weight on the back of her neck. Eyes that were closing in with every heartbeat. They hadn't even told anyone their suspicions yet; when they did, the pursuit would begin in deadly earnest.

And however well-trained a fighter she might be, she had no way to protect herself against magic.

CHAPTER ELEVEN

Haira [Miryo]

MIRYO HAD AMPLE OPPORTUNITY to doubt her decision as they rode east. The journey through Currel's rocky countryside was uneventful, verging on tedious, and gave her far too much time to question whether she should have gone north.

They traveled at a good pace, and by the fifth day were crossing the smoother, fertile lands of Seach's southern coast. The road was lined with thick hedges and low stone walls; it was very different from the mountainous lands around Starfall, or Tsurike Hall's airy forests in Insebrar, where Miryo had spent her first ten years. She rode upright in her saddle, drinking in the sights.

The road wound between farms and the occasional pasture. Often she could see people in the distance, hip-deep in the rapidly maturing grain. Farmers, of course, yet they seemed so different from the Cousins who performed the same work in Starfall's domain, simply because they weren't associated with witches. Miryo found herself squinting at these distant figures, and then realized she was trying to see if any of them had red hair.

The question of her doppelganger never left her mind for more than a moment. How had it spent the past twenty-five years? Where would she find it? It was, she figured, probably masquerading as a normal person. Would it be a farmer? Or had it taken up some craft? It would look like her, she remembered, and so she imagined herself in a dozen different contexts, each one stranger than the last. Miryo tried not to be distracted by these, and hunted the elusive flicker of instinct deep inside her mind.

It was extraordinarily difficult. She repeatedly considered backtracking and going north, where she had a more concrete lead to follow. She never did it, though. Having committed to this path, she was determined to keep to it.

For a while, at least. Until she could no longer stand to depend on the vague thread of direction that was all she had to guide her.

SHE WAS RELIEVED when at last they came to something other than a village or a farm, simply for the distraction from her own doubt. And also, she had to admit, because once those villages and farms lost their exotic aura, they all mostly looked alike.

Haira's capital consisted of a central keep surrounded by a city that sprawled across the forking of the Nuna and Tufa Rivers. Miryo and her companions had pushed to reach it that day, and so when they crested a ridge that gave sight of the city, the red-tiled houses were bathed in vivid sunset light, and the rivers blazed as if they were on fire.

"Beautiful," Miryo murmured, momentarily entranced by the sight. The Cousins, as usual, said nothing.

The vantage given by the ridge was deceptive; it was nearing full dark by the time they passed through the gates and into the bustling evening activity of the city. Haira was not a place that went to sleep with the sun, particularly not in the summer, when the nights were pleasant. Hawkers continued to cry their wares, often in Miryo's face, and the taverns and gambling halls along this main road over-flowed with light and laughter. She debated dismounting to lead her horse, but there were other mounted people in the streets, and she feared being crushed by the crowd if she went on foot. This was a far cry from Starfall, or the rural quiet of the previous days.

A woman careened out of a doorway to Miryo's right and almost fell under her horse. Miryo grabbed the woman's arm to pull her to her feet, and got drunken thanks in return.

"Tell me, where can I get a room?" she asked the woman, although by the looks of her she'd had enough beer to forget her own name.

The woman peered up at Miryo and grabbed the stirrup to steady herself. Miryo's horse sidled until she controlled it. "North," the woman said at last, having finished her examination of Miryo's face. "Not around here. In the bit between the Nuna and the Tufa. We like to keep our gam-bling and our housing separate, here." She grinned, and Miryo saw that she had lost two teeth at some point in her life. "Want me to show you?"

Miryo agreed warily. Having a guide through this crowd would be useful, but she knew that such offers were sometimes traps. *Well, if it comes to a scuffle, that's what I have two Cousins along for.*

The woman took her horse's bridle and began to lead the animal deftly through the streets. Miryo checked back periodically to make certain neither of the Cousins had gotten cut off by the crowd, but mostly she watched the woman for any sign of trouble.

She'd be a fool to try. No one knows I can't use my magic. All the people here look at me and see a witch. With two Cousins who, by their looks, are quite competent with their swords. Miryo shivered, although the air was warm. *Mother, I do hope they're competent. I assume they are, and if I'm wrong, I* don't *want to find out in the middle of an attack.*

They soon left the main crush behind, and Kan and Sai moved up closer to Miryo's sides. She began to breathe easier. The streets they were on were less crowded, but not deserted. It didn't feel like they were headed into an ambush.

A bridge loomed in the uncertain light ahead. The Tufa River rushed underneath, white-capped and energetic. Miryo's guide had released her horse's bridle; now she gestured for the three of them to follow her over the bridge. On the other side, they found themselves amid buildings with signs marking them as inns.

"Here you are," the woman said, indicating the buildings with a sweep of her arm.

"Any recommendations?" Miryo asked, having decided the woman was not a thief.

She shrugged. "I live here. I don't know." She scanned the street less drunkenly than she had Miryo's face a while before. "That one over there, I've heard it mentioned once or twice. Decent food. I could use a bite myself."

Miryo looked to the one she had indicated. THE DANCING FLAME, the sign read, with a cozy hearth painted above the words. She glanced back at Kan, who shrugged. Sai looked blank.

"Sounds good," she said at last.

Neither room nor food was too expensive, and by the time their bags were upstairs, the woman had ordered supper for all of them, a dish of rice mixed with vegetables. Miryo poked through hers cautiously, then took a bite; it was acceptable.

"What's your name?" she asked the woman, who was devouring her own food at a good rate.

"Anthia," she mumbled, wiping a drip of sauce off her chin.

"Thank you, Anthia. Are all of the folk here so helpful?"

The woman swallowed and flashed a quick grin at her. "Some of them. You kept me from falling under your horse, and so saved me from bruises, maybe broken bones. I figured you deserved something in return."

Miryo gave her a sharp look. Her voice had cleared of its slur with remarkable speed. "Somehow," she said, "I don't think that's quite true."

Anthia looked puzzled.

"You're not as drunk as you pretended to be. And you weren't as off-balance as you looked; I could tell that as soon as I grabbed you."

Anthia saluted with her mug of cider. "Sharp of you."

"So the question is," Miryo said, studying the woman closely, "did you fall into me on purpose, and if so, why?"

A shrug. "I wanted a better look at you, and it seems less strange if you pretend to be drunk. Drunk people act oddly."

"Why did you want a better look?"

Anthia gave her a half grin and took a sip of cider. "Tell you later."

"Tell me *now*," Miryo said.

"Not here," the woman said, still with that half grin, and flicked her eyes toward the few other patrons in the room.

Miryo stood. "Upstairs, then."

The Hairan seemed about to protest, but Kan had her arm by then, and propelled her firmly up the stairs.

Up in the room, Kan and Sai bracketed Anthia, but not too threateningly. The Hairan leaned against the wall and seemed much more amused than she had any right to be.

"I must say," Anthia murmured, looking at the Cousins on either side of her, "I didn't expect *this* out of you. I must be getting careless in my old age. Most people take far longer to get this paranoid."

"What are you after?" Miryo asked, her voice hard.

"Haven't you checked yet?" Anthia asked, cocking her head to one side.

"I don't know what you mean."

"Odd," Anthia murmured, her eyes narrowing. "Well, you look wet behind the ears still; you must not be in the habit yet." Abruptly Anthia was gone, and in her place stood a younger, cockier-looking woman with red hair and a triquetra pendant.

"Oh, Lady," Miryo murmured, sitting down hard on the bed.

"No, Terica's the Lady here. I'm Edame, adviser to her and her Lord husband."

"Miryo," she replied, standing once more. "I didn't realize."

"You weren't meant to. That was the point of the illusion. A tip, oh green one: If someone seems odd, check them for any kind of magic. Sometimes it'll be a fellow witch in disguise. Sometimes it'll be someone spelled by a witch, for any one of a number of purposes. Sometimes it'll just be somebody odd. But it's always good to know."

Edame didn't look much less green than Miryo herself; if the woman was a day over thirty, Miryo would eat her shoes. How she had gotten to be adviser to the rulers of a domain was a mystery, but Miryo recognized her name and knew she wasn't lying. "I'll keep that in mind. Now, what exactly *were* you doing?"

The witch shrugged. "The more feckless of Lord Mimre's two sons was gambling in that hall tonight. I was keeping an eye on him, at my Lord Iseman's request. Then, as I was leaving, I saw you, and I couldn't pass up the opportunity to investigate what a sister of mine was doing in town."

She's as prying as Morisuke—and she's not even a Head! "Well, my business is my own."

"Certainly," Edame said easily. "Still, can I offer you lodgings at the keep? The beds up there don't have lice."

"Kind of you, to point me to an inn with lice."

"All of the inns have them, except for the ridiculously expensive ones patronized by fat merchants. And even some of those."

Miryo found herself glancing at Kan and Sai. Both of them had on their usual faces, impassive and wary, but neither seemed to see a danger in the offer. Miryo didn't see any, either. And it would be good to save the money. "All right."

Edame nodded. "Excellent." She gestured peremptorily for the Cousins to take the bags. "Let's not waste any time; it'll take a while to get to the keep."

THE FIRE HAND took them through the northern and southeastern districts rather than fight the crowds in the southwest again. The central keep was just south of the fork in the river, nestled right up against the bank.

Not much of a "keep," Miryo thought, looking up at it. *I don't know much about warfare, but it doesn't look very defensible to me. Not with buildings crowded right up against its walls. I guess they're not worried about an attack.*

Edame roused a pair of stable boys to care for the horses and swept right on into the keep proper. Miryo tried not to scurry at the woman's heels, but she had a very swift stride. They whipped through one high-ceilinged hallway after another until Edame stopped dead and made an irritated noise. "Blasted woman. I can never find her when I need her." She sang a quick seeking spell, then set off again at the same brisk pace. Miryo felt the power move—primarily Air, and little enough that Edame didn't need a focus to handle it—and swallowed. Narika's warning was becoming more real to her. She *wanted* to be able to do what Edame had, wanted to disguise herself and find people she was looking for with the power that was her birthright.

Not yet, she said to herself, and gritted her teeth. *Not yet.*

She didn't realize how grim her expression had become until they came across Edame's target, and the woman flinched visibly at her look. Miryo smoothed her face hastily and attended to what the Fire Hand was saying.

"I *know* you don't have anything prepared," Edame said impatiently. "But you can put something together, surely. We're always housing visitors here. This is the domain capital, for Crone's sake! Don't tell me that you can't find a room for one of my sisters!"

The woman set her mouth in a sour line and managed a grudging curtsy. "I shall see to it, Edame-nai. If your guest could wait in the small salon, I shall send a servant to her shortly." Then she retreated, back stiff, before the witch could say anything further.

Edame made another sound of vexation. "I swear, that woman lives to make my life difficult. She hates me."

Miryo shot her a startled look.

Edame noticed; her scowl vanished, and she grinned at Miryo. "Lionra's really not that bad. I just give her a hard time. Come, I'll take you to the salon."

They had barely settled themselves on the comfortable divans in the salon when, as if summoned by magic, a servant appeared with iced fruit juice. Edame waved him away as soon as he was finished pouring. Then, toying with the stem of her goblet, she eyed Miryo. "I never did accomplish my original goal, did I? What *are* you in town for?"

Miryo sipped her own juice to buy herself time to think. Edame continued to watch her intently, which did not make it any easier. "Well," she said at last, taking a gamble, "I'm afraid you're just going to have to live with your curiosity."

Edame looked sour. "In other words, you're not going to tell me." Miryo nodded, and she sighed heavily. "You, I think, are trying to take all the fun out of my life. I bet you're going to end up in Air. You've got their habits already."

Miryo tried not to breathe a visible sigh of relief. Judging by her behavior so far, Edame was mercurial enough that she might have reacted much worse. How someone so seemingly unstable had gotten to such an important position was baffling.

"I'm assuming," Edame continued, "that you're not in a Ray yet. Yes?" Miryo nodded. "I thought so. You don't look as overwhelmed as most of the newly fledged do, but you've still got that faint air of 'just out of Starfall.' Whatever you're doing, enjoy this while you can; after you join a Ray you might not get to wander around very much. Unless you do pick Air, of course. Do you have any idea what you'll choose?"

The torrent of words was hard for Miryo to sort through, as tired as she was. She stifled a yawn and forced her mind to focus. Just because Edame hadn't pressed her earlier question didn't mean she wouldn't still try to get information.

"Not really," she said as soon as the threat of the yawn had passed. "I have quite a while before I need to choose."

"Wise child. You can change Paths, you know, although some Rays are more lenient about that than others. But I'd have to ask a Void Head to remember the last woman who convinced the Primes to let her switch Rays. They *really* don't like letting you do that. So be certain you know which one you want before you commit. Take the whole time if you have to, but be certain."

Miryo sipped her juice and wondered if Edame regretted her own choice. She certainly didn't seem to have the temperament for playing at politics—but she *was* a domain adviser.

She did not get a chance to investigate this. A servant entered then and curtsied. "Katsu, Nai, if you will follow me, the room is ready."

"I'll come with you," Edame said, standing. "Lionra's a good woman, but I want to be sure the room's acceptable."

More stairs than Miryo cared to think about later, the servant led her into a small but well-appointed sitting room. "Your bedroom is through there," she said, indicating a fretwork door, "and here is another for your servants. There is a private bath behind that door."

"Indoor plumbing and heated water," Edame said with a wide smile. "I love my Ray." She strolled around the room and made an ostentatious show of checking the mantel for dust. "It'll do," she said at last. "Tell Lionra I thank her. I know it's difficult, having to arrange things on such short notice." The servant curtsied again and departed, closing the door behind her. "Even though it's her job," Edame added.

The door opened again almost immediately and the Cousins entered, laden with the bags. Miryo showed them the rooms and left them to unpack. Edame was standing in front of the sitting room's fireplace, looking restless. "Thank you," Miryo said to the Fire Hand. "This is much better than that inn."

Edame snorted. "Of course it is." She cocked her head to one side and studied Miryo. "How long are you staying?"

"I was planning on leaving tomorrow."

"Stay one more day. You look like you could use the rest."

Miryo hesitated. She wanted to be on the road; she felt that any delay would cause her to lose the faint pull she had been following so far. But nine days in the saddle had left her feeling as though her spine had fused into a solid rod, and a rest would be more than welcome. "All right. I'll leave the morning after next, then."

"Excellent. I'm told my Lord and Lady have arranged for some special entertainment tomorrow night, although they refuse to tell me what it is." Edame flashed another quick smile. "I shall leave you to your rest, then!" With that, the Fire Hand swept to the door and out, leaving Miryo to collapse gratefully onto her bed's feather mattress, not even pausing for a bath.

LONG YEARS OF HABIT prevented her from sleeping late. Miryo was up not long after the sun, and she awoke feeling unbearably grimy. The rains on the coast had not made it over the hills, and the dust on the road the previous day had been appalling. That, combined with the sweat of a night spent indoors in a lowland summer, made her skin crawl.

Her first task, then, was to clean herself. Once that was done, Miryo felt much more inclined to face the day, and the volatile Fire Hand who would no doubt track her down during it.

Sai was in the sitting room when Miryo finally emerged, clean and dressed. "Where's Kan?" she asked the Cousin. "Checking on the horses?" Sai nodded, not looking up from the split she was mending in a saddlebag. She still hadn't spoken in Miryo's presence. Cousins were quiet, but she took it to extremes. Miryo left rather than engage in another fruitless attempt to start a conversation.

Once out of her room, she wasted no time in getting lost. She debated asking a servant for directions, but decided to wander for a bit longer; she wasn't too hungry yet, and the one task she wanted to accomplish today needed no special rush.

She emerged into an unfamiliar hall just as Edame began descending a staircase at the opposite end. "There you are!" the witch called out, hastening her steps. "Come with me. I'm off to see if I can discover what is afoot for tonight. Surely *someone* here knows; the servants know everything."

"Actually," Miryo said, forestalling her, "I was wondering if you could do me a small favor."

"Certainly! Provided you don't want me to convince Iseman to declare war on anyone."

"Nothing like that. I was just wondering—do they employ a court artist here?"

Edame snorted. "Every Lord and Lady in the east, and a lot of less important people, employ court artists. There are two here. One does tedious landscapes and the other specializes in overly flattering portraits of spoiled noble children. Do you have a preference?"

"The latter, if that's all right."

"Certainly." Edame gave her a curious look. "What do you need done?"

Miryo quirked an eyebrow and smiled.

"Your business again, is it? Miryo, I swear to the Goddess, you keep your mouth more tightly closed than any woman I've met. But so be it. I'll take you to Ryll. You're in luck, actually; he, unlike his colleague, is awake at this hour. Tothe never rises before noon if he can help it. And all his landscapes are sunsets because of it." Even as she spoke, Edame set off through another door, taking Miryo through a confusing knot of hallways before halting in an archway. "Are you in, Ryll?"

A thin, middle-aged man came out of a back room. "I am, Edame-nai. How may I help you?"

"You can't help me, not unless you know what's planned for this evening." He shook his head, and Edame sighed. "I thought not. Well, then, I'll leave my sister Miryo here, as she's the one who really wanted to see you. I'm off to find someone who *does* know." Then she was gone, leaving Miryo alone with the artist, who did his best to erase a long-suffering expression when he realized she was looking at him. "I'm sorry, Katsu. I forget my manners. Please do be seated. How may I be of service to you?"

"I'm told you do portraits," Miryo said as she took a chair.

Ryll nodded. "Do you wish me to paint one of you?"

"Yes and no. I don't need a painting, and in fact I won't be staying here long enough for you to finish one. If you could do just a quick sketch of my face, though, I would be deeply indebted to you."

The artist pursed his lips and studied her face. "In charcoal?" Miryo nodded. "This is possible. You are certain, though, that you do not want something more elaborate? I could arrange to have it shipped to you; even with just a sketch to work from I'm sure I could do a lovely portrait. You have such vivid coloring."

Ryll was evidently one of those men who did not find witches too intimidating to court. Miryo wondered if he had cast any looks at Edame. And how such looks had been received. "A sketch will be sufficient, thank you."

He bowed with good grace. "As you wish, Katsu. Would you like to begin now?"

"If you're free."

"I am always free to serve one of your sisterhood. If you haven't eaten yet, I can have servants bring food up while you sit for the sketch."

"That's very kind of you."

"Then come this way," Ryll said, gesturing her toward the back room. She glimpsed an easel and a half-painted canvas through the doorway. "We will get started right away."

IN THE END Ryll made several sketches for her, each at a different angle. He was more talented than Edame had given him credit for; the sketches, hastily done, were nevertheless quite recognizable, and the paintings in his back room were elegant. Miryo thanked him, and tried her best to get him to accept a small fee, which he refused with many bows and a few more attempts at flirting.

She took the sheets back to her room and debated venturing out to try and find Edame. She needed to know what would be happening tonight, after all. But the thought of navigating the keep's halls left her feeling drained. In the end the choice was taken out of her hands, because she fell asleep.

Nine days of travel had tired her out more than she had thought, and her sitting room was sunny and pleasant. Miryo sat down in a comfortable chair to consider her search, and woke up several hours later. The room had grown dim in the late-afternoon light, and no one else was there. Miryo stretched, wondering where the Cousins were, and went to bathe again. She knew her presence would be expected at supper tonight, and it would be better not to show up with an imprint of the chair's upholstery on her cheek.

Clean once more—she wondered if everyone here bathed several times a day in the summer, to alleviate the heat—she shook out the one nice dress she owned and looked at it ruefully. It was hardly the sort of thing she had hoped to wear for her first presentation to domain rulers. But there wasn't anything to be done; she had nothing finer. And it was too late now to ask Edame for another gown, even had she been able to overcome her pride.

A loud knock at the door made her jump, and then the witch herself swept in, holding an armful of fabric. "I was hoping I'd find you here," Edame said briskly. "Here, this ought to fit you—you're a slight thing, aren't you?"

Miryo took the proffered silk and shook it out. The dress was embroidered with silver thread, and quite a bit finer than the one she had just dropped on the floor.

"Good color for you," Edame said, smoothing out the dark gray silk. "Sets off your hair wonderfully. It will look much better on you than it does on the mousy brown creature who owns it. I'll convince her to give it to you as a gift."

"That won't be necessary," Miryo said hastily.

"Nonsense. You're a witch; you deserve to own at least one pretty thing, and depending on what Ray you choose you may never have the coin to buy it. Put the dress on. I've found out what Iseman has arranged for this evening."

"What is it?" Miryo asked as she stepped behind the painted dressing screen.

"Just you wait," Edame replied mysteriously. "Does the dress fit?"

Miryo emerged a moment later, tugging the sleeves straight. "It's a bit loose, but that's fine."

"Turn around." Edame fiddled with the intricate lacing of the back, which Miryo had not known what to do with. Hairan court clothing—even something as simple as this—was much more complex than she was used to. The fabric of the dress rose and fell and rearranged itself into a much more flattering shape. "Wonderful. You're a credit to Starfall. Now come quickly; we don't have much time before they sound the call to supper." Edame whisked her out the door and back through the maze of the keep's halls. After just a few moments they came to a gallery overlooking a hall, and Miryo heard a low murmur of voices.

The Fire Hand gestured for her to come look. Approaching the rail, Miryo looked down at the men and women in the room below and caught her breath. "Temple Dancers."

CHAPTER TWELVE

Dance [Miryo]

"NOT JUST ANY COMPANY, either," Edame said, looking smug. "These are the Dancers from the Sunset Temple in Eriot."

"Haira has its own company, yes?"

"Of course we do. We have the second largest population of Avannans in the land, second only to Eriot itself. You should hear Iseman go on about how Temple Dance is the purest expression of adoration of the Goddess. But this company is truly incredible. I saw them once, in Eriot, several years ago."

Miryo looked over the railing at the Dancers below. Uniform with their sleek, black-dyed hair and lithe bodies, they milled about below, stretching and preparing for their performance tonight. She'd learned about them, as she'd learned about everything else: somewhere between clergy and laypeople, Temple Dancers were a key element in the Avannan sect's religious practices. They were also disturbingly flexible, she saw as one of them began to stretch. She didn't think her own body would do that without serious magical aid.

"You've probably never seen a Temple Dance before," Edame said.

"No," Miryo replied, still watching them. "Avannan worship isn't that strong in Insebrar, and they tend to not perform for witches anyway. And of course they never come to Starfall."

"I'm almost tempted to keep you away tonight," Edame said with a smile. "This company is so good, they'll spoil you for anyone else."

"Do you know what they'll be performing?"

Edame glanced around, then leaned toward Miryo with a conspiratorial air. "The Aspects."

That broke Miryo's attention away from the Dancers in the room below. "Are you serious? I thought they only did that on Holy Days!"

"That, and when somebody with a lot of money requests it. Especially if that somebody is as devoutly Avannan as Lord Iseman is."

Miryo looked back down, trying not to feel awed. The Aspects of the Goddess were neither a rote Dance performed the same way by every company, nor a local tradition not found elsewhere. Every company had its own version, and every version was different. "Eriot's company was the first one to perform the Aspects, yes?"

Edame leaned against the rail and nodded. "Long, long ago. Their version is legendary. Avannans talk about it as if the Goddess herself comes down and Dances with them. The Aspects are one of the holiest Dances there is, and they do it better than anyone."

And Miryo herself would be seeing it tonight. She felt a quiver inside, and with some surprise identified it as excited anticipation. It had been a long time since she'd felt that way. More than a year. The stress of studying for her testing had damped her spirits considerably, and her doppelganger's existence had prevented the aftermath from being the joy it ought to have been.

"I'm glad I stayed," she murmured.

Edame laughed. "You'll be even more glad in a few hours."

THE ANTICIPATION of seeing the Temple Dancers distracted Miryo from her nerves over meeting two of the highest-ranking people in the land. The great hall was imposing, but not as grim as the hall the Primes sat in for rulings. Miryo could feel the eyes of the assembled people on her as she walked past them; they were used to Edame's presence, and no doubt other witches came through, but a new arrival was always an occasion for comment.

Iseman and Terica looked to have been cut from the same bolt of cloth. They were both tall and bone-thin; Ryll could have been their cousin. Both were dressed in long robes more elaborately embroidered than Miryo considered to be in good taste, but she kept this thought from her face. Hairans tended toward flamboyant, even gaudy clothing, and the Lord and Lady were far from the worst offenders in the hall. Miryo was grateful all over again for the dress Edame had found for her; at least it was subdued. Some of the color combinations out there that evening had never been intended by nature.

Miryo sat next to Edame for the meal, with Iseman and Terica on the witch's other side. The food was rich, much more so than she was accustomed to; the assault of spiciness and sweetness in the sauces was nearly overwhelming. Miryo had to be careful what she chose out of the available dishes. Hairans ate much as they dressed.

She made simple conversation with Edame and the

woman on her other side, but stayed quiet for the most part. She wasn't in a mood for chatter. Instead she entertained herself by trying to guess what was in each of the elaborate dishes served to the high table by men and women who were, in Miryo's opinion, the only tastefully dressed Hairans in the hall. She was grateful when the meal was over and they retired to a smaller hall nearby that had been prepared for the performance.

Iseman and Terica seated themselves in two thronelike chairs along one wall, in front of a mural that was probably the work of the landscape painter; it featured half-clad nobility lounging on a hillside in front of a fiery sunset. Edame, Miryo, and favored members of the court took chairs behind the Lord and Lady and to either side. Everyone else—lesser ministers, courtesans, hangers-on—was relegated to the galleries along the walls. They shifted restlessly, embroidered robes rustling in the otherwise silent room.

And then the Dancers entered, and all sound ceased.

For this Dance, all wore black. Their pale skin stood out in sharp contrast. Their clothing was as close-fitting as it could be without restricting movement, and unadorned; men and women alike wore pants and sleeveless vests. Every one of them was lean and fit, and nearly androgynous in their similarity.

They lined up facing the Lord and Lady of Haira, and bowed briefly. The priestess who accompanied them spoke a short benediction, dedicating the night's performance to the glory of the Goddess in all her five Aspects. Then she, along with the majority of the Dancers, retired behind the black curtain that had been erected at the back of the hall.

Only one young woman remained in front, and she seated herself on the floor. After a moment of silence, hidden musicians struck up a tune.

It was swift, light, and full of energy. The seated woman stretched one leg out, raised it, rolled back over her shoulder and sprang to her feet.

The Maiden, Miryo realized. Not all companies performed the Aspects in the same order, but she seemed to recall that Eriot's went in order of increasing age. She wondered where they would put the Warrior in that sequence.

The woman was still moving. She leapt about lightly, kicking her legs higher each time. When she was on the ground, her feet all but blurred with their fast, intricate movement. The music continued, ever more rapid; it sounded like a call now. And so it was: The Dancer's motions beckoned a man from behind the curtain. He came forward to join her, and the two whirled around each other in a dazzling display of agility.

Miryo was entranced. The Temple Dancers made their motions look simple, but she could guess at the strength and control they required. This was nothing like the country dances performed at festivals in rural areas, nor the courtly patterns trod by stiff-backed highborns. The steps were choreographed and rehearsed for weeks before they were ever performed for the public. And the training these Dancers underwent, if she remembered correctly, began when they were only five years old.

Others had come forth to join the two already on the floor. They moved in a circle around the first two, kicking higher with each turn. The music was a joyous celebration of the Maiden's youth and boundless energy.

And lacing through it all, expressed through the bodies of the Dancers, was the power of Fire. Its beckoning warmth called to her, entranced her, invited her to take hold—

Miryo stopped herself just short of drawing power, for what purpose she did not know, except to feel the thrill of holding it. *Goddess wept. If I did that, and it got out of control, here in this hall . . .*

She took a deep, unsteady breath, and tried not to think about that.

When the Dance finished, the performers retired behind the curtain and were replaced by two new Dancers, one man and one woman. The two of them struck up positions mirroring each other, and then the music began.

It began with flutes, a pair of them, playing a simple duet. The man and woman flitted around each other, skimming across the floor, barely touching it. They leapt, too, but where the previous Dancers had done so in sharp competition with each other, these two seemed to move for the sheer joy of it. The illusion that they were floating in midair at the height of each leap was so strong that Miryo almost suspected magical intervention, and for one, irrational moment feared that *she* was somehow doing it. Her entire body was tense with the frightened awareness that she might draw power, and yet she couldn't leave; it would be a horrible insult. All she could do was sit there, with a physical embodiment of the Element of Air being displayed before her, and fight not to reach for it.

The music turned, and so did the Dancers. Now they came together, and if Miryo had thought they were floating before, now they were flying. The man grasped his partner around her lean waist and tossed her about as though she were the feather she imitated. He gave the impression that he could, if he chose, fling her right up to the vaulted ceiling, and not even find it hard.

That Dance ended in a beautifully posed embrace, honoring the Goddess as Bride. Miryo gulped in air gratefully, trying to both gather herself and relax before they were replaced by their fellows.

Both of the previous Dances had been in a standard four-beat pattern, but now the musicians began a tune in three. The Temple Dancers glided across the floor in a waltz that was to stiff court waltzes what water was to glass. Round and round they whirled, every move flowing into the one that followed it. Where Miryo's heart had been set racing by the energy and freedom of the previous two pieces, now it was calmed—and that almost did her in. She just barely caught herself before she opened herself to the Element of Water. The beautiful, swirling patterns were more subtly seductive than the first two Elements had been. Her fingers clenched around the arms of her chair as she caught herself just in time.

She wasn't sure what to expect from the next-to-last Dance, for she suspected that it would be the one honoring the Crone. After all, the Earth did not move very much, and neither did most old women. The company chose to express the concepts of solidity and deep roots; the Dancers in this fourth piece moved into poses Miryo had not thought possible, and then held them as if they could stay there all day. The musicians switched to low-voiced instruments that resonated deeply in the hall. The quiet strength and determination of the Dancers impressed Miryo a great deal, and although she felt the power of Earth there, she also remembered the trial she'd undergone in Star Hall, and drew on that resolution to keep herself in check.

And then it ended, and she was safe. There was one Dance left, the Warrior, but there was no such thing as Void magic, no Void power, nothing to lure her to the edge of danger.

But she sat bolt upright as the first notes slashed through the still air of the hall. Electricity raced up her spine—not magical power, but something other, something from the core of herself. She was in no danger of working a spell, but her eyes were riveted on the scene in front of her as the Dancers expressed through movement their devotion to the Goddess as Warrior.

The Dance had leaps, but they were not frivolous, nor were they competitive, unless the Dancers were competing against themselves, each trying to outdo her own last display of strength and control. It looked like a fight, if fighting were art. The men and women on the floor leapt and rolled and came together with movements that were just a hair short of being violent. But there was no contention; there was only the bond of loyalty and fierce determination.

And then the music shifted, rising a note, and Miryo's heart rose into her throat. With that shift the music became sharper, even more fierce, and she suddenly felt a longing to be out of her chair, out of the castle, out on the road; she wanted to be riding to find her doppelganger this minute. The challenge sang in her blood, driving her to victory. With this feeling in her, surely she could not fail.

She tightened her grip on the chair until her knuckles

turned white and forced herself to breathe. *Not yet. You can't leave yet. Not today. Not now. But tomorrow . . .*

Tomorrow, I hunt.

The Dance finished abruptly in a final, breathtaking pose, and she unclenched her hands. They ached from the strain. Massaging them surreptitiously, Miryo eased back into her seat and glanced over to her left.

Edame, who appeared not to have noticed her various struggles, gave her a sour smile. "I could do without the Warrior Dance. It never seems to fit into the sequence, no matter where they put it."

This contrasted so sharply with Miryo's own reaction that she did not respond. She didn't exactly *like* the Dance, but it had roused in her feelings she could hardly contain. Edame, it seemed, did not feel that way. Which was not unexpected; the Warrior was not often honored in the witches' religious practices, because of her absence from their magic. Miryo's reaction was the odd one.

The priestess had finished her closing invocation, and the people in the hall began to move again. The Dancers emerged from behind their curtain, lining up to be presented to Iseman and Terica. First among them was the priestess, who exchanged warm words with the Avannan Lord and Lady before gracing Miryo and Edame with a chill nod.

"Blessings of the Goddess on the unbalanced," the woman said, and stepped aside for the company of Dancers.

Edame made a vexed sound. "I *hate* the ones who do that."

"Do what?" Miryo murmured, pitching her voice for only Edame to hear.

"Call us 'unbalanced.' At least most priests have the good taste not to be so . . . *open* about it. Look at the way she looked at us. Like we're wayward children who refuse to hear what the Goddess is trying to tell us."

Edame's description was an apt one. The woman's gaze had been faintly regretful, in what was quite possibly the most irritating way imaginable. "How many are like that?" Miryo asked. "I know some priests and priestesses don't approve of us, but the teachers never tell us how many are likely to make an issue of it."

The Fire Hand shrugged. "It depends on where you are, and what sect they're from. Less in Currel, for example, being so close to Starfall. Nalochkans aren't bad. Avannans are the worst. They click their tongues and shake their heads over whatever it is we're doing wrong—and of course no one ever *tells* us; we're supposed to guess that on our own."

"So they don't tend to make trouble."

"Not usually, no. But there are exceptions."

Miryo continued to nod and smile at the Dancers at they filed past. She wished the line would hurry up; she was still humming with energy. And dawn was hours away yet. Miryo took a deep breath and forced herself to sit quietly.

The line was nearly finished at last. It went in order of increasing rank, save for the priestess; the first ones presented had been those who did not even perform tonight. Now there were only four Dancers left, the last of whom would be the leader of the company.

The next-to-last woman froze when she reached Miryo.

She recovered smoothly, and bowed with perfect grace

to both witches. "Goddess be with you," she murmured, and moved onward. Miryo marked her, though, and her face, with a small scar on her chin. Tonight she would seek that Dancer out, and ask her why she had frozen, as if she recognized Miryo's face.

THERE WAS A RECEPTION afterward, of course; the visit of a company as famed as Eriot's was an occasion for celebration in this city so heavily populated with Avannans. And even those who did not honor Temple Dance as the highest form of religious adoration knew a social occasion when they saw one. The hall was filled nearly wall-to-wall with people.

Miryo detached herself from Edame as quickly as manners allowed and began to circulate. The Dancers were easy to spot; black hair was reasonably common in the eastern domains, but they were the only ones with bare, unadorned heads. Finding a specific black-haired Dancer, however, was much more easily said than done, especially in this crowd. Miryo was about to give up in frustration when Kan materialized at her side.

"Rice wine?" the Cousin said, offering her a goblet.

Miryo took it, distracted. "Kan, I need you to do a favor for me. Find Lionra, the seneschal. There's a Dancer in the company with a scar on her chin. I need to know what room she's in tonight. She's high-ranking, just below the company leader. Be discreet if you can." She could go to the company's leader and ask for the Dancer's name, but that would spark interest she would prefer to avoid.

Kan nodded and vanished into the crowd, leaving Miryo with wine she didn't really want. She continued to peruse the room, keeping an eye out for the Dancer, but before much time had passed Edame reappeared, looking irritated.

"There you are. I realize you are perhaps not planning on joining my Ray, but it will still do you good to speak with some people here. You should be seen." She took Miryo's arm and led her through the crowd.

Socializing was *not* what Miryo wanted to be doing at the moment, but Edame was impossible to argue with. She endured the next few hours patiently, watching the Fire Hand flit from group to group. Finally, pleading exhaustion, Miryo escaped to her own room.

Kan was not there, and neither was Sai. Miryo stood in the middle of the sitting room and fidgeted, wondering what to do. Should she go seek out the Cousin, or wait here for her to return? They could waste hours tonight chasing each other through the keep. She decided to stay where she was.

Her determination was sorely tested; it was nearly Low before Kan came back. Miryo braided and rebraided her hair repeatedly to keep herself busy. She was twisting it into a low bun when the Cousin finally entered and bowed. "I apologize for taking so long. The Dancer's name is Sareen. She has a room to herself in the western wing. It's next to the room of her company's leader, and two down from that of the priestess."

The snapping energy she had gained from the Warrior Dance was still with her, in full force now that she could do something with it. "Thank you. Take me there, please."

They encountered no one in the hallway. Miryo could hear the distant sounds of the revelry still going on. Before she was quite ready, she was in front of Sareen's door, and

Kan had retired to a nearby alcove. Miryo straightened her dress, then knocked on the door, hoping the Dancer was in.

She was. And she started again when she opened her door and saw Miryo.

"I would like to speak with you," Miryo said.

Sareen recovered and bowed. "Of course, Katsu. Please, come in."

The room was bare compared to Miryo's; this was the sort of housing that would normally be given to the lesser servant of a high-ranking visitor. Temple Dancers lived spartan lives. Were Sareen one of the younger Dancers, she would be sharing a room with two or three others. It was a mark of her status that she had even this room to herself.

There were two chairs; Miryo took one and gestured for Sareen to take the other. It felt strange. She still wasn't used to having rank herself, that people would wait for permission to sit in her presence.

"Twice now," Miryo said, having considered and discarded a more roundabout approach, "you've reacted oddly when you looked at me. Why is that?"

Sareen dropped her eyes. "My apologies, Katsu. I didn't mean to be rude."

"You needn't apologize. I'm just curious. Have you seen me before?"

"I don't believe so, Katsu. It's just that you remind me a great deal of someone I used to know."

I knew it.

Miryo swallowed her rising excitement and forced herself to speak casually. "Who?"

"A fellow Dancer. She used to be in training with our company."

Of all the professions Miryo had envisioned for her doppelganger, Temple Dancer had not been high on the list. It was almost as strange as imagining her double as a priestess. "How long ago was this?"

"Quite a while. Twelve years, maybe thirteen."

"And . . . she was your age?" Miryo had to hastily revise her sentence. Sareen would find it odd if she referred to the doppelganger as "it."

"A bit younger, Katsu."

Sareen looked to be in her late twenties. Which fit, of course; the doppelganger would be the same age as Miryo herself. She had to reach into herself for the calm of Air again before asking the next question. "Where did she go?"

Now the Dancer looked regretful. "I don't know, Katsu."

Somehow I didn't think it was going to be quite that easy.

"Did she go to another company elsewhere, do you think?"

Sareen shook her head. "No. Criel—our leader at the time—said she had a different calling. I don't think she's still a Dancer."

A different calling? Perhaps it *had* become a priestess, strange though it was to imagine. "Where is Criel now?"

"I think she's in Verdosa, Katsu—in the main temple there."

In the east. Miryo could not believe her luck. Or perhaps it wasn't luck; perhaps the thread she'd been following had been bringing her to Sareen and Criel, not to her doppelganger itself. No way of knowing, at least not yet.

Miryo realized Sareen was looking at her curiously. She cursed her lack of magic; if only she could use it, she could question the Dancer further and then "encourage" her to forget the conversation. But since the woman was likely to gossip, she didn't want to add fodder by asking more questions.

Sareen was still looking at her. Miryo put her frustration aside and stood. "Well, I won't take up any more of your time. I'm sure you're tired, after that performance. Which was quite beautiful, by the way—I count myself lucky that I was here for it." Despite the danger it had posed.

"It is how we worship the Goddess," Sareen said quite simply. "The beauty brings you closer to her." She bowed Miryo out of the room, and closed the door behind her.

It wasn't until Miryo was well away from Sareen's room that she realized she had never even asked her doppelganger's name.

CLIMBING AROUND on the rooftops in Starfall was one matter; the Cousins knew perfectly well that students went to the roof of their quarters for privacy and a look at the stars.

Climbing around on the rooftops of Haira's central keep was another matter entirely.

For one thing, it lacked the architecture of the students' quarters, which was well-suited to climbing and hiding. For another, Haira had guards who would be less inclined to look the other way if a mysterious silhouette appeared against the night sky. But Miryo needed fresh air, and quiet, and she was accustomed to doing her thinking while sitting on a roof. She took her chances with the guards and climbed out her bedroom window.

Outside, she took deep breaths and tried to calm her racing heart. She had *proof.* Her doppelganger existed, and someone had seen it. More than one someone. Miryo had not doubted the Primes, but somehow this confirmation made the whole situation more real.

Her doppelganger was out there. Somewhere. And she *was* going to find it. Because she refused to fail.

Criel, former leader of Eriot's company, would know where it had gone. What professions were there for thirteen-year-old former Temple Dancers? Many of them joined the clergy when they became too old to Dance, but Miryo had difficulty visualizing her double taking vows at that age. And why had it left the company in the first place? What "other calling" had it gone to follow?

These were all questions she could ask Criel when she got to Verdosa.

Now that she had a direction, Miryo could not wait for dawn to come. She did not regret this pause in Haira, but she was itching to get back in the saddle. She had to wait a few hours yet, though, before she could wake the two Cousins and get them on the road—

North.

Miryo's heart almost stopped.

North, not east. The pull had moved. And it was distinct; she wasn't imagining the change. Whatever was drawing her wasn't in the east. It was north, now—not the far north, but nearby. Toward Kalistyi, though maybe not that far.

It's on the move.

The pull *did* lead to her doppelganger; she was sure of it now. And it was moving. Heading west.

What's in the west?

Half the domains lay in that direction. It could be headed anywhere, from Starfall to Askavya.

But the thread that led to it was stronger than it had ever been before. Miryo was no longer afraid she would lose it. Whichever way her doppelganger turned, she could follow it. And it couldn't run forever. Eventually— *soon*—she would catch it.

Miryo rose and began to make her way back across the roof to her window. She hadn't gone far, knowing she didn't want any encounters with guards. Her mind and heart were both racing, but she made an effort to quiet them. She *had* to get some sleep tonight. Tomorrow would be early enough to get on the move once more.

And if I keep telling myself that, she thought wryly, *I might even begin to believe it.*

She did not sleep that night.

CHAPTER THIRTEEN

Hunters

MIRAGE DIDN'T WANT to stop in Angrim, but they didn't have a lot of choice. They still hadn't sent a bird ahead to Silverfire, and the horses needed the rest anyway.

Who am I kidding? I need the rest, too. I've been on the road just as long as Mist has. From Insebrar to Abern to Starfall to Insebrar again to here—I haven't really stopped since Chervie, and that little holiday got cut short.

They had been driving themselves hard since Starfall, first to reach Avalanche before he left Vilardi, and then to get to Miest before trouble could catch up to them. They had not told anyone of their suspicions, and there had been no sign of pursuit from Vilardi, but still the hairs on the back of Mirage's neck refused to lie down. She could not escape that hunted feeling, and it had begun to seriously grate on her nerves.

So this delay in Angrim, while frustrating, was also nice. It was a welcome chance to sit in something other than a saddle; to walk on her own two feet through the daylit streets of a town; to wake up in the same bed two mornings in a row.

Mirage slept for an exceptionally long time their first night in Angrim, and woke just before noon. She stretched luxuriously, legs dangling off the narrow bed. She'd recovered from the lump on her head she'd taken in that brawl, and her knee was mostly better, but they'd been two weeks on the road from Vilardi, and she didn't have much energy left. While these hours of sleep had not been strictly necessary—she'd gone on in worse condition before—they had been very pleasant. Her nerves had calmed as well. In the sunlit quiet of her room, she reveled in the lack of tension. She no longer felt as if she must check the road behind her for pursuit every few minutes. It was truly a relief.

All right, lazy. You've lounged around in bed for long enough; time to get up and get some things done.

She found Eclipse downstairs in the common room, enjoying an early lunch. He raised an eyebrow at her, but chose not to comment on her late rising; in a way it was a pity. Mirage was in a good enough mood that for once she wouldn't have retaliated.

The reason for his silence became apparent soon enough. He needed her in that good mood. "I've been checking the horses, and they need to be reshod before we head on."

The day was half gone, and his expression was wary. It wasn't hard for Mirage to figure out. "You want to stay an extra day."

Eclipse nodded. "There's a farrier who can do it today, but he shod Sparker last year and I *really* don't like his work. The one I'd rather get can't do it until tomorrow."

Yesterday Mirage would have snapped his nose off; yesterday she felt as though she were being targeted by an archer. "That sounds fine. It'll give me a chance to mend some tack and get everything else back in order. Have you gotten supplies yet?"

The look on his face was priceless. "You're not going to argue?"

"Not really. I don't think the extra day will hurt us, and I can certainly find productive ways to use it."

"I won't complain. Especially since I haven't even begun to get supplies—I woke late, too." His grin was not very repentant.

"No wonder you didn't chide me. I expected you to."

"I *can* chide you, if you'd like."

"No, thank you." Mirage stretched again and looked around the common room, which was empty aside from them; the inn did not begin serving nonguests until dinner. "This quiet is *nice*. Especially in light of our recent adventures. No brawls, no suspicious guards, and best of all, not a cockroach in sight."

He cocked his head and studied her face. "You're not feeling as edgy, are you?"

"Nope. Which is why I'm in a good mood. Take advantage of it while you can."

"Can I borrow some money?"

"Don't press your luck." They grinned at each other, in genuine, unadulterated good humor for the first time in a while.

Which was odd, given that as far as they knew, their situation hadn't improved. But the more Mirage thought about it, the more she felt pleased at the thought of staying in Angrim, maybe even wandering around the town a little bit, seeing what interesting things she might happen across. She'd been in Angrim many times before, but still . . .

You can't stay forever, she reminded herself. *You've still got trouble on your back.*

But since a certain amount of delay was inevitable, she might as well enjoy the respite.

MIRYO KNEW HER DOPPELGANGER was in Angrim the moment she rode through the gate. Its presence hit her with palpable force; every nerve in her body hummed before subsiding into a quieter but still noticeable murmur.

"It's here," she said to the Cousins, pitching her voice to just carry over the noise of the town.

They both glanced at her briefly, then returned their attention to the crowd with redoubled fervor. *I think they expect it to leap out and attack me right here. I wonder if it can tell I'm coming?*

"Let's find the house, and then we'll make a plan," she said, and began to press through the crowd.

The house in question was new, being a part of the Air Ray's plan to maintain places for witches to stay while they traveled. There weren't many of them yet; the money to build them came largely from the Void Ray, and they gave slowly. This one, though, had benefitted from donations from Fire. Angrim was the capital city of Abern, and often had witches on diplomatic missions passing through. So the house, instead of being a modest little waystation, was palatial. Since no one else was there at the moment, Miryo had no qualms about commandeering it for herself.

It was a good thing, she reflected, that her double was here, that the long chase was drawing to a close. She needed it to end; the stress and effort had taken their toll, and she had pushed a fast pace from Haira to here. Their horses were not in good shape. But once her doppelganger was taken care of, they could rest here for a few days, then ride at a more sedate pace back to Starfall.

She could even cast spells to make their journey easier.

Miryo allowed herself a small smile that was hardly sufficient to express the glee she felt at that thought. *Magic. My magic. Soon I'll be able to use it.*

They found the house without trouble. The place was quite large; Miryo was amused at the ostentation the Fire Ray seemed to think was necessary. Did traveling ambassadors truly need a multistory house just to stay in overnight?

She chose a bedroom and sat on the bed to ponder the situation while the Cousins brought the baggage up. Her double was in Angrim, but for how long? It hadn't shown any inclination to stay in one place for long before. She needed some way to find it, and quickly, but without scaring it off.

And what happens when you find it, little girl? Are you going to kill it on the spot?

That was another problem, one she hadn't let herself address before. How *was* she going to kill her doppelganger? Her magic couldn't be trusted, and the Primes had explicitly outlawed it for this task anyway. She had to do it herself; she couldn't use the Cousins. But what if it knew how to fight?

Look at it this way. You know nothing *about fighting. Therefore, it can't possibly know less than you do, and there's a good chance it knows more. If nothing else, it's got to have scuffled with local boys as a child. So chances are you're going to be at some kind of a disadvantage when it comes to blows.*

But it didn't have to come to an out-and-out fight. She had to kill it herself, but was there any rule against having someone else capture it first?

The Cousins could do that. They could take it prisoner and bring it back here, where Miryo could . . . dispatch it.

That hardly seemed fair.

Fairness doesn't enter into it. This is necessary. Besides, it'll get its fair fight, when the Cousins go after it. Once they have it prisoner, it's as good as dead anyway, so it's not that much different from me attacking and killing it on the spot. And, since she had already established that doing so would be one step away from suicidal, this was her only workable plan.

A knock sounded on the door. "Come in," Miryo said.

Kan entered and waited patiently.

"It's here," Miryo said at last. "I don't know where exactly, not yet. I'm going to go out into the town. You and Sai wait here. Prepare one of the attic rooms to hold a prisoner, as best you can."

"I'll do that," Kan said. "Sai will accompany you."

Miryo grimaced, but she wasn't surprised. Her efforts to convince them she didn't need a watchdog had comprehensively failed. "All right. I won't be gone long."

She went down into the streets, Sai ghosting along behind her in the midday crowd. *It's here, somewhere within these walls. No sense of direction, though; I must be too close. Real helpful. My instinct* would *choose now to desert me.*

What if I wander into it, here on the street?

The thought turned Miryo cold. She wasn't ready. Only Sai was here—not that a combat-trained Cousin was anything to sniff at. But it would cause all kinds of comment if there was a fight here on the street. And even if she didn't encounter her doppelganger face-to-face, what if a merchant mentioned to it that he had seen a woman very like it earlier that day?

Miryo turned on her heel and left the crowded street as quickly as she could.

Her feet carried her without any real sense of direction. She wasn't sure which way the inn was, and couldn't yet bring herself to ask Sai. As it was, her wandering brought her to a place she wanted to go.

She went up the steps and into the temple's cool interior without thinking about it twice. It was the first time she'd set foot in a temple not built for witches' use, and she gazed around it in curiosity. This one was pentagonal in layout, with a door at each corner; from her studies, she knew it was an unusual design. The interior face of each wall was devoted to a different Aspect of the Goddess. The middle was open to the sky; Miryo hummed and sensed the spell that covered the opening, keeping leaves and other such litter out. Rain, however, could enter freely, as could snow and birds, so the natural world still had access.

Standing in the sunlight, Miryo made a complete turn, looking at all five statues of the Goddess. Maiden, Bride, Mother, Crone, Warrior. She hesitated among them; the Warrior governed violence and death, but she could use the calm of the Mother's Water, or the solidity of the Crone's Earth. In the end she chose the Maiden's shrine;

that was her current stage of life, and determination and passion were what she needed at the moment.

Sai dropped back to give Miryo privacy as she prepared herself for prayer. Since the shrine was the Maiden's, purification involved lighting a candle and meditating briefly on its dancing flame before she carried it with her to the shrine proper.

Once there, she slid her candle into the holder provided and sat cross-legged, gazing up at the statue of the carefree, passionate Maiden.

Youngest, Lady of Fire, you who are the energy of determination and drive—help me. I need your attributes. I'm not sure I can do this.

I'm afraid. And I freely admit it. I'm afraid of failure; I'm afraid of success, and what it might cost me. I've never killed a person; I never thought I'd have to. I've never even seen anyone die. But if I am to use my gift, the gift that is my birthright and what I have struggled for all these years—I have to kill.

Maiden, Goddess, why did you make it this way?

It's one thing to kill the doppelganger as an infant, to go through the ritual before your gaze, your holy starlight, has fallen on the child's face. The baby has no soul when it becomes two, and so the double can be killed without guilt, and the witch-child taken outside to be presented to you. But I do not doubt that, in the years it has been alive, my doppelganger has been in that starlight—has bathed in your light.

Does that mean it has a soul?

If it has a soul, am I right to kill it?

The question had been gnawing at Miryo for days, twisting her up inside even though she tried to put it from her thoughts. Did her doppelganger have a soul? If it did, could she in good conscience kill it, and go on with her own life?

The Maiden gazed down at her, laughing and carefree. Not worrying about consequences.

All right. If a man attacked me with a sword, I'd defend myself. And if there were no way to keep myself safe other than killing him . . . I'd do it. If there were no other choice. Souls don't matter, in that situation—or rather, they do, *and I value mine above his. There is no wrong in killing when it is self-defense, when there truly is no other option.*

There is *no other option here. I kill it, or my magic spins out of control and eventually kills me, and maybe other people along with me. How many times have I caught myself almost reaching for power, the words of a spell on my lips, waiting to be spoken? As in Haira. One of these days I won't be able to stop myself. So I kill my doppelganger, or it kills me. Two choices. Because I have a will to survive, I know which one I will choose. And I will live with the deed. I do that, or I die.*

The Maiden smiled blithely.

Lend me your energy, Lady of Fire. Lend me your passion and determination. Do not let me lose sight of what I have fought for all these years.

"In your name," Miryo whispered, and stood. She backed out into the center of the temple, where she bowed to each Aspect, and then left, Sai following without a word.

HUNTERS OFTEN LAUGHED that every other person in Angrim was an agent. It wasn't all that far from the truth.

Angrim played buffer between not one but two nearby Hunter schools: Thornblood to the north and Windblade to the south. Since the two didn't get along, the town's narrow streets were infested with their people, keeping watch from the overhanging upper stories of houses and shops. And other schools, having a vested interest in keeping an eye on those two, also seeded Angrim with their agents. The result was a city in which half the inhabitants were spying on the other half. Even those who weren't hired to gather information still sold it as a hobby.

Because of this rampant intrigue, contacting a Silverfire agent was not so simple as it had been in Chiero. Mirage took the first step of the dance that afternoon.

"Beer and a leg of goat," she said, dropping onto a stool at an open-air bar in the eastern quarter, safely equidistant between the Thornblood and Windblade ends of the city.

The barkeep raised an eyebrow. "We don't sell goat here. Go to Razi if you want that."

"You should serve it; tastes better than lamb. But forget the food. I'll just have the beer."

He served it to her, and went about his business.

A little while later, Mirage spoke to him again. "Do you know any herb-women around here? I've been having some stomach problems."

"Where are you staying in the city?" he asked.

"The Fisherman's Hook," Mirage lied.

He nodded thoughtfully. "There's a woman two streets over, on Thimble Lane, who could help you. She'll probably prescribe urgony, though, so if you can't stand the stuff you shouldn't go to her. If that's the case, I suggest the one at the corner of Lord's Way and Axehaft."

"Axehaft? That doesn't intersect Lord's Way."

He smacked his forehead. "Fletcher, I meant. Fletcher Street."

"Thanks," Mirage said, and left.

She had to grin as she left. The elaborate steps she had to tread to meet the contact, though necessary, were a very silly game. The request for goat had marked her as a Hunter; the stomach upset asked after a certain contact. Since she had named the Fisherman's Hook, he knew she was at the Cracked Oak. Urgony meant the contact would come tonight. The misnamed street said how.

She visited the herb-woman on Thimble Lane, to keep up appearances, but conveniently forgot to take the medicine she prescribed. Then, after a solid dinner back at the Cracked Oak, she retired upstairs to mend tack.

An hour or so later, someone knocked on the door. One, then two quick.

Mirage rose and let in her contact.

"A 'female complaints' healer?" she said, raising one eyebrow mockingly. "What a dull disguise."

Wisp looked unamused, and since she had a face like a knife and had long since mastered the art of making her five-foot body seem ten feet tall, the look carried force. "I'm getting old. Climbing through windows is something I leave to stupid young Silverfires who need to show off their shadow-skulking. Stealth isn't all about hiding behind bushes, you know."

Mirage bowed. "Have a seat, then, and rest your old bones, which are no more decrepit than your tongue—and I see *that* hasn't lost any vigor."

That made Wisp grin, but only slightly. Her weathered face looked hard enough to fight a rock and win. A real smile might have broken it. "All right. What do you need?"

"Not much. A message to Silverfire."

"Which is?"

Mirage passed her the paper. The code on it was complex enough that Mirage always had to work to write in it; Wisp read it like ordinary lettering. "Huh. You bringing trouble down on us, girl?"

"I hope not," Mirage said. "But better to be safe than sorry."

"A good motto to live by, though not one most Hunters pay more than lip service to. Why in the name of the Warrior did you take this job?"

"You would have."

"Just because I was young and stupid doesn't mean you have to follow in my footsteps."

"Ah, but then you became old and wise." Mirage put her hands up in mock-defense against Wisp's glare. "I wanted a commission. And it looked like a challenge."

"You hate the witches. So why are you working for them?"

Mirage shrugged uncomfortably. She still couldn't explain it.

Wisp gave her a close look, and then nodded slowly. "All right. You're not the most levelheaded Hunter Silverfire's ever produced, but you're not entirely stupid, and you have a good instinct." Her face grew even more serious then. "Watch out, though. The city is crawling with those damn bastards."

"Those damn bastards," in Wisp's lexicon, meant Thornbloods. "More than usual?"

"A whole crew of them have been here for the last week

or so—between jobs, and champing at the bit. Watch out for them. I know you don't get along with their kind."

"I'll be careful."

"As if that means anything with you children. Five years out of school, and eager to prove you're the next legend. Burning Angrim down around our ears is not the way to do that."

Mirage grinned. "Trust me. I'm leaving the day after tomorrow. I'll do my best not to get into trouble before that."

MIRYO PACED RESTLESSLY, back and forth across the length of her room. It lacked an hour yet until her plan could be put into motion, and every minute grated on her nerves like a rasp.

I might well be flayed alive if the Primes find out about this.

She blessed the Goddess for sending her Kan and Sai. She doubted any two other Cousins would have gone along with this; more than a few would have turned her in on the spot. There were several witches in Angrim they could hand her over to.

She forced herself to stop pacing and took a deep breath.

You've made the plan. Now see it through.

A half hour before the appointed time, she went downstairs. The most convenient thing about living in a house constructed by the Fire Ray was that it had structures built in to accommodate spies. It was to one of those she went, and there, alone in the stuffy darkness, she closed her eyes and calmed her breathing. Now she just had to wait.

A clanging sound; that would be the gate bell. Miryo's breath caught.

Footsteps. Sai opening the door, welcoming the visitor. Two sets of footsteps, one of them quite faint. Then Miryo put her eye to the spyhole, bit one fingernail, took it out of her mouth, and watched.

The Hunter entered the room.

Kan, garbed in a newly bought dress, Miryo's triquetra pendant around her neck, inclined her head. That was the hanging offense, right there. The penalty for masquerading as a witch was severe. And *very* few Cousins would have agreed to it. But Miryo couldn't bring herself to say to the Hunter, "Find someone who looks like me." Nor could she show the drawings; the effect would be the same. So she needed a substitute witch, and since Sai hardly ever opened her mouth, it had to be Kan.

"What is it you want done, Katsu?"

The disguised Cousin held out one of Ryll's sketches from Haira. "This woman is in Angrim. Find her. Bring her to me. Do not kill her. You have two days to carry this out. Your fee will be ten up front, and fifteen more upon completion."

The Hunter took the paper, and although the mask hid her expression from sight, Miryo received an impression of surprise, and perhaps even triumph. "I accept. You'll have her within a day."

CHAPTER FOURTEEN

Capture

MIRAGE DID NOT SLEEP in again her second morning in Angrim. Early rising had been a habit for as long as she could remember; Hunter trainees never lingered in bed, and neither did Temple Dancers, so she had been four the last time anyone let her sleep in regularly. Even when flat on her back in Silverfire's infirmary, she had woken early. Now it was an ingrained reflex.

She went around to the back of the Cracked Oak's courtyard and found a bent horseshoe tossed against the wall. The message had gone out without trouble, then. Wisp was always reliable.

The market streets of the city were already filling up; vendors were opening their stalls and laying out their goods, and a handful of enthusiastic buskers were warming up on the corners. The snatches of music they played followed Mirage as she bought saddle oil and strong gut cord, reminding her of the witches she was tangling with. It was a discordant note in an otherwise sunny and pleasant morning.

It was still early, and her shopping was done. Eclipse had promised to take care of the rest of it. She could return to the inn, but before she did so, there was one other stop she wanted to make.

Angrim's temple had always been one of her favorites. The open pentagonal layout felt less confining than most temples. Her company of Dancers had performed a specially designed Dance here once, a little over a year before she left them. That had been one of Mirage's first major public performances, back when she was Seniade, back before Criel had come to her and offered her a chance at her long-buried dream.

She brushed the ghosts of the past from her mind and returned to her purpose.

There were a variety of ways to purify oneself for presentation to the Warrior. For general worship, people often went through an exercise of controlled breathing. But the Hunter schools were descendants of ancient Warrior cults, and so Mirage showed her devotion in a different way.

The moves she performed were simple, but she put all her concentration and effort into each one. This was more than just purification; it was the beginning of her worship, and it demanded the best she had to give.

There were several patterns of movement to choose from, depending on the devotee's purpose in coming. Mirage chose the pattern of supplication. It was far from meek in tone—the Warrior didn't value meekness very highly—but the entreaty in it was plain. And then, pattern finished, she saluted the statue at the heart of the shrine. Since no one was there to watch, she made it the full, formal, Hunter's salute. Then, for good measure, she pricked her finger on her dagger and pressed her bloody fingertip to the wood rail that surrounded the shrine. It was stained with the small blood offerings of countless previous devotees.

Then Mirage knelt and prayed.

Warrior. Lady of Blades. Huntress and Protectress.

I got myself into this situation. I know that perfectly well. And it's up to me to get me out of it; I do not seek your aid in that.

But you are a warrior, not a murderer. You value a fair fight, or so the clergy tell us. And so I have to ask that you grant at least that much to Kerestel—Eclipse—and me.

Fighting the Wolfstar: that would be fair. Fighting Cousins: that would be fair. But fighting the assembled forces of Starfall would not be fair. Even if it's not all of them, even if it's just a faction, that is not a fair fight; it's slaughter. I'm no more immune to magic than the next person, whatever people say about me. And neither is Eclipse. If we go up against the witches, we're dead.

Please, grant us this much. Grant us at least a fighting chance.

Mirage lifted her eyes to the statue of the Warrior. Unlike many, it did not depict her in any fighting pose; instead she stood upright, sword raised before her face, eyes gazing outward with calm readiness. The look on the Goddess's face gave Mirage strength.

We will do what we can. If that's not enough, then so be it. But please, Warrior, at least give us that fair chance.

I promise I will use it well.

SOMETHING OF THE QUIET she had gained in the temple stayed with Mirage as she returned to the Cracked Oak. The clamor of the streets did not bother her; the annoyance of an overturned wagon of beer kegs did not touch her. She entered the inn feeling calmer than she had in some time. If trouble awaited her, at least she had made her peace with the Warrior.

The common room was deserted; those who wanted breakfast had eaten it and gone, and the rest had not yet risen for lunch. One of the servants had pushed several tables to the walls so she could scrub the boards of the floor, but had left the job half done; the bucket sat abandoned in the middle of the open space. Mirage, carrying her purchases, passed it on her way to the stairs.

Halfway there, she spun and threw the flask of saddle oil.

The Hunter behind her ducked it, but Mirage had bought herself time to draw her sword. And then she was backing up, retreating from the blur that was his attacking staff.

The floorboards were still damp; that was all that saved Mirage a moment later. Another Hunter leapt out from behind one of the overturned tables, but skidded on the boards, and thus gave her just enough warning to drop into a sideways roll. And as she came to her feet, Mirage realized just how much trouble she was in.

Hunters.

Four of them.

Thornbloods, her mind told her coolly, and then she was retreating again, trying to keep distance and the remaining tables between her and her attackers. Two were armed with staffs; two were bare-handed. *No blades? Why not?* She sidestepped a staff blow at the last moment, so that the man went reeling off-balance. *Thornbloods almost always use blades.*

Sword against staff. Mirage tried to cut through his

weapon, but it had been well-hardened, and for a Thornblood he did remarkably well at catching most of her
blows on the staff's iron bands. He wasn't quite quick
enough with the unaccustomed weapon, though. Mirage
swung at his right side, but disengaged before he had even
fully blocked it, then drew her elbow back and turned the
motion into a quick jab that found a weak point in his
leather armor. He collapsed, and then Mirage was running, vaulting a table to get clear of the other three.

She maneuvered to keep the unarmed pair, a man and
a woman, away from her back, so she could concentrate
on the other staff fighter. He was better than his friend.
Mirage had to leap over the butt of his staff and immediately block the descending upper end. The effort jarred
her arms, and all she gave in return was a tiny slice along
the back of his hand. She did the same to the other hand
a moment later, but it was minor damage at best, and his
friends were about to enter the fray.

Void it—I've got to get free of this! Mirage looked for
an exit and found none. And in her moment of distraction, the staff fighter struck twice: slamming the elbow
of her sword arm, and then knocking her blade clean out
of her hand.

The other Thornbloods charged. Mirage created her
own exit; she rushed the staff fighter, who had not expected such a move, and shoved him into the unarmed
man. She failed to break free, though, and found herself
fighting the other bare-handed Hunter, a woman, while at
her back the men rose to their feet.

She feinted right, as if to bolt for the door; behind her
she heard one of the men shift. Then she reversed direction and headed left, toward the stairs. Two steps into

her flight she spun and kicked the bucket of soapy, dirty water. It flew into the face of the staff fighter, blinding him. The woman charged in. Mirage wasn't afraid. She'd bet on herself in a one-on-one fight any day, so long as she didn't have a concussion going into it. But the story would change quickly when the other two got back into the fight.

She broke two of the woman's fingers just as the staff-man arrived. His first blow she dodged, but the second clipped her in the diaphragm; she spun out of that and hook-kicked him in the kidneys, but he hardly grunted. His retaliatory blow, while not very strong, was enough to send her off balance and rolling to the floor. Mirage came up right next to a table and leapt onto its top, but the unarmed man had anticipated that, and was waiting for her there. His roundhouse kick threw her right back onto the floor.

Another roll, but she was hurting now, and the Thorn-bloods knew it. They spread out around her, trapping her near the overturned table, and advanced steadily. Mirage spat blood and forced air back into her lungs. There would be no backup coming for her. She had to finish this now, before they finished her.

The broken-fingered woman was the weakest link of the chain. Mirage targeted her. She got in one good kick, but it wasn't enough to take the woman down, and then the staff smashed into her lower back. Her spine erupted in agony. She snarled it away and spun, slamming her stiffened hand into the back of the staff fighter's neck. The woman kicked the back of her knees and sent her to the floor. A boot caught her chin and she flew backward, hitting the floor hard, and before she could force herself to her feet there was a sharp pressure on the small of her back, and someone twisted her arms painfully behind her. Mirage tried once to heave the weight off and got her face slammed into the floor. Then the female Thornblood knelt in front of her.

The woman wound her unbroken fingers in Mirage's hair and dragged her head up so she could see. Mirage spat more blood at her, but the woman ignored it, instead reaching up to pull the mask of her head covering down.

"Ice," Mirage mumbled painfully.

The Thornblood smiled. It was not a pleasant expression. "I've been looking forward to this for a while," she purred.

"I see it only took three friends to get your nerve up," Mirage said, putting as much acid into her tone as she could.

Ice was not perturbed. "Ah, this was not just personal. This was a job." Her smile got nastier. "There's a witch who wants to see you."

Then Mirage's head was slammed into the floor again, and she passed out.

THE MIRROR IN Miryo's bedroom was enchanted. She discovered this by accident; she was humming to calm her nerves while waiting for the Hunter to return, and the sound caused a resonance. The spell was one that caused the mirror to show various rooms in the house.

Of course. Can't expect a Fire witch to go skulking in stuffy closets. That's for the Cousins. She can sit up here and spy in comfort.

The enchantment didn't even require power to get it started, just a snatch of the proper music. Miryo, inferring from the type of spell and the tastes of Fire witches, figured the key out easily, and spent some time playing with the mirror. It reminded her of all she stood to gain.

There was a commotion in the house's courtyard; she could hear it through the window. Miryo shifted the mirror to see from above the front door, and found herself staring. Not one but three uniformed Hunters were out there, two of them carrying bodies. What in the Crone's name had happened?

She redirected the mirror again as they came inside and went to the room where Kan was waiting. No polite salutes now; the two Hunters at the back, both men, dropped their burdens while the woman Miryo had hired strode forward. She was obviously nursing an injured hand and more than one bruise, but arrogance was written in every line of her body.

"We've got her," she said without ceremony. "Within a day, as I promised. Now heal me and my friends."

Miryo bristled at her tone. Who was she, to order a witch around? Not that Kan was really a witch, but the Hunter didn't know that.

Rudeness is the least of your problems. Kan can no more heal them than I could direct an army. But she can't admit that, and I can't do anything to help her. Not until my doppelganger is dead. Miryo eyed the two bodies on the floor, neither of which was moving much. One was a man, also in Hunter uniform. The other was bundled up so that only her boots were visible, but Miryo didn't need a face to know it was her double.

Goddess. I'm not ready yet. I can't just walk in there, stab her, and heal those Hunters.

"I'm afraid I cannot do that," Kan was saying with

laudable poise. "Here is your payment, as I promised. I will give you coin for a healer as well, but I have pressing business I must attend to."

"For the Warrior's sake—at least heal *him*!" The female Hunter pointed at her motionless companion on the floor.

"He was not hired for this job," Kan said coldly. Her eyes dared the Hunter to argue. "You were the only one contracted. His injuries are none of my concern."

"He's going to *die,* Katsu." The term of address was ground out between her teeth. "That bitch stuck a sword in his gut. No healer is going to be able to fix that. He'll take an infection and rot to death. I don't care if you didn't hire him; you still ought to heal him."

"We'll pay for the service," one of the other Hunters said.

Miryo felt a sudden pain and realized she had chewed one finger until it bled. She could not take her eyes off the motionless Hunter. *Oh, Lady—I just can't do it yet! Not even to save that man! I want to use my magic, but I can't, not yet. Please, Mother of us all, I'm just not ready. Forgive me. Forgive me. I cannot kill it yet.*

Kan had been thinking fast. "I cannot," she said gently. "I *must* continue on to other things. But one of my sisters of the Water Ray lives on Upper Cart Lane, which is not so far a walk from here. Take him there, and she will heal him. Tell her he was hurt in the employ of Miryo."

Rage was still plain in the female Hunter's posture, but she bowed jerkily. "We will do so, Katsu. Good-bye." They picked up their unconscious companion and left.

Miryo waited until they were out of the courtyard, and then ran down the stairs to the waiting Cousins. "Put it in the attic room," she said, not looking at the body on the floor. "I'll deal with it shortly."

MIRAGE AWOKE to pain. She immediately pushed it to the back of her mind. The last thing she had seen was Ice's vengeful face, so this was no time for weakness. She had to be alert.

At least no one had blindfolded her. Not that there was much to see. The floorboards in front of her nose were dusty, but disturbed by footprints. The musty smell of the air suggested an attic. And the quality of the light suggested that it was afternoon, so either she was still in Angrim, or she'd been kept unconscious for more than a day. The former seemed more likely.

She shut her eyes again, partly to calm her headache, and partly to concentrate on sound. She could hear no one in the room with her. Of course, given Ice's words, a witch might be watching her magically. But she'd have to take that chance.

Rolling over brought more pain, of course, but that was to be expected. The room was tiny, with a sharply sloped ceiling, and empty save for a door. Nothing for her to work with.

Mirage twisted her hands behind her, testing the ropes binding them.

If a Thornblood tied these, they're even more worthless as Hunters than I thought. The ropes, while not loose, were definitely workable. With an ease born of long, painful practice, Mirage dislocated both of her thumbs and set about wiggling out of her bonds.

In moments she was free, but as she reset her thumbs and examined the rope around her ankles, footsteps sounded on the stairs outside the door. With one last, quick glance around, Mirage twined the rope loosely around her wrists and lay back down, more or less in the position she had been in when she awoke.

The only difference was that now she could see the door.

The visitor was not Ice, nor any other Thornblood. Red hair, clothing good but practical; probably a Cousin. Mirage suppressed a shudder. *Am I better off, or not? Which would be worse—Cousins, or Ice?*

No time to dwell on it. The woman was bending down to examine Mirage; she'd see the loose rope in a second.

Mirage slapped her hands hard against the floor and threw her weight onto them, kicking upward with her still-bound feet. She was lucky. The Cousin was unprepared and her aim was good; her heels struck the woman's head and sent her careening backward into the wall. She fell to the floor and Mirage was on her in an instant, clipping her hard behind the ear. She wouldn't be waking up anytime soon.

Mirage searched her clothing and swore. *Unarmed. What kind of Cousin goes around unarmed? Unless she's a witch, but I can't believe it of her. No pendant, and she doesn't move like a witch. She's combat-trained, I'd bet on it. I'm just lucky she thought I was still unconscious.*

Swiftly now, she untied her feet. There had been a definite thump when the Cousin hit the wall, and another when she fell; someone might come to investigate. The room's one window was much too small for Mirage to fit through, and looked out onto an unhelpful brick wall. She'd have to find another path of escape.

So she tied the unconscious Cousin with the ropes that

had bound her and slipped out the door. It opened onto a very short hallway with two more doors off it. They looked like more attic rooms, so she headed for the stairs at the other end.

The floor below was much more habitable, with a staircase to the next floor down at the other end of the hallway. But before Mirage could decide whether to investigate the rooms along the hall, go out the window, or head downstairs, one of the doors opened and another red-haired woman stepped out.

Void it. Mirage charged her. But this one was more ready than the first; she whipped a knife out as Mirage approached.

The woman's speed was no match for Mirage's. As the woman thrust with the knife, Mirage dodged to the inside. One hand seized control of the knife, while the other slammed into her collarbone.

This second Cousin collapsed with a cry of pain. Mirage kicked her in the head and put her out, too, but now her nerves were humming; with that noise, more Cousins would be arriving within seconds. No time to tie up this one, and no point. Mirage scooped up the knife and ran.

THE HOUSE DID NOT CONTAIN a religious shrine, but it did have a room for working spells, which was much the same. Miryo went there immediately after ordering the Cousins to take care of the doppelganger.

She knelt in the center of the room. Triquetras done in Elemental colors encircled her; she spared them a brief glance before ignoring them entirely. Her mind focused on a single thing.

Maiden. Bride. Mother. Crone. Warrior. Be with me.

Miryo took a moment to calm her breathing and her heart. Both were racing, after the scene with the Hunters. The knowledge of what she was facing didn't help her any, either.

Forgive me. I should have helped that man. He was seriously injured, and needed healing. But I had not prepared myself properly, and so I could not—would not—help him. I was too weak.

Please, Lady of Five Faces, help me not be weak now. My doppelganger is upstairs. I must—no, I will kill it. It hurt that man, nearly killed him; it has probably done the same to others. I, however, wish to help those in need, wherever they may be. I know now that I can serve you best as a witch of the Air. And this is the first step in that service.

I go now to execute my doppelganger. Be at my side, Goddess, as I wield the knife.

MIRAGE SPARED a quick glance out the hallway window as she turned the corner. As she had hoped, she was about to reach the ground floor. A straight run for the front door seemed her best option. Hopefully the house's remaining defenses would not mobilize in time to stop her. And hopefully she wouldn't run into anything worse than surprised Cousins.

But luck, which had been with her so far, now deserted her. She reached the bottom of the stairs, turned a corner, and found herself face-to-face with another red-haired woman.

The triquetra pendant that hung around her neck drew Mirage's eyes like a magnet.

"Warrior," she whispered. "You're the witch who had me taken."

MIRYO STOOD FROZEN, numb, barely able to feel the dagger in her fingers. She had thought she was prepared for the shock of seeing her doppelganger. She was wrong.

Her doppelganger's flame-colored hair was cut close to her head, but the hue was like hers. Its body was hard muscle, but the proportions were the same. And the face she saw was her own. Not similar: *identical*. Battered though her doppelganger was, its face was hers. Miryo's skin crawled as she stood in the hallway, staring at herself.

Its eyes—gray, like her own—widened in shock. It was even less prepared for this than Miryo herself.

"Who *are* you?" it whispered, body tensed and wary. Miryo realized for the first time that it, too, had a knife in its hands. "My—my sister?"

"No," Miryo said, responding automatically. She couldn't make herself move. "Not sisters. You and I— we're the same person."

One pale eyebrow rose in a manner that was eerily familiar.

"You're my doppelganger. My double. Made when I was five days old. Only you were supposed to be killed then—doppelgangers are always killed—but you survived. Somehow. But I have to kill you now." She closed her mouth with a snap to keep herself from babbling more.

It brought the knife up defensively. Miryo eyed the blade and swallowed; it looked *very* competent. And it had nearly killed a Hunter. How was she supposed to stand against it?

"So you murder babies," the doppelganger said coldly.

"It's not murder!" Miryo protested. "It's done before the child is presented to the Goddess. So there's no soul when one body is killed."

"I've been in starlight since then, more than once. Do you want to bet that I still have no soul?"

That hit *far* too close to home, even after Miryo's resolution to put the question behind her. "It doesn't matter. I *have* to kill you. As long as you're alive, I can't control my magic. So either I kill you now, or I cause a lot of destruction and probably hurt or kill other people before I die, myself." The word "kill" stabbed her every time she said it.

"And I'm supposed to believe you."

"You don't want a demonstration, believe me." Miryo clamped down on the trembling part of herself and matched her doppelganger, glare for glare.

"So why don't *I* kill *you*? That should solve the problem, shouldn't it?"

Miryo's heart thudded painfully. She didn't have a prayer of matching it in a fight, and now she'd admitted her magic was not stable. And she had a sick suspicion that neither Kan nor Sai would be appearing to help her.

The courage of her convictions held her up. "That's not the way it goes. You're a doppelganger. A copy. Not a real person. You were never meant to live."

It stared at her as though she were babbling nonsense. The expression, its familiarity, unnerved her, but she refused to show it; any hint of weakness and this thing would exploit it. Miryo kept her jaw firm and did not look away.

The doppelganger straightened suddenly. "All right," it said, and tossed its knife casually to the floor in front of Miryo. Then it spread its arms wide. "Do it."

Miryo stared at it in complete shock. "What?"

"Kill me," it said grimly. "Stab me in the heart. If you truly believe what you're saying, then it should mean no more to you then tearing up a sheet of paper. Do it. Stab me in the heart."

Miryo stepped forward, over its discarded blade. Taking a deep breath, she raised her own knife, lining its tip up with her double's chest. It could undoubtedly strike the weapon from her hand, but it made no move to do so.

Her doppelganger gave her a twisted smile. "Think of me, whenever you cast a spell."

CHAPTER FIFTEEN

Path

NEITHER OF THEM MOVED for an eternity. Then the witch swore an oath Mirage never would have thought she knew, and dropped her dagger to the floor.

"I can't do it," she said.

Mirage breathed for the first time in what seemed like a year. *Warrior, but I hate bluffing.*

The witch looked up, and her eyes narrowed. Mirage was not yet over the indescribable shock of seeing her own face, down to its expressions, on someone else. Other thoughts bubbled at the edges of her mind, but she kept them ruthlessly quashed. *Deal with this first.*

"You knew I wouldn't," the witch accused, that voice so like a trained version of Mirage's own.

She shrugged, trying to make it look casual. "I couldn't, were I in your place."

The other woman thought about that for a moment, then gave a sour half grin Mirage's muscles knew very well. "Is that really how this works?"

"Looks like it. Lucky for me, too, since I was kind of gambling my life on it. But I knew I couldn't kill me, so I figured you couldn't, either."

"I *am* killing myself, though," the witch said wretchedly. "By not killing you. One of these days, I'm *going* to cast a spell. I can't keep stopping myself. And if that doesn't destroy me outright, other witches will step in. They can't take the risk of letting me run wild."

Mirage's gut clenched. Her double had not been lying; the hopelessness in her eyes was very real. The woman's hands, hanging limp at her sides, trembled faintly before she closed them into fists. Mirage almost smiled at that; she wouldn't want to show weakness, either.

She is *weak, though,* a corner of her mind whispered. *She can't use magic. You could kill her right now.*

In theory, yes. In practice, no. The feeling of recognition was too strong, the sense that here was something she had been missing all her life, searching for without knowing it.

A witch. After years of telling people she had no connection to them.

But however much she hated being wrong, she couldn't just write this woman's life off. No more than she could *really* surrender to death at the witch's hands. So that left her with only one option.

Not a very good one—but it's all I've got.

"Look," she said into the dead silence. "You believe what you're saying, I'm sure. And maybe the rest of Starfall thinks it's true. But it can't hurt us to look again.

"So how about this? We promise not to kill each other. Instead, we look for other answers, other ways out of this they may have ignored or missed." She paused, biting her lip as she watched the other woman's reaction. "And if it looks like time is running out, we'll reconsider."

The witch's eyes widened. For an instant hope lived in her eyes, before dying again. "But witches have been doing things this way for centuries—there's got to be a reason. And people who know *far* more about this than I do have sworn there's no other way."

"Ah, but they lack one thing we have." Mirage smiled, putting as much certainty behind it as she could. "Each other. Am I right? None of them have had their doppelganger there."

"But you don't know anything about magic."

"Do you want to pick the knives up and start over? Our chance of success at this may be tiny, but at least it's a chance. And it might even leave us both alive."

The witch swallowed, visibly torn. Then she straightened her shoulders. Mirage approved of the grim determination in her eyes, even if there wasn't a lot of conviction there. "All right. We can try."

THEY TOOK CARE of the unconscious Cousins first. Miryo was appalled to see the ease with which her doppelganger had taken them down.

Her double checked the two women over with a professional eye; she set Kan's broken collarbone as though she had done this more than once before. "They'll be fine, except for the break. They both might have concussions. But I tried not to kill them—I just needed them out of the way."

Miryo nodded, wondering how on earth she was going to explain the current situation to the Cousins. *But that's a problem for later.*

Once the two women were laid out more comfortably, they fetched a bottle of rice wine and took it to the study, the very room where Kan had, in Miryo's name, hired the Hunters. The irony amused Miryo in a grim way. They dragged chairs to the hearth, where a small fire was burning, poured themselves glasses of wine, and finally sat down to talk.

Miryo broke the silence first. "All right. Let's start at the beginning. What's your name?"

"Mirage," her doppelganger said.

Only one group of people in the world took names like that. "You're a Hunter."

"You didn't know?"

"I had no idea." Miryo laughed without humor. "No wonder you were able to hurt those other Hunters so badly. Unless you had help?"

Mirage shook her head, that familiar wry grin on her face. "You hired Thornbloods. They're not as good as they like to think they are."

"I only hired one. It's lucky for me she thought to bring friends, or you might not have ended up here at all."

"Luck." Mirage snorted. "Ice is a coward. She knew I could take her in a fair fight; I'd bet on myself against any one other Hunter, and probably any two Thornbloods. Had she come after me alone, I'd've killed her on the spot."

Miryo felt an odd sort of pride. *Of course. I don't want my double to be a second-rate anything. She* should *be that good.* But she was also disturbed; the casual way in which Mirage spoke of killing was completely alien to her. It reminded her that, although they were technically the same person, they were not identical. *Which makes sense. We had very different upbringings, after all.*

Then what Mirage had said registered. "You knew that Hunter?"

"We're old enemies," Mirage said shortly. "Our schools don't get along, and she's a bitch. You could have saved yourself a lot of trouble by just sending a messenger, you know. I probably would have come, and then we'd all have avoided this mess."

And then that Hunter wouldn't be dying from a gut wound. But it's too late to fix that now. Miryo's inward laugh was bitter. *And hopefully I won't* have *to do this again.*

"So I know you're a witch," Mirage said. "Your name?"

"Miryo." It was only when she said it that she noticed the similarity. They both pursed their lips, and then laughed nervously at the other's expression. "But you weren't always called Mirage. You used to be a Temple Dancer, right?"

"How did you know that?"

"While I was following you, I got to see Eriot's company perform the Aspects. Afterward I talked to one of the Dancers—Sareen, I think her name was."

"Sareen. There's someone I haven't thought about in years." Mirage looked pensive, then banished the expression. "My parents named me Seniade."

The words jolted Miryo. "Your parents?"

"The people who raised me for a few years, then sold me off to the Temple as a Dancer when their farm died out from under them and they couldn't afford to feed themselves, let alone a child." Mirage shrugged, apparently undisturbed by the story. "One of the priestesses told me I was never their child to begin with. I certainly didn't look anything like them. I only saw them a handful of times after that, though. The Temple, and then Silverfire, were my real family."

Miryo looked at her thoughtfully. *It's still so strange. As if I'm seeing myself, had I lived a different life.*

Mirage lost patience with the meditative atmosphere at the same time Miryo did. "So," her double said briskly, as if this were simple business, not anything important. Probably to cover the tension still in the air. "Start from the beginning. Who was my mother? Besides a witch, of course. And how exactly did I come to be?"

"It's a long explanation," Miryo said.

"Do I look like I'm going anywhere?"

They were, after all, discussing their lives—and their fates. Miryo nodded. "All right. My mother—*our* mother—was called Kasane. She was a Water Hand, living in Insebrar. I have no idea who our father was; probably some man from her village. When she found out she was pregnant she went to Tsurike Hall, because you're supposed to be at one of our halls when you give birth. That's so you can keep the infant out of starlight for five days; they've got windowless rooms for it."

"So that the child won't have a soul yet."

"Exactly. There's a ritual they do, the night of the fifth day, that creates the channel for magical power. But it's got a side effect."

"Me."

"You," Miryo agreed. "Well, sort of. I guess you could say it makes *both* of us, out of the original child. But only one of the two has the channel for magic. The mother kills the one that doesn't—remember, no soul still—and then takes the witch-child outside to be presented to the Goddess."

Mirage sat back in her chair, fiddling with her wine. "So what happened? Why am I still here?"

"I have *no* idea," Miryo replied. "Maybe the Primes know; they didn't say."

"Maybe Kasane forgot to kill me first. Or botched the job, although I don't have any lethal-looking scars, at least not that I've noticed. How is it usually done?"

Again the casual attitude toward killing. Miryo suppressed a shudder. "I didn't ask."

"Great. And the body?"

"Disposed of, I assume. I don't know how." Miryo kicked herself for not asking these questions of Narika when she had the chance.

"So death and cleanup are two things we should think about," Mirage said.

"I have a feeling that list is only going to get longer," Miryo said grimly.

"It's a pity my 'parents' are dead. I never got a chance to ask them where I came from, how they ended up with me. And no one at the Temple cared much; I was hardly the only foundling there. Is Kasane dead, too?"

"A few years ago."

"You don't seem too grieved."

"Witches don't have very close relationships with their daughters," Miryo said. "The babies are raised by the Void Hearts, at the domain halls. My mother was transferred later to Trine; I stayed in Insebrar. We get ten years of schooling in a local hall; then they take us back to Starfall, and we spend the next fifteen years there."

Mirage whistled soundlessly. "And I thought Hunters trained for a long time. We start at ten and finish at twenty. So you've just graduated, as it were?"

"Pretty much. Would have, if it weren't for you." Miryo felt less bitter over it, though, than she had.

"What happened?"

Miryo described the testing procedures, glossing quickly over the preliminary questioning and the Elemental trials. "And then they open the channel that was created in the connection ritual. It's blocked, you see, until you're mature and can handle it. And even then some can't; the power kills them. I survived, but got blasted, and that's how they knew you were alive."

Mirage held up one finger to pause her for a moment. "What happened right before that?"

"Before the power? The Elemental tests. They're tests of character; you have to be determined enough, but able to bend, and to stay calm, and to fight back when necessary."

"I count four Elements. What was the last one, Void? What happened in that one?"

"They showed me a glimpse of the Void." Miryo shivered at the memory.

"And what trait does that test?"

Miryo opened her mouth to respond, and froze. She closed her mouth slowly, then said, "Wholeness of self."

"Interesting." Mirage's eyes narrowed. "This was shortly after Midsummer?" Miryo nodded. "I felt it. I was riding along the road, minding my own business, when I felt this weird . . . presence. As if an old friend was there with me—but gone an instant later. I barely had time to register that, and then I keeled headfirst out of my saddle and didn't wake up for a day."

"It hit you less hard, then; I was out for longer. But I was the one the power went through." The skin between Miryo's shoulderblades crawled. "Weird. I didn't know it would affect you. Though I guess it makes sense. It's probably a function of the same thing that's sending my magic askew."

"Which is?"

"The way it was described to me was, you're a part of me. Of my mind. And it takes total concentration to work magic. Since you're a part of me that I can't focus, you make it impossible for me to control the power I draw."

"Can't you just not work magic?" Mirage asked.

Even the suggestion made something twinge, deep inside. Miryo flinched, and saw her doppelganger see it. She took a steadying breath, than said, "No. It's . . . I feel it there, all the time. The Elements are the world we *live* in, you know. They're all around us. There's an energy to them, and I can feel it now, and I keep wanting to reach out to it. And it's getting harder and harder to stop myself."

"I'll knock you out, if you need," Mirage offered. Her tone was light, but Miryo had no doubt she meant it. Then the Hunter started in her seat. "Warrior's teeth. I forgot about Eclipse."

"Another Hunter?"

"A year-mate. I'm working with him on . . . well, it would take too long to describe it now. I've got to go talk to him. Otherwise he's going to find out I was kidnapped by Thornbloods, and then there'll be *real* trouble."

She did not say it, but the words still hung in the air. *Do you trust me enough to let me leave?*

Miryo looked at her doppelganger, weighing it in her mind. This would be a perfect chance for Mirage to flee. But then again, she could hit Miryo over the head and stroll out at any time, if she really wanted to escape. So there was little reason to assume that she wouldn't come back.

"This house is on Lilac Row," she said finally. "Go left out the front door, and you'll be on Lord's Way."

Mirage nodded. "I'll be back soon."

MIRAGE GOT SEVERAL STREETS away before the shaking overtook her.

She leaned against a wall and closed her eyes, trusting her instincts to warn her if trouble came. Her first thought, oddly enough, was that she should go back and apologize to those men in Enden.

Them, and damn near everyone else I've known in the past twenty-five years. Well, twelve really; I got to dye my hair black when I was a Dancer.

That was irrelevant, and she knew it. Her thoughts refused to behave, though. A suspicion she had been denying her entire life had suddenly burst into reality; that was enough to send anyone into shock.

Warrior's teeth. I am a witch. Well, not a witch, but damn near. Part of me is. Goddess. I was expecting the other shoe to drop, but I thought it would have to do with the assassination. Instead, a steel-toed riding boot I never saw materializes out of nowhere and kicks me in the head.

And there's a whole different kettle of fish. Can I tell Miryo about the commission? Regardless, how am I supposed to continue with that and find a way out of this lovely mess we're in?

A chill ran down Mirage's spine, and she opened her eyes. *Tari-nakana was tracking me. I wouldn't want to bet this had nothing to do with it.*

She needed some time to sit alone and think all of this through, but it would have to wait. The sun was setting;

Eclipse would be taking Angrim apart stone by stone before much longer. Mirage pushed her roiling thoughts down, straightened her shoulders, and headed for the Cracked Oak.

The common room had been straightened up; there was no sign of the battle that had disrupted it earlier that day. None of the patrons so much as glanced up as Mirage passed through the common room.

Eclipse was not upstairs, although her lost sword was. Mirage swore and headed back down, strapping the blade on as she went. The innkeeper, when she hunted him down in the kitchens, had no idea where Eclipse had gone.

Void it. He's gone after the Thornbloods already.

MIRYO PACED back and forth in the study, using the beat of her steps to organize her thoughts. That was the idea, at least. It was failing miserably.

How do I explain this to the Cousins? How do I explain it to the Primes? *I've got to find Ashin, and ask her what she knows. She knew that Mirage was alive—but there was more to it than that. She was anticipating something, I know it. But I have no idea what it is.*

She kept pacing mostly as an outlet for the quivering that threatened to overtake her muscles. After all that preparation, steeling herself to kill her doppelganger, this sudden change in her path was more than a little disorienting. She had no second thoughts about her decision; she had known, when she looked in Mirage's eyes, that she faced a person. Not a copy. And she couldn't kill her without at least trying to find a different solution.

Dealing with the consequences wouldn't be easy, though.

Miryo made herself halt, put her hands over her face. She took two deep breaths, steadying herself. She needed to stop this nervous mental twitching and come up with a useful plan.

She didn't make very much progress before a hand clamped over her mouth from behind.

"Do not move," a low voice growled. "And *don't* try to sing. I'll take your throat out before you can get two words into your spell."

Miryo felt a dagger point prick her neck and did not doubt him. She was torn between nodding to show her agreement, and remaining still, lest he think she was trying something. She decided not to move.

The hand vanished, but an instant later he was prying her jaw open and a shoving wad of cloth into her mouth. It choked Miryo, but she kept silent. When she was securely gagged, her attacker spoke again.

"Don't make a sound," he said, voice grim. "You will nod yes or no to my questions, and make no other movement. Did you hire Thornblood Hunters today?"

How am I supposed to answer that? It was yesterday, not today, and Kan did the actual hiring, albeit while sort of pretending to be me. So do I say yes or no?

The man had no patience for her indecision. He grabbed her shoulder roughly and swung her around to face him.

Her worst fears were confirmed. The intruder was a Hunter, fully uniformed. And while she didn't think he was one of the three men from earlier in the day, she had no doubt that the rest of the Thornbloods were less than happy about the treatment of their own. The look in his eyes was cold as steel, and as unforgiving.

For a moment, at least. Then his eyes shot open, and his knife hand dropped to his side.

At that instant, the door swung hard into the wall. The Hunter spun around, drawing his sword. Miryo tried to yell a warning and choked on the gag. Without even looking, he snapped his left arm around and put the dagger back to her throat. She froze.

Mirage took one look at the two of them and fell against the door frame laughing.

Should I be relieved, or offended?

"Eclipse," Mirage said when she had air to speak, "take that gag out of her mouth. She's not going to cause any trouble."

Eclipse? Her partner. I'd better not tell him I thought he was a Thornblood.

"What's going on?" he said roughly, not moving either blade an inch. "Who in the Crone's name is she? Are you even who you look like?" His sword arm extended as though he expected Mirage to attack.

"Take the gag out, Kerestel," Mirage said, not laughing anymore. "I understand that this looks strange, but it does have an explanation, however odd. I *was* waylaid by Thornbloods, but that's over with, and we can deal with them later. I promise Miryo won't cast a spell."

Miryo's earlier trust in her was repaid. Eclipse wavered for a moment, then reluctantly sheathed his blades. He pulled the gag none too gently from her mouth, and did not apologize for the rudeness.

"Sit down," Mirage said. "This will be a shock."

CHAPTER SIXTEEN

Kan

A LONG STRETCH of explanation later, Eclipse had not run screaming from the room. He even seemed to accept what they had to say, at least provisionally. Mirage was relieved. Although she had allies, he was one of her few friends; she would need his support to get through this. Especially since he too was blood-oathed to the commission.

And I have yet to figure out where I stand with Miryo. Or where she stands with me.

The witch was, as far as she could tell, being completely forthright. And her attitude had changed since their encounter in the hallway; she *saw* Mirage now, as a person instead of a thing.

Although I have the feeling that her prior attitude didn't come easily to her. It was something taught to her by the Primes, not something she believed in herself. Which is lucky for me, since it meant I could bluff her.

The three of them were sitting in an arc in the study, looking at their boots or the wall or random spots on the ceiling. No one had spoken for a while. The only sound Mirage could hear was the buzzing of an insect against one of the windows, fighting to get out into the darkening sky.

"There is one other thing," Miryo said at last. Mirage looked at her sharply. "I haven't mentioned it before now because I'm still not sure what it means. But before I was tested, one of the witches at Starfall was acting strangely. Ashin-kasora, the Air Hand Key. She was very much on edge about my testing. It looked like she couldn't decide whether I was fated to sprout wings or die on the spot. It sort of makes sense now; she knew you were alive, Mirage. And she must have known I'd be sent to kill you. But still it feels like she's expecting . . . something else. I really don't know what. My best guess is that she suspected we'd end up where we are now."

"In cooperation. Where is she, do you know?"

"No idea. Askavya, I was told, but that was a while ago. She disappeared right after my test, you see, before I'd even woken up."

Mirage glanced at Eclipse, who was looking alert and thoughtful. "We could try to find out where she is."

He returned her glance with interest when she said that. Mirage knew what he was thinking. But could they trust Miryo that far?

The two events were almost certainly related. Which meant she didn't have much choice.

Mirage cleared her throat and addressed Miryo again. "Were you familiar with Tari-nakana?"

"I didn't know her personally, if that's what you mean. But I do know who she was. Does this have to do with her death?"

"Very much so. She was assassinated."

Miryo's eyes widened. "She *what*?"

"By a Hunter. A Wolfstar." Mirage outlined their trips to Starfall and Vilardi, and Avalanche's role in the matter.

"So how is this related?"

"There's two angles. First, Tari-nakana was tracking my movements before she died. I know this because I found a list in her study that matched my recent itinerary."

Miryo's eyes narrowed. "So Ashin wasn't the only one who knew about you."

"It looks that way. The second angle, though, is . . . well, not dubious; we're fairly certain of our conclusions. But I don't know if they're tied in with our situation. We think the Wolfstar was hired by witches."

Miryo became very still. She did not so much as blink. Mirage, waiting for a response from her, doubted she was even breathing.

"An interesting theory," the witch said at last, and her voice was so carefully controlled Mirage could guess at the roiling emotions it was masking. "Would you care to back it up?"

Mirage explained their reasoning as thoroughly and carefully as she could. Miryo had to be reeling at the idea; it was comparable to someone telling Mirage that a Silverfire Hunter had killed the person employing him as a bodyguard. Not impossible, but certainly shocking. She owed it to her double to prove the accusation was well thought out.

Miryo listened, stone-faced. When Mirage was done, she closed her eyes as if in pain, then opened them grimly. "I see. I can't say I like the idea, but . . . well, a year ago I wouldn't have believed you at all. But there's something about the way Ashin disappeared—it's not unusual; vanishing without telling anyone where you're going is standard behavior for an Air Hand, but I still thought there was something off about it. As if she had not just left, but had . . . fled."

"Do you think she expects what Tari-nakana got?" Mirage asked.

"I don't know. But they both knew you were alive." Miryo looked pensive, then shook her head with a sigh. "I'll have to think about this. So what do you do now?"

"We haven't told our employer yet," Eclipse said. "There were a few things we wanted to take care of first."

"We were headed for Miest," Mirage elaborated. "We need to talk to Jaguar, the head of Silverfire. He's the one who tapped us for the commission; he may know something more about the situation. And, to be quite honest, we wanted our defenses in place before we started flinging accusations about."

"Defenses?"

"Our school is more than just the place where we learned things. If one of our people gets into trouble because of something he did in the course of fulfilling a contract, he can petition Silverfire for help. I don't know if we'll need it, but I'd rather be prepared."

Miryo nodded. A wry grin slipped across her face. "Do you think they'd let me join you in hiding?"

"We'll make sure it doesn't come to that."

"I hope not. Since it'll take a while to be certain whom I can trust among the witches. And loyal though Kan and Sai are, I don't know that the Cousins will be much help to me, either. But there's not much point in worrying about that right now. I'm too tired to think very straight anyway."

"I could use sleep, too," Mirage said, touching the

bruises on her face gingerly. "An afternoon of uncon-
sciousness just doesn't cut it. When do you think you
could be ready to go tomorrow?"

"I'm coming with you to Miest?" Miryo looked
surprised.

"Not quite all the way. I'm not taking you into the
school itself; you look *far* too much like me for that to be
a good idea."

"And there's no way you could disguise me?"

"Remember that we're talking about a nest of people
trained to notice things like that. If they saw through it,
we'd be in more trouble than I even want to *think* about.
Bringing a witch into Silverfire is not the way to increase
my already scant popularity."

Miryo rubbed her eyes and yawned hugely. "All right. I
can be ready by noon, I think. It would be sooner, but it's
going to take me a while to explain all this to the Cousins.
They've been unbelievably cooperative so far—and I've
been doing some strange things—but this is pushing it. I
have no idea what I'm going to say to them."

"They have a right to object?" Mirage asked, surprised.
Maybe Cousins aren't the mindless sheep I'd thought.

"Technically, no. Some witches don't even like them to
offer opinions. But I haven't demanded blind obedience
from them yet, and I don't want to. The problem is, if they
think what I'm doing is truly stupid, they may send word
to the Primes."

Mirage was pleased to hear that Miryo treated the
Cousins like people. Perhaps she'd even be willing to explain who—or what—they were. But that was a question
for later. "What would the Primes do, if they knew?"

Miryo rubbed her eyes again. "I don't know. I'm kind

of afraid to think about it. This little hunt wasn't a suggestion; it was an order. If they decide I'm a danger to those around me, they may try to resolve the issue themselves. They'd probably kill you on the spot."

"Is there anything I can do to help?"

"Not really. I'm just going to have to talk to the Cousins. I need to know where they stand before I can plan anything else."

She isn't comfortable enough with this situation to want me there. Fair enough; I would have preferred to talk to Eclipse in private myself. We'll learn to trust each other. Hopefully.

"Where should I meet you tomorrow?" Miryo asked. "Here, or where you're staying?"

Mirage looked to Eclipse, thinking it over. "Somewhere else," he said firmly.

"Outside the city," Mirage agreed. "We don't want to show up here, not if this is to be kept quiet, and we also need to make sure the Thornbloods aren't aware of what's going on." She smiled thinly. "Not yet, anyway. I have every intention of sitting Ice down for a little chat someday. At the point of a blade."

She was aware, as she said that, of a slight stiffening in Miryo's body. *Interesting. Another thing she's not comfortable with. Most witches aren't violent. I wonder if there's anything she does that will make me feel the same way?*

Aside from magic, of course.

"There's a line of six or so elms on the west side of the north road," Eclipse offered. "Would that work?"

"I can find it," Miryo said.

"Noon, then," Mirage agreed. "We'll see you there.

But send word to us at the Cracked Oak if anything goes
wrong. Or just come find us, if it's really critical."

"I will," Miryo promised.

DESPITE HER EXHAUSTION, Miryo did not sleep when the
two Hunters had left.

*I've done nothing physical today, yet my arms and legs
feel like lead. First time I ever knew that sitting around
doing nothing could be so draining. Then again, there
was that tiny bit of excitement in the hallway. That would
never have anything to do with me feeling like the walking
dead. Of course not.*

She paced the study at a slower rate than before, more
mindless wandering than steady movement. She clasped
her hands behind her back and ambled around, staring at
the floor, trying to force her exhausted mind to work.

Oddly enough, she felt liberated. Her problem had not
gone away; on the contrary, it had complicated itself horribly. And they might still end up back at square one, if
they didn't find a way through this. But the feeling of a
sword hanging over her head had vanished. She might
not have to kill Mirage. That single thought kept running
through her head, lightening her heart. Miryo realized
that she was humming under her breath, and the tune was
a song of praise to the Goddess.

As soon as she realized this, something shifted. Miryo
felt herself reaching for power, for what use she didn't
know; she just thirsted for its touch. She cut herself off
abruptly, sweating, and stood in the middle of the room
trying not to shake.

No. No. You've made it this far; you'll damn well keep

going. You will not *pull power. That's just asking for trouble, and you know it.*

Intellectual knowing was one thing. The reality of the hollowness in her stomach was another. Miryo pressed the heels of her hands to her eyes, refusing to let herself break down. She had gone twenty-five years without magic, and had only truly tasted it once since then. Surely another few weeks would not kill her. Surely.

But Goddess—I want it so badly.

Bitterness washed over her. *Why did Mirage have to do that to me? Bluffing me out like that, telling me to kill her—damn her to* Void *for that. It could have been easy, over and done with. I might never have looked back. But I'll never know. She had to come along and make me think about what I was doing. Make me see her as a person.*

Miryo slapped the stones next to the fireplace, hard. The shock helped clear her mind. Then she sat down in one of the chairs and made herself take deep, calming breaths. She knew herself. Had she killed Mirage, doubts would have plagued her for the rest of her life. Her doppelganger had done her a favor, even if it was one loaded with extra trouble. But that didn't stop her from yearning momentarily for the simple answer of a knife in the heart.

Well, I could always kill myself. *That would take care of it.*

She was jolted out of that morbid thought by the door opening. Miryo leapt to her feet to find Kan standing just inside the room, looking at her.

Or maybe she'll *kill me.*

Kan did not actually look angry. Not yet. Of course, she didn't yet know what had happened. The Cousin stood in the doorway, arm in a sling to protect her broken collarbone, and looked at Miryo.

"She's not dead," Miryo said, deciding on bluntness as her best option.

Kan blinked.

"Come in. Sit down. Do you want me to get you something—tea?" Miryo considered slapping herself, in the hope of finding more rational things to say. "Of course not. You want an explanation. Please, sit down, and I'll try to give you one."

She noticed the pronoun. I'm sure of it. Which means I'll have to tell her everything—or close to it. Not about Tarinakana, I think. Not unless it's absolutely necessary.

"I was going upstairs to kill her. I caught her in the hallway—lucky, really, or she would have been gone. But . . . I couldn't kill her. And I don't just mean physically, although there was that, too. I just couldn't make myself do it."

Still Kan said nothing.

"Look, I know that the Primes know a damn sight more than I do. And I should believe them when they tell me this is the only answer. But in my heart, I cannot accept it—not without at least *trying* to find another way. I just can't believe that the Goddess intended this. Mirage is a *person,* not a thing. She's not just a copy of me. I had that knife in my hand, and I looked at her, and I couldn't do it. Not yet. We're going to try and find another solution. And if that doesn't work, well, we'll go back to where we started. I can't possibly be at a worse disadvantage than I was in that hall, so I'm not really losing anything. And I just couldn't live with myself if I didn't try to find another way."

Kan sat, stone-faced. Miryo looked at her. And then, when the silence became too much, she asked, "What are you going to do?"

The Cousin stood and walked away, going to face a bookcase. Miryo bet she wasn't looking at the books. Several moments passed before Kan turned back to face her.

"I understand," Kan said. Miryo had to strain to hear her voice, even in the quiet of the room. "I understand, but I do not—cannot—agree. I think you should listen to the Primes. I think that ignoring them is a serious risk."

Miryo nodded slowly, a sinking feeling in her stomach. "You'll report me, then."

"No," Kan said, and the floor slammed back into place beneath Miryo's feet. "I'm supposed to serve you. I'm also supposed to serve the Primes, who commanded me to ride with you. I understand what you're doing, and why, but I do not agree with it. What then should I do?" She paused, closing her eyes. She tried to lean her head back in thought, but a spasm of pain crossed her face and she straightened, looking at Miryo. "This much I can offer you. I will not report you, but neither will I go with you. I will remove myself from the situation."

Miryo swallowed hard. She spread her hands in her lap, laying them on her knees, and was proud that they did not shake. "I understand."

"Sai will come with me," Kan said, answering the question Miryo had not yet asked. "We will neither help you, nor get in your way."

"Thank you," Miryo said, and she had never meant the words so much in her entire life. "I will not forget this. And if the Goddess smiles on me, and I come out of this in one piece, I will do whatever I can to repay you. Regardless of whether I turn out to be right or not."

Kan nodded.

Another awkward pause. "Good night, then," Miryo said, and left the room.

She had been in her bedroom for a few minutes when she heard Kan's footsteps in the hall. They stopped outside; Miryo would have wagered the Cousin had her ear to the door. Then the footsteps went away, and after a moment she heard a door shut.

Miryo began throwing her belongings into her saddlebags.

ECLIPSE RESPECTED Mirage's obvious desire for silence on the way back to the inn. They had one short discussion when they reached the room, on the topic of whether or not she would allow him to see to her injuries. She claimed to be fine, and cited her success against the Cousins as proof, but Eclipse knew better. More than any other Hunter he'd met, Mirage was able to ignore pain. On several occasions during their training, she'd dismissed broken toes and cracked ribs as minor inconveniences. So he put his foot down, and she conceded.

He washed her face and inspected it. She was developing some lovely bruises, but her nose hadn't been broken, and neither had her jaw. He prepared a tea to help her concussion, then made her strip down and let him check her other injuries.

Mirage had a special penchant for breaking ribs, but for a change she'd stayed in one piece. Her arm was also intact. A low whistle escaped him when he saw her back, though. Any harder and the blow would have damaged her spine or her kidneys. She had been damned lucky.

Eclipse let her pull her shirt back on then, and they began packing in silence. Mirage's face was impassive behind the bruises. At last, though, he had to ask the question that had been in his mind since they left the house on Lilac Row.

"Do you think she'll be there tomorrow?"

Mirage answered without hesitation. "Yes."

"You trust her that much."

"I'm not sure it's possible for me to not trust her." She paused. "Does that make any sense?"

"Yes, but I'm still not sure you should believe it." Eclipse tucked his weapons-cleaning kit into his saddlebag and then sat on the bed, looking at her directly. "You two aren't identical, you know. There's no way you could be. You grew up completely differently."

"I know. But I still feel, gut-deep, that in many ways we're the same. Maybe more of a person's character is inborn than I'd thought. Or maybe each of us was somehow influenced by the upbringing the other had. Whatever it is, I can tell already that despite our differences, we're more similar than not. So I know she'll be there."

"Because you would be."

"I would bet you any sum of money that she's weighed the situation in her mind and come to the same conclusion I have. Although we take a risk by doing this, what we stand to gain outweighs it. So we'll stick with our decision until something changes the balance."

The reasoning was so typically Mirage that Eclipse had to snort. "It's that kind of thinking that put you through such misery in childhood. You could have stayed a Temple Dancer."

Mirage flashed him a quick grin. "But I wanted to be a Hunter. And the cost was worth it."

"Your evaluation of cost is not that of a sane person."

"It was worth it in the end. I went through some trouble at Silverfire, but it ended eventually, and now I'm where I want to be. More or less. If you leave out the bit about my life being in imminent danger."

"Sen, you'd be *bored* if your life weren't in danger."

Another grin. He was glad to see her mood improving. She hadn't said anything outright, but he could tell that she wasn't happy to discover that the whispers about her being a witch were peripherally true. It had produced a brittleness in her manner, probably too subtle for Miryo to see—after all, she had only just met Mirage. But he, who knew her well, could see it, and he was relieved that it seemed to be fading.

That, or she was just putting up a better mask.

He'd keep an eye on her, just in case.

THEY'D SET THE MEETING time for noon the next day, but Mirage and Eclipse left the inn before dawn. They departed in stealth, heading for one of the lesser exits from the city. Neither knew if the Thornbloods were aware of Mirage's escape, but they agreed it was better to take the precaution. It meant that Mirage got very little sleep that night, but Eclipse could stand guard while she napped and waited for Miryo to arrive.

That was the plan, anyway. They arrived at the line of elms around dawn to find Miryo already there.

Mirage raised an eyebrow at her from the back of her

horse. She was amused to see that Miryo could interpret the gesture perfectly. "I talked with Kan—the one whose collarbone you broke. Sai doesn't talk if she can help it. Anyway, Kan said she wouldn't help me, but neither would she cause me trouble. She's just staying out of it. So they won't be coming with us."

"And you decided you wanted to sleep under the stars."

Miryo grimaced. "I trust Kan. Mostly. I just decided I should get out while the getting was good. Just in case she changed her mind, or Sai didn't agree with the plan."

"Wise of you." Mirage stifled a yawn and considered her options. She was tired, but there was no point in wasting good daylight when they could be riding. She could always doze in the saddle. "If you've got your horse, then, let's get moving."

CHAPTER SEVENTEEN

Experimentation

HEAT POUNDED MIRYO throughout the day, and combined with the hard pace the Hunters set, it drained the energy from her. She refused to complain, though. Luckily Mirage called an early halt in a sheltered copse. Miryo wondered why they had not stopped in a town; they could have reached one before nightfall quite easily. She kept her mouth shut, though, as they set up camp. The two Hunters handled their horses with an easy, unconscious competence that made her envious. Then again, if what little she knew about Silverfire was correct, her double had been on the road more or less constantly for the past five years. Miryo was similarly competent with the things she did every day.

They took a light supper around the fire, still not talking much. Then Mirage revealed her reasons for stopping early, outside of a town.

"Right," she said. "Time for us to work on this magic thing."

Miryo stared at her. "Work on it? What *exactly* do you mean by that?"

Her apprehension was justified. Mirage shrugged.

"You say your magic spins out of control because of me. Has it ever actually happened?"

"Only during the ritual itself."

"And you weren't paying much attention then, I'd imagine. So it's worth our time to test it. I'm not saying I think you're imagining the problem; it's just that we should have a better idea of exactly what happens. We're isolated here. We can go away from Eclipse and then the worst thing we can damage will be some farmer's pasture land."

"And ourselves," Miryo pointed out acidly.

"We'll do something small. Then it won't cause much havoc if it gets out of control."

Miryo compressed her lips and stared at her doppelganger. Narika's words about the time and practice needed to learn fine control danced in her memory. Keeping a spell small wouldn't be half so easy as Mirage seemed to think.

But you need to do this; she's right about that. And she's not afraid of it. Do you want her to think you're *scared?*

"Come on, then," she said at last. "I want to get well away from here."

They left the horses and Eclipse behind. The latter seemed none too happy with the situation, but he said nothing. Miryo and Mirage walked through the woods in silence, Mirage leading the way, until they found a small gap in a grove of aspens where a thick carpet of grass had sprung up. A quick circuit revealed they were a good distance from any fields, so they settled themselves on the ground.

"You pick what we do," Mirage said. "I have no idea how this works."

Miryo considered it. *Small, so we don't need a focus. And nondestructive. Right, so Fire's out of the question.* Healing Mirage's face came to mind, but she thought about what could go wrong and decided against it. "Levitation," she said at last. A brief search netted her a fist-size piece of shale, which she set in the grass several feet away.

"What do you want me to do?"

"I'm almost tempted to tell you to do nothing, so we can see what happens with that. Luckily for us, common sense overrides my stupidity. You should probably concentrate on the rock. And me. I don't know if you'll be able to feel what I'm doing, but if you can, try not to interfere with it."

Mirage answered with a sharp nod. *She's as edgy as I am. But at least I know one thing: she'll be able to focus well. Nobody could get far as a Hunter if they couldn't concentrate.*

Miryo closed her eyes and took a few deep breaths to center herself. Then she opened her eyes and focused on the rock.

It was over in a heartbeat, and Mirage was picking shards of shale out of her hair. "I assume that wasn't the intended result."

"Not at all," Miryo said, disgruntled. It had happened so quickly she could hardly sort it out. She had reached for power, and sung the phrase, but then it had *twisted* away, like a cat that didn't want to be held. "Did you feel anything?"

Mirage looked thoughtful. "Not at first. Just that you

were concentrating. Then it felt like someone had punched me in the gut, and the rock blew up."

"Interesting. It sounds like the power snapped sideways into *you* for a moment. I didn't know it could do that. You can't draw it on your own; you don't have the channel. But it seems it can come into you through me."

"Maybe if they trained the doppelgangers in magic, then, there wouldn't be this problem."

Miryo was skeptical. "I find it hard to believe nobody thought of that. And it's not just a matter of that one channel; you're not structured to work magic. I can't explain how I know that, but I can sense it, like the way I sensed where you were."

"So that's how you found me. I was wondering." Mirage leaned back and pondered the bits of stone on the ground. "It's still worth a shot, though. If you explained what you were doing, I might have a better chance of not interfering with it—or tossing the power back to you when it slides over to me."

A disbelieving laugh slipped out of Miryo. "It's not that easy. I've been training my whole life. I can't duplicate that in a night, any more than you could teach me how to fight."

"Right, but wrong." Mirage's tone was brisk. "I couldn't teach you how to fight; that takes time and practice. But I *could* teach you a basic stance, how to hold your hands, maybe some simple blocks and attacks."

Part of Miryo rebelled against that notion; magic wasn't that easy. But it *was* true that the basic principles could be explained quickly. Explained, but not necessarily understood. She'd be drawn and quartered by the Primes if they found out she'd been spilling trade secrets, but she was already on track for that anyway. A little more couldn't hurt. Too much. "All right. I can try. But it begins with drawing power, and I *really* don't think I can describe how I do that. It's just there; I reach out and take it."

"It doesn't begin there at all. Where are you pulling this power from?"

"The Elements."

"And where are *they*?"

Only then did Miryo realize how much knowledge she took for granted. She'd known things like this before she was ten. "They're in the world around us. They're what the world is *made* of, really, though each one has a specific prime source. The sun is the prime source of Fire, the sea is Water, the wind is Air, and the ground itself is Earth."

"And Void?"

"Unworkable. It's the thing that *isn't* the world; how can you touch that? The Primes have a trick of showing you the Void—that's what they did in my testing—but we can't go there, or use it, or do anything with it."

It wasn't easy, reducing her education to a summary. Miryo was painfully aware of how much she was simplifying things. She could hardly do otherwise, though, so she forged on ahead. "Anyway. That's basic magic. For bigger things, or more complicated ones, we use a focus. Stones, feathers—you've probably seen them."

"Up close and personal, when I was blood-oathed to the commission."

"That one's a complicated spell. It uses all four Elements to bind you, and foci for each one."

Mirage held up one hand to stop her and closed her

eyes. "Earth—the crystal?" She cracked one eye long enough to see Miryo nod. "Was the blood Water?"

"Fire, in that case; blood is one of the rare foci that can serve for more than one."

"So Water was, what, the bowl?"

Miryo felt proud. "Exactly."

"Where was the Air?"

"The witch's breath. Spells themselves are sung, but spoken words are an Air focus."

"So what exactly does a focus do?"

The answer to that question had filled an entire lecture when Miryo was ten. Since then, though, she had thought of a much simpler explanation than the one Kibitsu-ai had used. It wasn't perfect, but it would do for now, and no one had to know how badly she was butchering the true complexity of it. "Think of it like juggling. You can't hold five balls in your hands, but if I were to toss them at you one at a time, you could keep them all in your control, ready to be taken hold of when needed. That is, assuming you can juggle."

Mirage grinned. "Believe it or not, that was part of our training. Juggling is excellent for building coordination."

"So you see what I mean."

"Yes. I think so, at least, although I get the feeling you're leaving the better part of it out."

Miryo grimaced. "I am, but the full, technical explanation would take about four hours and would confuse you horribly."

"We'll skip it, then."

"Do you have any other questions? I understand this stuff so well, I have trouble figuring out what I need to explain."

Mirage considered it. "None that I think are relevant enough to ask right now. You can't have gotten much sleep last night, so you need more tonight."

"As if you don't?" Miryo raised one eyebrow pointedly at her doppelganger, and they grinned at each other. "All right. We'll give it one more shot. Try . . ." She considered it. "If you feel the power coming into you again, try to not fight it. I don't think it will hurt you, and it may rebound to me of its own accord. We can hope."

Mirage nodded again and closed her eyes.

Focus. Concentrate. This is easy. You should be able to work this spell without thinking. Miryo exhaled, then took a breath and sang.

This time it was not quick. Miryo could feel trouble building with horrifying clarity. She tried to cut the spell short, but power was surging through her and couldn't be walled off. Wind kicked up around the clearing, bringing down leaves. Mirage's eyes shot open, then narrowed; she opened her mouth to say something to Miryo, and then a huge gust of air slammed into her and threw her across the ground into a tangle of underbrush.

The wind died. Miryo cursed and leapt to her feet, going to her doppelganger's side.

Mirage was swearing a blue streak and fighting her way out of the tangle. "Nettles," she spat when she had regained her feet. Already blisters were beginning to rise on her hands and face. "Just what I needed."

Well, at least my training will do some *good tonight.* Miryo cast about and found a patch of dock leaves. She pulled a few and offered them to Mirage, who took them with sour thanks.

"What was that you said?" Mirage asked as she rubbed the leaves over her blisters.

Miryo blinked. "When?"

"While I was still in the nettles. Misetsu and something."

"Oh. Misetsu and Menukyo. First witch and her eldest daughter. Witch swearing. We're all descended from those two."

"Great. I don't suppose we could call back their spirits and ask them what in the Warrior's name is going wrong?"

"Sorry, raising the dead isn't a spell anybody's worked out." Miryo took a deep breath, quelling her frustration. "I think that's enough for tonight. And I'll try to come up with some better way to do this."

ECLIPSE DIDN'T QUESTION the explanation he got of the evening's antics, but watching him, Miryo suspected he knew just how much they were leaving out. Mirage either didn't notice or didn't care; she seemed mostly interested in finding a stream to bathe her blisters in.

Which left Miryo alone with Eclipse for the first time since they'd met—when he'd held a knife to her throat.

"I know Sen—Mirage," he said bluntly as Miryo was brushing leaves off her clothing. She tensed at his tone. "And I'd bet she's made some sort of bargain with you, about what you two will do when you know you're running out of time. But I can promise you this: Sen will never admit it's too late."

She straightened slowly, wondering if this was about to become real trouble. The two Hunters were good friends.

Eclipse might get the bright idea that he could save Mirage trouble by killing her.

But if he were going to do that, he wouldn't have given her this kind of warning. Would he?

"Perhaps," she said, keeping her own tone level. "We'll see."

Eclipse sighed in frustration. "It's a virtue and a flaw; she won't give up on something she thinks is important. It's gotten her through some tight situations before. But I've always told her that one of these days she'll commit herself to something impossible, and kill herself trying to do it. And I have a bad feeling that time's come."

Miryo wanted to argue that, but she held her tongue. *Let him talk,* she told herself. *Find out how he feels about all of this.*

"Void it," he muttered, glaring at her, but more in irritation than anger. "I'm wasting my breath, aren't I? You two are too much alike. You're probably as damnfool stubborn as she is; you probably think of this as a challenge you can't pass up. Well, it was worth a shot. I'd rather not see you both get killed."

That was a sentiment Miryo couldn't argue with. But still she stood quiet, waiting for the rest of it.

"I'll be honest," Eclipse said after a moment, his voice low. "If I had to choose between you two, I'd have Sen live. Of course I would; she's been my friend for twelve years. But . . ." He growled under his breath. "Warrior's teeth. I'd rather see her live. But I'd rather see *you* live than both of you die."

It was helpful, but not enough. Miryo had to know what he was planning to do. "There's one way out of this," she said. "Have you thought about it?"

His eyes flicked up to hers. "Of course I have."

Stiff silence. "And?"

The words came out of Eclipse slowly, grudgingly, but they came. "I'm not going to kill you." He sat down on a saddlebag, lacing his hands together into a knot. "If only one of you is going to live, I'd rather it was her. But I won't kill you to save her."

Tension drained out of her shoulders. "I'm glad to hear it," she said wryly.

He managed a grin. "She'd never forgive me if I did, anyway. Just . . . Void it. For once, admit when you're in over your head. Heads. Both of you. Don't you both die just because you won't give up."

"I don't plan on it," Miryo said. "But I won't give up, either, not easily—you're right about that. It's too important." She smiled briefly, without humor. "If we fought, Mirage would win. But I don't know if we will. These days, I can hardly predict what *I'm* going to do, let alone her."

She finally felt relaxed enough to sit down, and settled herself on one of the bedrolls Eclipse had laid out while she and Mirage were off playing with out-of-control spells. "I'm not going to waste time worrying about it right now, though," she said, thinking about those spells. "Better to work on finding a solution."

Eclipse sighed again at that. "You sound like Sen."

"Well, we are the same person. Kind of." Miryo cocked her head to one side, studying him. "It's strange, though; I sort of know her, and I sort of *really* don't. Would you be willing to talk?"

"About her?"

"You seem like you're pretty good friends, and—I

don't know. I feel kind of strange, questioning her." Miryo glanced off in the direction Mirage had gone, wondering how long her double would take bathing. "Or maybe another time."

Eclipse shook his head. "No, she's in a mood where she doesn't want to deal with other people. She won't be back for a half hour at least. I'd be happy to talk." He gestured for her to sit on a log, and settled himself on the ground. "What do you want to know?"

MIRAGE DUCKED HER HEAD into the stream and held it there as long as she could before coming up for air. The cold water cooled her temper, even if it didn't fix her skin.

She sat on her hands to avoid scratching them or her face and leaned her head against the tree at her back. Random muscles in her legs twitched: another side effect of the spell backfiring. She shuddered at the memory of the power sliding through her, pulsing in her blood. *All those years saying I wasn't a witch, and now look at me.*

Miryo didn't seem bothered by the strange behavior of the power, but she was more used to that kind of thing. Mirage had to admire her double's guts, agreeing to try spells despite the risk. It reminded her of her training days at Silverfire, when the students had learned to do a dive-roll from the back of a moving horse. They'd practiced the rolls from a standing position, and then from a stationary horse, but when the time came to do it in motion her muscles had still frozen with fear. Only reminding herself of what her fellow students would say should she balk had made her commit to the roll.

Maybe that was what had motivated Miryo.

Now that she'd thought of it, Mirage suspected her guess might be right. If she put herself in Miryo's shoes, and imagined what her own attitude to magic would be in that place, she could understand her double's actions.

Warrior's blade, but we're a stupid pair. I'm glad Eclipse is around to keep us sane, or we'd kill ourselves, just because neither of us would admit to being overmatched.

"TELL ME ABOUT her childhood," Miryo said.

Eclipse wasn't surprised at the question. In her place, he would have wanted to know the same thing. Unfortunately, there was only so much he could tell her about it. "I wasn't there for most of it. She didn't come to Silverfire until she was thirteen."

"I want to know about that, too," Miryo said, sitting forward in interest. "I know she was a Temple Dancer, but how did she end up as a Hunter? I thought the schools didn't take trainees older than ten—eleven at the most."

"They don't. Sen was . . . an exception." Eclipse laughed briefly, shaking his head. "I don't know why I still call her Sen. She just made such a vivid impression on me back then, when she came to Silverfire, before she earned her Hunter name. That's when we became friends."

"You're year-mates?"

Eclipse nodded. "But she and I are better friends than most. A *lot* of people didn't like her being accepted so late; she didn't have any friends when she showed up. But I . . . well, I admired her. All these people trying to make her fail, to drive her out, and I think she didn't even *see* them half the time. Just blocked out everything that wasn't a part of what she needed to do." He grinned as a memory returned to him, even though it was kind of a painful one. "There was this one master, Talon—he figured out early on that the quickest way to make Sen do something was to tell her she was too weak to do it—"

He broke off as Miryo laughed. "What?"

The witch waved a hand, indicating he should continue. "Just seeing similarities, is all."

"I hope you never went through anything like she did," Eclipse said, a little grim, even after all this time. "Talon went too far, always telling her she wasn't good enough. Had Sen convinced she hadn't yet proven her right to stay. She damn near broke herself trying to satisfy him. In the end, Jaguar even brought in a witch to heal her when she ripped her knee apart from training too much."

The amusement drained out of Miryo's face at his words. Watching it was strange; Eclipse still hadn't adjusted to the likeness. It was as if he were seeing Sen with long hair.

No, not quite. More as if he were seeing Sen the way she might have been, had she not come to Silverfire. The challenges she faced there had put a hardness in her, a streak of self-reliance that made her difficult to befriend. Eclipse was the only person who had really gotten inside that defense. Miryo was softer, more open; her life had not driven her to be so skeptical of those around her.

Miryo spoke, breaking his reverie. "She's good, isn't she? I saw the Thornbloods when they brought her in. She did quite a bit of damage before they took her. And there were four of them."

Eclipse snorted. "It would *take* four Thornbloods to take her down. Partly because they're not great Hunters, and partly because you're right: she's that good. I think that's why Jaguar let her into Silverfire. She was already strong and agile from being a Dancer, and she's got reflexes you wouldn't believe." He paused as a thought came to him. "Then again, maybe you would." He held out his hands, palm up. "Put your hands over mine, just barely touching."

Miryo did so, plainly curious.

"I'm going to try and slap the backs of your hands," Eclipse said. "When you feel me move, you try to pull away faster, so I miss. Got it?" Miryo nodded. "Okay. Ready?"

His hands flashed out and slapped hers smartly.

"Okay, now you see how that works. I guess you never played this as a kid? We'll do it for real this time." He repositioned his hands beneath hers.

And slapped her hands again.

They went through this twice more before Miryo dropped her hands and gave him an ironic look. "I don't have her reflexes, do I."

The difference was unmistakable. "I guess not. She must have gotten it from the Dancer training, before she got to Silverfire." But he knew as he said it that it wasn't true. Sen couldn't sing, and Miryo didn't have the reflexes. It had to be a part of their condition—but why?

Miryo didn't look like she believed the excuse, either. She chose not to comment, though. "So if life was so hard for her at Silverfire, why did she come? She had to have known it wouldn't be easy."

"Oh, she knew it, all right. I think she was just crazy." Eclipse shook his head in bemusement. "She says she'd always wanted to be a Hunter. Like that was what she was meant to do. She didn't mind being a Dancer, but it wasn't her choice. Then the woman who led her company called her in one day, completely out of the blue, and offered her a chance to be a Hunter." He shrugged. "She took it. And never looked back."

"Looking back feeds doubt," Miryo said softly, gazing off into the shadows. "And sometimes you can't afford that."

Her meaning was obvious. Eclipse watched her, and worried. They weren't going to give up. And he could only hope that one of them would be left standing when it was done.

CHAPTER EIGHTEEN

Silverfire

POWDER IN HER HAIR dulled its color to brown; makeup gave her cheekbones she'd never been born with, and at the same time downplayed her eyes. Despite it all, Miryo couldn't help but feel the innkeeper's eyes lingered on her a moment longer than they needed to.

Void it. My horse isn't even stabled, and already my disguise is cracking.

She couldn't figure out how. Granted, the pool she'd used for a mirror that morning had not been great, but she'd been impressed with Mirage's skill in changing her appearance. The powder couldn't take a lot of abuse before it would start to brush out, but it had the advantage of being temporary; she'd rebelled against truly dyeing it. It didn't have to last long. All she had to do was get a room at the inn and stay in it, and touch up the powder at need.

But the innkeeper was looking at her already.

Had sweat begun to streak the makeup? The day was still young, but already it was hot. She had split off from Mirage and Eclipse earlier that morning, riding to Elensk while the two Hunters visited Silverfire. She still wished she had gone with them; her doppelganger had spent many of her formative years there, and so Miryo was naturally curious to see the place. But Mirage's concerns were well-grounded, and so Miryo stayed away. She had wanted to just camp somewhere, but Eclipse had pointed out that it might cause trouble if a patrol of trainees from Silverfire came across her.

So here she was, in town and disguised. In theory. Perhaps not so well as she had thought, though.

The realization hit her like a falling tree branch. *It's not your appearance, idiot; it's your behavior. You've seen for yourself how many mannerisms you two share. How many times do you think he's seen Mirage, with Elensk this close to the school? That's why he's looking at you sideways.*

I knew *spending the day in a town full of Silverfire agents was a bad idea.*

Quickly Miryo recalculated. And so when the innkeeper quoted the room price to her, she put on the expression she could least imagine on her own face or her double's: petulance.

"Per *night*?" she said, deliberately imitating the accents she'd heard from the petty highborns in Haira. "Well, at least it covers the bathhouse as well, right?"

Irritation flickered in his eyes. "I'm afraid we have no bathhouse, goodwoman," he said. "I will have a maid bring up a tub and hot water, though."

Miryo was surprised to notice how much the lack of the honorific "Katsu" grated. It had been hardly any time since her testing, and yet already she took the term for granted. But no time to mull on that; she had an act to keep up. "No *bathhouse*? Sweet Maiden, what kind of backwater place is this? And I'm going to have to put up with another five days of this before I get to Dravya!"

"I apologize, goodwoman. I'm afraid this is a small town, and a small inn."

"I don't need *you* to tell me that." Miryo put as much aggravation in her sigh as she could. "Well, I don't suppose I'll find better in a pest hole like this town. And I'll be gone soon enough—thank the Bride. Now where's my room?"

She dropped the pose as soon as the door was shut behind her. Her jaw ached, and she rubbed it absently; maintaining that expression had been surprisingly hard. And what a silly way to behave! Blaming that poor man for not running a city-class inn, when he lived in a small town. She wished she could apologize.

It was barely noon. Mirage and Eclipse would not be back until tomorrow, which left her with the remainder of today and part of tomorrow to kill. Somehow.

She had lunch first, sequestered in her room; then she had the maid bring up the promised tub and water. Miryo dismissed the girl's offers of help, and as a precaution locked the door behind her. She didn't soak in the tub, lest the steam interfere with her disguise; she was capable of touching it up, but not redoing it from scratch should it become ruined. Instead she stripped down and took a thorough sponge bath, fiercely scrubbing away the layers of dust that had built up during the ride. Then she touched up her disguise, called for another bath, and used this one to clean some of her belongings, remembering too late that a true highborn would have had a servant do it. By the time she was done it was vaguely dinnertime, and she called for the maid to remove the tub and bring supper. She ate. The dishes were taken away.

And then Miryo was out of tasks to occupy herself, and the boredom set in.

IT HAD BEEN three years since Mirage visited Silverfire, and a full five since she had lived there, but she still remembered every tree and stone in the lands surrounding the compound.

I bloody well ought to. We spent enough time doing training exercises out here.

She and Eclipse hastened their pace along the road; now that they were so close to their goal, neither of them had the patience to wait. They flew along, kicking up clouds of dust as they went. Mirage resolved to make sure Mist and Sparker were treated well while they talked to Jaguar. The horses deserved some rest, and weren't likely to get it anytime soon.

The tower with the bells and the dovecote was the first thing to come into view, poking up from the horizon. Then there was a dark smear, slowly growing; that was the small wood along the back edge of the compound, where students learned how not to sound like crippled cows when sneaking around. Mirage even knew the exact moment she would see the small guard tower and wall that straddled the road. They had always struck her as an odd paradox; they didn't do much to guard entry to Silverfire, yet anyone who thought he could sneak in was sadly mistaken. The structures themselves were there mostly to give students practice sneaking in and out.

A whoop sounded from the tower as they approached. Mirage squinted and saw a limping figure emerge, waving energetically at them.

"Warrior's blade, Mirage, you cost me ten silver! I bet

you'd be here a month ago!" Viper hobbled forward another few steps and moderated his voice now that they were in range. "Both of you at once? Man, what a treat!"

Eclipse glanced at the leg Viper was favoring. "What's up with you?"

"Took a spear to the thigh." He put on a woebegone expression. "A witch healed it, believe it or not, but it still takes a while to get totally better. So here I am, serving guard duty on the infants." A sharp whistle sounded then, and his head whipped around. "Speaking of which. There's a class of fourteens coming through, and I've got to be 'on guard.' Come by after noon, though; it's been a dog's age since I talked to either of you." That said, he hobbled back to his tower.

Mirage nudged Mist forward and frowned to herself. *He expected me? Why? Does everyone know we're on this commission?*

The question would have to wait until after their meeting with Jaguar, so she put it from her mind and raised her head, taking in the view of Silverfire with warm appreciation.

She was an itinerant Hunter; she had no home. But if she had to name the place closest to her heart, it would be here. Up ahead were the shale walls of the barracks; Mirage could just see her old room, high up on one corner, and she smiled at it. Opposite was the small building where students had classes. Silverfire provided its trainees with a decent education, but since they rarely took jobs involving high-class society, book-learning was not of paramount importance. More of their lessons were conducted elsewhere in the compound.

Such as in the salle, just past the class building. Indoor

practice was held there, but in fine weather—or often in poor weather—the students trained outside, in the hard-packed dirt ring next to the salle. Behind that she could see the archery range, and the mounted combat arena, and then the wood.

They stopped first at the stables, just inside the yard. Farther back were the school stables; these up front were for visitors only. They were staffed by successive shifts of trainees and one old Hunter.

"Good to see you," Briar said laconically, taking the reins of their horses in his scarred, three-fingered hand. "Here for Jaguar, right? He's been waiting."

"Is he with anybody now?" Mirage asked.

Briar rolled his eyes around, considering it. "No. No outsider, at least, and he'll kick a student out for you."

Mirage grinned. "Thanks. Treat the horses to something nice; we've been hard on them lately."

That earned her a sharp look, and then a scrutiny of Mist that took in everything from her dusty forelock to the tiny scrape on one back hoof. "You better not be treating her badly."

"Treat Mist badly? I know better than that. You'd take a horsewhip to me if I lamed her."

"Damn straight." He tugged on the reins of the horses and vanished into the stables.

They continued onward, past the barracks and the infirmary. Mirage shielded her eyes with one hand as they approached the building at the tower's base and glanced upward. Sure enough, there was a young man up there, plastered to the side of the tower and looking petrified. *Must've lipped off to one of the masters. Poor sod. I won-*

*der how many trips he's made up there—and how many
he has left?*

Then they were inside the building, and blinking in the
dim light. She could just barely make out a thin shadow
behind the desk. "You took long enough getting here," he
said curtly. "We got your message days ago."

"Delays happen, Slip," Mirage said. Her vision was
clearing now, showing her a tiny, rail-thin man sitting
bolt upright behind a stack of papers. His knifelike face
marked him as the twin of Wisp, Silverfire's contact in
Angrim.

"You do this on purpose, don't you?" Eclipse
complained.

"Do what?" Slip said blandly.

"Make it dark in here. You like us being blind when
we walk in."

"You knew what it would be like. Haven't you learned
to close your eyes before you come in? Stupid boy."

Just as sweet as Wisp. Mirage grinned to herself. "Is
Jaguar free?"

By way of an answer, Slip cocked his head to one side.
A moment later, they heard a faint *bong* from overhead.
"Now he is. You saw the idiot outside?" He barely waited
for them to nod. "Five years here, and still an idiot. That's
his third session with the tower this month. Talon sent
him for ten climbs this time. Says he'll make it fifteen,
next time, and twenty after that. Warrior save us all. I keep
hoping the stupid git will fall off and make us all happy.
Why Jaguar hasn't thrown him out I don't know. But he's
done now—that was ten—so go on upstairs."

"Ouch," Eclipse murmured in her ear as they left Slip's
domain. "Ten trips—that *hurts.*"

"And fifteen in store," Mirage muttered back. She imagined she could hear the boy's feet against the shale of the walls, climbing down from the belfry. "For his sake, I hope he learns to keep his mouth shut."

And then they were at the top of the stairs. They both paused and straightened their dusty clothing. Then Mirage raised one hand and knocked.

"Come in," Jaguar called.

He didn't look surprised to see them. Of course not; knowing him, he'd known they were approaching before they even spoke to Viper. Silverfire's Grandmaster had not earned his position by being a stupid or inattentive man.

Mirage and Eclipse saluted him. He stood and returned it, master to student, then sat once more. "Stand free," he said.

They stationed their feet apart and clasped their hands behind their backs. No one really relaxed in Jaguar's presence, even with permission; it just wasn't possible.

Jaguar eyed them for a moment, then nodded. "Start talking."

MIRYO WISHED she could sleep. It would make the time pass more quickly. But despite being exhausted by the trip, she could not seem to fall asleep. It was too early, and she had too much on her mind.

She didn't dare go down and socialize in the common room. Aside from concerns about her disguise, it didn't remotely fit the persona she'd adopted, that of a young woman with pretensions to rank. Neither could she chat with the maid, even supposing she wanted to. She started to review spells in her head—a reflex left from the crush of the days before her test—but she immediately started to reach for power, and cut herself off, sweating.

Crone have mercy. It's getting harder to resist.

The brief taste from that night in the wood had only sharpened her longing for magic. Which she ought to have expected. It was logical, really.

But logic did nothing to soften the bite.

Miryo paced the room for some time before finally stopping, swearing, and kneeling to pray.

Goddess. Please, oh please, hear my prayers.

Help me hold on. I can't give in now, not when we maybe have a chance to make this better.

Or have I got it wrong? Maybe this really is *the way you intended things to be. I feel like there should be another answer, but every time I look, I feel like I'm slamming my head against a brick wall.*

Thinking about that put an uneasy feeling in Miryo's stomach. What if she and Mirage failed? What would it mean? None of the options were reassuring. It might mean that the answer had been there, and they had simply been too stupid to see it in time. Or perhaps the Goddess intended for things to change, but not at their hands. Or the Goddess liked things the way they were.

Separation and death, a denial of the self—I can't *believe that.*

Miryo firmed her jaw. *I've committed myself to this path, Goddess. So either give me the strength to see it through, or convince me that I'm wrong.*

It was more a demand than a prayer, but it hardened her resolve, and maybe that was enough.

*   *   *

"WE THINK WE KNOW who the Wolfstar is," Jaguar began when they were done with their report. "They have one, twenty-nine years old, named Wraith. He hadn't done much to earn his name, or so we thought until recently. It seems he inherited in full measure the Wolfstar tendency to hide his tracks. But only for a while. After enough time has passed, he feels free to boast."

"Boast?" Mirage said, not bothering to hide her contempt. "When you're an *assassin*? That's stupid. It's not as if there's a limited term on revenge."

"He's aware of that," Jaguar said dryly. "It came out in this last year that he was behind the death of Lady Anade of Razi. Tangle, Cano's Cloudhawk, went after him; he had a personal attachment to the late Lady. Wraith killed him a few months ago."

Mirage whistled soundlessly. She knew of Tangle; he was one of Cloudhawk's gems. And if Wraith was twenty-nine, he had to have killed Anade when he was just twenty-one. Her fight with him took on a whole new light—not that it excused her losing him in Vilardi.

"He'll come after you," Jaguar said. "You, Mirage, are far too distinctive to fight unmasked and not be recognized. Now that he knows you're on his trail, he *will* be coming for you." The Grandmaster's eyes were unforgiving as he looked at her. "He's your concern. We'll do nothing to help you against him. You knew when you took the commission that it entailed Hunting the Hunter responsible."

"I understand," Mirage said calmly. *He may be good, but I nearly had him in Vilardi. He'll not escape again.* "We weren't looking for aid there."

Jaguar nodded; he would never have expected another

answer. Silverfire Hunters were taught to handle their own problems whenever humanly possible. "To the remainder of the commission, then. What do you plan to do?"

"We'll tell our employer about our suspicions," Eclipse said. "In person, if we can arrange it; I don't like this communication at a distance. I want to see her face—whichever one of them it is—when we tell her."

"And then what do you expect?"

"Not sure," Mirage replied. "I get the impression that our employers are few; I don't think they'd look so hunted if they had numbers on their side. Who their opponents are, and how many, and how powerful, we don't know. That'll affect how much trouble *we* face."

"We're Silverfires, though, and that should count for something," Eclipse added. "Even if there's trouble between our employers and the Wolfstar's, they may acknowledge Hunter neutrality and leave us out of it. We aren't bonded to anyone; we do the job we were hired for, impartially."

Mirage could not have said what it was that raised the hairs on the back of her neck. Jaguar's expression gave nothing away. If he reacted, it was with no motion larger than an infinitesimal flicker of an eyelid. But something got her hackles up, and she gave the Grandmaster a hard look.

"We *are* impartial, aren't we?" she asked him. "Unless there's a reason you picked us."

Jaguar dropped his eyes to his desk. It was as close to looking guilty as she'd ever seen him. After an excruciating pause, he said, "It was Tari-nakana that brought you here."

Mirage carefully unclenched her hands and flexed the

tension out of her fingers before replying. "I thought that was arranged by my company leader."

"It was arranged *with* her. Tari-nakana—Tari-nai at the time—proposed it in the first place, and negotiated with me to accept you here."

Her first thought, irrationally enough, was that it was good no one else at Silverfire had known of that. *Red hair alone had people whispering about me. If they'd known that, whispers would have been shouts.* Everyone *would have wanted me thrown out. Or dead.*

"I believed when I chose you—and still believe now—that your impartiality isn't endangered," Jaguar continued. "You knew nothing of Tari-nakana's involvement. Her tracking of your movements was almost certainly just a continuing interest in your career, and without further evidence, there's no reason to believe it relates to her assassination."

In a moment of spontaneous, unspoken accord, neither Mirage nor Eclipse said anything. They had further evidence, sitting just a short ride away in Elensk. But despite the loyalty Mirage owed to Jaguar, and despite the trust she had in him, she was not ready—not yet—to tell him about Miryo.

"Do you know why Tari-nakana wanted me here?" she asked.

Jaguar looked her in the eye and shrugged. "For the obvious reasons. You were—and are—ideally suited to being a Hunter. You were a good Dancer, but your talents wouldn't have been fully used there. She saw that, and for whatever reason took a personal interest in seeing you where you belonged."

And if that's the whole story, I'm a Thornblood.

"One other thing," Mirage said, and again she was not sure why she spoke. "We met Viper on the way in. He said he'd been expecting me. Why? Does he know about this commission?"

She didn't imagine it; Jaguar's eyes widened fractionally. "You *haven't* heard, then."

Mirage relaxed her hands again. "No." *What was I supposed to have heard?*

Jaguar didn't answer; he just stood and beckoned for the two of them to follow him.

They left his office through another door, this one opening on a staircase leading upward. It took them to the dovecote, and the balcony around it, which overlooked the salle's outside yard, the archery range, and the mounted combat field.

The practice yard was crowded. At the far end a young man was going through a spear pattern with methodical slowness; the weapon's length had earned him breathing space, but the rest of the yard was packed. A small clump of students, marked as fifteen-year-olds by the stitching on the backs of their jackets, were reviewing knife patterns together. A solitary twelve-year-old was falling, over and over again, plainly trying to learn to do it right. And on the side closest to them, the newest crop of trainees were sparring.

Jaguar directed their attention to the pair on the left edge. "Tell me what you see."

Mirage looked down. The padding they wore masked them thoroughly. She thought they might be girls, but young as they were she couldn't be at all sure. They still moved with the hesitancy of trainees who had not adjusted to the fact that they were supposed to hit people, but she could see they were beginning to get over it.

"They're not half bad," she said after a moment. "Still a little reluctant to hit each other, but they've learned to keep their guard up, and I can see some of the others haven't. The taller one will be a good kick-fighter if she works at it."

Jaguar nodded, and glanced at Eclipse.

"They move like Mirage," Eclipse said.

Mirage stared at him.

"They've got her reflexes, her agility. They may not be used to hitting each other, but they already understand fighting in a way none of the others do. They're naturals. Like Mirage."

Mirage's eyes were pulled inexorably back to the padded, androgynous figures below. *Like me. Warrior's soul. Are they—*

"The shorter one has reddish-brown hair," Jaguar said. "The taller has brown hair, but only because she dyes it. There's another at Windblade, and one at Thornblood."

Doppelgangers. Goddess.

His eyes flicked to Mirage. "You know something about this."

It was a statement, not a question. And it put Mirage in a horrible position. It was one thing to not tell Jaguar about things he was unaware of; it was another thing entirely to lie directly to him. And yet she could not begin to fathom the trouble that could result if she told him what was going on.

Neither of them moved for a long moment. Then, at last, Mirage dragged her eyes away from the doppelgangers in the yard below and faced the Grandmaster squarely.

"I do," she admitted in a low voice. "But for the sake of . . . many things, I cannot tell you right now. Not until I clear up another matter."

"You owe me certain loyalties," Jaguar said. His voice was unexpressive; she could not tell if he was angry or merely reminding her.

"I know," Mirage said, and tried to put strength into her voice. "But this other matter takes precedence. I swear by the Warrior's soul, I owe you an explanation, and you'll have one. But not now."

"And what if you don't survive this commission?"

Mirage quirked an eyebrow at him sardonically. "Wraith isn't going to take me down. But just in case the witches do, I'll arrange for you to get an explanation anyway. Will that do?"

He searched her eyes for a moment, then nodded. "It will. For now."

CHAPTER NINETEEN

Doppelganger

Night was deepening, and Miryo was contemplating trying to sleep, when she heard a faint noise behind her.

She turned around just in time to see the window swing inward. Reflexively, not even thinking about it, something in her reached for an annihilating rush of power, to obliterate the intruder—

She choked it off, barely, as Mirage appeared in the window and climbed into the room. Miryo stood, trying to calm her breathing, wondering if Mirage noticed, as her doppelganger came forward. Eclipse followed her in, and shut the window behind himself.

One look at Mirage's face was enough to tell her that her attempts to calm herself might be wasted. *They weren't supposed to be back until tomorrow. What happened?*

"There are more of them," Mirage said curtly.

"More of them?" Miryo repeated, not catching on.

"Doppelgangers. At least four. Two at Silverfire, one at Windblade, one at Thornblood. Nobody's guessed what they are, at least not as far as I know, but Jaguar at least knows there's *something* strange about them. He asked me. I didn't tell him." Mirage's eyes held a cold stoniness

Miryo could sympathize with. Her own eyes would probably look the same, once she got over the shock.

"Crone's teeth—where did they come from? Tarinakana didn't have any children." Miryo's breath caught, probably because her throat had closed off. "But Ashin has a daughter."

Mirage's eyes flicked to meet hers. "Would you recognize the girl if you saw her?"

"I don't know. I've never seen her. But if she looks like Ashin, probably."

Her double turned to face Eclipse, who was still standing by the window. "What's the schedule like for first-years?"

"Forest riding, every morning. And it's not evaluation time."

"Perfect." Mirage turned back to Miryo. "Get your stuff and meet us on the west side of town. We'll ride to Silverfire tonight and check the two of them tomorrow."

The innkeeper would no doubt wonder why his spoiled, prissy guest was departing well after sunset, but that had suddenly been demoted in priority. Miryo nodded. "I'll be there in less than an hour."

THE RIDE WAS CRAZY. Miryo wondered whether being a Hunter was always like this—skulking about, climbing through windows, and leaving town in the dead of night. And whether being an Air witch was anything like it. If so, her life was going to be very hard on the nerves.

They circled around Silverfire, giving the compound a wide berth, and approached the wood from the back. When they neared it, they left Eclipse with the horses. Mirage led Miryo forward on foot, creeping through the black murk of the trees. Miryo stumbled along in her wake, trying not to make too much noise, but it was hard; the ground was tricky and uneven. She had wandered around at night before, but generally either in Starfall's well-kept grounds or on its roof. Here, in forest as near to trackless as made no difference, she had more trouble. She kept misjudging where exactly the ground was, and staggered as a result.

The twentieth or thirtieth time she did this, Mirage paused. Miryo cringed, imagining what her double must think of her. She hated being incompetent.

"Walk toe-heel," Mirage advised, and continued on.

Miryo tried this and found it peculiar but helpful. The motion tired her legs, as they were unused to it, but walking toe-heel allowed her to find the ground with her foot before committing her weight to it. She still cracked twigs and rustled in the leaf mold, but she didn't sound quite as much like a drunken donkey, which made her feel a good deal better. It gave her hope that she might, with practice, learn to do this well.

Sometime later Mirage paused again. "Wait here," she murmured, and then she was gone, swallowed up by the blackness. Miryo strained her ears, trying to track her by sound, but heard nothing more than the occasional rustle that might have been a squirrel.

Then Mirage was back. "Follow me."

They went on only another ten steps before stopping again. "Can you climb trees?" Mirage asked.

Well-kept garden trees in Starfall, yes. But it couldn't be harder than Starfall's roofs. "I'll manage."

They scrambled up into the branches. It wasn't as difficult as Miryo had feared. In fact, the tree seemed to have been discreetly pruned to make climbing easier. Her suspicion was confirmed when Mirage led her onto a small platform nestled among the branches.

"Observation post," her doppelganger explained. "The masters come up here to watch trainees, during evaluations."

Miryo wrapped her cloak more tightly around herself and squirmed around until she was comfortable. "What time will they be riding through?"

"They leave Silverfire at First. Depending on which route they go, they'll be here a half hour to an hour after that. They'll pass by here, though, no matter which path they're sent down."

By Miryo's reckoning, it was now somewhere between Low and Dark. They had at least four hours to kill, stuck in a damp, dark, cold tree. She sighed and squirmed a little bit more, then laid her head against a branch and tried to go to sleep.

She probably dozed, but it was hard to tell. Every time she opened her eyes, she saw Mirage, a motionless black shadow against the black of the tree. Miryo wondered if her double was sleeping at all.

"Is it always like this?" she asked at last, voicing her thought from before.

Mirage didn't answer immediately, and Miryo thought for a moment she'd nodded off, or hadn't understood the question. Then the shadow shrugged. "Depends on what you're doing. Some jobs are more . . . lively than others."

"Do you ever get a rest?"

A snort answered that. "I was supposed to, back before Midsummer. I'd ridden from one end of the land to the other, with three back-to-back jobs. Then Eclipse showed up with the commission."

"And you've been on the road since then?"

"Yeah."

Silence; even the wind had died down. "Do you enjoy it?"

Mirage laughed softly. Miryo couldn't quite guess the meaning of that; it didn't sound bitter, but neither was it particularly amused. "Yes. Probably more than is good for me. I'd like a rest, but I also feed on the challenge. I was bored stiff for a while, earlier this year. Getting the commission gave me more energy than a month of relaxation."

"I've wondered about it myself. I've got to choose a Ray, you know, and I'd been leaning toward Air. But I didn't know how I would take to being itinerant."

"Not everyone likes it. The masters at Silverfire try to make sure that students who don't, either take another profession or transfer to one of the schools we're friendly with." Mirage cocked her head to one side, and Miryo felt her double's eyes on her. "You might enjoy it. I do, after all. But I don't know if that's one of the traits we share."

"Well, I'm getting a sample of it, running around with you."

"And what do you think?"

Miryo grinned, even though Mirage couldn't see it. "I think I like it more than is good for me."

That was the last they said for a while. Dawn came an hour or so before First; just as Miryo was able to see Mirage clearly, her double said, "We need to stay quiet from here on out. If anyone comes through and suspects we're here, I'll go down and talk to them. You have to stay as still as possible."

Miryo nodded.

It was harder than she'd expected, though. Her legs became stiff, then threatened to cramp; she stretched them surreptitiously, but winced at every scrape of her boot against the platform. Mirage didn't look at her, or say anything; still, Miryo could imagine her thoughts. She finally started meditating, just to take her mind off her growing discomfort.

She was jolted from this exercise by Mirage's hand on her wrist. Miryo came alert, and eased forward on the platform, putting herself in a position to see the riders as they passed by.

They were strung out along the trail, each several minutes behind the last. Three went by before Miryo felt Mirage's touch again. The rider who appeared was a thin, wiry girl, with close-cut brown hair.

When the girl had passed, Miryo glanced over at Mirage and shook her head.

Two more riders passed. Then Mirage tapped her wrist again.

Miryo hardly needed the touch. The girl's cropped hair was a darker red than her mother's, but it did little to disguise her; she might as well have had Ashin's name symbol tattooed on her forehead, so striking was the resemblance.

They had to stay in the tree as the remainder of the class passed; then they climbed down and left as quickly as possible. No one crossed their path on the way out. Mirage nodded wordlessly to Eclipse as they took their horses' reins; then the three of them mounted and rode swiftly away from Silverfire.

AT FIRST THEY RODE with little or no sense of direction. It didn't last, though. Before long Miryo pulled herself straighter in her saddle and chose for them all.

"Aystad," she decided. "There's a Void Hand there who might be able to tell us where Ashin is."

"That was sudden," Eclipse remarked.

Miryo smiled thinly. "It's quite convenient, really. Back when I decided not to kill Mirage, I had no idea what I was going to do next. There was far too much we needed to do, and no way to sort through it. The problem's solving itself, though. Things keep falling out such that I don't really have much choice in what step I take next."

"And that doesn't bother you?"

"I can't do much about it, can I? So I might as well accept it."

Mirage tuned them out and rode in an unseeing haze. Her eyes were fixed on the road ahead, but in her mind all she could see were the two girls. The two doppelgangers. Fighting. Moving like her, Eclipse had said.

It irritated her, perversely enough. She'd grown up with the stigma of being red-haired and unusual, and although she had hated it, it had formed a very real part of her identity. She simply wasn't quite like the other Hunter trainees. She was fast and strong, and fighting just made sense to her. It was instinctive. And that was something that set her apart.

So now you're upset that you're not unique anymore. Get over yourself.

All kinds of new questions were cropping up now. Why

did doppelgangers have these qualities? Why were they fast, and strong, and natural fighters? Were those traits somehow anathema to magical ability?

Maybe when we find Ashin-kasora, we can convince her to bring us her daughter—both of them—whatever. It's possible that there is a solution, but it has to be done before that second ritual. If that were the case, it was too late for Miryo and Mirage, but at least they could do something to help those other girls.

And somehow, in the middle of all this, she would have to deal with Wraith.

Something slammed into her chest.

WHAT THE—

Miryo's horse reared, nearly throwing her. She hauled sideways on the reins as the gelding came down and just barely avoided trampling Mirage.

Mirage. On the ground. With—

With an arrow in her chest.

Another shaft streaked through the air and buried itself in a tree next to her horse's head. Miryo's gelding bolted.

The animal plunged off the road, leaping a rock and then narrowly avoiding a tree. Miryo hung on for dear life, hauling on the reins, staying low in the saddle lest a tree branch slap her down. She had to stop her horse. Mirage was somewhere behind her—

Dead.

She snarled. *Can't be sure of that. I've got to get back.*

Her gelding stumbled, and finally she was able to rein him in. He'd run quite a distance in his panic. Miryo twisted in her saddle, trying to spot the road through the patchy trees. The ground was too broken, though, and she couldn't be sure of her direction.

Steel crashing against steel was her guide. In the split second before her horse ran, Miryo had seen the uniformed and masked Hunter who had shot her double down. He and Eclipse must be fighting. So all she had to do was find them, and she'd find Mirage.

She kicked her horse into motion.

The rough terrain confused her, though; she kept being led astray. Under her breath, Miryo muttered a stream of increasingly vicious curses. *I don't have this kind of time to waste!*

Then she crested a small rise, and saw the fighters.

Eclipse had crowded his horse close in against the other Hunter's, trapping him against a sharp spur of stone, and the two of them were fighting furiously. But their struggle had carried them away from the road, and Mirage was nowhere in sight.

Miryo swallowed hard, forcing tears down. Then she took a deep breath and began to sing.

She meant to craft a holding spell, to stop the two combatants. Within three words, though, it was gone. Without even meaning to, Miryo reached up to the sun above her and the earth below her and the wind around her, and pulled them together into a spell of destructive force. Her control was poor, and the energy surged wildly, straining against her fragile hold.

Miryo was past caring.

Mirage had taken an arrow to the heart. If she was not dead, she was beyond Miryo's ability to heal. And so Miryo had nothing to fear; she drew the power in to crush the Hunter before her.

He drove Eclipse back with a furious attack. And in that moment, Miryo gathered the maelstrom of nearly uncontrollable energy; it was oscillating violently, slipping out of her grasp, but she focused every fiber of her being to unleash its fallout on him.

And then she twisted desperately, wrenching the power sideways into the ground with an effort that made her entire body scream. The earth exploded into fire and dust, but through it she could still see the figure that had leapt from the outcrop and slammed the Hunter off his horse.

I don't believe it.

Miryo stared, through the pounding of her sudden headache, as her doppelganger rolled to her feet and drew her sword in one swift motion. *I saw her go down. She can't be here—not fighting.*

But she could not deny the evidence of her eyes. Mirage had leapt off the spur of rock as the Hunter neared it again, and with her momentum had wrenched him to the ground. It was a miracle she hadn't landed on his drawn sword. Beyond them Miryo could see Eclipse, slack-jawed with startled disbelief, staring at the two of them.

And now they were fighting, and Miryo finally saw what Eclipse had meant when he said Mirage was good. Wound or no wound, she was fighting, and even Miryo could tell that she was brilliant. She flowed from one motion to the next like liquid lightning. The other Hunter looked clumsy by comparison, and slow with the shock of seeing her. He sliced at her side, but she was long gone; then she leapt forward in his cut's wake and nearly impaled him. Only a quick twist saved him. And now Mirage had him on the retreat, and she pressed her advantage.

She cut high, low, and then low again. Somehow he

had gotten a dagger out, and was using it to parry some of her blows, but Mirage's speed made her one blade seem like three. He took a nick to one hip, and then another on his shoulder. A thrust nearly caught him in the face, and he wasn't fast enough to avoid a slice along his cheek and ear. Part of his mask flapped free. Beneath the blood Miryo could see a grim, hard expression.

Mirage kicked dust into his eyes. He shut them and for a moment seemed to be fighting by hearing alone. But it wasn't enough; within a moment he'd lost his dagger, and a finger with it.

He howled and charged forward, opening his watering eyes. His momentum and greater bulk knocked Mirage off-balance, and the two of them went sprawling, blades flying across the ground. He should have kept his feet and his sword, though. Before he'd even finished rolling, Mirage was on her feet.

She waded in with a swift flurry of kicks. They caught him in the face, the chest, the groin; even where she was standing Miryo could hear bones breaking. The Hunter was barely putting up a token resistance now. And then Mirage slammed him onto his back, knelt on his chest, and drew her dagger. Miryo closed her eyes as she slashed it across his throat.

CHAPTER TWENTY

Misetsu

"THAT'S TWICE!"

"You're seeing things." Mirage refused to look at Eclipse as she retrieved her sword from the dust.

"*No.* The first time, *maybe,* that explanation would fly. But not now. He shot you down, Sen, and there's a hole in your jacket to prove it."

Now Miryo stepped forward, looking from one to the other of them. "What do you mean, 'the first time'?"

Mirage shot Eclipse a furious look, but it didn't silence him. And somehow hitting him didn't seem like a reasonable course of action. Since she couldn't think of anything else to do, she just stood, trying not to shake, as he answered Miryo's question.

"It was when we were students. She got into a fight with this other trainee. He hit her and killed her. I ran to get a master, but when we came back, Sen was on her feet again, and fighting him."

"He didn't kill me. I was just stunned."

"Not a *chance,* Sen. Even then I knew what a broken neck sounded like."

"And now it's happened again," Miryo said, her voice

faint. "I saw that Hunter shoot you. You were dead before you hit the ground."

"I *wasn't* dead."

Eclipse laughed wildly. "What are you going to say— the arrow bounced off you?"

Miryo held up her hands to silence both of them. "Please—just *think* about it. This would explain so much."

Mirage's eyebrows shot upward. "Like *what*?"

"Like how you didn't die twenty-five years ago. Maybe Kasane *did* kill you, and then you came back to life."

That produced a momentary silence. Then Mirage shook her head. "But how could I have ended up unkillable? Is there some spell that would do that? No, it doesn't make sense. Besides, if I'm invulnerable, why would the Primes send you to kill me?"

"Maybe they didn't know," Eclipse said.

But now Miryo was shaking her head, eyes wide with appalled understanding. "No, the Primes knew. But you're not completely invulnerable, either. When they sent me after you, the one thing they emphasized above every- thing else was, *I had to kill you myself.*"

More silence. Then Eclipse said, "So if I were to attack her—"

"You stay away from me," Mirage snapped. "I'm damned if I'm going to let you test this theory on me." The very thought made her gut clench. She could still remem- ber, though she had tried to forget, the sickening crunch in her neck as Leksen's foot collided with her jaw. That, and now the impact of the arrow, and the hot, spreading pain, and the blackness.

"It makes sense, though," Eclipse said.

"Except that neither of you has given me a good answer for how I ended up like this."

Miryo snorted. "We've already got ten thousand unanswered questions. What's one more or less?"

Mirage cleaned her sword of dust and her dagger of blood, then sheathed them both, the familiar tasks hiding the shaking of her hands. "Fine. So I'm hard to kill. What now?"

She succeeded in turning them from the subject, at least for the moment. The glance Miryo sent at the corpse on the ground looked involuntary, as though it drew her eyes against her will. "Is that the Wolfstar?"

"Wraith. Yeah. You can tell by his uniform."

"So your commission is finished."

"Only partly," Mirage said, grateful to be discussing something other than her deaths. "There's still the matter of who exactly hired him. Eclipse and I will write to our contact while you go see yours. Then we can decide whether to go after Ashin or our employers first." She snorted. "Assuming, of course, that *Ashin* isn't our employer."

Miryo gave her a startled look. "Do you think she is?"

"Not any of the ones we've met so far. From your description, she sounds too straightforward to be our first witch, and too confident to be our second. So there are at least four of them involved, counting Tari-nakana. But probably more than that, since there are four doppelgangers that we know of."

"Yeah. I'm trying to think of who else has a daughter the right age." Miryo pondered it, then gave it up with a shake of her head. "I'll have to think about it. What should we do with him, though?" Again that involuntary glance, her eyes sliding sideways.

"We strip him," Eclipse said. "The uniform marks him, and generally the only way to get a complete one is to kill its owner. So that'll be proof of his death. The body, we'll bury." He raised one eyebrow at Miryo's reaction. "You seem surprised."

"I guess I just didn't expect you to show him that kind of respect."

"He was doing his job. Just as we are. I personally wouldn't have accepted a commission to kill Tari-nakana, but that's not an issue worth defiling his corpse over."

Mirage watched Miryo's reaction with interest. *Did she think we'd leave him for the crows? I didn't much like him, but that's not a fate he deserved.* It seemed that her double had in fact expected something of the sort.

Miryo closed her eyes, swallowed once, and opened them again. This time she looked at the body quite deliberately. "All right, then. Let's get this done and move on."

SNATCHES OF CONVERSATION kept drifting to Eclipse's ears. He tried not to look as though he were eavesdropping, but it was hard; he wanted to hear what they were saying.

He could tell Miryo's voice from Mirage's. They were very similar, of course, being built of the same basic stock, but Miryo was a witch, and it showed. Mirage lacked the trained mellifluousness her double had. And there was a near-permanent edge to Mirage's voice that Miryo didn't have.

But the more they talked to each other, the more they

began to sound alike. Not entirely, of course, but their tones did shift together. Eclipse had heard it before; people often picked up intonations and speech patterns from those around them. But it was more disturbing, hearing it from two voices that were so similar at their core.

He wondered if it was possible Mirage could pick up all the qualities of Miryo's voice. She had a tin ear, probably caused by the same division that made Miryo's reflexes ordinary. But could either of them develop to match the other? Or was there a basic divide between them, caused by the ritual that had made them two?

That was, in part, the topic of their conversation tonight.

Earlier in the evening they had experimented once more with magic. Miryo had described what happened to the spell she had built during Eclipse's fight with Wraith; she hadn't really been in control, and had barely managed to divert the energy when Mirage reappeared. She had speculated, however, that had she completed the spell while Mirage was dead—or whatever—it might have worked. Mirage, of course, had flatly refused to test this theory. But they had compromised: Eclipse knocked her out, then moved back a safe distance while Miryo tried a spell.

It backfired. Miryo hadn't seemed surprised, but it was hard to tell; the fallout had all but completely paralyzed her, so her expression was a bit stiff. The spell's effects had only worn off a little while ago.

Eclipse snorted at the memory. The growing rapport between the two occasionally left him on the outside, but they needed him around; without him, they might start trying some of their more crack-brained ideas. Like getting Mirage drunk. Miryo thought the alcohol might interfere with the power sliding into her, but Eclipse had gotten her to postpone that particular test. Permanently, he hoped.

"I don't know how we'd do that, though."

He blinked and came back to himself. What had Mirage just suggested?

His year-mate shrugged. He pulled his eyes away and watched her out of his peripheral vision. "You're the witch," she said. "Can't you put something together?"

"It's not that easy," Miryo said, shaking her head. "You don't create a new spell by experimentation, you know."

"Oh, right, because I know *so* much about where spells come from. Does a little bird deliver them?"

There was real bite in Mirage's voice, but Miryo just rolled her eyes, unfazed. "No. They're created by intuition, mostly. Although that's not the way my teachers put it. I never quite understood how this works, but apparently, every so often, there's a witch who just finds herself following a pattern nobody's used before. And it works. They say it's a matter of closeness to the Goddess. That's the way Misetsu got started. Her faith was strong enough that she received the gift of magic, and the ability to pass it on to her daughters. We're all descended from her."

"So new spells aren't something you can create at will."

"I'm afraid not. Still, the idea's worth looking into. Maybe someone else can find a way to make it work. It runs counter to the way I've been thinking, but we haven't had any luck so far combining our efforts. So maybe separating us completely *is* the solution."

Separation? Eclipse tried not to show his interest.

After all, he wasn't even supposed to be listening. But as a potential answer to their problems, it had merit. As near as anyone could tell, the difficulties they were having were caused by the remaining connection between them. Severing it—if that was possible—might fix everything.

He wondered how *they* felt about that. What existed between them was not quite friendship, and not quite sisterhood; it was something different, and as far as he could tell neither of them ever thought about it. They had just accepted it as a matter of course, within a day of meeting. But how would this separation change that?

He couldn't guess. He knew, however, that if a permanent severing was the only answer to their problems, they would both accept it without question. It was a cost they'd be willing to pay.

ONCE MORE THEY split up. Miryo rode directly into Aystad, while Mirage and Eclipse circled around to a different gate. There was less need for it, since Aystad wasn't a Hunter town like Angrim and Elensk. But caution seemed to be ingrained in the Hunters' bones, and Miryo was beginning to behave that way, too.

She found the Twin Hearths, her designated inn, and took a moment to get her luggage into her room. She didn't bother to unpack it, though. That was another thing she was beginning to pick up. She'd skipped out of enough places in the middle of the night lately that she knew better than to get settled in.

Then it was time to find her contact, Yaryoki. The names and locations of all the Void Hands was one of the things she'd been drilled on and tested over, but just because she knew the streets' names didn't mean she could find them.

Aystad was a horribly tangled town. Miryo at least had the sense to ask her innkeeper, and he was very obliging, but following his directions turned out to be impossible. By the time Miryo found Yaryoki's house, nearly an hour later, her temper was frayed quite thin.

She took a moment outside the low garden wall to straighten her hair and calm herself. Then she walked in.

The perimeter spell tripped as she passed through the gate. Miryo kept her steps slow, to give the Cousin time to get to the door. It opened before she reached it, and the short, stocky woman inside bowed her in without a word.

Perhaps it was the way the Cousin seemed unaccountably tense. Perhaps it was the way she didn't ask Miryo's name, as if Yaryoki had been expecting her. Whatever it was, though, instinct prompted Miryo to draw herself suddenly erect as she was conducted into the sitting room.

Where she bowed to the Primes.

BEING AROUND MIRAGE had taught Miryo how to control her expression better. She was proud of herself as she straightened; that control, combined with her sudden suspicion before she walked in, allowed her to face the Primes without flinching, or showing any sign of surprise that they were here, in Aystad, in Yaryoki's house. Expecting her.

Satomi, of course, was in the center. They sat in an arc of high-backed chairs; the resemblance to their formal seats in the hall where they had sent her on her hunt was not accidental. Magical lights cast the room into stark relief. The effect left her feeling as though there was no place to hide.

"We are concerned," Satomi said.

Void it.

"The Cousins were sent with you for protection. We began to worry when they were seen by a Void Hand, and you were not in their company. We investigated."

So Kan and Sai had been found. Miryo wondered, rather belatedly, where they had gone after they left her.

Satomi's eyes were completely expressionless. "You have found your doppelganger."

"Yes." *No point in denying it.*

"And it is not dead."

Miryo found herself flinching at the pronoun. She had grown used to thinking of Mirage as a person; it was jarring to speak with someone who didn't. But Satomi was waiting for an answer. "No, Aken."

She expected the Void Prime to ask her why, and in fact was marshaling her arguments. Not that she thought they'd work, but it was worth a try. Satomi, however, surprised her by staying quiet. It was Rana who spoke next.

"We understand," the Water Prime said, and Miryo's jaw almost hit the floor. "It is difficult. To face one so like you in appearance, to strike that blow, is not an easy thing to ask."

"You must do it, though," Koika put in. "This task has been given to you. It is your responsibility to fulfill it."

Miryo could already see what they were doing. Next it would be Shimi. And, right on time, the Air Prime spoke up. "There are no other options. None. We have searched for them, through the centuries, and found none. Misetsu established the pattern for us, and we must continue to follow it if we wish to survive."

And then, of course, came Arinei, giving her the final

exhortation. "This is all that remains between you and the power that is your birthright. All you need do is reach forth and take it. Then you will be a witch—as you have strived to be, all these years! That dream will be yours!"

Empathy, resolution, reasoning, and a grand vision to round it off. All nicely matched to their Elemental roles. Miryo hoped the cynicism she felt didn't show in her eyes. It would make them very unhappy.

Of course, so would what she was about to say. "So you say. But I'd still like the chance to investigate it myself, before I go kill a part of me."

"Your doppelganger is no part of you. It was separated out in infancy for a reason."

"What reason, Shimi-kane? That's one of the things I wonder about. And I'm afraid I can't quite agree that she's no part of me." No visible reaction when she called Mirage "she," but Miryo knew they'd noticed. "You see, I've met her. I've looked her in the eye. And that's something none of you can understand. You've not been there, looking at your own reflection made flesh."

"Wrong," Satomi said.

The word brought Miryo's head snapping around to face the Void Prime. It broke the tenor of their little speeches so far. Satomi wasn't speaking from a script now; she was talking to Miryo directly.

"What?" Miryo said.

"I have been there. I looked my doppelganger in the eye. And I hesitated. For an entire day I talked to her, and I questioned everything exactly the way you have. But in the end, I chose to complete my task. Will you hear why?"

The floor had dropped out from under Miryo's feet. Satomi's doppelganger had survived? How? Presumably the way Mirage had, of course, but . . . Miryo tried to envision it—the Void Prime, twenty-five and idealistic, looking for a way out. And then accepting that there wasn't one, and killing her double.

"Yes," Miryo managed to get out. And then a belated, "Aken."

Satomi closed her eyes for a moment. When she opened them, they were as cold as ice.

"Centuries ago," she began, "in the days when the land was still joined into three great kingdoms, a woman dwelt in the southern mountains. She was a hermit, and a devotee of the Goddess in all her Aspects. Despite her young age, she was known for her faith, and her love of the Lady who watches over us all."

Misetsu, obviously. Miryo knew the story. But she kept her mouth shut; no sum of money would have persuaded her to interrupt Satomi right now.

"One evening, as the stars were beginning to emerge, this woman climbed to the top of a crag and stood there, singing praises to the Goddess. And such was the joy and devotion in her heart that her song changed, and became something more. And she saw that around her the starlight had begun to grow; it filled the air, and formed into threads, and began to dance around her.

"She stood there the whole night through, singing. When the dawn rose, she sang one final praise, and then fell asleep, there on the rock where she had stood. In the evening she awoke, and the gift of magic was strong inside her, and the Goddess had given her the name of Misetsu. In the weeks and months and years that followed she continued to hear the Goddess's voice in her heart, and thus created the first spells and enchantments."

Now Satomi's voice changed, and Miryo realized the story was diverging from the one she had always been told. "She had daughters, three of them. And the Goddess showed her how to pass her gift on. One by one, as her daughters were born, she sang the spells over them. And she found, to her surprise, that as she did so, each child became two. This puzzled her, but she chose to raise all of them as her own."

Goddess, I wish Mirage were here to hear this. Wait— no, I don't. I'm not sure what the Primes would do to her.

"Twenty-five years later," Satomi continued, "she began to discover her error. For the time had come for her eldest daughter, Monisuko, to wield her magic."

Monisuko? I thought her name was Menukyo.

"To Misetsu's horror, her daughter's magic raged out of control. And before long, it slew both her and her double. Misetsu grieved, but attributed the disaster to imperfect faith. Her next daughter, Machayu, would do better."

Machayu. Still no Menukyo. But I bet I'm going to hear how they ended up deciding to kill the doppelgangers.

"Machayu also died, and her double with her," Satomi said. Miryo wasn't surprised. "But Misetsu did not give up. She prayed tirelessly, and sought a way to make it possible for others to wield magic, so the gift would not end with her. It was after Maiyaki, her third daughter, died, along with her double, that she found the solution. With the death of the doppelgangers, magic became stable. Misetsu, now aged and weary, lived just long enough to see Monisuko's eldest daughter, Menukyo, become a full witch."

She paused to give Miryo a searching look. Miryo stood still and tried to show no expression. *And there's Menukyo. Not the eldest daughter. The eldest granddaughter.*

When Satomi did not speak again right away, Miryo risked a question. "But why must the doppelgangers be killed? What did Misetsu learn that made her think that was the only way?"

Satomi gave her a brief smile, but there was no humor in it. The Void Prime's eyes were hard and flat, as if holding emotion down by will alone. "When I was sent after my doppelganger, the answer to that question was given to me before I left. I felt, based on my own experience, that it would be better if those after me did not know. It seemed kinder. But I question my decision, now. It is my dearest hope that I will never again be required to send one of our own on this task, but I will advise those who come after me to tell those sent. It is imperative that our young witches understand why they must kill their doppelgangers."

Miryo stilled her hands and waited, motionless, for her answer.

"The answer we give comes to us from Misetsu, from her last writings before her death. 'The doppelganger is anathema to us. It is destruction and oblivion, the undoing of all magic. It is the ruin of our work, and the bane of our being. It and our magic will never coexist, and its presence threatens all that our powers can do.' So wrote Misetsu, five days before she died."

Silence. Tension. Miryo suddenly blinked, and forced air back into her lungs.

Merciful Mother. I thought—I mean, there was obviously trouble, but—

"The doppelgangers are a danger to us *all*," Satomi said. "That is why we must kill them. If we do not, all that we are will be destroyed." Her expression was grave, and only now did Miryo see something human in her eyes, too deep to be identified. "Do you understand?"

"I do," Miryo managed. Her voice was little more than a strangled whisper.

"We will give you another chance," the Void Prime said. "You see, now, why you must kill your doppelganger. For your sake, for the sake of us all, do it without delay, and return to us. If you do not, we will take steps, for our own protection."

In her mind's eye Miryo saw Mirage, but the image had subtly changed. Mirage. Not just a part of herself, but a danger. Carrying in herself the seeds of destruction for Starfall. It was a part of what she was. Could that ever be fixed?

Goddess. This choice—Mirage, or all that I've held dear—

"I understand, Aken," Miryo whispered. She felt dead inside. "May I be excused?"

Satomi nodded. "May the Goddess walk with you."

CHAPTER TWENTY-ONE

Faith

PERVERSELY, MIRYO FOUND her way back to her inn without difficulty. She paid no attention to where she was headed, but within a few minutes of leaving the Primes she looked up and found herself in front of the Twin Hearths.

Her feet felt like lead as she walked in. She had a private room on the third floor, with a sitting room and a bedroom; the sitting room had a fireplace. Miryo doubted any fire could melt the ice in her gut, but she craved the warmth. So she forced herself up the stairs, one step at a time, eyes on her feet, and focused only on that fire.

"Are you all right?"

Miryo looked up. She had just entered the sitting room. Mirage was on her feet by the fireplace, giving her a look of clear worry. Miryo shut the door with exaggerated care and said, "Yes. Mostly. The Primes were there."

"The *Primes*?" Mirage led her to one of the chairs and got her to sit down. "Here?"

"Yes. Or I thought so; they were probably just projections." She hadn't even thought to check for spells. But would it have mattered? "Satomi—the Void Prime—she had to kill her doppelganger when she was my age. And Menukyo wasn't the eldest daughter; she was the eldest granddaughter. Misetsu watched all three of her daughters die, because of their doppelgangers, before she figured out what was wrong."

Miryo got to her feet, and was surprised to find she was steady on them. She walked a few steps away, into the middle of the room. She couldn't bring herself to turn and look at Mirage. "They've looked. Truly, they have. And they finally told me why. You—" She looked at the ceiling and swallowed painfully. "Doppelgangers are the antithesis of magic. Your very existence puts all magic in danger. That's why you have to be killed."

She never even heard Mirage move. But one minute she was standing, looking at the ceiling; the next, hands slammed her into the floor, grinding her face against the carpet, and twisted her arms painfully behind her back. Miryo's mind snapped out of its fugue and straight into fear.

"I have a theory," Mirage breathed into her ear, voice low and hard. "I think that just as you can kill me, I can kill you. And I'm the only one who can do it. And, you know, maybe I should. All my Hunter training tells me to do it. You're a threat to me.

"It wouldn't even be very hard," she continued, and her words had an edge to them that made Miryo's blood turn to ice in her veins. "Your Cousins aren't here—and they couldn't stop me anyway. You have no magic you can depend on; you're practically defenseless. Killing you would be *easy*. And it would solve so many problems."

She paused. Miryo tried desperately to breathe, but all she could manage were shallow, panicked gasps. *Oh, Goddess, she's going to do it—*

Then the pressure on her arms eased slightly. "But

before I was a Hunter, I was a Temple Dancer," Mirage said. "And that means I have faith. Faith that the Goddess didn't mean for things to be this way. Faith that she wouldn't give her children a 'gift' that requires them to kill. Faith that, if we search, we *will* find another answer. And that even if we don't succeed, it's still a cause worth dying for."

Another pause. Miryo expected Mirage to let go now, and when she didn't, her fear grew stronger. Never in her life had she been so terrifyingly aware of the fragility of her body.

"So I have faith in the Goddess," Mirage went on. "But that's not really enough, is it? Because this is in the hands of three people: the Goddess, myself, and you. I trust the first two. Can I trust you, though? Can I rely on you to listen past the persuasive words, the simple way out? They sound so plausible, so convinced of their own truth. Thinking past their boundaries won't be easy. And I don't know that you can do it."

Miryo licked her dry lips and tried to speak. It took several attempts before her voice would work. "I can. I will."

The pressure increased sharply, making her hiss with pain. "Why should I believe you?"

"I swear. On my soul. Satomi still regrets what she did—I saw it in her eyes, at the end. She's never come to terms with it. I don't want to live like that. I'd honestly rather die. It would be *better* to die, fighting for a better way, than live knowing I betrayed myself and the Goddess."

She waited, barely breathing. The words were unplanned, but true. Only now did she understand what she'd seen in Satomi, so deeply buried. And she didn't want to end up that way.

Then, slowly, Mirage released her arms, and knelt on the carpet beside her.

Miryo sat up, blinking sweat out of her eyes, and faced her doppelganger. Mirage looked drained, but she nodded. "Good. I knew you felt that way—well, I was pretty sure—but I had to make you say it."

Well, at least that wasn't an afternoon stroll for her, either. Miryo brushed her damp hair back and managed a wan grin. "If nothing else," she said, listening with some detachment to the rasp in her own voice, "we'll live on in infamy."

Mirage gave a short, harsh bark of laughter. "Well, that's better than nothing, I suppose."

Miryo tried to fight the pull of her own weariness, then gave up and rolled over to lie flat on her back. "Crone's teeth, all two of them. I didn't get to ask about Ashin." She laughed at herself, flatly. "You think they would've told me?"

"You're asking me? I've never met these women."

"Probably not. Void it. How are we going to find her now?"

"I don't know. Our contact offered to meet us in Talbech. We can try to make her tell us."

"If she knows."

"I think she probably does." Mirage leaned back against one of the chairs and wiped her own brow clear of sweat. "Mind if I think out loud?"

"Not at all," Miryo said. She considered sitting up, but the floor was far too comfortable.

"Good. My mind's too shot to work without help right

now." Mirage's laugh sounded more like a croak. "So. Kasane has a child. She does the ritual, kills me—we assume—and I somehow end up with my foster parents in Eriot. Good so far, except we don't know how I got there. I'm five; my parents send me off to be a Temple Dancer. I stay there until I'm thirteen. Tari-nakana sees me, recognizes what I am, and makes sure I become a Hunter. Why?"

"Because you're good at it."

"Right. Then, soon after that, several *other* doppel-gangers don't die."

"I can believe you were an accident, but it stretches credibility that all of *them* were, too."

"But we're dangerous to witches, or so the story goes. So letting us survive isn't a very good thing to do."

Miryo snorted. "That's an understatement. The Primes are not going to be happy with either of us. Letting you live is pretty much equivalent to an act of war."

Mirage held up one hand to silence her, and dropped her head, thinking. When she lifted it once more, there was a gleam in her eye Miryo didn't like. "An act of war."

"More or less."

"And they'll try to stop us."

"I wouldn't bet against it."

"So they're likely to try and kill us." She smiled without humor. "Like Tari-nakana."

It was so obvious Miryo should have thought of it sooner, but she could hardly wrap her mind around the idea of the Primes doing something like this. *"They hired Wraith?"*

"Of course. Tari-nakana knew about me and did noth-ing. And soon after she finds out about me, other doppelgangers start to survive. They must have found out *something* of what she was doing, and took steps to stop her."

"Which would be why Ashin has so conveniently vanished. If she was working with Tari-nakana, her life is in danger, too. Assuming the Primes know about her."

"The real question, then, is *why*. Do these people not know the risk involved?"

Miryo shook her head. "I can't quite believe that. But we know the risk, and that hasn't changed what we're doing."

"They don't have our incentive."

"You expect me to know Ashin's mind? Or Tari's? We're still going to have to talk with Ashin to figure this out completely. They must have some reason for what they're doing, or they wouldn't endanger the witches this way."

"So we'll go meet our employer and confront her. We need to talk to Ashin as soon as possible, and chances are these women know where she is." Mirage stood with a burst of energy Miryo envied. "Can the Primes track us?"

Miryo groaned involuntarily as she rolled over and rose to her knees. "No. Normally, yes, but not with us. If they try a searching spell, it'll get confused, because as far as it's concerned we're one target in two places at once. It can't cope with that."

"Even if we're together?"

"Doesn't matter. We're still the same thing in two places."

"So we're safe from that, at least. But we'll need to watch out for mundane spies." Mirage extended her hand to Miryo and helped her to her feet. "We need to get out of Aystad right away. Are you up to riding tonight?"

"Given what we're facing?"

Mirage smiled briefly. "Okay. We'll push our pace, then, and be in Talbech by late tomorrow."

"I'VE GOT a plan."

"Do you, now?" Miryo was flat on her back on her narrow bed, feet propped up on a saddlebag, and wanted nothing more than a nap. Mirage's energy never ceased to amaze her.

Energy, or that damnfool stubbornness Eclipse complained about? Maybe she just refuses to be tired.

"How do those alarm spells you people set up work? Where are they normally located, and are they set off when you cross a line, like a trip wire, or do they sense more generally than that? And do they just go off, or do they give information about who's there?"

The questions gave Miryo a mild headache—or maybe it was just the sudden flashback to being questioned by the Keys. "They're like a trip wire that resets itself. It goes off when you cross a border. I'd be able to tell you where it is; I can sense magic, even if I can't work it. And they usually just indicate how many people have crossed it. Anything more than that and the spell starts being really complicated. Most witches don't bother with anything more than the basics."

"But they *do* tell you how many people. Void it. I was hoping they wouldn't." Mirage bit one knuckle, then shook her head. "Eclipse will just have to stay home. She's expecting two people—it'll be you and me."

Miryo looked at her sharply. "What are you going to do, dress me in his uniform?"

"Not a chance. I'm through with beating around the bush. They know about us; I'm sure of it. Why bother pretending? We'll just go in there and confront her."

"She'll have magic, you know. You may not want to be *too* forceful."

"She'll have a hard time singing if I hit her in the throat."

Miryo flinched. *Goddess. I keep thinking I've gotten used to her, and then she says things like that.*

Mirage didn't seem to notice. She sat down and leaned her elbows on her knees. "So. The things we want to know are: Where Ashin is. Why they're doing this. If they have any ideas about how to fix us. Anything else you can think of?"

"If there are any other doppelgangers."

"Good one. I assume they put all of them into Hunter training, but that might not be the case."

"I somehow don't get the feeling they'll tell us who is involved with this."

"If they do, they're idiots. The Primes want to get their hands on us already; giving us names would make us an even bigger liability. I was trained to deal with torture, but you weren't, and even I'm not unbreakable anyway."

Trained to—Bride's tears. I'm glad I didn't have her childhood.

But I won't tell her that they have other ways of making us talk.

Mirage cracked her back, then stood up briskly. "Let's get ready. I'm sick of wasting time."

*   *   *

THE NIGHT HAD CLOUDED over and the streets were black as pitch. Mirage liked it that way. She was in full uniform, and it was better if people didn't see her. They started asking questions if they did.

Miryo had argued against the uniform. But Mirage had wanted to wear it, for a variety of reasons. It made her look more intimidating, for one thing; people had trouble dealing with a faceless woman. And given what they were planning, a little intimidation couldn't hurt. Besides, she preferred to be in uniform for situations like this. It put her in the right mind-set, and gave her confidence. Which also couldn't hurt.

"Where are you?" Miryo whispered, glancing around.

Mirage slid right up behind her. "Here."

Miryo jumped. "Goddess. I can't see you in this blackness. Were you there all along?"

"Yes," Mirage lied.

Miryo shook her head and walked on.

Behind her, Mirage grinned to herself. It wasn't very nice, playing with her double's mind like that, but she couldn't resist.

One last corner, and then they were there. Mirage waited as Miryo cocked her head to one side. The witch hummed softly, then nodded. "It's a simple ward," she whispered. "An alarm, nothing more. She won't know who we are."

Mirage nodded. "Let's go, then."

They crossed the boundary swiftly and sped to the door. Mirage waited, motionless, listening with all her skill for footsteps. They came, at last, and she tensed her muscles.

The Cousin who opened the door never stood a chance.

She wasn't fight-trained, like the ones Miryo had with her in Angrim; she was a simple maid. Mirage had a hand over her mouth before she even finished opening the door.

"Fetch your mistress," Mirage said in a low voice. Behind her, Miryo was keeping back, the hood of her cloak pulled low. "Tell her there are visitors. *Nothing* more than that. If you say anything else, it'll go badly for you. Do you understand?"

The Cousin nodded convulsively.

"We'll be in the sitting room. Now go," Mirage said, and released her.

The woman fled. Mirage led the way into the house, Miryo on her heels, and searched for the sitting room. It didn't take long to find; the house was not large. Glancing about, Mirage suspected that it, like the house in Ravelle, was the home of a witch. Whether or not it was the property of the woman they were meeting tonight remained to be seen.

Enough speculation. Mirage stepped back as Miryo seated herself in the most impressive chair in the room. By the way it was positioned, their contact had obviously meant it to be her own seat, when they came at the appointed time later tonight. Mirage stationed herself behind it, and then they waited.

Before long, she caught the sound of hurried footsteps on the stairs. Two sets, one of which—the Cousin's—scurried away down the hall. The other stopped for a moment, then continued on with a more measured, deliberate tread. And then the door swung open.

"What do—" she said, but she got no further.

Miryo stood up, and it was clear by the look on the other witch's face that she recognized her, but had *not* expected to see her here. She had taken the time to put on the illusion, Mirage saw, despite the fact that it had been compromised in Ravelle. She must not want her real appearance known. Mirage didn't blame her.

"What are *you* doing here?" the witch said. She had recovered her composition admirably.

"We have questions for you," Miryo said, and Mirage took a step forward.

The witch's eyes shot between the two of them. And then they widened hugely. "Dear Goddess. You—"

Then, to Mirage's surprise, she began to laugh. Wryly, not hysterically; she leaned back against the door frame and smacked one hand against the wall. "What beautiful luck. We hire Hunters, and don't even realize who one of them is. I wish you people wouldn't wear masks." Then she straightened and looked at Mirage. "What do you say we trade? You take off the mask, and I'll drop the illusion. Deal?"

Miryo glanced back to Mirage, who gave her an imperceptible shrug. She could see no harm in it.

"Excellent," the witch said, as Mirage reached up to remove her mask. And the illusion vanished from her face.

"Ashin!" Miryo blurted. And then a muttered "kasora," as if she couldn't decide whether to include it or not.

So this is Ashin. Mirage supposed the odds worked out; this wasn't either of the two previous witches, and she doubted there were many of them in this group. *One hurdle cleared, then.*

"So," Ashin said, brushing her hair back from her high-boned face, quite unlike the face of the illusion. "It looks like we both got a surprise." She looked at them and shook her head wonderingly. "It's amazing. You really do look the same. You *would,* of course, but it's one thing to know that, and another thing entirely to see you standing side-by-side." She gestured for them to sit. "Well, Miryo, I said I'd talk to you after your test. I guess now is the time."

"SO YOU DIDN'T KNOW who you'd hired?" Mirage asked the Air Hand Key.

Ashin shook her head. "No. It was stupid of us, but Tari was the only one who knew where you were. It seemed safer that way—we couldn't betray you—but then when she died, we lost you completely. We went ahead and hired Silverfires, but with you and your partner always wearing masks, we had no idea who we had. It was pure chance that we got you." She paused. "Or maybe not. You're good—or so I'm told—so it makes sense that your Grandmaster chose you."

Technically he'd chosen Eclipse, but that didn't mean Jaguar didn't have her in mind. "*Would* you have hired me, if you had the choice?"

"I haven't thought about it. Maybe, since you're involved anyway. It doesn't matter, though; it's not something I can go back and change."

Straightforward, just as Miryo said. I hope she isn't the brains of this operation; she seems to be a good person, but she's not nearly devious enough to run a subversive campaign. "Did you know the Primes were behind the assassination when you hired us?"

Ashin flinched visibly. "You're sure of it, then?" Mirage nodded. "We suspected, but we weren't sure. That's why we hired Hunters; we needed to *be* sure. Void." She sighed. "Well, I don't think anyone will be surprised to hear it's true."

"They killed Tari-nakana because of this, then," Miryo said.

"Of course. Well, sort of. They'd found out that Tari knew about a living doppelganger. It happens, sometimes, that a child somehow slips through, but a witch who finds out about one is supposed to report it. Tari didn't, which meant that she was entertaining heretical ideas. They had her killed to prevent her from causing further trouble."

Electric fire shot up Mirage's right arm, making her clench her hand.

What in the Void was that?

A tension she hadn't even realized existed melted out of her bones, and with the relaxation came understanding. The blood-oath, the spell that bound her and Eclipse to investigate the assassination, had been fulfilled at last.

What a shame that talking about her achievement would only bring the Primes down on her head all the faster.

Look on the bright side. That's one less sword hanging over my head.

She dragged her mind back to Ashin's last comment. "But she'd already caused trouble, hadn't she?"

"Yes. She was the one who began arranging for other doppelgangers to survive. We don't think they were aware of that at the time, though. Otherwise they would have tried to get her to talk first, to name her accomplices. But they know now. Otherwise they wouldn't have searched her home."

Looking for evidence. Mirage nodded. "So how many of you *are* there, in this little conspiracy?"

Ashin gave her a measuring look. "I don't think I'm going to tell you that."

Mirage grinned. It was good to know Ashin wasn't an idiot. "All right. How about a different question, then. Are the other doppelgangers out there children of your little conspirators, or did you find a way to make *all* doubles survive the ritual?"

"We know you let your daughter's doppelganger survive," Miryo said.

Ashin smiled faintly. There was a definite tinge of ruefulness to it. "Of course I did. If I believe in this, I should believe in it enough to commit my own child to it. But some of them, I'll admit, aren't ours."

"And how are you arranging that?"

"The same way you made it," Ashin said to Mirage. "As far as we know, anyway. When a doppelganger survives, it's because the child was touched by starlight before the ritual."

The implications hit home quickly. "So she has a soul when she's divided."

"Exactly. And this is important because it puts an interesting twist on the way your lives work. You two share one soul, you see. And so you're the only people who can kill each other. If anybody else tries, you just come back, because the other half is still around."

"We found *that* bit out the hard way," Miryo said dryly.

Ashin looked disappointed that her declaration hadn't been met with more shock and amazement, but she went on. "The immediate effect is that when the mother kills the doppelganger, it comes back to life a little while later."

"And then what?" Mirage asked. "How did I end up with foster parents? Why wasn't I just buried?"

"That's a very good question, and one we'll probably

never know the exact answer to. The doppelgangers are given to the Cousins to dispose of, you see. Unfortunately, we don't know which one tended Kasane. But you can bet the Cousins are in it up to their eyebrows, or at least some of them are. Every time a doppelganger survives to adulthood, it's because a Cousin took her elsewhere, and didn't report her to the Primes."

Mirage was amused by that. *So much for the Cousins as the mindless, eternally obedient servants. I wonder how many witches realize all the tricks their subordinates are up to?*

"I just wish that the Cousins would talk about it," Ashin said with a frustrated sigh. "We have a few on our side, but they claim to know nothing. The Cousins know more about what goes on at Starfall than anyone likes to think about, but they refuse to talk. Some of them help us, though."

"You've been arranging for this with other witches' children, then?" Miryo asked.

"Yes," Ashin admitted blandly.

"And this doesn't bother you at all."

"Are we supposed to let them continue on, just as we have for all these centuries? No. We're doing them a favor. Things will be better this way."

"Only if we find an answer," Mirage said, and put some bite in her voice. "I don't suppose you happen to have that up your sleeve?"

"I'm afraid not."

"But you think there is one."

"Of course. Why else would we be doing this?"

Miryo seemed to find Ashin's attitude as irritating as

Mirage did. "What if Mirage and I die, though? Then what?"

The Air Hand Key shrugged. "Then someone after you will find the answer. One of the pairs we've arranged for. The Goddess will not let things continue on this way forever; eventually she will show us how things were meant to be."

Warrior's teeth. She'd make a good siege general. Throw bodies at the problem, and one of these days some of them will break through. Just don't count the casualties.

And as if Miryo and I didn't have enough pressure on us before. Now it's not just "find an answer or die," it's "find an answer or children will die, too."

"What makes you think there's an answer?" Miryo said.

"Did the Primes feed you that quote from Misetsu?" Ashin asked. When Miryo nodded, she snorted. "Crone's stick. You should read the rest of what that woman wrote. She may have been devout once, but magic went to her head; all the later stuff reeks of pride. You can bet that by the time Monisuko's opening ritual came around, Misetsu wouldn't have heard the Goddess if she'd had all five Aspects shouting in her ear."

Mirage could believe it. She'd seen Temple Dancers, who devoted their lives to honoring the Goddess, lose their way to the seduction of praise. It happened to the clergy, too. There was no reason it couldn't happen to a witch.

"You think she was wrong about doppelgangers, then," Miryo said.

"Of course. She couldn't find an answer—because she

wasn't *listening*—and so she found an easy way out. Then she made up something suitably frightening to justify it."

Mirage doubted the story was that simple. But she didn't want to argue it too closely; she *hoped* Misetsu had been wrong.

"We've been trying to think of a solution," Miryo said. "Obviously. We had thought that what we maybe needed to do was divide ourselves completely. Find a way to cut the connection that remains between us."

Ashin looked dubious.

"You don't think it will work?"

"It *might* work," the Key said. "But so would killing Mirage—if your only goal is functional magic."

"It's one up on the old system; it leaves us both alive."

"But it doesn't really *gain* you anything."

Mirage raised one eyebrow at her. "And what do you think there is to gain?"

Ashin got up and began to pace, hands clasped neatly behind her back. "I don't know. Not specifically. But think about it—the priests and priestesses all turn their noses up at us and call us unbalanced. Why? What's lacking in us? I'd bet anything it has to do with the doppelgangers. We're losing whatever's in you. It might be the physical attributes. You have speed, and strength—you're born fighters."

"So I'm the brawn, and Miryo's the brain?"

"You're not stupid; don't act like you are. You know as well as I do that idiots don't make good Hunters. You're fighting, and she's magic, but you're both intelligent."

Mirage conceded that with a nod. She had made the comment deliberately, intending to provoke Ashin.

"What about putting us back together, like we used to be?" Miryo asked. "That doesn't lose anything."

"Been tried. It didn't work. The Path of the Head's of the opinion it *can't* work—the magic won't flow in that direction, if that makes any sense. It's like canceling a spell outright, instead of counteracting it. Just can't be done."

Mirage's spirits sank at the witch's words; for just an instant, she'd hoped that Miryo had hit on the solution. Her double seemed equally depressed. The room was momentarily silent. Then Miryo roused herself again. "Another question. Has anyone ever figured out why we only have daughters?"

Ashin nodded approvingly at her. "Not that I'm aware of, but it's a good question, and I wouldn't be surprised if it's a part of this same issue. Lack of sons would definitely qualify as an imbalance, at least in my book."

"How are we supposed to fix it, though? Are all you people crazy enough to risk your lives for a heresy you don't even fully understand?"

The Key shrugged. "We haven't thought of anything. But we've been trying. And we may not have an answer, but we *do* have faith in the Goddess."

Mirage smiled sourly. Her own arguments sounded flimsier, coming out of someone else's mouth. "You don't think separation is the answer, though."

"I don't see how it would right the balance. It seems that separation loses you just as death does."

Now it was Mirage's turn to stand and pace. "But it's the only answer we've *found*."

Ashin looked at her directly. In her eyes Mirage saw conviction, and determination, and a blindly trusting faith that frightened her with its unquestioning intensity. "But it's not the only answer out there. I'm sure it's not. You'll just have to find the right one."

Uh-huh. And it's going to be that easy, I'm sure.

"What do you have planned?" Mirage asked her bluntly.

"'You' meaning 'you and your friends,' I assume." She hardly waited for Mirage's nod. "We're not certain. We'd like to go on as we have, and save more doppelgangers, but it's much more dangerous than it used to be."

Not surprising. Mirage glanced over to Miryo and raised an eyebrow.

"Our best bet is to hole up, I think," her double said. "To get off the road and really work this through. We'd have to find a place we're not likely to be tracked down. Does Silverfire have anything like that we could use?"

"Yes, but I don't think that's a good idea." Mirage sat down and twiddled her mask between her fingers. "Hunter security is good, but it can be broken, especially by magic. And they'll be expecting something like that." She realized that she had wrapped her entire head covering around her left fist. She pulled it off and folded it neatly. "Our best bet would be somewhere else, somewhere remote."

"The mountains?"

"Maybe. I'd favor the ones here in Abern. I know a few folk who live there; they might be able to set us up." The itinerary from Tari's study was in her saddlebags, so hopefully no one would be able to make the connection to her earlier jobs. Mirage wondered briefly if she should demand protection from Ashin as one of the three boons she and Eclipse were now due. *No, no sense in it; they want us alive anyway. Save the boons for later. And hope there will be a later.*

"Hiding is a good idea," Ashin said, nodding. "We can get in touch with you through the paper you have."

"And if we think up anything that requires your help, we'll contact you."

The Hand Key nodded again. "May the Goddess be with you. I'm sure she'll give you an answer."

CHAPTER TWENTY-TWO

Flight

"DOES ASHIN FRIGHTEN YOU as much as she does me?"

Miryo had to laugh, despite the tension weighing on her. "Yes. She's so single-minded it's unbelievable. There's the problem, which she knows; there's the solution, which she's looking for; and there's the Goddess, who will make it all okay."

"When you put it that way, she doesn't sound all that different from us. But somehow . . . I don't know. I think it's the way she's willing to gamble so many lives, including her own daughter's, on this."

"Yes." Miryo fingered the tail of her braid, twisting it around her finger. "Maybe that's the only way to do it, though. There really *is* a problem. The clergy have been saying so forever, and we've been ignoring them. I think that 'unbalanced' thing *must* have something to do with this. Which is encouraging, in a way; it means that we *are* right, at least in thinking that the current situation is wrong."

"Whether any of our hypothetical solutions are right is another story."

"I guess we'll find out." She glanced up sharply as a rumble of thunder reached her ears.

Mirage also looked up and made a sour face. They were in a large, open field probably intended for grazing, though at the moment no livestock were in it. There was no shelter to be had, other than the low stone wall at their side. Miryo, considering the incoming weather, wished they had gone ahead and pushed to reach the next town, but Mirage had advised keeping as low a profile as possible.

Eclipse approached their campsite as a second roll of thunder began. He had been some distance away, bathing in the stream; he ran a hand through his wet hair and gave the sky an irritated look. "I might have saved myself the walk, and just waited for the rain to wash me off."

"Two baths won't kill you," Mirage said.

Ill weather might make them all sick, though. Miryo glanced at the wall. "Could we rig up cloaks over this? That might give us at least a little bit of shelter." If there was a more exposed place to camp within a hundred miles, she'd be surprised.

"We can try," Mirage said. And, as Miryo had hoped, the Hunters were able to set something up. They weighted one edge of their cloaks onto the wall with loose stones, and set their saddles on the inside of the other edge, forming a sloping roof. It would hold for at least a while, provided the winds didn't become too strong.

"I refuse to do this again," Miryo said when they were finished. "Dye my hair; Void it, cut off my nose and I won't complain. I just want to sleep in a building."

"It won't be bad after tonight," Mirage said. "Soon we'll be in trees again, and then we'll be able to set up something much better. Besides, the bad weather probably won't last long. Summers have been dry, lately."

"All the more reason we're due for a wet one." Hearing the whine in her own voice, Miryo grimaced. "Sorry."

"I can hardly throw stones at you for being in a bad mood. I feel the same way myself."

Eclipse glanced at them both, but said nothing. He had reacted little to their account of their meeting with Ashin. Lately he seemed to have assumed the responsibility of keeping them in one piece until they found their answer or killed themselves trying. Beyond that, he was keeping his mouth shut. Not long ago, such behavior would have intimidated Miryo, but she was becoming accustomed to him. He had begun treating her the way he did Mirage. This made things a little problematic for Miryo, who didn't understand him the way her doppelganger did, but she just followed Mirage's lead: If Eclipse's silence didn't bother her, Miryo wouldn't worry about it, either.

Mirage tapped her on the arm. Suppressing a sigh, Miryo got up and followed her out from under the shelter of the cloaks.

They had agreed to pray together every night, in hope of deriving some kind of inspiration from it. Miryo wasn't sure how productive it would be, but it couldn't hurt. If nothing else, it meant she'd at least go to the Goddess's arms with a good record of piety.

She banished such negative thoughts with a grimace. *Thinking like that won't get you anywhere.*

The first sporadic drops of rain began to fall. Miryo knelt on the ground at Mirage's side, looked at the sky, and began to pray.

I DON'T THINK this is doing much good.

Mirage suppressed a sigh. It wouldn't help to let Miryo

know her heart was not truly in their prayers. It wasn't that she didn't care; her life was on the line, after all. She just didn't get the feeling that kneeling out here in the mud was getting them anywhere.

Once again she turned her mind to the ins and outs of their problem, in hope of having some sudden revelation that would make everything clear. No such luck. Separation still struck her as their best option, but Ashin hadn't favored it, and Miryo seemed to agree with the Key. They'd spent the ride so far cooking up bizarre schemes for making Mirage a part of the casting process instead.

She still had to shudder at the proposition Eclipse had put forth. He hadn't meant it seriously, but the potential consequences didn't bear thinking about. He had suggested that they try to create the channel for power in Mirage.

I can just see me spawning another one of me—of us—whatever. Three people with one soul. As if two aren't enough. And we'd still have an antimagical doppelganger around, which wouldn't solve anything.

Miryo had tried teaching Mirage to sing a spell, but that had been a miserable failure. Not only could Mirage barely tell one note from another, she found it impossible to remember the proper order of the syllables. The language used for magic was not easy to learn, and small errors had meaning. She'd accidentally said "kosuda" instead of "koshuda," and Miryo had fallen about laughing. According to the witch, she would have been summoning fish instead of a wind.

What else was there? They had already tried being in physical contact, the same night she had Eclipse knock her out. None of it was working.

Mirage realized her breathing had quickened. She forced herself to slow down. *Even if I can't concentrate, I shouldn't distract Miryo.*

She knew that Eclipse thought she had become resigned to dying in the attempt. He was wrong, although Mirage could not have said exactly why. She had said at one point that it was because "die trying" wasn't even an option; she *would* succeed. That wasn't quite it, though. And it wasn't Ashin's blind belief that the Goddess would make it all right.

Maybe it's just that I can't believe I really might die.

Oh, and this *is a cheerful train of thought.*

She shook the gloomy feeling off with an effort. Even as she did so, the intermittent drops from the sky became a real rain. Mirage sighed inwardly, but said nothing; Miryo was deep in prayer, and she would stay out here as long as her double did.

But Miryo was in fact *not* deep in prayer. She was looking at Mirage.

When she realized this, Mirage blinked. Miryo's eyes slid quickly away, but Mirage had to grin. "Have you been praying?" she asked.

Miryo looked uncomfortable. "I . . . I just can't concentrate. I'm sorry if I distracted you."

At that, Mirage laughed outright. "And here I am, kneeling in the rain because *I* don't want to interrupt *you.* What a stupid pair we make."

"Do you want to go back in?"

"No, I'd rather sit out here in the mud." Mirage snorted and got to her feet. "Enough of this. Maybe some sects would tell us suffering is good for the soul, but I think the

Goddess will understand if we forgo this in favor of not catching cold."

THE RAIN, which had been showing every sign of blowing through quickly, changed its mind and camped out over the road they were taking. It did not improve Miryo's mood. She had hoped for a while that it would be possible to teach Mirage the words and pitches of a spell, and that this might be the answer to their problems—or at least the right idea—but she finally had to concede defeat. Her doppelganger was trying, but she didn't have the ear, or the voice.

Well, at least twenty-five years of study accomplished something. *Even if I can't use it.*

She found she was chewing on one thumbnail and made herself stop. *Fine, so that idea won't work. Think of another one. You haven't tried everything, and maybe something you think is completely outlandish will turn out to be the answer. You'll never know until you try.*

Of course, trying might well kill her.

But if I don't try, I'll still end up using my magic by accident. I know I will. I almost bit my tongue off last night, trying to keep myself from interfering with the rain. During the fight with Wraith, it felt so good *to pull power. Even though I didn't really have it under control.*

I'm going to get us killed.

For a while she rode with the fond fantasy that the Primes knew the key to solving it all, and were keeping it from her out of a spiteful desire to undermine the Goddess's gift. She particularly enjoyed the idea of hitting Shimi over the head with something large and heavy;

the Prime was one of the few reasons she still wasn't sure about joining the Air Ray.

Shimi wasn't a truly bad person, though, and there could definitely be worse Primes. Miryo still remembered Ikkena-chashi, the Earth Prime who had preceded Koika during the first two years Miryo had been at Starfall. That woman's heart had been carved out of stone—assuming she had one to begin with. And Ashin would make a *miserable* Prime. Her temper got the best of her much too often. Shimi would likely be succeeded by Naji, though, who was the current Heart Key, and who would make a very good Prime when the time came.

And thinking about that is getting you nowhere. *Stop wasting time.*

A fat splat of water hit Miryo in the face at that exact moment, and she bit back a swear word. Then, with a sigh, she bent her mind once more to the task of finding a way to stay alive.

AT LEAST we've got trees over our heads. That makes it better. Sort of.

Just keep telling yourself that.

Mirage stared fixedly at a spot between Mist's ears and did her best to ignore the rain. It was doing nothing to lighten her mood.

Travel conditions were becoming increasingly worse as they moved into the foothills of western Abern, where the road was, often as not, a thin sheen of slick mud over slate. Mirage cast a watchful eye to her right. The path dropped away into a short, crumbling slope, and then flattened out into a streambed. With the dry weather lately, flash flooding was a distinct possibility. And that was the last thing they needed today.

Then they rounded a bend in the road, and Mirage changed her mind. *No,* this *was the last thing we needed today.*

Three Cousins, mounted on horses, were in the road, blocking their path.

Lightning cracked overhead as the two groups stared at each other.

"We have a message," the center one said at last, pitching her voice to carry through the worsening rain. "Will you hear it?"

After a moment, Miryo nudged her horse forward, until she was just in front of Mirage and Eclipse. "I will."

"From the Primes: 'We gave you one final chance in hopes that you would understand and return to us. We grieve that you chose to ignore our words. Now we are forced to take steps on our own.'"

Mirage didn't wait to hear a single word more. She lunged forward, grabbing the bridle of Miryo's horse, and kneed Mist sideways off the trail.

She took the Cousins by surprise. Mirage risked a single glance behind her as she threw her weight backward in the saddle; they were still on the road, in disarray. Then Mist's footing slipped and Mirage had to concentrate on riding her horse down the soaking wet, disintegrating slope.

Somehow they made it to the bottom in one piece. Mist gave a convulsive leap as she hit the foot of the slope and cleared most of the stream; to her right Eclipse had ducked low over the neck of Sparker, who was doing the same. Miryo's horse floundered through the water behind them. And then Mirage heard shouting on the road above. She looked back and up in time to see a knot of Cousins appear on the path, behind their original position, and plunge down the slope after them.

Void it. They had reinforcements.

Eclipse swerved right, and Mirage followed him. Dead ahead the land climbed sharply up again, and even if the horses could manage it in this rain they would lose too much time.

Mirage was worried. All three of their horses had been on the road for a long stretch without real rest; how would they hold up in an extended chase? Already Miryo's gelding was falling behind.

Then a roar up ahead drew her attention forward.

The land in front of them dropped away again. The gully wasn't nearly as steep, but it was filled nearly to the top with rushing, churning water: flooding from the rain. Mirage gritted her teeth and cued Mist with her heels; the only way across was to jump.

Mist cleared it. An instant later, so did Sparker.

And then, behind them, a crack, a horse's scream, and a squelching, rolling thud.

Mirage reined Mist in so hard the mare stumbled. She looked back over her shoulder, and her worst fears were confirmed.

Miryo's gelding was flailing in the mud, screaming in agony; one foreleg was clearly broken. Next to him, facedown and unmoving, was Miryo.

And just past her, on the other side of the stream, ten or twelve Cousins.

Mirage knew what she had to do. But she sat there, motionless, staring at the form of her fallen double.

Miryo wasn't moving.

"Come *on*!" Eclipse roared.

The Cousins would be clearing the stream any second.

"Move your Void-damned ass!"

Mirage closed her eyes. *Warrior have mercy. I do what I must.*

She slammed her heels into Mist's sides, and the mare leapt forward, into the teeth of the wind, away from the stream. Away from Miryo.

Leaving her to the Cousins.

NOT ALL OF THEM stayed behind at the stream. Mirage heard splashing, and guessed that at least a couple had not made the jump; of those who did, some reined in around Miryo's fallen form, and the rest pursued the Hunters across the muddy ground.

Eclipse led the way, up a gentler slope and into the shadows of the trees beyond. Mirage was hard on his heels. They slowed as they passed between the first trunks; one misstep in here and their horses would go down. The only bright side was that it would slow the Cousins just as badly. And the two Hunters were more accustomed to riding under bad conditions than the witches' servants; in wooded terrain like this, they had the edge.

The chase stretched out, with pursuers dropping away one at a time, fanning out to cover the area more thoroughly in case the Hunters diverged from their course. Mirage was numb inside; she let Eclipse choose their way without even paying attention to what he was doing.

She'd left Miryo behind.

There had been a dozen Cousins there. Not odds Mirage favored. Had she ridden back to the stream, even with Eclipse at her side, she would have gone down.

But she had left Miryo behind.

The betrayal stabbed her, a razor-edged knife twisting in her gut. She could go back; she *would,* later, and try to rescue her double. But at that moment, when Miryo had gone down, Mirage had ridden on. Leaving her behind.

Light pierced her eyes. The clouds that had blanketed the sky all day were breaking up; rain still fell, but in the west the sky was clearing enough to let the sun through. It was later in the day than Mirage had thought. And they had just ridden out of the trees. Up ahead Eclipse twisted around in his saddle to look back at her.

"Have we lost them?" he asked.

They both reined in to listen and heard a crashing not too far behind. "No," Mirage said grimly. "Although most of them are gone."

The two Hunters urged their horses forward again, making for another small wood visible in the distance. They had not covered even half the ground to it, though, when behind them three Cousins broke free of the trees and sighted them with a triumphant cry.

The Cousins' horses were fresher than either Mist or Sparker. Mirage, looking ahead, realized that they would not make the next patch of trees in time.

An unpleasant grin crossed her face; she was barely aware of it.

She cued Mist to slow ever so slightly, so that the lead Cousin would catch up to her sooner. Up ahead, Eclipse did not notice. Mirage kicked her left foot clear of the stirrup for just a moment, and then hooked her toe back in from the other side, so that the stirrup was twisted around.

The first Cousin had almost drawn abreast.

Mirage suddenly pulled her horse up short. As she did so, she swung her right leg clear of the saddle; her left foot in the twisted stirrup and her hands planted on the saddle's cantle gave her a pivot point for a roundhouse kick that took the Cousin completely by surprise. Mirage's foot slammed into the woman's shoulder and threw her backward, clean out of her saddle and onto the ground. Her last sight, as she whipped her right leg around to drop herself back in the saddle, was of the woman rolling into the path of the second Cousin on their trail.

Eclipse had finally noticed what she was doing. He was pulling Sparker around in a circle, but Mirage kicked Mist forward and caught up to him. An unpleasant thud behind them told her the fallen Cousin had tripped up her compatriot's horse.

Which left just one.

They reached the wood. Mirage reached up for a low-hanging branch and pulled herself out of the saddle and into an elm. Eclipse had anticipated this one; he grabbed Mist's bridle and kept the mare moving forward, deeper into the wood.

The Cousin raced closer.

Stupid. One Cousin against two Hunters?

The woman didn't stand a chance. As she rode under the tree, Mirage dropped. The horse reared at the unexpected weight on its hindquarters. As she and the Cousin fell, she made sure the other woman ended up on the bottom. Her head slammed into a rock. Mirage didn't even have to knock her out.

She took a moment to scan the muddy field they'd just left. Some distance away, she could just see a Cousin rising unsteadily to her feet, cradling a broken arm.

There was no one else moving.

Mirage turned and jogged deeper into the trees to find Eclipse.

"I'M GOING with you."

"*Void* you are."

Eclipse grabbed Mirage's arm as she took hold of Mist's bridle. "You, alone, against how many Cousins? You're good, Sen, but not that good."

She gave him a quick grin, even though it was the last expression her face wanted to assume. "I'll be quiet."

"You'll be *dead*. And that's what they want."

Mirage shook her head. "Miryo's the only one who can kill me, remember? Ashin confirmed it. And according to Miryo, they can't magically force her to kill me if she doesn't want to. A spell like that has to have something to work with."

"So then they lock you in a cell until her magic kills you both. Great alternative."

Mirage wrenched her arm free of his grip with a violent twist. "What do you want me to do? Let her rot in their hands? Run away? Warrior damn my soul *black* if I do. I left her there on the field because I didn't have any other choice, but now I do. I can sneak up to them, and try to get her loose."

"Let me go with you, then."

"No." Mirage shook her head emphatically. "Two people are more noticeable than one."

"And two people can kill more other people than one can."

"I hope to kill as few people as possible. Besides, Kerestel," and she took care to soften her tone, "I need you to do something else."

"Ah. Here comes the thinly disguised excuse to keep me away."

"It's not an excuse. I *need* you to go back to Silverfire."

He stared at her. "What? Why?"

"The other doppelgangers. Jaguar needs to know about them, and about me. The Primes will learn they exist eventually—if they don't already know—and they will find them. That can't be allowed to happen. If Miryo and I go down in this, those girls have got to be around to keep trying for an answer."

She could tell by his face that he did *not* like hearing her talk about dying. "That can wait, can't it?"

"No. Please, Kerestel, do this for me. I've got to know that they'll be protected."

He dropped his head, then kicked a rock suddenly. "I don't like it. Letting you ride off alone is a *shitty* idea."

Mirage reached out and lifted his chin so she could look at him directly. In his eyes she saw worry, even fear. For a brief moment it warmed the cold place inside her, to remember that he was her friend, and would ride with her into the middle of a nest of Cousins and Primes if she would only let him.

"I've got to do this, Kerestel," she whispered. "I left Miryo there. I owe a debt to her. To her, and to the Goddess."

He hugged her suddenly, fingers digging into the muscles of her back. "Don't get yourself killed just because you expect to. You're better than them, Sen. Find a way through and come back alive."

Mirage blinked back unexpected tears and nodded. "I'll do what I can."

CHAPTER TWENTY-THREE

Power

SATOMI WAS MANY DAYS' ride away, but the image of her in the mirror was very nearly as intimidating as the Void Prime in person.

"We regret that you forced us to this," Satomi said.

Miryo shrugged, meeting the woman's pale green eyes without fear. She was done with playing the role of obedient underling. Satomi knew that she had pitched her lot in with Mirage and Ashin. It didn't much matter what she said now. "If you say so. I followed the only course I saw that did not dishonor my commitment to the Goddess."

Satomi's expression was hard and cold, unmoved by Miryo's words. "If you were truly devoted to her, you would heed the words of her chosen one, Misetsu. Instead, you took a different path, turning your back on us and placing everything the Goddess has given us in danger."

"The Goddess gives you doppelgangers, and you kill them."

"She separates them so that we may be refined for her gift. She divides that which might hinder us."

"So you think." Miryo shrugged again, carelessly. "I think you're wrong. But that's kind of obvious."

The Void Prime was less than pleased with her unruffled attitude. Miryo wondered if she could tell it was all a facade. In truth, her heart was beating triple time; her hands would be trembling if she didn't have them clasped in her lap. It was taking every ounce of control she had to keep her voice even, to meet the eyes of the projection without flinching or looking away.

"For the sake of what you once were," Satomi said, "and in remembrance of the promise you once showed, I tell you that I do not relish what we must do."

I just bet, Miryo thought cynically.

As if she had heard that thought, the Void Prime's eyes hardened. "You will tell us everything you know about the heretics Tari subverted before her death. It will go easier for you if you tell us willingly, but whether you do or not, we *will* get that information."

"And then what? You'll kill Mirage? You can't. I'm the only one who can do it, and I refuse."

Satomi shook her head. "No. We cannot permit you to live; you will spread the poison that Tari began. And so we will kill you both." She arched her thin eyebrows at Miryo. "Did the heretics not tell you that? You are the only one who can kill your doppelganger, and it is the only one who can kill you—but that assumes you wish to leave the other one alive. All we need do is kill you both at once, and our problem is eliminated."

What little self-assurance Miryo had vanished with a sickening lurch. For the thousandth time since she woke up, she remembered her fall from her horse: pitching forward, putting her arms out to catch herself, one hand skidding in the mud, and the ugly, hot crunch in her neck. Then blackness. And waking up to find herself surrounded by Cousins.

What had been abstract theory up until then had become very real. She could not die, save by Mirage's hand. Or so she had thought.

"Kill us both?" she repeated, her voice a strangled whisper.

Satomi nodded grimly. "You are an abomination: one soul in two bodies. If you will not cooperate with us, we will kill both bodies. I will regret losing a witch of your potential talent, but you have turned your face to the darkness."

The Void Prime had to be lying. Or did she? Miryo swallowed against the sick feeling in her gut and met Satomi's pale green eyes squarely. She was damned if she'd let the woman know how afraid she was. "What you see as darkness, I see as light. I would not trade that for your way; I would not 'return' to your side even if you let me."

"As you wish." Satomi's voice was as cold and sharp as a knife of ice. "You will be dealt with accordingly."

"WE CONTINUED TO SEARCH, but found no tracks beyond that second wood," the Cousin said. She stood at attention, arms stiff at her sides; her shame at her failure was written in the formality of her posture.

Satomi nodded. "And how many did you lose?"

"Two, Aken. One at the river, when her horse fell, and another when she was knocked off her horse and trampled."

Twelve against three, and two Cousins had died. And only one capture to show for it. Satomi could not bring herself to rebuke the woman, though; two of the three had been Hunters, and one of them had the advantages that came with being a doppelganger. That did not excuse the Cousins' failure, but it did much to explain it.

For the hundredth time, she wished she could be there to handle this in person. But she could not risk approaching the doppelganger so closely. None of them could.

"Keep Miryo drugged," she said at last. "Her magic isn't stable, but she may attempt to use it anyway. Bring her south to us as quickly as you can."

"And the other?"

"Shimi-kane is tracking it now. We will contact you again when we have its location confirmed."

The Cousin nodded. With a single note, Satomi ended the spell, and the woman's image vanished from the mirror in front of her.

She sat for a moment, staring at her own reflection in the glass. One hand came up to brush back a few strands of her pale, fiery hair. No white in it yet; after the last half year she felt as though there should be. The discovery of Tari's heresy had pained her deeply, bringing up long-buried memories of her own doppelganger. And that had been just the beginning of her problems.

Satomi truly wished that Miryo could be made to understand. She wished that for *all* the heretics, but Miryo above the others. The young woman showed so much promise; she was bright, and adaptable, and devoted. But she was also, in the end, flawed. She had come to believe wholeheartedly in the lies Tari had spawned, and she would not listen to reason. Satomi grieved that she must kill Miryo, but there was no choice. She could not place the survival of one talented young woman above the continuation of Starfall itself.

The alarm on her personal quarters tripped. Satomi composed her face, then rose and went to admit Shimi.

"It worked," the Air Prime said. "The man is heading north, quite rapidly."

Satomi studied her colleague closely. There was a glint in Shimi's pale, cold eyes she did not like. Arinei had been upset over Tari's betrayal, but that was nothing compared to Shimi's fury when she learned that Ashin was a part of it, too. The Air Prime was furiously bent on seeing all of the heretics destroyed. Her goal was not wrong, but Satomi would have to watch her and make certain the woman did not carry it too far. This needed to be a careful bloodletting, not a bloodbath.

"And have you succeeded in spying him out?"

The Air Prime dropped her eyes. "No. Not yet."

Of course not. None of them had seen him in person, and secondhand descriptions were nowhere near as helpful in directing spells. Again Satomi cursed the circumstances that kept them remote from the actual events.

Shimi didn't seem worried. "I'm certain it'll be with him. Our informant says they're close friends, and they've been traveling together for some time. I doubt the doppelganger will have abandoned his side now, when it needs an ally."

Satomi could only hope she was right. If the doppelganger had split off from the other Hunter, they would have a difficult time finding it. "Very well. Spell to Tsue and inform her. Have her send a detachment after him—no, more than a detachment. They'll need to gather more of the Cousins in the area, if they're going to take the doppelganger prisoner. The rest will bring Miryo south."

*   *   *

MIRAGE WATCHED from the shadows as several mounted figures rode out through the gates. She could not see them well, but they were almost certainly Cousins. It was dusk already; she wondered at their late departure. What moved them, that could not wait until morning?

When they were out of sight, she dismissed them from her mind. They might return, and she'd have to keep an eye out for that, but in the meantime, her concerns were with the ones still in the house.

The building in front of her was a large, dim bulk in the fading light. It belonged to Linea, the Lady of Abern; she retired there occasionally for foxhunting and parties. Now, however, it lay empty, and the Cousins had appropriated it for their own use.

A faint, almost imperceptible pull had drawn Mirage there, leading her on when the tracks she was following became too faint to trust. She suspected it was the same connection that had led Miryo to her. And it had brought her here, to the forested fringe around the house, but now it had failed her.

Not completely; she could tell that Miryo was in the house. But there was nothing beyond that. No sense of her double's specific location.

Mirage gritted her teeth. *Not good enough.*

She closed her eyes and focused on the sensation she had been following. It was weak, and hard to pay attention to; it faded whenever she directed her attention to it, like a light so dim it only shone in peripheral vision. But Mirage was determined not to accept that. She concentrated on thoughts of Miryo: her appearance, her voice, the way she behaved. The ways in which she was different from Mirage. The strange feeling Mirage got every time she went to do something and found Miryo had done it already.

Give over, Void it. Where is she?

There.

Mirage's eyes shot open. Western end of the house, top floor but below the attics. Not quite on the corner.

Now she just had to find a way in.

She hummed the way she had heard Miryo do, but felt nothing. Not surprising; it would have been too much to ask that she be able to sense any alarm spells. She'd have to walk in blind, and hope to outrun pursuit.

Wait. Think about that. There weren't any witches there when you were ambushed. You're lucky there weren't; one spell and you would have been out of your saddle, on the ground next to Miryo. So if there weren't any witches there, will there be any here?

That seemed downright stupid. Why not send a witch to help capture them? Miryo couldn't cast reliable spells, but she could still wreak havoc trying. Why wouldn't they send someone to deal with that?

"The doppelganger is anathema to us. It is destruction and oblivion, the undoing of all magic. It is the ruin of our work, and the bane of our being. It and our magic will never coexist, and its presence threatens all that our powers can do."

She heard Miryo's voice, recounting Misetsu's words, as if her double were standing next to her. Mirage actually jumped, then made herself be still.

Could that be it? If I'm a danger to them, and to their magic . . . they may be afraid to put a witch anywhere near me.

If that's the case, there may well not *be one in the house.*

She couldn't be certain her logic was correct.

But does it matter?

Not really.

Mirage would go in after her double whether there was an alarm spell or not. She considered that, and found it acceptable. Stupid, but acceptable.

She stood there in the shadows for a moment longer. Exhaustion permeated her body; she'd driven herself hard to get here. Mist was in poor shape. Mirage was in worse.

But she had been even more worn down before, and she knew how to deal with it.

Mirage closed her eyes and went inside.

There was a place within her, one she had found years ago, when she first made the commitment to be more than an ordinary Temple Dancer. It had served her well during the extra training she put herself through. When she went to Silverfire, it was all that had kept her going during the days when the students gave her the worst they had, when the masters demanded more and faster progress from her, to prove her right to stay. There was a place inside where she could go and not feel pain or weariness, where she could put them aside and focus on the task before her. It was an internal emptiness, a clean space where all of that melted away. Mirage closed her eyes and found that place. She took three slow, deep breaths, and felt her exhaustion drop from her. Her muscles were loose, relaxed, but ready to leap into motion. She could be tired later. Right now, she had something she had to do.

Mirage opened her eyes and looked at the house. Miryo was in there.

She began to run.

THE STABLE LAY at the house's southeastern corner, and the shadow of its wall made a good hiding place. Mirage cursed the weather for clearing; the moon was bright, and made sneaking in more difficult. But she had gotten this far without any sounds of alarm, and she thanked the Warrior for that.

Inside the stable, she made a quick count of horses. Five of them, all with Starfall's markings. Did that mean five Cousins? They might have lost some horses along the way, either at the stream or in tripping over fallen bodies. *Well, assume at least five. And hopefully not more than ten.*

She left the stable and ghosted around its side, into the shadow of a huge tree. There weren't many lights in the house, and most of them were clustered up near the top of the western end, where Miryo was being held. Unsurprising.

Still, there might be Cousins lurking elsewhere in the house; she couldn't see the windows of the northern side. And Mirage didn't relish the idea of wandering through the entire place, trying to find staircases to get her up to the top.

The answer was right in front of her—or rather, above her. The tree's branches overhung the southern wing; they would give her an easy path to that roof. Then she could find a way to climb the wall of the main body of the house, and thus gain the roof. If nothing else, she could break in a window there; she'd at least be closer to her destination.

Mirage grasped the branches and swung herself up into the tree.

She landed, cat-soft, on the roof, and ran along it to the shadow of the higher section. Still no alarm. And there was a drainpipe, right in front of her, which led straight up, and looked sturdy enough to climb.

Lucky for me Linea's not a fanatic about security.

The drainpipe took her up to the roof without trouble. She ran along its crest, staying as low as she could; all it would take was one Cousin outside and looking up to give her away. But she made it to the house's western end, and slid carefully down to the edge that overhung the top-floor windows.

She could hear Miryo's voice, muffled through the window. Mirage glanced down and scowled. Someone—probably one of the Cousins—had nailed the window shut. She couldn't care less about Linea's opinion of the modification, but it meant that getting into Miryo's room would not be quick. And she couldn't afford to be slow.

After a moment, she slid sideways, to the next window. It too had a light—both of the ones flanking Miryo's did—but she could hear no voices.

Mirage lowered her head until she could peer in.

A woman was in there, sitting on the floor. Her back was to the window, which was encouraging; she was sharpening a sword, which was not. But she had left the window open a crack, and Mirage, eyeing the gap, calculated that she could get in quickly enough to take down the Cousin without a prolonged fight. She hoped.

Through the window, take her down. Then next door, hope there's not more than one Cousin in there. If you're lucky, it'll go quietly enough that the others won't know what's happened.

If you're not lucky—you'll deal with it.

Mirage took a deep breath, held it, then expelled it slowly. She grasped the gutter, tested to be sure it would hold her weight, and then swung her legs down, placing her toes silently on the windowsill. The Cousin had not turned around. Mirage lowered one hand and grasped the window's edge.

Then she yanked the window up and threw herself through.

The Cousin, to her credit, was on her feet almost instantly, but she was looking too high; Mirage rolled across the floor and surged upward, grabbing the woman's sword hand. She kicked the Cousin's feet out from under her and twisted the captive arm around as she did so. Her opponent fell to her knees without too much of a thump, and then Mirage cracked her over the head with the pommel of her own sword. The Cousin went limp.

One step down, lots to go.

Mirage lowered the body to the floor and tossed the sword under the bed, where it wouldn't be found immediately if someone wanted to use it.

Next door, someone began to sing.

AT LEAST they were feeding her. Miryo had wondered if they would, when night fell and no food came. But a Cousin had finally appeared, bearing a tray with bread and a bowl of soup. No fork, knife, or spoon.

As if I could threaten anyone with them.

The Cousin watched her as she ate. She had not drawn her short sword, but one hand rested on the pommel. Miryo did her best to ignore her guard, but it made eating difficult.

Finally she broke the silence. "What's your name?"

A suspicious look from her guard.

Miryo held up her hands. "I'm just wondering."

The Cousin considered that for far too long. Finally she opened her mouth to let out one word. "Tsue."

"Tsue. Thank you." Miryo sopped a piece of bread in her soup and ate it. "Tsue, how many Cousins died in the ambush?"

The woman's eyes hardened.

"I had hoped none," Miryo said quietly. "I don't have anything against you. You're just doing your job, and I'm just doing what I think is right. But I take it that someone did die."

At last she got a grudging nod. "Two."

"Their names?"

"Yun and Gau." Tsue's jaw tensed. "One at the stream. The other in the chase."

Meaning that Mirage had killed her. "I'm sorry. I can promise you that Mirage—my doppelganger—didn't deliberately target her. She doesn't kill unless she has to."

No response to that. Miryo finished her meal in silence and waited for Tsue to remove the bowl and tray.

The Cousin, however, stayed motionless. Finally, after an excruciating pause, she reached into her belt pouch and removed a small flask. "You must drink this. By the order of the Primes. I almost put it in your food, but . . ."

She didn't finish the sentence, but Miryo could guess, and she was grateful for Tsue's honor. "What is it?"

"A sleeping drug."

Not a poison, then, although Miryo hadn't thought it would be. "It's not necessary."

"The Primes have ordered it."

"Tsue, what am I going to do? Overpower you all single-handedly? As if I could. You could take me down in your sleep. And as for my magic . . ." She snorted. "I might as well kill myself on the spot and save the trouble."

Tsue didn't look forgiving.

"All right. What if I gave you my sworn word I will not attempt to cast any spells?"

The Cousin shook her head. "The Primes have ordered it."

What a good little drone you are. Miryo sighed and closed her eyes. She could see the path all too well: she would be drugged and taken to Starfall, tied to her saddle. They'd revive her enough to eat, but she'd be dosed again before she could get too lucid. Once they got that potion inside her, her odds of escape went to nil.

Unless, of course, Mirage came after her. Ever since the confrontation with Satomi, Miryo had half hoped her doppelganger would stay away. It wasn't likely, though. Which meant that Mirage would probably be captured as well.

Fine. Then you do something about it. Now.

She had offered to give her sworn word, but she hadn't actually done it.

Miryo opened her eyes and gave Tsue the most sincere look she could manage. "May I have just a moment, before I drink it? I'd like to pray."

The Cousin gave her a long, searching look, and finally nodded. She took a step back—just one—and waited.

Void it. I was hoping she'd leave the room.

Miryo, robbed of the privacy she'd hoped for, turned and went to the window. Outside she could see the moonlit ground, but not the moon itself; that was on the other side of the house. She looked through the panes of the glass at the sky, envisioned the stars there, and closed her eyes.

Here goes nothing.

Miryo began to sing.

She kept it as quiet as she could; her hands, clasped near her mouth, helped muffle the sound. She got a good distance into the spell before Tsue realized something was happening.

"What are you doing?" the Cousin snapped, stepping forward.

The game was up. Miryo spun to face Tsue, singing full-voice now; as the Cousin lunged at her she dodged. It was a ridiculous chase, trying to keep out of Tsue's hands while fighting to control the power. No, not to control it; that was beyond her. She just had to direct it, to make certain that someone else—Tsue—took the brunt of its force.

The power built to a crescendo, and Miryo realized she had no idea what it was going to do.

Through the roaring in her head, she saw the door fly inward hard enough to rebound off the wall. And there, so suddenly and unexpectedly Miryo almost didn't believe her eyes, was Mirage.

One instant her doppelganger was in the doorway; the next, she twisted and threw herself violently to the floor. And even as she did so, the energy of Miryo's spell broke its bounds and shot outward in an expanding ring of razor-edged fire.

Tsue had only begun to scream when it hit her.

The world swam around Miryo. Blackness threatened at the edges of her vision. She took deep gulps of air, reaching out for something to steady herself; there was nothing nearby, and then suddenly Mirage had an arm around her, holding her up.

"Warrior's teeth," her doppelganger swore, looking around the room.

Miryo's vision was clearing. All around, at chest-height, there was a band of destruction. Her spell had ripped into the walls, and through them; the ragged edges were dancing with rapidly spreading fire.

She forced herself to look to her left.

Tsue's body had suffered the same fate as the walls. The spell had caught her squarely, and had ripped her upper body apart.

"This place is going to be covered in fire and Cousins in about half a second," Mirage said.

Miryo complied numbly as her doppelganger dragged her toward the door. They made it to the hallway, and stopped there.

Two Cousins in the room to one side had been coming to investigate the noise. They had gotten no farther than the doorway; the spell had caught them there. As far as Miryo could see in either direction, the energy had torn through the doors and walls. She wondered how far the destruction stretched.

"Not this way," Mirage muttered, eyeing the growing flames. She pivoted and dragged Miryo into the other neighboring room.

For a moment Miryo thought the body on the floor in there was also her doing. But this woman, she saw, was intact, and still alive.

"Can you climb?" Mirage asked.

Miryo swallowed the urge to laugh hysterically. "Yes."

"Out the window and onto the roof. If you go to the eastern end, there's a drainpipe that will take you down to the southern wing. From there you can climb the tree down to the ground."

"What about you?"

Mirage nodded at the unconscious Cousin. "I've got to take care of her."

As she went to the window, Miryo saw what her doppelganger meant; Mirage had pulled a thin rope out of somewhere in her clothing and was knotting a harness out of it. She glanced up and scowled at Miryo, standing there. Only then did Miryo realize Mirage was wearing her uniform, but without the mask. Her pale skin looked even whiter against the black. Almost as pale as Miryo herself felt.

"Move!"

She moved. Miryo leaned out the open window and saw that it would be no trouble at all to get to the roof. At least, it wouldn't have been trouble under normal circumstances; now, however, her hands were shaking, and her vision was fogging, and she couldn't forget the sight of the fallen Cousins.

"Fallen?" Say it. They're dead.

Miryo took a deep breath and climbed out the window.

She made it to the roof without losing her grip. Below, she saw Mirage pushing the Cousin's limp body out the window; Miryo hoped the rope was long enough to reach the ground.

Then she turned her face away and climbed.

Linea's manor house was simple compared to Starfall. The roof was too steeply pitched for Miryo to stand on, so she pulled herself up to the ridge and began to walk along there, one slow, unsteady step at a time.

There are at least three Cousins still alive in that house. And they're probably looking for you.

Miryo ran.

She didn't allow herself to think about it; she just focused on the far end and started running. Later, the memory would terrify her, but now she simply did it and ignored the risk of falling. When her foot finally slipped, she was already above the southern wing. She turned the slip into a slide down onto one of the attic window gables, and from there went farther down to the edge of the roof itself.

The drainpipe was there, as Mirage had promised. Miryo glanced back and saw, to her relief, that her doppelganger was following. Then she swung her legs over the edge and began to climb down.

The house was well and truly on fire by the time they reached the ground. Mirage pointed, and Miryo saw several figures emerging from the house's main door.

"They'll find the other Cousin," Mirage said. "Let's get horses and go."

They went into the stable and stole two horses. Mist, Mirage said, was in the woods, but was worn out from a hard ride. They would pick the mare up and bring her along without a rider.

"What about the other horses?" Miryo asked.

"I cut their saddle girths. *Move,* Void it."

With the last of the momentum she'd gained on the roof, she pulled herself into the saddle and let Mirage lead her away from the blazing house.

CHAPTER TWENTY-FOUR

Void

"What do you need?"

Mirage swallowed before answering, in an attempt to keep the thickness out of her voice. She was exhausted from riding, but she didn't want Wisp to know that. Not that it was possible to hide much from the older Hunter.

"Refuge," she said, and was reasonably pleased with her crisp tone. "For at least a few days. Me, and one other person. And no questions asked."

Wisp raised one eyebrow. "No questions. I see. And I'm supposed to hide you. From whom?"

"That's a question."

"Damn straight it is, and I intend to get an answer to it. For one thing, I've got to know who I'm hiding you *from,* if I'm to do it right."

"Hiding us from everyone would be a good start."

That didn't amuse Wisp. "You answer my question, or there's no deal. You've barged in on me, ignoring the methods you're supposed to use, and now I get the feeling you're dumping a bucketful of trouble on me. This has to do with the commission, doesn't it?"

"Jaguar agreed Eclipse and I could claim refuge if necessary. Are you going to disobey him?"

"Your 'other person' isn't Eclipse. And yes, I damn
well *will* disobey him if I have to; there may be a better
way to handle this problem than straight refuge." Wisp
glared at Mirage. "This has to do with your commission.
Tell me."

Mirage thought about continuing to refuse, and gave
the idea up. On a good day, she might be willing to face
Wisp in a contest of wills, but not now. She had to save
her energy for her real enemies. "All right. The ones behind the assassination are after me."

"Why?"

"I killed their Hunter. Wraith."

A slight flicker of an eyebrow was the only sign of
surprise Wisp showed at the name. "And?"

"And about ten thousand other things I won't go into
now. I don't have the time, and frankly, it's personal
enough that it's none of your damn business." Mirage
summoned all her energy to glare back at Wisp. No way
in the Void was she going to explain the doppelganger
issue.

"Fair enough," the Hunter said after a pause. "Answer
me one thing, and then I'll give you your help. Who's
after you?"

Mirage considered it for a moment, and finally decided on honesty. Lying wasn't going to make her any
safer. "The Primes."

She'd never seen Wisp show visible shock before.
"*All* of them?"

"All five."

"Void." The old Hunter exhaled slowly. "You don't
do trouble by halves, do you?" Mirage didn't bother to
answer that, and Wisp didn't seem to expect her to. "All

right. You and one other person. Why in the Warrior's name did you pick Angrim for your hideout? Those damn bastards are all over the place, and if rumor's to be believed, one of them sold you out. Nobody knows to whom, but I'm guessing it's the Primes."

Sold me out? Ice. I will rip that bitch's guts out and hang her with them. Mirage gritted her teeth and tried to focus on the immediate issue. "Probably. They came after me awfully fast."

"So why are you sitting still? They've got spells they can use to find people. You're stupid to stay in one place. Only way you're going to stay safe from them is to keep moving, as fast as you can."

"They can't find me."

Wisp raised an eyebrow.

"It's part of the stuff I can't explain to you now. Just trust me on it. Eclipse is on his way to Silverfire, so ask Jaguar if you want the whole story; he'll have it soon enough."

"Don't think I won't do just that." Wisp tapped a finger against her jaw, then nodded. "How about you be a priestess for a while?"

Mirage blinked. "What?"

"I can hide you at the temple. They've got cells for the ones who've taken vows of silence, and I can get you a pair of those. You wear a hooded robe and don't talk to anyone, ever, or even leave your room if you don't want to. Is your friend male or female?"

"Female."

"Good. You can be neighbors. If it were a man he'd be stuck on the other side of the compound, and that would make things more difficult."

Given how Miryo was behaving right now, splitting up would be more than just difficult. Mirage did not want to leave her double alone for very long. "That'll work. Where should I meet you?"

"At the temple. Midnight. Bring your friend."

WHEN MIRAGE RETURNED with news of a plan, Miryo simply nodded. She trusted her doppelganger to arrange things; she herself didn't have the resources to hide them both. Or even just herself. She really didn't have any resources, period. And it was easier to just accept what Mirage had set up.

The irony of their hiding spot did not escape her. Miryo felt a nearly overwhelming urge to apologize to the silent, cloaked figures who lived along their corridor. They came here for a life of peace and meditation, living to honor the Goddess, and here she was, in their midst, her hands stained with the blood of women who had just been doing their jobs.

Goddess, I swear on my soul, I never meant to kill them.

But it felt so good, to finally do *something, and touch the power I can feel all around me. . . .*

Tsue's choked-off scream echoed in her memory, and she flinched.

The old Hunter with the hatchet face had given her an odd look before leaving. Miryo had been hidden beneath a hooded cloak, so she doubted the Hunter had seen her clearly. Still, she could not shake the suspicion that Wisp had somehow guessed what lay so heavily on her heart. Which was nonsense. But the idea would not leave her alone.

"Void it," Mirage cursed softly, and Miryo jumped. "I should be sent back to Silverfire to be retrained. I bloody forgot to keep the paper with me when I came after you."

Miryo felt dead. "So we don't have any way to contact Ashin." The desire to try the spell herself welled up inside her, and she gagged. Mirage didn't seem to notice.

"I'll go find Wisp this afternoon and get her to send a bird to Silverfire, for Eclipse when he gets there. That way he can tell Ashin, if he hasn't thought of it already. It's not perfect, but it's the best we can manage."

Miryo shrugged. If she had hoped to conceal her apathy from Mirage, though, she was disappointed. Her doppelganger gave her a sharp look. "What's bothering you?"

What do you think? Miryo couldn't bring herself to say it.

Mirage guessed anyway. "The Cousins."

Miryo stood and walked two steps to the wall of her cell. They were not supposed to be in here together, talking, but it was an hour for private meditation, when they were unlikely to be interrupted, and they were keeping their voices low. "I can't be as calm about it as you can."

She half expected her doppelganger to be unsympathetic; how many lives had Mirage taken? A few Cousins were nothing, especially in their situation. But Mirage nodded. "No, I understand. Believe it or not, I still dream about the first man I killed." Miryo looked at her in surprise, and Mirage shrugged. "The rest don't bother me as much—Wraith, for example—but the first one does.

I didn't even know his name." Her eyes dropped to her boots, and she sighed. "You can tell yourself that it was self-defense, and that will help. A little. If you hadn't cast that spell, getting you out of there would have been a lot more difficult. And odds are good I would have had to kill those Cousins anyway."

At least it would have been you, and not me.

She was well aware that she had once been at least superficially prepared to kill her doppelganger. Questions of self-defense and so on had bothered her, but she had thought she had come to terms with them. It had been easier then, though. She had seen Mirage not as a person, but as an obstacle to be eliminated.

That was the problem. Tsue had been a person. And so had the other Cousins, even though she hadn't known their names.

Mirage stood and laid one hand on her shoulder. "I know it's hard. And nothing I can say is going to make it any easier for you. But please, before you beat yourself up over it, remember that it *was* self-defense. And defense of the other doppelgangers and their witches, whose lives are also at stake."

Then she slipped out the door and left Miryo to her thoughts.

WISP WOULD EVISCERATE Mirage if she kept breaking contact protocol, so she had to jump through the usual series of hoops, though a different set from those she'd used the last time she was in Angrim.

At least it gave her something to do. Getting out of the temple and back into it without being identified or trailed by Thornblood people let her feel that she was accomplishing something useful, instead of sitting in her cell, waiting for—

For what? A miracle?

They were no closer to finding an answer than they had been when they faced off with knives in a hallway here in Angrim. With the Primes pressing them, they had no leisure to think, to experiment. They just kept on having to move, constantly running to stay alive.

Mirage kicked herself mentally. *You're not running now. You're sitting in a temple. Complain about having to sit still, or complain about not having time to sit and think, but for the Warrior's sake, don't do both at once. Idiot.*

And one task was even more important than figuring out the answer to the doppelganger problem. Not more important in the long term, but more important in the short term, because without it, they weren't going to accomplish a damn thing, whether they were hiding in a temple, racing along a road, or sitting in a library with all the collected knowledge of the world available for their use.

She had to get Miryo back on her feet.

MIRYO'S SLEEP THAT NIGHT could barely be called sleep. It was a shallow doze plagued by horrific memories: breaking her neck at the stream, hearing Satomi condemn her, killing Tsue and the other Cousins.

She lay in bed and stared at the ceiling, wishing she dared climb up on the temple roof. It had always been her instinct, when she wanted to think something through. Was it some spillover from Mirage's Hunter training?

No, because it went back further than that; she'd been climbing roofs since her double was a Temple Dancer.

She went up there because it brought her closer to the stars, the eyes of the Goddess.

And yet, was under the eyes of the Goddess where she really wanted to be right now, with the blood of the Cousins on her hands?

Miryo pressed the heels of her hands into her eyes and rolled over in her narrow, hard bed. No. Not the roof. Not with her memories of the last time she'd been on a roof.

Instead, she pulled on her robe and went into the hallway.

She was not the only person awake; the hermits under a vow of silence sometimes walked the corridors or the gardens as a form of moving meditation. She passed by two others, whether men or women she could not tell, making no acknowledgment of their presence, as they did not acknowledge her. They walked in their own minds with the Goddess.

Miryo envied them.

Low came and went, and still she walked. It had been at least an hour, as near as she could judge it, since any other priestesses had gone by. She was alone in the halls of the temple.

Then she turned a corner and found someone else there.

The hooded figure paced forward steadily, but, unlike the others, stopped instead of passing her. "I take it you can't sleep."

Miryo swallowed, trying to slow her pounding heart, and said, "Not really."

Mirage tipped her head up enough to peer out from under the hood. "I figured as much. Nightmares?"

Miryo glanced away, unable to meet her double's gaze.

"Of course nightmares." Mirage held out her hand. "Come with me."

Miryo looked at the hand for a long moment, pale and barely visible in the dim light of the hall. She wondered where her doppelganger wanted to lead her, and almost asked.

Instead she took Mirage's hand, and followed her silently through the corridors of the temple.

MIRAGE FELT MIRYO TENSE the minute they passed through the archway into the pentagonal sanctuary of the temple. Moonlight spilled through the opening in the center of the roof, creating a silver island in the center of the floor. Along the walls, the five figures of the Goddess stood in shadow.

"I know you don't want to be here," Mirage said quietly, before Miryo could speak. "You're not a devotee of the Warrior. You feel like having blood on your hands means you don't belong in a place like this. But that's exactly why you should come." She turned and faced her double, saw the stricken expression on Miryo's face. "We haven't prayed since the ambush. I won't say we *need* to; this isn't about obligation. But I want to, and I think you do, too. Even though you're telling yourself you don't."

Miryo stood motionless for several heartbeats, looking almost like a statue herself. Then she nodded, slowly, stiffly. "Yes." She hesitated. "Thank you."

They made a circuit of the sanctuary. Mirage bowed to each of the five Aspects, while Miryo touched her heart. The moonlight reflecting off the floor of the temple cast the faintest of glows onto each statue, so their faces were just discernible in the darkness.

Then Mirage spoke again. "Do you want to pray to any one of them, or all together?"

She could see Miryo thinking it over. "All five."

Including the Warrior. Mirage nodded, and the two of them together went into the center of the sanctuary, where they knelt, pulled their hoods forward, and began to pray in silence.

Some time passed—at least a quarter of an hour, by the movement of moonlight across the floor—before Mirage became aware of eyes on her. She glanced up and found Miryo looking in her direction.

"What is it?" she asked.

"When you were a Temple Dancer," Miryo said, "was this how you prayed?"

Her voice was hesitant, yet behind it lay a kind of unconscious conviction. As if she knew the answer before Mirage gave it.

"No," Mirage said. "Sometimes, yes, and sometimes we went to regular services. But other times—for me, most of the time—we prayed as Dancers."

"What does that mean?"

"We prayed with our bodies. Not with our voices or our minds. We Danced. Together, or alone, following the music in our hearts."

The words were a poor description for it; usually only Avannans or other Dancers understood. But Miryo was nodding, and the unconscious conviction had grown visibly stronger. "Witches do something like that. Usually alone. We just sing. No words, ordinary or magical; whatever notes and sounds seem right. It's not a spell. It's prayer."

Mirage cast a glance around the temple. The Aspects of the Goddess gazed back at her in the reflected moonlight. Even the breeze had died; there was no sound from the town outside.

She began to strip down to the Hunter uniform beneath her robe. "Do you want to take turns, or do this together?"

MIRYO STOOD in the center of the room, the moonlight casting her shadow onto the stone, and closed her eyes.

Mirage stood nearby, eyes also closed.

For several heartbeats, the two of them stood, silent and motionless, and composed themselves.

Then they began.

Miryo was tentative at first, her voice hardly more than a whisper. She was not accustomed to an audience. But Mirage was not listening to her, not consciously. Each was in her own place, speaking to the Goddess in the truest way she knew.

Miryo sang with no particular plan. Her voice strengthened as she went along. Mirage, moving in a circle around her, also began hesitantly; her motions became more assured with every step she took.

Goddess, Miryo prayed through her wordless song, *forgive me for what I have done. I meant Tsue harm; I wanted to do something that would get her out of my way. I succeeded, but at a far higher price than I had intended. Forgive me for that. And forgive me for the joy*

I felt when I held that power. I took pleasure in acting, if not in the act. Please, forgive me. I beg you.

Mirage, too, sent up a prayer, writing it in the air with her hands and her arms, the angle of her head. *Help us, please. Don't let us lose our momentum. For our own sakes, as well as those who will follow us, we* cannot *afford to let this go. Too much depends on it. Please, help us keep our course.*

And, behind it all, from both of them: *Give us the answer. Please. There* is *another way; show us the path to it.*

Miryo's singing took on a sense of direction. It was the progression she had seen in Haira: the Aspects of the Goddess, from youngest to oldest. Four of them she sang, from Maiden to Crone, while Mirage moved around her. The doppelganger made no sound, but her dancing provided a sharp counterpoint to the notes Miryo sang; the kicks and leaps, with their fierce, hard perfection, were sworn to the spirit of the Warrior.

Their separate prayers flowed into each other, creating a single plea, sound and movement, voice and flesh. The styles were different; Miryo sang the four, while Mirage danced the Warrior, but the rhythm that underlay them was the same.

And then they felt the change.

To Mirage, the air became filled with an electric energy. Her tired body took on a sudden drive that lifted her to greater heights, as it sometimes did in battles, in Dances, when words and thought dropped away and there was nothing but the movement. To Miryo, however, it was something more.

Without intending to, she lowered the guards she had placed so carefully on herself, and reached for power.

Panic tried to claw its way up her throat, but faded to nothingness before it could paralyze her. Miryo knew, distantly, that she should be afraid; this was not in her control, and she did not know what it would do. But the strange purity of mind that had overtaken her would not allow her to fear. She watched, with detached immediacy, as she sang onward, and the power took shape around them.

Mirage leapt into the air, a spinning, kicking leap, and did not land again. The power that filled the air around them lifted her up. She danced on, with nothing beneath her feet but air, and also found she could not fear.

The energy pulsed into visibility. Miryo, singing full-voiced to the four Aspects she had invoked, was also lifted from her feet; around her she could see the shining strands of power. Earth, Water, Air, and Fire; they wove a dizzying, exhilarating web around her and Mirage, and together they wept at the beauty.

And then, through those strands, something else.

Void, Mirage whispered in her mind, and Miryo recognized it as well.

The four concrete Elements and the one that was not pulsed in counterpoint to each other, a pulse that fit the rhythm they had created. And still Miryo sang, and still Mirage danced. The tornado of energy around them was not even remotely in their control, but they had created it, and it continued to draw on them, feeding its own growing power. The strands of the Elements spun them around each other in a dizzying circle, and the air grew to an incandescent white glow.

Goddess—
Show us—
Show ME—

The white fire tore through them, a blinding rush of pure energy, and all thought disappeared into the flames.

CHAPTER TWENTY-FIVE

Mirei

A CRASH BROUGHT ECLIPSE to his feet, sword in hand.

He dropped the blade an instant later, wondering how in the Warrior's name Mirage had suddenly appeared in his room in the middle of the night.

"Sen?" he asked, baffled.

From where she knelt on the floor in the dim light, she lifted her head, one inch at a time, and as she did so something around her neck fell down to dangle freely, drawing Eclipse's eyes.

A triquetra pendant.

"Miryo?" he said uncertainly.

The pendant was *all* she was wearing. She knelt there, half lit by the moonlight through the window, and he grew more confused the more he looked at her. There was no way Miryo could have picked up those muscles, but the woman's hair was long, not cropped. And why would Mirage be wearing that pendant?

And what was it in her face that made him so unsure?

Eclipse voiced a question he had never expected to have to ask. "Who . . . which one are you?"

She stood, slowly, and looked down at her hands and arms with a completely unreadable expression. "Either," she said, and her voice had the well-trained tones of a witch. "Or neither." She laughed faintly; it had a disbelieving sound. "Does it matter?"

"What?" he whispered.

She looked straight at him. "She gave me the answer, Kerestel. I prayed for an answer, and the Goddess showed it to me."

Then she fainted.

"I DON'T UNDERSTAND," Eclipse said.

She raised one eyebrow at him. "Yes, you do. You're just having trouble admitting it."

"You're . . ."

"One person. As I used to be. I was praying—both of me were—was—whatever." A grin bloomed involuntarily on her face. "I don't think grammar can cope with this. I was praying to the Goddess, and it occurred to me—to the Miryo part of me—that I wasn't praying the way I really wanted to. Ought to. So as Miryo, I sang, and as Mirage, I danced, and I listened to the Goddess with all of my heart. And she made me whole again."

The wonder of it had still not faded from her mind. She slipped one arm free of the blanket Eclipse had given her and stared at it in the light of the candle. A part of her calmly identified it as her own, while another part marveled at the smooth, hard lines of her muscles.

"And you remember both," Eclipse said.

"Of course."

He bit his lip and looked at her, perplexed. "What am I supposed to *call* you?"

The answer was there when she reached for it; the name had come to her during the ritual, but she had not looked for it until now. "Mirei." She smiled involuntarily. "The Goddess gave me the name. As she renamed Misetsu, back when this all began."

He swallowed. "It . . . works. I guess. It's kind of both of you."

"In more ways than you know." She held her hands out to him, palms down. "Try me." He placed his hands under hers, and then tried to slap them; he missed, but only barely. "I'm going to have to watch out for that. It's possible that I'll improve again, when the Miryo bit of me stops interfering with the reflexes Mirage had, but I don't know. I may be permanently watered down."

He managed to dredge up a smile from somewhere. "At least it'll be more fair for the rest of us." The smile faded. He hesitated for a moment, then looked at her directly. "So what happens now?"

She hadn't thought about it yet. "I think . . . I still need you to go to Silverfire. I could send the message to Jaguar magically, but I don't think that would go over well."

"You could deliver it in person."

Mirei shook her head. "I can't. There's . . . too many other things I have to do."

The pause betrayed her, or maybe he would have guessed anyway. "Warrior. You're going to do something stupid, aren't you?"

"Not stupid. Necessary. I've got the answer, but that only solves half the problem. I have to convince the others, or it's worthless."

" 'The others'?"

"The Primes. I could work this as an underground rebellion, but it would be long, and painful, and probably very bloody. If I can convince the women at the top, right from the start, it'll be better for everyone."

"And they'll be *so* happy to see you, I'm sure."

"I've got magic now. I can defend myself."

"Against five Primes at once?" He shook his head. "You've never been that stupid before. Why start now?"

Can I even make him understand? I suppose I have to try. Mirei took a deep breath and let it out slowly. "Kerestel—Eclipse—this is what I have to do. Never in my *life* have I felt it so clearly, seen so perfectly what it is that I should do. The path is there, in front of me. I can't say that I know where it leads. But if I don't follow it . . ." She shrugged, hands gesturing to show her loss for words. "I have to." A smile flickered across her face. "Hey, it's a challenge. And you know how I love challenges."

He looked at her silently for a very long time. Mirei met his eyes, but not in confrontation; she merely let him read whatever he saw in her expression.

At last, reluctantly, he dropped his eyes and nodded. "All right. I guess I know better than to try and stop you."

Relief washed over her. She had any number of ways of stopping *him,* should he try to interfere with her, but she didn't want to use them. Far better that he should agree. "There's a few things I need to do, then. Do you still have my saddlebag?"

She had given him most of her baggage when they parted after the ambush. "Yes."

"Good. That takes care of clothing, then." She wondered whether the clothing she had been wearing in Angrim was lying on the floor of the temple, or if it had been burned away in the fire that had transformed her. "And I'll need to borrow your weapons."

He looked surprised. "You have magic now, don't you?"

"Yes, but it's not always the best way of handling things. And I need the Primes to see that I'm both Miryo *and* Mirage."

"Take them," he said without hesitation. Mirei was again relieved. She had been wary of asking for two reasons; the part of her that saw him as Miryo did was reluctant to ask a favor of someone she did not know all that well, while the Mirage part of her knew Hunters disliked lending their blades.

"Thank you," she said sincerely. "Do you have the paper we were given in Corberth?"

"In my bag."

"I'll need that before I leave. I have to write to Ashin and the others, so that they'll know what I've figured out. I'm also going to give you a copy. I don't want to risk this information getting lost."

She did not add, "in case I die," but Eclipse was capable of filling that in for himself. His face grew grimmer, but he did not comment. "How are you going, then? Do you need a horse?"

"No. It'll take too long. I'll go the way I came."

As she said that, the shock that had been lurking in the back of her mind came explosively to the fore. She saw a fainter cousin of it on Eclipse's face. "Isn't that . . . I thought moving living creatures like that was impossible."

So did I. Mirage had known it, but Miryo had taken it for granted; only now, as she thought about what she had done, did the full import hit her. Even when the Primes had appeared so suddenly for her testing in Starfall, they had walked in; a spell had simply kept her from noticing.

"It's supposed to be. I . . ." Her voice trailed off as she closed her eyes and thought back. "I know how I did it. And I can do it again, to get myself to Starfall."

For a brief moment she considered explaining to him how it worked, and what had changed, but she decided not to. *He should know, eventually. But if I tell him now . . . no. After I'm done in Starfall. Otherwise I'll never get out of here.*

And the witches deserve to know first.

"If you're sure," he said uncertainly. "Can you depend on a new spell like that?"

"Yes," she said, without hesitation. "I remember what I did, almost as well as I remember how I made myself one again. It'll work."

He trusted her enough to accept that. "All right. Do you want to write to Ashin now, or later?"

SHE SAT, STILL WRAPPED in the blanket, and stared at the enchanted rice paper that would take her message to Ashin.

Crone's stick. Where to start?

All the things she wanted or needed to say crowded into her mind, making thought momentarily impossible. Mirei gritted her teeth and forced herself to focus. *One thing at a time. Go in order.*

She bent her head and began to write.

Ashin:

> *The Primes sent Cousins to ambush us and take us prisoner. They were going to interrogate us for information on you, and then kill both of us; it's apparently possible, if you kill both at the same time. They may be aware of the existence of the*

other doppelgangers. Eclipse is going to warn the Grandmaster of Silverfire, who has two of them under his training. You should see to the others, and to their witches.

But I have found the solution.

Misetsu was almost *right. She didn't lose the voice of the Goddess as thoroughly as you thought. She simply misinterpreted what she sensed. "De-struction, oblivion, undoing"—it's the* Void. *That is what we lose when the doppelgangers are killed. That is why, until now, we've only been able to touch four of the Elements.*

The doppelgangers are not meant to remain separate. Yes, they're divided, but only for a time: when the witch is opened to magic, she is ready to rejoin with her other half, and become a single person again.

That is what I have done.

Since being rejoined, I've begun to work magic that incorporates the Void. I suspect, although I'm not certain, that when I have children, I'll have sons as well as daughters. How exactly all of this interrelates is for the Path of the Head to sort out; I admit that I'm really just feeling things by instinct.

Following this message are the notations for the spell that made me whole. It's complex, and requires the participation of the doppelganger— not in song, but in movement. *And that's why previous attempts failed; I bet you anything they treated it as song alone, and left out the physical part. But the doppelganger represents the*

Warrior, and the Warrior is movement as well as Void.

> *Copy the notations at the bottom, and distribute them as widely as you can, so they won't be lost. I'm headed south to see the Primes. I don't know how well they'll receive this news, but I'll find out. Wish me luck.*
>
> *—Mirei*

She set to work writing down the pitches and syllables that had guided the power to rejoin her two halves. Though she had sung the spell only once, it was burned into her memory; she wouldn't forget it anytime soon.

A part of her watched the process of notation with detached curiosity. She had yet to adjust to the way things seemed both familiar and yet strange. She still grieved for the deaths of the Cousins she had killed, but the acceptance her Mirage side had of these actions tempered her guilt and kept it from paralyzing her. Likewise, the part of her that had been trained as a witch wrote out the spell without a second thought, but that which had been a Hunter found it intriguing. Then she recorded the movement, dredging up long-buried memories of Dancer notation. Ashin would have to find someone to interpret it for her.

When she had finished, she sang the message to the paper's counterpart. She had no idea which of the conspirators had it, but the information should reach Ashin soon.

Eclipse was downstairs, getting food for her. It was very late, or perhaps very early; the bells had rung

Dark not too long ago. Soon the inn's staff would be waking and beginning the day's chores, but right now everything was still silent.

Mirei rose and found her saddlebag on the floor. She worried briefly for Mist, then dismissed the thought; Wisp would take good care of her horse. And besides, the mare needed the rest. She unbuckled the flap of the bag and found her spare uniform on top.

Mirei fingered the windsilk thoughtfully. She had intended to go to Starfall armed, but dressed normally. Now, she reconsidered.

Well, I am a Hunter, as well as a witch. Maybe if I wore it without the mask?

That seemed the better plan. If she showed up masked, it would cause alarm; witches didn't appreciate Hunters skulking around their domain any more than Hunters wanted witches in their schools. The uniform would still spark unease, but enough people would recognize her face that she could get through to the Primes. She hoped.

Besides, you want to wear it.

She grinned and began to dress.

ECLIPSE GAVE MIREI a long, serious scrutiny. It was nearly dawn, and she stood in the center of his room, dressed in Hunter uniform, his weapons strapped to her hips, the triquetra pendant around her neck. Her hands hung at her sides, relaxed; her posture had the loose wariness of a cat.

"You're sure you know what you're doing?" he felt compelled to ask, one last time.

Mirei nodded, and there was no hint of doubt in her eyes. "I do."

He swallowed and forced himself to accept that. He was afraid for her, but also proud; only rarely had he seen someone with her kind of certainty and resolve. It had produced in her an aura of peace, and a readiness for whatever might come.

"Goddess walk with you," he said at last. "She has so far."

"Thank you," Mirei whispered, and gave him a tight embrace.

Then Eclipse stepped back, retreating to the dubious safety of the wall. She had said the spell would work, but after all the previous backfires, he still felt a reflexive need for shelter. Mirei seemed to guess his feelings; she smiled. Then she took a deep breath and began to sing.

And not just sing; her body moved as well, arms carving a pattern in the air, as no witch before her had done.

It didn't take long. A few heartbeats later, she was gone, and the air around Eclipse shifted, rushing to fill the gap where she had been.

Eclipse exhaled slowly, and sent up one last prayer.

MIREI APPEARED in the middle of the forest. It took her a moment to orient herself. She was on the northern side of the mountains, surrounded by trees just becoming visible in the light before dawn. She took a deep breath, inhaling the familiar and yet strange scent of Starfall's forests; a part of her felt as if she were home.

Around her, the sentry spells roused.

Void it. They recognize me as something odd. Not student, not Cousin; witch, but odd. And I left the token with Eclipse.

She reached out, humming, and soothed the spells. They subsided, mostly; her magic was effective, but not quite the same as what the spells were keyed to. It had to be the Void influence. Mirei grimaced. She'd have to watch out for that, or they'd bring a guard down on her head.

In the meantime, she needed to decide what she was doing.

It was not yet dawn. Mirei considered proceeding on toward the settlement to the south, but decided against it almost instantly; many witches preferred to work elaborate spells at night, under the light of the stars, and as a result slept late in the morning. She might arrive at Starfall to find everyone in bed. And while that might be amusing, it wasn't precisely the effect she wanted. Besides which, she was bone-tired.

Mother's mercy—it was tonight *that I was in Angrim. I've been one person for less than half a day.*

The rejoining felt natural enough that she took it purely for granted. But although that ritual had infused her with energy, self-translocation turned out to be an incredibly tiring spell. She'd be well-advised to rest before going to face the Primes.

A few minutes of wandering in the brightening woods oriented her more specifically. She was in a familiar area; there was a spring nearby, with clean, sweet water. It was sheltered enough to provide a good place for her to sleep, and in the afternoon or early evening, she could move on. She even scrounged some blackberries, which she could eat when she awoke.

She found the spring, erected a minor ward to alert her if anyone approached, and curled up to sleep.

She awoke with a start around noon.

Hunter instincts brought her awake within a heart-beat, and immediately she began to move. Her ears strained, listening for the sound of approaching feet, as she found a good tree and pulled herself into its con-cealing branches.

She heard nothing.

A moment later, though, a red head appeared, below her and slightly to one side. Mirei recognized her: Ganchise, an Earth Heart. Spells masked any sounds she might make. The part of Mirei that was a Hunter sneered at that; the spells made the witch lazy. With-out them, she'd sound like a drunken donkey, crashing through the woods that way.

The witch nosed around for a while, but Mirei had taken care not to leave any noticeable signs of her pres-ence. Even the berries were concealed under a bush. At last Ganchise shrugged, muttered something the spell muted, and moved onward.

Up in her tree, Mirei exhaled. *I'm going to have to be more careful. I must have set off one of the wards; she was clearly looking for me, and not just passing through. I'll have to do better than that.*

She was awake now, and wouldn't be going back to sleep anytime soon. With a sigh, Mirei settled herself on the tree branch to wait.

And pray. As long as she had the time to kill, it couldn't hurt.

I'm here, Goddess. At Starfall. I'm going to talk to the Primes. Please, let them listen to what I have to say. Help them be rational. They're frightened of doppelgangers; they may be frightened of me. But I'm not here to hurt them. Please, help them see that.

I don't want this to come to trouble.

As the sky began to darken, Mirei rose and made her way up the mountain.

CHAPTER TWENTY-SIX

Starfall

MIRYO'S KNOWLEDGE TOLD HER which way to go; Mirage's kept her hidden and quiet as she moved. She passed a group of unarmed Cousins, off on some errand; Mirei concealed herself and waited until they were some distance away before continuing on. It couldn't hurt to be careful.

That same thought provoked her, when she came to the mountain's peak, to not declare herself to the guards.

The two women flanking the road were more of a formality than anything else. They existed to welcome and guide the infrequent visitors to Starfall, not to keep anyone out. And there was no wall around the buildings, which took up the space of a small town. There was one small ward, more a strengthened version of a sentry spell than anything else; Mirei, having learned from her past mistake, managed to soothe it into tranquility without setting off any ripples of unfamiliarity. It was accustomed to letting witches through, and it recognized her as one of them.

Which, technically, I am. Satomi gave me the pendant, although I imagine she'd like to take it back.

Full dark had descended by the time she reached the

cluster of buildings that was the heart of Starfall. Mirei was just as happy; it made sneaking in much easier. She eyed the place from the shadow of a tree and put together her strategy, based on Miryo's knowledge and Mirage's skill.

Now, the question is, where are the Primes right now? I probably won't find them all in one place. Satomi might be in her office; I should start there. If I can get her to listen to me, she can call the others to a formal audience or something.

But how to get to Satomi, without going through everyone else first?

Mirei studied the buildings. The answer was quite obvious, and didn't even require a spell. *At least years of climbing the roof will be good for something. If I can get onto the well house, that support they built across to the students' hall when the wall started to weaken will get me to that line of sculptures. From there, the roof should be no problem.*

Good. Now do it.

She slipped through the shadows to the well house's side. There she paused; a pair of Cousins were chatting inside, and she didn't want to risk them hearing her. Before long they left, and she lifted herself up to the well house roof.

One side sported the lower end of a buttress that ran the short distance to the students' hall. Now it became Mirei's road. She reached the shadow of the wall and found easy climbing there; it was one of the sections with sculpture, which made for good handholds. It took only a moment, and then she was on the familiar terrain of the roof.

She arrived at the building's far side and considered

her next options. A series of shallow scissor arches connected the students' hall to the main building where much of Starfall's administrative work went on. Satomi should be there. Mirei walked along the edge of the roof, trying to remember the layout of the interior, until she came to the arch that would likely bring her closest to the Void Prime's office. Then, checking first to ensure that no one was looking, she ran across.

Halfway across, she again experienced that strange dichotomy. Mirage thought nothing of this stunt; Miryo was amazed at the casual attitude she took toward it.

With that thought, one foot slipped.

Mirei caught her balance, exhaled once, and ran onward to the safety of the other side. *I need to stop doing that. What if I find myself distracted in the middle of a spell? That wouldn't be good at all. I need to stop thinking about what I'm doing, and just* do *it.*

She gave herself a moment to rest, then searched for an open window. When she found one and slipped through, she found herself in the exact hallway she had hoped for.

From here she proceeded carefully, listening for voices or footsteps. The administrative hall was generally a busy place, filled with Heart and Head witches going about their various tasks.

Now, however, it was dead quiet.

In fact, Mirei saw no one at all in the halls.

Her confusion was completed when she peered around a corner to the door of Satomi's office and found no one there. She had expected the Void Prime to be working; she usually was, at this time of night. But the customary guard of two Cousins was absent from her door.

So where in the Maiden's name is she?

The realization smacked her, and Mirei felt extremely silly. Tonight, if she was counting the days right, was one of the nights when the Primes held court in the ruling hall. There they made announcements, heard cases, and dealt with the affairs of Starfall itself. All students were required to attend, and many witches currently at Starfall did as well.

You should have remembered that, idiot. Start thinking more clearly, or you'll not have a snowflake's chance in a bonfire of convincing the Primes of anything.

At least, she reflected wildly, this would save her some trouble. All the Primes would be in one place, and she'd get her formal audience.

She took a moment to quell the absurd laughter welling up inside her. It was nerves, and nothing more. She couldn't let them interfere.

When she felt calm, she set out again, this time to the adjoining building where court was in progress.

Two Cousins stood on guard outside the hall's door.

Mirei eyed them and wondered what to do. Present herself to them, and ask to be announced? Freeze them with a spell? *No, the Primes would sense that. Void, every witch in there would sense that.*

The question was, then, did she want to be announced or not?

I think not.

Applause from inside the hall gave her the cover she needed. Mirei put on a burst of speed, and before the clapping died down, both of the guards were unconscious, without any magic at all. She took a moment to lay them to one side before facing the door.

Deep breath. Straighten your uniform; you want to look good.

She had never done anything quite like this, in either of her lives. Adrenaline raced through her, making her muscles tingle. She had to consciously stop her hands from trembling, and keep them away from the hilt of Eclipse's borrowed sword.

Let's go.

She sang, and the doors, carved with the symbols of the Elements, swung open.

The voices inside the hall died down as she began the long walk down the aisle. Witches and students filled the benches to either side of her; heads turned to look as those in front realized something was happening. Before Mirei had passed the second rank of grave slabs, there was silence. She stepped evenly, deliberately, her heels tapping on the stone in the silence of the hall.

Whispers rose and fell in her wake as women recognized her.

The Primes, at the far end of the hall, rose from their chairs. Mirei kept her eyes on Satomi, standing dead center, outlined by the unadorned blackness of her Elemental banner. To their credit and her relief, they waited until she had reached the front before saying anything.

She stopped in front of their dais and bowed.

"What are you doing, Miryo?" Satomi asked in an icy voice.

Mirei smiled at her, trying to fight down the whirlwind of nerves and exhilaration inside her. "Wrong."

The Void Prime's eyes narrowed, and in them was a touch of fear. "The doppelganger, then. You have no right to wear that pendant."

She grinned again. "Not that, either. Can't you guess?"

Murmurs from behind her. Mirei spread her arms wide. "Miryo. *And* Mirage. And proof that we've been doing things wrong for all these centuries."

The murmurs rose. Satomi gestured sharply, and the assembled witches and students fell silent. "What have you *done*?" the Void Prime whispered, almost spitting the words out. "Combined yourself with an outsider—a *Hunter*? This is an abomination!"

"No worse than you've done," Mirei shot back. She tried to stay restrained, but failed; her voice grew louder. "Would you like me to start listing the actions *you've* taken? Would you like me to tell these women about Wraith?"

"We need not listen to your lies," Arinei snapped above the rising noise.

"Lies? I am Mirage *and* Miryo. I know what you have done."

She was ready to say it, to expose the Primes' assassination of Tari before the listening witches, and damn the consequences. Before she could, though, Satomi stepped forward, green eyes glittering with hard fire. "We have done what we must, for the safety of all. There is no choice. 'The doppelganger is anathema to us. It is destruction and oblivion, the undoing of all magic. It is the ruin of our work, and the bane of our being. It and our magic will never coexist, and its presence threatens all that our powers can do.' So wrote Misetsu—"

"Five days before she died. Yes, you told me that before. And I believed it then, but now I know it's wrong. Misetsu ought to have listened better when the Goddess spoke to her." Mirei pitched her voice to cut through the air of the hall. "Destruction. Oblivion. Undoing. *Void.*

"*That* is what we are lacking. *That* is why the clergy call us unbalanced. *That* is why we have no sons. We are crippled in our ignorance, and yet we think that ignorance is power. For centuries now, we've turned our faces from the rest of the power that should be ours."

"The Void is untouchable," Koika said. "It is nothingness. You cannot work with nothing!"

"*You* can't," Mirei said, with a reckless grin. "I can." She looked up and around, eyeing the ruling hall with calculated distaste. If she had to do this publicly, then she'd better exploit the theatrics of it. "I've never liked this place. So why don't we go elsewhere? Let's adjourn to Star Hall, and I'll show you just what I can do." She directed her smile right at Satomi, let it widen slightly. "Follow me however you can."

Then she sang herself out.

MIREI STAGGERED when she appeared on the center dais, breath ragged in her chest.

Goddess, I hope the Primes don't realize how hard that is. I can't afford to let them think I'm tired.

She waited, slowing her breathing, for the others to arrive. It would take a few minutes; they, unlike her, would have to walk. Adrenaline still flooded her body, but she was grateful for it. Without it, she might fall over.

Noise outside the hall alerted her. Mirei spared one last glance upward, into the unfathomable blackness of the hall's crossing, imagining the stars above. *I've come this far. Please, Goddess, don't desert me now.*

The Primes led the way. Satomi, Mirei saw, chose to

enter from the branch of the hall dedicated to Fire; she wondered briefly if that meant anything. At least she wasn't entering with Shimi. The look in the Air Prime's eye was murderous.

As the other four raised themselves onto columns of Elemental light, just as they had during Miryo's test, the Void Prime stalked up onto the dais and opened her mouth to speak.

Mirei sang two quick notes and twisted one hand through the air, and the witchlights in the hall went out.

She heard involuntary gasps from the Primes, lit from beneath by their shining columns. Then Koika's voice sounded, and the lights came back up, giving her a better look at the absolute shock on the five women's faces.

"This is what I mean," Mirei said, hoping her own surprise wasn't visible. She hadn't known she was going to do that. In fact, she hadn't known she *could*. It seemed the Goddess was still with her. "Void magic is the undoing of magic."

She had hardly any warning before Shimi began to sing. Mirei had just enough time to identify the spell as an immobilizing one; then words were flying out of her mouth and her body was in motion, slightly different this time, canceling the Air Prime's spell.

That was a different phrase. So they don't all cancel the same.

Shimi's eyes looked like they were going to fall out of her skull. It was a fundamental truth that magic could be counteracted, but never canceled. And Mirei had just turned that on its head.

"This is what Misetsu didn't understand," Mirei said. The branches of the hall were filling up. She couldn't spare the attention to be sure, but it looked like all the witches from the ruling hall were entering the branches for their Rays. The Void witches made a ring around the Primes, and the students were packing in at the back of each branch, eyes wide. There were even Cousins, squeezing into the spaces behind the columns. "Doppelgangers *are* the undoing of magic. As you have just seen."

The reaction was not what she had hoped.

It was even worse than she had feared.

Miryo had never been in a true battle of any kind, physical or magical. So it was purely Mirage's instincts that guided Mirei when terror possessed the Primes' faces and the spells began to sound.

She flew into motion, singing frantically, body twisting, slashing through spells right and left. They came only from the Primes, and for that she was grateful; had any other witches joined in, she would have been dead. As it was, only the power of the Void and the other women's fear of it saved her from the Primes' spells. Ordinarily she would never have stood a chance against the five of them, not together and probably not alone, but she had canceling magic, which they had never seen before and did not know how to react to. A spell that took them twenty pitches to construct, she could cut through in four.

Her canceling could overpower any one of them. But only barely, and they soon realized that just as well as she did.

They began to sing together.

Mirei didn't even recognize what they were constructing. That made things worse; if she didn't know what it was, she couldn't cut it effectively. And the odds of her managing to outmuscle all five Primes in concert were beyond bad.

She saw the look in Shimi's eyes, and knew she wasn't likely to survive whatever they were building.

I can't stop them.

But I can try to turn them.

Mirei didn't let herself consider what she was about to do. She took a deep breath, prayed to the Goddess, and threw her voice into their spell.

She did not seek to cancel it; she didn't have the strength. Instead, she did something even more reckless: she wove herself and her power into the spell they were building. Satomi was at its head, and so she found herself in direct competition with the Void Prime for control of the energy.

She and Satomi faced off across the central dais. Electricity surged up Mirei's spine; her movements had closed in to nearly nothing, but the energy she was channeling lived in them just the same, suffusing her body until she knew she might well die of it. The two witches stood at the heart of a vortex of power that was spinning wildly out of control; Mirei couldn't take it from the Void Prime, but her efforts threatened Satomi's grip.

If this goes on, Mirei realized, *we are* all *going to die.*

Any of the witches in the hall could stop her. Mirei could not see them through the lightning swirl of energy that surrounded her, but she heard no voices beyond the six of them, and felt no interference. No one was going to risk touching this maelstrom.

She could not take it, and Satomi could not hold it.

Mirei looked the Void Prime directly in the eye. The anguish she saw there struck her like a physical blow.

She wants *to believe. She wants to admit I'm right, and that she was right to doubt. But she also wants me to be wrong, because if this is truly the way, then she failed the Goddess when she killed her doppelganger.*

She could not spare a single instant to speak. All of her voice, all of her energy, was bound up in the spell cracking the air around them. She could only communicate with her eyes.

Give it to me, Satomi. Give me the power, and let go of the past.

Please.

PLEASE.

The power slipped into her control.

Mirei acted with the instantaneous decisiveness of a warrior in battle, with the educated instinct of a witch. The moment the power slammed into her body, she hurled it in the only direction still safe.

Up.

And the top of Star Hall shattered.

With a scream of magic, Mirei summoned what energy she had left and threw a barrier over the dais.

Epilogue

HER BARRIER FAILED, but it didn't matter. More than one witch in the assembled crowd kept her head well enough to sing one into being. The stones and glass that had made up the crossing rained down and were deflected by the layers of energy that sheltered the dais.

Mirei stood, trembling, and watched them fall.

When the last fragments had settled, she took one deep, shuddering breath. Then her legs folded beneath her, and she sat down hard on the surface of the dais.

Across from her, Satomi was weeping.

The other Primes were in equally bad shape. Rana and Arinei were sitting, like Mirei; Shimi and Koika were still standing, but none of them were on their columns of light anymore. Those had vanished at some point, Mirei wasn't sure when. Possibly when she had hurled the power upward.

A hand touched her shoulder.

She turned to find Eikyo there. And she had no sooner looked at her friend than she was enveloped in a crushing hug.

"Goddess," Eikyo said into Mirei's shoulder. "You . . . I can't believe it." She laughed abruptly and lifted her head, looking at Mirei. "Except I kind of can. You never liked taking rules for granted." She glanced around at the wreckage. "I can't believe they *attacked* you."

Mirei stood unsteadily. "I should have expected it. I just didn't realize how much it would frighten them, how much . . ." Her voice trailed off, and she had to cough to get it working again. "Goddess. What a mess."

She stepped off the dais, employing what will she had left to keep herself on her feet. Rana, Arinei, and Koika she ignored; if there was any trouble left, it would come from Shimi. The Air Prime stared at her as she approached, her eyes wild with shock.

Mirei gritted her teeth and managed a bow without falling over. "Shimi-kane. I am sorry for what has happened. I understand that you were doing only what you thought was best."

The Air Prime didn't respond. Mirei was not even certain the woman had seen her.

After a moment, Mirei bowed again, turned, and climbed the dais once more. Eikyo stood back as she went to Satomi and knelt at her side.

"I don't understand," the Void Prime whispered. For the first time since Mirei had known her, she looked old; exhaustion and pain had drained the color from her face, leaving it bloodless and worn. "You're right. I know you are. But why didn't she tell us before? Why let it go on like this, for so long?"

Mirei had no ready answer for that. She had found the solution, but not the reason. "Aken . . . I'm not a priestess. I don't know." She closed her eyes and tried listening. No divine revelation occurred to her, but she did come up with an idea. Whether it would do Satomi any good was questionable. "The clergy tell us that the Goddess, though Mother, is not our mother. She won't hold our hands and walk us through life. We have to rise and fall on our own successes and mistakes. I'm sure she grieved to see us go wrong, but she wouldn't do anything to change it. Not until we were ready to listen."

Satomi shuddered. "That's harsh."

It *was* harsh. Mirei didn't have anything that would soften it, either.

The dust had cleared. She glanced around and saw witches on every side, staring at them. Rana was at Shimi's elbow, trying to get her to move.

"Aken?" Mirei asked softly. "Can you get up?"

The Void Prime looked around for the first time. She winced when she saw the destruction Mirei had wrought, but waved off her half-formed apology. "No, you did right. That power had to go somewhere. It was you, me, or the roof." She declined a hand and pushed herself to her feet. "We can always rebuild the roof."

Then she looked at Mirei and firmed her jaw. "Tari and her . . . compatriots. They've arranged for the survival of other doppelgangers, have they not?"

"Yes, Aken."

"Good." Her eyes were still weary, and full of pain, but they also held conviction Mirei could only admire. "It's a start." She turned a full circle, facing all of the assembled witches, students, and Cousins in turn. They quieted when they saw her on her feet and alert. "Come with me, then. There's a good deal more we must discuss." The Void Prime stepped off the dais and over a low spot in the ring of rubble that surrounded it. The crowd of women parted to let her through.

Mirei, still on the dais, cast her eyes upward. The walls vaulted skyward, and then ended abruptly in a jagged, shattered line. High above, she could see the glimmer of the stars: the eyes of the Goddess, watching them all.

She smiled to herself, then followed Satomi out of the hall.

Glossary

Ai—the honorific used for an unranked witch of the Void Ray.

Air—one of the five Elements. Air is associated with the Bride. Among the witches, the Air Ray is itinerant, and serves anyone in need.

Akara—the honorific used for a Key of the Void Ray.

Aken—the honorific used for the Prime of the Void Ray.

Anade—the former Lady of Razi. Killed by Wraith. Succeeded by Cano.

Arinei—Prime of the Fire Ray.

Ashin—Key of the Air Hand.

Aspect—one of the five faces of the Goddess. The Aspects are the Maiden, the Bride, the Mother, the Crone, and the Warrior.

Atami—Key of the Water Hand.

Avalanche—a Hunter of Silverfire. Formerly employed by Tari.

Avannans—members of a religious sect that honors the Dance as the highest form of adoration to the Goddess.

Bonded—a term used for Hunters who take permanent employment with a single individual.

Briar—a Hunter of Silverfire. Stablemaster at the school.

Bride—the second Aspect of the Goddess, associated with marriage and the Element of Air.

Cano—the Lord of Razi. Successor to Anade. Served by a Cloudhawk, Tangle, now deceased.

Chaha—the Lady of Kalistyi.

Chai—the honorific used for an unranked witch of the Earth Ray.

Chakoa—the honorific used for a Key of the Earth Ray.

Chashi—the honorific used for the Prime of the Earth Ray.

Chime—a division of the clock developed in Insebrar; each lasts three hours. In order, they are Low, Dark, First, Mid, High, Light, Late, and Last.

Cloudhawk—one of the Hunter schools, training bonded spies, who are often employed by Lords or other powerful figures.

Cousin—term used for the servants of the witches.

Criel—a former leader of the Sunset Temple company of Dancers in Eriot. Now serves as a priestess in Verdosa.

Crone—the eldest Aspect of the Goddess, associated with wisdom and the Element of Earth.

Dance—an art practiced in some temples (especially Avannan temples) to honor the Goddess.

Dark—the second chime of the clock, corresponding to 3 A.M.

Domain—the primary political unit. Formerly the fifteen domains were subsets of three large kingdoms, but those realms fractured centuries ago.

Earth—one of the five Elements. Earth is associated with the Crone. Among the witches, the Earth Ray serves the land itself, working to prevent droughts and other natural disasters.

Eclipse—a Hunter of Silverfire. Year-mate of Mirage. Formerly called Kerestel.

Edame—Fire Hand. Domain adviser to Lord Iseman and Lady Terica of Haira.

Eikyo—a witch-student in her twenty-fifth year. A friend of Miryo's. Intends to join the Earth Heart.

Elements—the substances that make up the world. Each has a variety of symbolic associations. The five Elements are Fire, Air, Water, Earth, and Void.

Fire—one of the five Elements. Fire is associated with the Maiden. Among the witches, the Fire Ray serves the rulers of the land as advisers.

First—the third chime of the clock, corresponding to 6 A.M.

Freelance—a term used for Hunters who work for hire in short-term jobs.

Governor—an individual who rules over a region of a domain, answering to a Lord or Lady.

Hand—one of the three Paths. Witches of the Hand carry out the work of their Ray, usually in other domains.

Head—one of the three Paths. Witches of the Head conduct the research and recordkeeping of their Ray, often in Starfall or one of the domain halls.

Heart—one of the three Paths. Witches of the Heart are the organizational and administrative structure of their Ray, and often live in Starfall.

High—the fifth chime of the clock, corresponding to noon.

Hinusoka—a witch-student. Died during the final test of passage.

Hunter—an individual trained by one of the Hunter schools. Hunters may be trained in a specialty, such as spying, assassination, bodyguarding, or mercenary soldiering, or they may generalize. Some are bonded; others are freelance. All Hunters are highly skilled at individual combat. Their training lasts for ten years, ending at the age of twenty.

Ice—a Hunter of Thornblood. Year-mate of Lion. A long-standing enemy of Mirage's.

Iseman—the Lord of Haira, and husband of Terica. A devout Avannan.

Itsumen—Key of the Void Hand.

Jaguar—the Grandmaster of Silverfire.

Kai—the honorific used for an unranked witch of the Air Ray.

Kan—a Cousin. Assigned to aid Miryo in her search.

Kane—the honorific used for the Prime of the Air Ray.

Kasane—Air Heart. Mother of Miryo.

Kasora—the honorific used for a Key of the Air Ray.

Katsu—the honorific used for a witch of unknown or un-decided affiliation.

Kekkai—Key of the Fire Heart. Successor to Tari.

Kerestel—the former name of Eclipse.

Key—a witch who leads a Path. A new Prime is selected from among the ranks of the Keys of the appropriate Ray.

Kimeko—Key of the Void Heart.

Kobach—a noble, now deceased. Tried to usurp the lord-ship of Liak from Narevoi. Killed by Mirage in Haira.

Koika—Prime of the Earth Ray.

Lady—the ruler of a domain, if female; the highest political rank.

Last—the eighth chime of the clock, corresponding to 9 P.M.

Late—the seventh chime of the clock, corresponding to 6 P.M.

Light—the sixth chime of the clock, corresponding to 3 P.M.

Linea—the Lady of Abern.

Lion—a Hunter of Thornblood. Year-mate and lover of Ice.

Lionra—the seneschal of Haira Keep.

Lord—the ruler of a domain, if male; the highest political rank.

Low—the first chime of the clock, corresponding to midnight.

Mai—the honorific used for an unranked witch of the Water Ray.

Maiden—the youngest Aspect of the Goddess, associated with youth and the Element of Fire.

Makiza—the honorific used for a Key of the Water Ray.

Marell—a Silverfire agent. Stationed in Chiero.

Mari—the honorific used for the Prime of the Water Ray.

Menukyo—a witch. According to legend, the eldest daughter of Misetsu.

Mid—the fourth chime of the clock, corresponding to 9 A.M.

Mimre—the Lord of Seach.

Mirage—a Hunter of Silverfire. Year-mate of Eclipse. Formerly called Seniade.

Miryo—a witch-student in her twenty-fifth year. Daughter of Kasane.

Misetsu—the first witch. A holy woman in the area now called Starfall who received the gift of magic for her piety.

Morisuke—Void Head. Stationed in Samalan to provide information to witches traveling to or from Starfall.

Mother—the third Aspect of the Goddess, associated with family and the Element of Water.

Nai—the honorific used for an unranked witch of the Fire Ray.

Nakana—the honorific used for a Key of the Fire Ray.

Nalochkans—members of a religious sect that denies the Warrior Aspect of the Goddess.

Narevoi—the Lord of Liak.

Narika—Air Head. Often works to recruit new witches into the Air Ray.

Nasha—a Silverfire agent. Stationed in Handom.

Nayo—the honorific used for the Prime of the Fire Ray.

Nenikune—Void Heart. Keeps the Starfall infirmary.

Onomita—Key of the Fire Head.

Path—one of the three divisions of a Ray, each dedicated to a different function. The three Paths are the Hand, the Head, and the Heart. A Path is led by a Key.

Perachi—Water Hand. Serves the people of Samalan.

Prime—a witch who leads a Ray. Together, the five Primes rule the domain of Starfall, and the witches who serve in other domains.

Ralni—the Lord of Insebrar.

Rana—Prime of the Water Ray.

Ray—one of the five divisions used among the witches, corresponding to the Elements. Each Ray serves a different subset of the world. A Ray is led by a Prime.

Ruriko—Void Heart. Secretary to Satomi.

Ryll—one of two court artists employed at Haira Keep. Specializes in portraits.

Sai—a Cousin. Assigned to aid Miryo in her search.

Sareen—second highest-ranking performing member of the Sunset Temple company in Eriot.

Satomi—Prime of the Void Ray.

Seniade—the former name of Mirage.

Shimi—Prime of the Air Ray.

Silverfire—one of the Hunter schools, training freelancers who do a variety of work. Their school is located a short distance away from Elensk in Miest. They have a longstanding rivalry with Thornblood.

Slip—a Hunter of Silverfire, retired from active work. Twin of Wisp. Jaguar's secretary.

Stoneshadow—one of the Hunter schools, training bonded assassins, who are often employed by Lords or other powerful figures.

Talon—a Hunter of Silverfire, retired from active work. Teaches unarmed combat at the school.

Tangle—a Hunter of Cloudhawk. Served Lord Cano of Razi; killed by Wraith.

Tari—Key of the Fire Heart Path; now deceased.

Terica—the Lady of Haira, and wife of Iseman. A devout Avannan.

Thornblood—one of the Hunter schools, training freelancers who do a variety of work. Their school is located north of Angrim in Abern. They have a longstanding rivalry with Silverfire.

Tomichu—Void Head. Keeps the common library at Starfall.

Tothe—one of two court artists employed at Haira Keep. Specializes in landscapes.

Tsue—a Cousin.

Ueda—Key of the Earth Heart.

Viper—a Hunter of Silverfire.

Void—one of the five Elements. Void is associated with the Warrior. Among the witches, the Void Ray serves the witches themselves, handling the internal affairs of Starfall and its people. Alone among the Elements, Void does not make up a part of the physical world, but rather represents that which is not the world.

Warrior—the fifth Aspect of the Goddess, associated with death, warfare, and the element of the Void. Alone among the Aspects, she does not stand for a stage in the cycle of life, but rather for the end of that life.

Water—one of the five Elements. Water is associated with the Mother. Among the witches, the Water Ray serves the common people of the land, often living in the larger villages and towns to heal diseases and handle other problems.

Willow—a Hunter of Silverfire. Year-mate of Mirage and Eclipse.

Windblade—one of the Hunter schools, training freelance bodyguards. Their school is located south of Angrim in Abern.

Wisp—a Hunter of Silverfire, retired from active work. Twin of Slip. Stationed as an agent in Angrim.

Wolfstar—one of the Hunter schools, training freelance assassins.

Wraith—a Hunter of Wolfstar. Assassinated Lady Anade of Razi.

Yaryoki—Void Hand. Stationed in Aystad.

Yuri—Water Head. Teaches history at Starfall.

Acknowledgments

I would like to thank everyone who critiqued this novel and gave me encouragement over the years, especially Jason Pratt.

I'd also like to thank Alasdair Brooks, for the unwitting loan of his finds tent at Castell Henllys, where I wrote substantial portions of the later chapters. It was the only place in the entire camp where I could plug my laptop in, and also the only place with chairs. I am very grateful for these things.

Final thanks, of course, go to Devi Pillai and Rachel Vater, for being the ones to finally get me over this hurdle.

extras

orbit

meet the author

MARIE BRENNAN holds an undergraduate degree in archaeology and folklore from Harvard and is now pursuing a PhD in anthropology and folklore at Indiana University. Find out more about Marie Brennan at www.marie brennan.net.

introducing

If you enjoyed **WARRIOR**,
look out for the sequel

WITCH

by Marie Brennan

FOR EIGHT DAYS, Mirei thought she could relax.

Those days weren't empty of stress; her very presence at Starfall was a source of tension for the witches around her. Her life was no longer in danger, though. Her magic was under control and the Primes were no longer planning to execute her; on the whole, her situation had improved. And so Mirei began to relax.

But on the ninth day, a Cousin woke her with a message that she was needed in Satomi's office. That alone was a sign of trouble. Mirei had gone to that office every morning since coming back to Starfall, and given that she didn't sleep in, she was always there by First at the latest. If Satomi had sent a servant to wake her early, then there was trouble bad enough that it couldn't wait.

Mirei sent the Cousin away and dressed as quickly as she could, throwing on the first thing that came to hand. It was a lightweight blue dress, on loan from some witch, or perhaps another Cousin. Miryo's clothing, left behind when she went in search of Mirage, didn't fit her muscled shoulders, and the only clothing of Mirage's she had was her Hunter uniform. Wearing that only stirred people up even more. As did going armed; Mirei had to stop herself short of taking the sword that leaned against the wall by her bed. There might be trouble, but she sincerely hoped it wasn't bad enough that she would have to kill anyone.

And you'd look like an idiot, wearing a sword over a dress.

Unarmed, she left the New House, the residence for newly tested witches who had not yet established homes elsewhere. It was only a short walk from there to the main structure of Starfall, a rambling complex filled with offices, libraries, and classrooms. The hour was early enough that few people were about, for which she was grateful. They still stared at her, and it brought back surreal memories of her childhood as Mirage. People had stared at her then, too, for the fiery red hair that made her look like a witch. She'd snarled about it for years, only to find out that she *was,* in a sense, a witch—or rather, the other half of one. Getting over *that* revelation had taken a while.

Ruriko was waiting in the outer office, surrounded as always by piles of paper. She exchanged one look with Mirei; Ruriko could say more with one look than most women could with a speech. Then the secretary waved her through, into the Void Prime's office, and turned back to her work.

The interior room was one Mirei had never seen before

eight days ago, yet it had become familiar with startling speed. As a witch-student who had not yet been tested, Miryo had never been summoned to this inner sanctum, with its elegantly tiled floor, shelves of books, and tidy sheaves of paper. She'd spoken instead with the unranked witches who taught her classes, or occasionally the Keys who served the Primes and ran much of Starfall's business. Since returning as Mirei, though, she'd spent much of every day here, sitting in one of the high-backed chairs, trying to help quell the trouble she'd caused.

Satomi was alone inside—another worrisome note. Usually other people were present for these meetings. The Void Prime stood next to the window, gazing out over the predawn landscape. She, too, was much more familiar than she had been—enough so that Mirei could read the tension in her body, even though she was trying to hide it. Satomi had the kind of face that registered age by acquiring more dignity, rather than lines, but today she looked old and tired.

The door closed softly behind Mirei; she waited, then ventured to speak. "Satomi-aken. What's happened?"

Satomi's voice was quiet, flat, despite its richly trained tones. "Shimi is gone."

"Gone?"

"From Starfall. She left in the night." Satomi turned away from the window. The lamps in her office, lit against the early morning darkness of the sky, made her look even paler than usual, and painted her delicate features with shadows. The unrelieved black of her dress only accentuated it. Black was her Elemental color, and she'd always worn it on ceremonial occasions, but she hadn't put it off since Mirei came to Starfall. Mirei suspected it was in mourning for all the doppelgangers who had died. Or, perhaps, for her own.

The Void Prime crossed to her desk and picked up the single sheet of parchment that lay on it. She scanned it, not appearing to really read the words, and then handed it to Mirei.

> *I have left, and will not return. I refuse to remain in company with that abomination. The doppelganger is taken out of us for a reason; to bring it back in is rankest heresy. It must be destroyed. To state that it is the Warrior and the Void is no argument in its favor—on the contrary, that is exactly why we must get rid of it. It is the destruction of life, the destruction of magic, the antithesis of everything that is this world, and if we welcome it back in, we will have committed a terrible sin. It will not be enough for that monster to leave. We must destroy it, and remove this horror from the world.*

Mirei shook her head in disbelief, putting the sheet back down. "She almost sounds like a Nalochkan."

"She was raised in Kalistyi," Satomi said grimly. "The Nalochkan sect was as strong in Kalistyi when Shimi was a child as they are now. Clergy never come into our halls, of course—Nalochkan or otherwise—but the influence still penetrates."

"You mean . . ." Mirei fumbled for words. She wasn't awake enough yet to handle this rupture to the tenuous peace. "She can't actually *share* their beliefs—can she? To disavow the Warrior, to say she's not even part of the *Goddess*—" It would be radical enough in an unranked witch; though the witches didn't call themselves a sect, they had their own approach to religion, and rarely strayed from it. For no less a woman than the Air Prime, one of the five women who ruled Starfall and its people, to show such allegiance to an outside sect—

Satomi turned back to the window, placing her slender hands on the sill. When she spoke, her voice was low, betraying her tension. "No. I would not say she shares their beliefs, not to that extent. But the influence is there. And we of Starfall have never given as much attention to the Warrior as we do to the other four Aspects of the Goddess; the Void has, for us, been as much practical as theological. We neglect it, as we neglect the Warrior. And for someone like Shimi, who needs a reason to believe you are anathema . . . it would be easy to magnify that divide. Especially when she grew up surrounded by Nalochkan beliefs."

Mirei sank into a chair. When other witches were there, she behaved more formally, but in private Satomi allowed her some liberties. "I don't get it. You had doubts, sure, but you killed your own doppelganger. I can understand why you didn't want to believe that I was right—it meant that you were wrong to kill her. But what's Shimi's reason? Why won't she believe?"

"Because she *didn't* kill her doppelganger." Satomi bowed her head. The two of them had never addressed this issue directly, not since the Void Prime told Miryo of her own doppelganger's death. Mirei had only come to understand it fully when she and Satomi fought in Star Hall. Then she had realized the cause of the Void Prime's reluctance to accept what Mirei had to say. "I remember looking at her, and I remember recognizing her as the other half of myself. In the end I convinced myself that she was a threat I must eliminate—a threat to all of us, not just myself—but that memory came back to me when you told us what you had done. Shimi has no such memory. It is easier for her to believe that doppelgangers are anathema, when the alternative is such a radical change."

"But what does leaving accomplish, except to openly declare her opposition? If she's so worried about what's going to happen, then she should stay and try to minimize the chaos. She's one of the five most powerful women here—"

Mirei stopped mid-sentence, because Satomi had turned around, and her pale green eyes were full of fear she had not shown before.

"Ashin sent us the list," the Void Prime said.

The words didn't register. "The list?"

"Of the other doppelgangers. Who they are. And where."

Mirei's heart skipped a beat, painfully. The list. The Void-damned list. There were other doppelgangers out there, alive—the nonmagical halves of witch-daughters. A group of conspirators among the witches had arranged in secret for them to survive the ritual where they were supposed to die, because the conspirators were convinced they *shouldn't* die. And they were right; Mirei had proved it. But prior to that, Starfall had branded those witches as heretics, had even assassinated their leader. One of Mirei's tasks in the last eight days had been to communicate with Ashin, the Key of the Air Hand, and the only one of the conspirators she knew personally. She had been trying to convince the woman that it was safe, finally, to admit where the doppelgangers were.

It seemed she'd finally succeeded.

"Shimi has it," Mirei said softly.

"Ashin wrote to us last night, after we sent you away. Shimi had no chance to make a copy of the list, but she wouldn't need to; we spent hours discussing it. She knows where they are."

Suddenly Mirei couldn't bear to be sitting; she rose to her feet and moved a few steps away with quick, tight strides that barely helped to ease her tension. Her boot heels clicked on the tiled floor with shocking loudness. "She'll go after them. But no—she can't kill them. Not without the other half of each pair, the witch-daughter. She'd have to kill both at once, for them both to stay dead." Her gaze snapped up to meet the Prime's. "You have to protect them."

"I've already taken steps," Satomi said. "And will take more, after I speak to the other Primes, which will be soon. As for the doppelgangers themselves, we'll write to the witches that are nearest to them, send them after the children. If they move quickly enough, we should be there ahead of Shimi, or whomever she has sent in her stead."

For a moment that seemed like an ideal solution, heading the Air Prime off at the pass. Then Mirei had a brief, vivid memory of standing on the balcony of a tower at the Hunter school of Silverfire, watching two young girls train below, listening to the Grandmaster of the school say, *"There's another at Windblade, and one at Thornblood."*

"Bad idea," she said.

Satomi paused on her way to her desk, shoulders stiff with affront. "I beg your pardon?"

"No way in the *Void* is that going to work. Not for all

of them. You're going to send a witch into a Hunter school and have her say, 'Sorry, I need to walk off with some of your trainees'?" Mirei shook her head, knowing her fear was making her be rude. "They'll throw her out on her ear. *If* she's lucky."

"They will not have a choice," Satomi said crisply. "We will use magic if necessary."

"Oh, even better. You send witches into three different Hunter schools and have them throw spells about before they run off with trainees. Aken, you'll start a *war*."

The Void Prime raised her eyebrows in startlement. "They would be that angry?"

"We do *not* like witches interfering with us," Mirei said. The word "we" came out reflexively, and she saw Satomi notice it. But Mirei was as much a Hunter as she was a witch, the Mirage part of her had lived that life, as the Miryo part had lived here in Starfall. "They might not be able to stop you. But trainees belong to their schools, just as much as our daughters belong to Starfall. Stealing them away—you're talking about offending not one but *several* groups of trained assassins, mercenaries, and spies who already don't like you very much. You do *not* want them angry at you."

Satomi's hands clenched on empty air, a gesture of frustration and impotence. "Then what do *you* suggest? We can't just leave them there for Shimi to take."

The answer was obvious. "I'll go after them."

"No. It would take too long for you to get there."

"It would take me no time at all."

Mirei saw the heartbeat of incomprehension in the Void Prime's face, before Satomi realized what she meant. It was an understandable blindness; translocating living things was supposed to be impossible. And so it *had* been, until Mirei recreated herself out of Miryo and Mirage. That rejoining gave her access to the magic of the Void, believed untouchable until then. Satomi was not yet accustomed to allowing for that in her plans.

"You could bring them right back here!" the Prime said, hope lighting her eyes. "We wouldn't even have to wait!"

Mirei almost agreed. Then instinct murmured in the back of her head. She was still learning what she could and could not do with Void magic, but one thing she had learned was how exhausting it was, especially translocation.

She had to shake her head. "No. I don't think I can move more than just myself."

The hope in Satomi's eyes withered.

"Maybe I'll be able to someday," Mirei said. "But I'd rather not experiment with something that tricky yet. I can take myself to Silverfire now, though. There are two there, right?" Satomi nodded, not that Mirei needed the confirmation. "I need to talk to Jaguar anyway. He knows he's got two of them, and that they're like me—that is, like Mirage was. If he'd hand them over to anybody, it would be me. So I can get them to safety, and then go after the other ones." She thought it over, grimacing. "Wind-blade, I can probably manage; we're friendly with them. Thornblood will be a different story. Their people hate my people's guts. But I'll figure something out."

Satomi pulled herself up, spine straightening from its momentary slump. "The rest are fostered with farmers, tradesmen, the like. We can take care of those."

"Fine." Mirei's mind was already racing, thinking

ahead to what she would need. Translocate to Silverfire, then ride to Angrim—that would take about four days. Fortunately, both Thornblood and Windblade were just outside of Angrim, so she could kill two birds with one stone. Then—assuming she found a way to steal a girl out of the hostile territory of Thornblood—the long ride back south to Starfall, where the doppelgangers could be protected. Once she got away from Angrim with the other pair, they could pick up an escort of Cousins, or even other witches. Just in case Shimi, or anyone else, tried something. There could well be Thornbloods on her tail at that point, and who knew how many witches out there might agree with the Air Prime about the new situation?

But her experiences as Mirage told her how well plans survived actual testing. Better to stay adaptable. "Give me a sheet to communicate with you," Mirei said. The written word was slower, but on the road, it would be an easier spell to manage than bringing Satomi's image up in a mirror. "I may have to play things by ear. And you can get in touch with me if anything else happens here."

Satomi nodded. "Very well. Bring them back to us, as quickly as you can."